CW00435676

Copyright © 2016 by Owen Nichols

All rights reserved. No part of this publication may be reproduced, distributed, or transmitted in any form or by any means, including photocopying, recording, or other electronic or mechanical methods, without the prior written permission of the author, except in the case of brief quotations embodied in critical reviews and certain other noncommercial uses permitted by copyright law.

Cover design by Black Dima

Clock image; Madison Frye Photography ©

Blue background & hand; Dreamstime.com ©

London image; 123rf.com ©

For Emma and Josh.

With all that I am.

And in loving memory of Gi and Grampa.

Gramps, you'd have loved this, Gi, not so much...

Fifty Two Weeks of Murder

Prologue

I have lived a privileged life. Born into wealth as old as the divisions that mark the Counties. Educated by the finest minds in the world, not because of my intellect, limited as that is, but through right of birth. I have dined with Kings and Queens, played cards with Presidents and hunted Pheasant with Princes. I've flown a helicopter along the Colorado River before touching down to enjoy a Champagne breakfast with my beautiful wife, great cliffs of the Grand Canyon towering above us. I've seen the moon rise over the dunes of the Sahara Desert as if imitating the sun, the pale orb seemingly close enough to touch as I rode my camel to meet the bedouins who would be our host for the night. I've scaled the Pitons at St. Lucia, slept with the Inuit under the Aurora and walked among the remains of Machu Pichu as the sun crept over the ruins of the Inca's.

Ashes.

All of it ashes in my mouth, tainting my soul with its sullied grime. We scrape and claw at life, desperately clinging to some hope that it means something. That your suffering has a purpose and meaning that will become clear to you when the time is right. I have everything, yet realise that I have nothing. If I have nothing, then how can anyone less privileged than me have anything? We tread water every day, slowly drowning as we wait for someone to rescue us. To save us. You must do this yourself. We must all do this ourselves.

Sixty years ago, there were two and a half billion people on Earth. Now there are seven billion. We spread like a cancer, a writhing tumour leaching through the planet sowing death, destruction and pollution. We will reap what we sow and soon this planet will slough us off like a putrefying skin. Every species, except for Homo sapiens, lives in accordance with its niche, taking only what it needs. They each have a purpose, are part of a larger ecosystem which will not survive without them. We, however, are more akin to a virus, tragically aware of the fragility of our host, yet too wilfully negligent to act.

We are the most violent and destructive organism on Earth. More have died on the battlefield since the Second World War than died during that War itself. Life is cheaper than ever before. Who will notice a few lost souls? Who will mourn their loss when there are so many of us?

As I thought upon this, I realised that murder cannot be the sin Civilisation would have us believe. The Constitution gives us moral guidance, a set of laws we willingly abide by. An abstract principle made flesh, adhered to because we allow it to govern. Killing, however, is not amoral. We stand and watch, mute, as we allow those all over the world to kill and torture yet apply a different moral code to ourselves. We pass judgement passively, imbued with a soporific cowardice, too numb to care or act. When did we become so desensitised to the world around us?

You will invest more money and time catching me and my disciples than you will supporting the NHS. You will waste so many resources attempting to catch me that more people will die in a hospital bed, or lack thereof, than could otherwise have been saved. You would be wise to leave me alone. This is no idle threat.

Allow me to set us on the path to freedom. To redemption. Let me show you how.

*I felt real emotion for the first time last night as I start us all on the path to true civilisation. A giddying rush of energy and surging joy, infusing my very being with its purifying essence. I'd planned this moment for many years. Fantasy turned reality. Fantasy turned truth. I'd chosen my prey long ago and stalked him carefully. I wanted it to be just right. I wanted **him** to be just right. Someone who passes judgement on us all. Who is he to do that? We allow men like him to Judge because we don't realise that there is another option. A lion doesn't require absolution as it feasts on its prey so that it may survive. Nor should we. Belief defiles sound reason and*

7

thought. We believe in our higher purpose, but lose the true reason for our existence.

I followed him as he left work and pounced before he could unlock the door to his Bentley. The Bentley you all bought through your passive acceptance of this society. He danced wildly as the electricity from my stun gun coursed through him and I knew my actions to be right and true.

It was a short drive to Wimbledon Common, his body limp in the back of the van as I parked by Caesar's Camp. The setting was perfect. As I pulled the wooden cross from the back of the van, he woke and I could see the fear in his eyes as he realised his fate. He kicked and bucked against his bonds and adrenalin pumped through me.

I was alive!

Dragging him from the vehicle, he tried to kick me, but was no match for my strength, my purpose and my will. A swift boot to the head made him groggy enough to tie his wrists to the cross, spread-eagled and helpless as I secured his ankles to the base. I waited then, listening to the Common. Heard the sound of traffic far off, a gentle background hiss from the A3. Like the tinnitus I suffered as a child – a tinnitus for our world.

The constant thrum of progress holding us back.

The hour was late and we were alone, so I waited some more. I wanted him to know his fate. It did not take long for consciousness to take him in its chilling grip. It took delightful moments for him to realise where he was and what was going to happen. Terror and agonising pain gave him strength as he struggled.

Jesus wore a crown of thorns, but I'd given my own spin to the punishment and given him a gag of thorns, the thick needles tearing the inside of his mouth, his screams muffled by the dense foliage. Despite his pain, he managed to scream some more as I nailed his wrists and ankles to the cross, the crunch of steel through bone a

8

wonderful undercurrent to his wails of despair. Disappointingly, he fainted after the wrists and I had to hammer his ankles to the wood in an odd silence, the nail slipping once on his slick blood as it poured in rivulets from the wounds. I made sure to avoid the arteries. I didn't want him bleeding out too soon.

Using the winch on the van, I raised the cross and beheld the glory of my work. The bible made real. The word of God before me. I savoured the moment, seeing my work made true. As he woke, whimpers of delightful suffering dancing through the night, I played the role of Longinus and pierced his side with a lance, blood splashing warm on my face, his essence feeding my own. The blood, as Jesus' did to Longinus, opened my eyes and cured my blindness. I saw the world for what it was. I saw clearly the path we must all take. Know me, for I am fanatic. Born again.

The deed done, I recorded the moment and present to you my work. This will be your task. To carry out your own rebirth. To descend into the deepest recesses of your soul and take charge. To begin your pilgrimage and seek true humanity. To become truly **humane***. This will not be without hardship but I will be here to support you and make it easier to join me and begin the human devolution. Each week I shall reward those who prevail most beautifully.*

With money.

Five million pounds sterling.

Each week, I shall present a new trial. For one year, we shall test ourselves with new challenges and when this is done, we shall see a new society take shape. The world will recoil in horror, but, in time, they will venerate us as saints. They will see our work and be grateful for the courage we show.

It is time for you to rise up. Weak. Destitute. Outcast. Alone. You are none of these. Not anymore. Our species begins anew and it is time for you to take your rightful place. This week you shall present the greatest works of man turned real. The written word made flesh. I have shown you the Bible reimagined. Now it is your turn.

Let the fifty two weeks of murder begin.

Week One

Chapter One.

Anders kept her breathing steady as she ran through the trees, enjoying the sense of isolation gained from climbing the walls to Richmond Park before the gates were opened. Her feet kicked up mud and splattered her legs as she pushed herself harder, aiming to reach the Richmond Hill Gate before the warden opened them up. As she burst through the woods, Anders took the worn path along the grassland, startling a herd of deer that nestled along the edge of the trees. Antlers pierced the sky as a large stag stood to attention, glaring angrily at the interloper. The deer had resided here since Charles I built the park in the Seventeenth Century, its thousand hectares three times the size of Central Park in New York and providing the animals shelter from modernity for almost four hundred years.

Giving the stag a wide berth, Anders picked up the pace. A heavy mist clung to the ground as the low morning sun dappled through the trees, a lazy attempt to banish the fog that showed little sign of relinquishing its grip on the grass. Anders thought it beautiful and slowed a little to enjoy the view. Large tower blocks ringed the red brick walls, but the Royal lands stubbornly resisted the march of progress and remained a resolute obstacle to the brick and tarmac jungle that encroached upon its majestic beauty.

Before Anders approached the wrought iron gates, a thickset warden came from his outpost and started unlocking them, giving Anders a rueful smile as she came to a halt by the black iron bars. Since an incident of vandalism the previous year, the pedestrian gates had remained closed at night.

"Morning miss," he said, amusement softening his voice. "Summer months we open early, so how are you going to get out in the winter?" He pulled the well-oiled gates smoothly open and beckoned Anders through.

"Same way I got in I guess," she replied enigmatically and waved a cheeky farewell. She could feel his eyes on her back, her sports bra showing the curled scars that laced her narrow shoulders, criss-crossed in angry welts around her frame, a particularly large one curling around her neck to her ear. Anders was used to it and paid the stare no heed. Her mind was focused on the run, the feeling of freedom and release gained from the activity.

Early morning traffic crawled by as she ran past old buildings, hotels and pubs. To her left, trees, grassland and shrubs lining a steep slope gave lie to the fact that she now lived in London. The sun, finally lifting itself from its slumber, shone brightly and chased away the fog, showing the meandering river below her in all its twinkling glory, boats bobbing gently on the water as it reflected the sun in a thousand diamond shards of light. Pushing herself for the last leg of the run, Anders bent her head and sprinted the last half mile, grinning with pleasure as her heart pounded in her chest at the effort.

Anders' apartment was on the top floor of a newly furnished block and she took the stairs two at a time, pulling out her key as she reached the final flight. Letting herself in quietly, so as not to wake anyone, she padded through the brightly lit open plan kitchen and living space, slipped past the bedrooms and into the workroom at the end of the corridor. In stark contrast to the Spartan décor of the flat, the room was cluttered with hundreds of books, piled high in stacks reaching to the ceiling. One wall lay bare and Anders had screwed a large whiteboard to it. The board lay blank and unused for now. In one corner nestled a large oak desk and a comfy chair, but Anders was focused on the Mu Ren Zhuang in one corner.

Closing the thick wooden door behind her, she moved gracefully to the corner. Her run had barely made her sweat, so she practised on the wooden training dummy until her slender wrists hurt and sweat dripped from her forehead, going through motions well practised by years of discipline. Train hard, fight easy, her drill sergeant had yelled at her each day and she had taken his words to heart with everything she did.

Her training done, she left the room and made her way to the bathroom and showered, enjoying the biting heat of the scalding water as it soothed out tightened muscles. Skin red from the shower, she wrapped a towel under her armpits and made her way to the bedroom, knocking on two doors in the hallway as she passed them.

"Wake up minions, big day today!" Anders cried and was greeted with groans of despair that only the newly woken can muster. Chuckling softly, she entered her bedroom. It was neat and clean, with a large walk in cupboard to store her clothes and some shelves where her favourite books were kept. The shelf and its contents were the only concession to personality and the rest of the room looked bare and unlived in.

Anders pulled on a silk blouse and suit trousers as she heard the thumps and bangs of the house waking up. Drying her long brown hair and pulling it into a pony tail, she applied some light make up, critically appraising herself in the mirror; a habit as old as Anders was. She was happy with her appearance now, despite the thick scar that snaked up from her collar, but it was a habit that was hard to break. A loud banging broke her from her reverie as Cassie pounded on the bathroom door.

"Aaron, hurry up!" she yelled. A loud raspberry from the bathroom made Cassie sigh with frustration and her bedroom door slammed in anger. Smiling to herself, Anders made her way to the kitchen and poured a bowl of cereal for Aaron and switched on the coffee machine for herself, the strong aroma of coffee bean wafting through the kitchen. As the machine percolated happily, she reached into a cupboard and took out her Estradiol and Medioxyprogesteroneacetate tablets and swallowed them quickly as she scanned the room.

Though she preferred a less cluttered environment, her workroom notwithstanding, the realities of children meant that the space was often covered in toys and discarded clothes. She scooped a few items up and placed them back in the toy box as Aaron burst into the kitchen and sat at the table, his legs barely reaching the floor and swinging back and forth as if to keep jogging. He was only seven, but tall for his age with blonde hair and brown eyes. Freckles peppered his nose and cheeks. He had an infectious energy and a gentle nature that always brought light with him.

"Morning Bumble," he said as he poured milk over his cereal and a good portion of the table as well. Anders leaned down and gave his forehead a kiss as she tousled his unruly hair, noting the Captain America t-shirt that she'd put in the wash the day before. He must have crept out sometime in the night and rescued it in their constant game of cat and mouse to have the item cleaned.

"Morning sleepy head," she replied as he shovelled the cereal into his mouth before wrinkling his nose in disgust.

"Ugh," he said. "Why can't I have Frosties?" Anders smiled as she sat opposite him and sipped her black coffee, one leg tucked under herself and elbows resting on the table as she cradled the mug.

"Frosties are for weekends and holidays," she declared.

"That's mean," responded Aaron as Cassie walked in, her blonde hair still dripping from the shower. She was dressed in her café work clothes and had been liberal with the application of dark eyeliner.

"What's mean?" she said, helping herself to some coffee from the machine.

"I'm a horrible mean Ogre," replied Anders, amusement crinkling her startling green eyes.

"What's an Ogre?" asked Aaron. Cassie pulled a chair out and sat at the table, arms curled around the steaming drink.

"It's a big green warty ugly thing that will eat you up!" she declared, poking Aaron in the ribs much to his delight.

"Bumble isn't ugly," he said through a mouthful of food. "She's pretty." Anders laughed and stood up to make his sandwiches for school.

"Flattery will get you far Honeybun, but it won't get you Frosties."
Aaron sighed theatrically and managed to spill some milk on his
trousers. Anders handed him a cloth and told him to wipe his pants.

"They call them trousers here," said Cassie with a rueful smile.
"Pants are what the Brits call their underwear." Aaron screwed up
his face.

"That's silly," he said. Anders chimed in as she wrapped up Aaron's
peanut butter and jelly sandwiches.

"You know what else is weird? Jelly. They call it jam here."

"That's not as silly as calling something I wear on the outside the
same as what I wear on the inside." Cassie grinned mischievously
and beckoned Aaron closer with a conspiratorial wave of her finger.

"You wanna know what a fanny pack is here? Fanny means…"

"That'll do Cassie," rebuked Anders good naturedly, concealing a
grin as she packed Aaron's bag for school.

The banter continued for a while until Anders declared that Aaron
needed to get to school. Cassie found his bag and shrugged into a
leather jacket as she ushered him out of the door. Aaron stopped to
give Anders a hug and she lifted him from his feet in a bear hug,
much to his squealing delight.

"Be good," she said and kissed his cheek. "I'll see you later." Cassie
leaned forward for a hug and Anders slipped her some money. "Toy
R Us on the way home. There's a skateboard there he's been after
for a while, third one up, second one in. Special treat for his first day
at school. Get a safety helmet as well."

Cassie took the money and smiled sadly.

"You shouldn't spoil us," she said softly as Aaron waited for the lift
in the hallway, humming tunelessly to himself. "You've done more
than we could have asked for." She looked suddenly vulnerable and
Anders' heart almost broke at the sight.

"You're my family now," she said simply. "It gives me the greatest pleasure." Cassie hugged her briefly, thanked her again and went to take Aaron to school. Anders quickly tidied up the kitchen and then slipped into the workroom. On the desk sat her Warrant card and she picked it up, recalling the oath that she'd taken a few days ago. She'd sat in the office of the Director-General of the NCA while he gazed on with a smirk as she raised her palm and recited the oath from memory. It spoke of fairness and integrity, diligence and the duty to uphold fundamental human rights.

As she said the words, her mind had raced back a decade to when she'd given her Federal Oath under very different circumstances in Quantico. She'd been a raw recruit, full of excitement at the possibilities that lay ahead. That oath had ensured her unwavering commitment to upholding the American Constitution and her willingness to defend it against all enemies. She felt a tinge of sadness at how things had changed but pushed such thoughts away. Life was all about change. She knew that better than anyone. Making the changes that mattered and dealing with the things you can't change is what really counts.

Checking that the lights were all off, Anders grabbed her jacket and pulled on a pair of boots before taking her purse and checking its contents. Slipping her watch onto her wrist and turning it so that it faced inwards, an old habit from her time in the army, Anders left the flat. Locking the door behind her, she took the stairs to the exit and made the short walk to the tube station. It was her first day of work, and, despite her morning exercise, she still had plenty of adrenalin left to feel nervous.

Chapter 2

The original Scotland Yard had been named because its rear entrance had backed onto a street called Great Scotland Yard. The location had moved several times since then and picked up the moniker New Scotland Yard in 1890. The return to Curtis Green building in twenty sixteen had allowed the "New" to be dropped and the building was now simply Scotland Yard. The three hundred and seventy million pounds raised from selling the previous Met offices had gone into refurbishing the new one, yet the exterior still looked drab and dour.

Anders had elected to stop at Waterloo and walk along the embankment to the Yard. She enjoyed the bustle of the streets and made a mental note to take Cassie and Aaron to the London Eye as she walked past. Aaron would enjoy the macabre London Dungeon that had moved to the Eye from London Bridge and Cassie would enjoy the Aquarium that was found next to it. A biting wind snapped at her jacket and she pulled it tight as she leaned into the blast. In typically British fashion, the day was breaking its earlier promise of sun, and dark, forbidding rainclouds started to loiter with intent. Walking along Westminster Bridge, she gazed at the Houses of Parliament and wondered at the history of the city. Modern skyscrapers tore at the skyline, visionary designs of glass and steel that sought to escape the clutches of the ancient buildings littering the streets. Anders loved the clash of ages.

Scotland Yard was located a short walk from the bridge and she paused briefly as she came into its shadow. The building was large and square, with rows of evenly spaced windows and little character. The impressive Ministry of Defence building crowded over it and Anders chuckled at the bombastic contrast. Before she could move on, a deep, yet cocksure voice boomed from the riverside, the cockney accent clear over the traffic.

"I thought I recognised that sweet ass from across the river!" Anders turned to see a large, immaculately dressed figure cross the street and move nimbly towards her, idly flicking a cigarette butt away as he weaved through the traffic. His suit was cut to show his broad shoulders and trim waist, a gold necklace flashing in the light against his dark skin. He walked with a swagger and opened his arms in greeting as he reached Anders. She grinned as she saw him and embraced the younger man with joy.

"Jesse," she said. "I had no idea you were in London. Don't tell me you've turned from the dark side!" Jesse shrugged easily and gave a wicked grin.

"You're out of touch Special Agent Anders," he replied. "I'm all out of that business, going clean and straight. Found me a cushy job with your new boys." Jesse laid an arm around Anders as he guided her into the building. "I ain't no Blackhat nomore, but you know you can't go around calling me Jesse. It's Crackers my little angel." Anders stepped to the security desk and signed herself in before allowing Jesse to show her to the offices. The large atrium was bustling with the change of shift and a few surreptitious stares were directed at Anders. Within law enforcement, she was both curiosity and legend.

"I'm no Special Agent now, Jesse, and I told you when I arrested you that your mother gave you that name for a reason and it wasn't so you could change it to Crackers." Jesse laughed and kept pace with the banter. His company was easy and he held no grudge for the past. Besides, he would owe her for many more years to come.

"Hell, you'll always be the most special of Agents and you know it," he said wistfully as he took her to the lifts. She gave him a knowing look and he sighed theatrically before pushing open the door to the stairwell and graciously waving her down.

"It's a long way down," he moaned as they descended deep into the concrete bowels of the building. "Seems the Met don't like the NCA in their building for some reason."

It really was a long way down and Jesse was breathing heavily as he slammed open the door to their offices by leaning wearily on it. Anders was admonishing him for his smoking as they walked into a large open space that was well lit and filled with new equipment but couldn't disguise the fact that it was as far away from the Met officers as possible.

To the right of the entrance lay two offices, separated from the room by glass partitioning. In the middle of the hub, several desks were spread out, one of which was piled high with computer monitors connected like a web and a stack of magazines and junk. Anders guessed that to be Jesse's station. The other tables were bare and unclaimed. At the back and to the left, several corridors ran off to different areas. Anders had studied the plans and knew that the two at the rear led to firearms and training and the other to the forensics suite. The ones immediately to her left linked to the holding cells and interrogation rooms. The entire structure was steel and concrete. Functional and nothing else. One wall was for posting evidence, ideas and chronology and it was currently bare.

"Mal!" called Jesse. "We have our latest recruit!" A head popped out from the office closest to the entrance and gave them both a big grin. It disappeared briefly and there was a whispered conversation before Mal stepped out. He was tall and filled the doorway, his rolled up sleeves showing thick knots of muscle attached to large hands designed for the more practical application of police work. Despite his fearsome build, his broad face was open and kind, with a beard that was peppered with flecks of grey. His voice, when he spoke, was suffused with the lilting tones of the Welsh Valleys. His eyes were sharp and piercing and Anders saw a core of steel within them.

"Welcome," he said as he shook her hand in a meaty fist. "I'm delighted to meet you. I'm sure Jesse…"

"…Crackers…" Mal gave him a weary look and turned back to Anders.

"…has given you the lowdown of the team." Anders smiled as she allowed herself to be guided into the office closest to them. Jesse took the opportunity to get to his desk and start work.

"He's told me of his conquests since he returned to London and then regaled me with his thesis on the evils of stairs, but that's pretty much it." Mal chuckled as they entered the office. It was decorated with warmth and care. There were throws on comfy sofas, rugs on the floor and bright paintings hung on walls. Behind a small desk sat an elegant and well-groomed woman who looked to be in her early forties, but was most likely older. She had taken care of herself and took pride in both her appearance and her work. She gave a warm smile to Anders as she entered and stood to greet her. She was much shorter than she looked and Anders towered over her, despite not being that tall herself.

"You must be Assistant Chief Constable Anders," she said, clasping Anders' hands in her own. She was well spoken, her inflection laced with wealth and class.

"Just Anders please ma'am."

"Anders it is," she replied. "I'm Abigail Philips. I'll be helping you with your investigations. I'm a…"

"Psychiatrist ma'am. I studied your work at Quantico. Your research into child abuse helped me to build several profiles during my time there." Abigail chuckled modestly and glanced slyly at Mal.

"I like this one. She can stay," she declared before giving Anders' hand one more squeeze and returning to her desk. She glanced up as they made to leave. "I'm told you like coffee. There's always a mug and a chat here." Anders nodded her thanks as Mal ushered her out of the room.

"Sharp as an axe that one," he muttered fondly as he gave Anders the tour of the station. They were clearly old friends. As Mal showed Anders her new workspace, he spoke rapidly of the project they were undertaking. His enthusiasm was infectious and Anders found herself excited to be at the spearhead of this undertaking. Only Jesse, Abigail and Mal were there, but the hour was early and Anders had wished to arrive before everyone else. Mal's crumpled jeans, flannel shirt and dishevelled look spoke of someone who spent more time at work than at home and she guessed that he would always be here before her.

"So, this is our second day of operations. We're in the Met's building, but we are NCA. We have our own operational independence. Technically, I'm the highest ranking officer in the building, but we'll keep out of their way as much as possible." He led her through the desks and into the forensics lab, clearly honoured to be leading this new taskforce. As they walked past Jesse, he winked at Anders and she smiled back, glad that he was now putting his considerable skills to good use.

"The NCA has been operational since twenty thirteen, but it took a few years to get us up and running. The Director-General's baby as it were. This is the lab," he said and opened his arms to display the area proudly. His soft accent was easy on the ear and Anders took a moment to realise that he'd been expecting a response from her. The room was larger than shc'd imagined, having studied the plans, and extremely well furnished. Two metal tables with drains below them were in the centre and each wall was festooned with equipment, from PCR machines and spectrometers to electrophoresis kits. Anders could see where the budget had gone and was suitably impressed. She gave him a cheeky grin and nodded her approval, a stray lick of hair escaping her pony tail as she tucked it behind her ear.

"I'm impressed," she said. "No coffee machine though." Mal grinned even wider and gave her a devilish wink.

"Follow me. If you want to be truly impressed that us Brits can do coffee then I shall show you our finest brew!" He swept past, gesturing for her to follow and she almost had to sprint to keep up with his long, loping strides as he made his way down the concrete lined corridors. Entering the main area, Anders saw a group of people standing around Jesse and chatting. He was holding court and embellishing his misdeeds with a light touch that made the others laugh. He often aimed to misbehave, but his breezy personality always helped him get away with it. Mostly. As Mal and Anders entered, the conversation was cut short and the group turned to appraise the newcomer. Mal clapped his large hands thunderously together and walked confidently towards the trio.

"Excellent!" he declared. "Just in time to meet our new Assistant Chief Constable!" As Anders walked to the group, she could sense the hostility from at least one of them. The most openly hostile was a female, slightly taller than Anders, slim with pinched cheeks and stern features. Blonde hair framed her face and her eyes were a piercing blue. She'd have been considered attractive if it weren't for her icy demeanour, a coolness that spoke of selfish determination. She looked to be in her early thirties.

"This is Lucy Colohan," Mal said as he made the introductions. "She used to be part of Special Branch until we poached her." Anders made to shake her hand, but Lucy merely raised hers in greeting, pursing her lips even tighter and gazing openly at Anders' scar. Oblivious to the slight, Mal introduced the giant that stood next to Lucy, dwarfing her with his height and build. Mal was tall but this man made him seem merely average.

"This is Barry Eisenfield, ex, er, military and all round expert in tracking down the lowlife's we'll be chasing." He had short black hair kept in a neat buzzcut and sported a nose that had been broken on several occasions. He had a full mouth that was always quick to smile and sparkling eyes that held an intelligence unexpected in such a brutish figure. He wore a tight fitting shirt with short sleeves that allowed his muscles free rein to intimidate or impress. Usually both. A large tribal tattoo snaked its way around his right arm and Anders could see the end of it crawling up his neck in a strange parody of her own scar. He held out a welcoming hand and gave a warm smile as Anders took it, her own delicate hand dwarfed by his. When he spoke, it was with a deep rumbling bass and always tinged with mirth.

"I hear you were with the Eighty Second Airborne," he said. More of a statement than a question. Anders nodded. "Came across you guys in Iraq during the "Surge." Operation Fardh al-Qanoon saw some pretty intense fighting, but you boys came out of it alright." Anders, seeing the way he carried himself, the gently patronising tone of another military force and reflecting on the barely noticeable pause in Mal's voice, took a guess as to his army background and gave him a warm smile.

"We did ok," she replied. "Spent some time with your lads securing the Helmand Province. You did alright yourselves." Barry let out a guffaw of laughter and clapped down on her shoulder with a loud thump, rattling her teeth with its force. He was interrupted by a sour voice as Lucy groaned.

"Not another one. Nothing better to do after leaving the army?" Anders shrugged easily, refusing to be baited by her aggression. She'd come across it oftentimes. It wasn't going to change.

"Plenty of transferable skills. Besides, I was FBI before I joined the Eighty Second. Wanted to make up my own mind about what we were doing over there."

"So why are you in London now then?" The curt question came from the third member of the group. He was skinny, with a slight frame and a face that could be handsome when he smiled. It was such a rare occurrence, however, that Jesse joked he didn't actually know how to make the necessary movements required for one. He wore a baggy suit that was ill fitting, but his eyes were sharp and his movements constantly stilted as if he was always holding himself back. Mal put a patronising arm around him, earning a grumpy scowl in return. It clearly tickled Mal to gently push his buttons.

"This here is Duncan, Abi's brother and all round nice guy, once you get through his incredibly prickly exterior. Ex CID, they're all like that. Part of the training. And you don't have to answer his question."

"That's ok," replied Anders. "It's a fair question. I was born here, moved to America when I was six and felt that it was time to come home." Duncan looked like he was going to respond when Jesse cut him off.

"Buckle up kids, we got our first case!" He was staring intently at the screen, sifting through the morning reports from HOLMES to determine which cases they might be interested in. Mal instantly changed demeanour, his lightness replaced with a business-like efficiency.

"Show me," he said and moved round so he could look at the screens, taking out a pair of wire rimmed spectacles that instantly aged him.

"Murder at Wimbledon Common," said Jesse. "Looks like some kind of crucifixion." Mal gazed at the report for a few moments before standing up and removing his glasses.

"Jesse, tell Helen and Ben to get their act together. I want them at the Common in thirty minutes. Barry, requisition an area van, we'll all go together. Lucy, Duncan, get to the lab and pull out all of the boxes in shelves one through to eight. Get them in the van. Anders, sift through the prelim's, give me a rundown on the way." As the team moved to their tasks, each of them showed the calm efficiency of trained and competent professionals. Anders found it reassuring as she stepped closer to Jesse while he printed off the details for her. She nodded at Lucy and Duncan as they strode to the forensics lab.

"I'm guessing they don't like me so much." Jesse gave a snort of contempt.

"I wouldn't worry about those two if I were you. Duncan's pissed because you have what he considers to be his job and Lucy hates you because, well…" He suddenly paused, unsure of what to say.

"Well what?" prompted Anders, her tone dangerous. Jesse grinned at her.

"You're just so much prettier than Lucy. It must be eating her up inside."

"Don't make me punch you again."

"Ooh Agent, you know I like it rough." He ducked swiftly as Anders aimed a half-hearted swipe at the back of his head.

"Get me the info," she said, holding back a smile. "We've a crime scene to get to."

The Interview

Part 1

The Home Office was located on Marsham Street at Westminster. It was a long, rectangular building with an open glass front, each segment crossed with wooden lattices. Black bollards lined the front to prevent a car bomb attack and the roof jutted out ever so slightly, filled with stained glass to allow the sun to shine below in a myriad of colours. It was a modern and sleek building, yet strangely muted as if afraid to display the wealth that had gone into its creation. At a cost of over three hundred million pounds, Anders wondered where the money had actually gone. Planning and red tape, she mused as she walked to the bustling main entrance, the heels of her shoes clipping loudly on the concrete walkway.

Making her way to the main desk, she announced that she was here to see Director General McDowell and was swiftly ushered into a lift and brought to a conference room by a nervous staff member who quickly slunk away once he'd knocked on the black, panelled door.

"Come in," shouted a deep voice from the other side, his voice muffled by the door. Anders stepped through and found herself in a large room with huge windows that overlooked a small, elegant garden at the rear. The space was dominated by a large, glass desk and behind it sat three figures. As she entered, they stood up and the largest of the three moved towards Anders and took her hand.

"Miss Anders, we are delighted to meet you. Please, sit down." He had a Scottish brogue that made his accent hard to decipher, but carried a genuine warmth and an easy going personality that ensured he was popular in any company. He'd come through the ranks of the police force over a thirty five year career and carried those decades effortlessly. He introduced himself as Director General McDowell and gestured to the two other members of the group.

"This is Francis Cooper of Her Majesty's Inspectorate of Constabulary and this is Justine Barrett, our current Home Secretary."

"For now," Justine said sardonically as she held out a hand in greeting. She was a consummate politician, well dressed and mannered and of indeterminate age. She could have been anywhere between forty and sixty.

"Ah yes, the upcoming elections," said McDowell as he sat down. "I'm sure the country will vote wisely as usual. Makes me glad I'm not involved in politics."

"I hired you," fired back Justine and McDowell shrugged as if to say such things were of no concern to him. Anders liked him immediately. Harder to like was Cooper. He was dressed in black and had an unctuous look about him. He virtually sneered at Anders and ignored her outstretched hand. Taking it back, she pulled out her chair and smoothed her dress down as she sat facing her three interviewers. McDowell opened a large dossier in front of him and started the questioning.

"So what do you know of the NCA?" he asked. Anders had been in London for several months and had used that time to read up on British law and its tangled web of enforcement agencies. Her response was quick and sure.

"Operational in twenty thirteen, it was formed to provide an umbrella force that would be involved with counter terrorism, organised crime and human, weapon and drug trafficking. Essentially, it can be tasked to investigate any crime. Your tabloids have dubbed it the British FBI."

"Indeed," he said. "You forgot to mention the part where we started with half of our initial budget." Barrett gave him a pointed look and he smiled easily, clearly comfortable with using his charm to escape censure.

"I believe the Home Office had a nine billion pound budget in twenty twelve. I'm sure resources were stretched thin," responded Anders diplomatically, but with a sly grin. Barrett stifled a laugh and appraised Anders with fresh eyes. McDowell smiled and winked.

"So, eventually the bean counters gave me some decent funding and I came up with an initiative. A task force that picks its investigations and can be sent anywhere in the country to quickly manage our more difficult assignments. You'll have the best resources and any law enforcement agency at your disposal. You've applied for the post of Assistant Chief Constable, though you realise it's a meaningless rank for the team."

The influx of American crime shows had led the public to believe that a plain clothes detective outranked a uniformed officer, but in Britain, they did not. The task force was to be given a high enough rank to ensure cooperation at any crime scene or local police force. It also meant that they had automatic authority to extend detention of a suspect to thirty six hours and authorise PACE house searches. Whilst the rank was high, the pay wasn't and any authority overruled by an officer of equal rank. Anders nodded her understanding and McDowell continued, reading through his notes from the dossier.

"Says here you were born in London before moving to America thirty years ago. Shone academically and majored in Forensic Pathology and Psychology by the age of eighteen? Impressive."

"So you're a freak and a genius? Or just one of those?" It was the first time that Cooper had spoken and his insidious tone was hostile and condescending. Barrett gave him an evil stare and apologised to Anders.

"You'll have to excuse Cooper, he likes to be challenging."

"Not a problem ma'am," Anders said and turned to McDowell so that he could continue. Unfortunately, Cooper had slid the dossier over to himself, pulling it across the table with a solitary finger that suggested he didn't want to sully himself with its contents, and led the questioning.

"You joined the FBI, then took some time out to go to the army and kill a bunch of Iraqi citizens before heading back to the FBI again." He peered up at her, disdain in his features. "Why did you join the army?"

Anders, despite her loathing of the man, smiled and kept her voice neutral and her hands on her lap, one tucked into the other.

"An opportunity came up and I took it. I had done some work with their MPs as a cross department training exercise and I was invited to join. The Agency saw it as an opportunity to foster good relations with the armed forces."

"Must have been hard," said Barrett, an expression of sympathy on her face.

"No harder than anything I'd come across before," replied Anders pointedly.

McDowell dragged the dossier back to himself with a scowl at Cooper and took the lead once more.

"Looking at your record, it's impressive. You have one of the highest conviction rates in the Agency."

"I had a great team," replied Anders, glad to be getting back to ncutral territory.

"You came top of the class for all combat disciplines and profiling." A snort of derision from Cooper.

"Bit manly isn't it? All that combat." Anders gave him a level stare.

"I wanted to make sure that any prejudices against me were purely that." Barrett smiled at her reply but Cooper continued, jabbing a finger down on the glass table as he spoke.

"Here's my problem. You may have the highest conviction rate, but most of those you caught were killed during arrest. Bit convenient isn't it?" Anders sat back in her chair, putting some distance between them. She wanted to remain passive against his questioning and knew that he was trying to goad her.

"I was tasked with tracking down the most violent offenders in America. Serial killers, serial rapists, repeat offenders. They didn't oftentimes come quietly." Cooper leaned forward and steepled his fingers together, nestling his chin on them.

"Ah yes, the old "Justified homicide". Difficult to have a fair trial if you're dead."

"Each case was closed only after a full investigation of the evidence. No killing was found to be unlawful and every case had sufficient evidence for a successful conviction had they been alive." Cooper chuckled. A laugh without humour. As he spoke, he reached into the dossier and pulled out a sheet of paper.

"Still. I think you're a killer Miss Anders. You may wear a badge and hide behind the law, but you've killed more people than all the criminals you've caught combined, certainly when we take your military record into account." He slid the sheet of paper across the table with a sneer. Anders didn't need look at it to know what the picture was. It had been splashed across every web page and newspaper across the globe. "And this? This just proves it."

The picture was a photograph of Anders. It had been taken just as she had burst from a house in suburban America. She was half naked, her torso exposed to show strips of skin hanging loose from her side. She was drenched in blood, her hair matted with gobbets of gore and carried a small child who had thrust his arms around her neck and buried his face in her protection. Anders gripped him tightly, her bloody hands leaving dark smears on his white shirt, a shocking contrast of purity and death. What struck most about the image wasn't the blood or the damage wrought upon Anders. It was her eyes. They were wild. Full of animalistic rage and fury. The eyes of a killer.

Chapter 3

Caesar's Camp at Wimbledon Common was now Hole Ten of the London Scottish Golf Club and it consisted of a rolling plain of fresh cut grass surrounded by dense trees and shrubs. On the Southern side, a small road wound round the edge of the Common, lined with huge Victorian houses that had been turned into smaller flats for larger profits. To the North, the common continued to slope down until it reached Beverly Brook. Anders had frequently jogged around the area and often hopped over Robin Hood Gate from Richmond Park and skirted along the shallow river. As they pulled up in a large police van, Anders reflected how close she had been to this site only a few hours ago.

The road had been blocked off by area cars, their lights flashing silently onto the red bricked houses. Police tape had cordoned off the entire area and Anders could see the silhouette of a crucifix as the sun shone behind it. For those opening their curtains that morning, it must have presented quite a shock. It was a very public killing.

Mal sat with Barry at the front of the van and a sullen silence had dampened the mood in the back as Lucy had glowered at Anders, who carefully ignored it. While Barry parked the van, Mal jumped out and made for a cluster of men who looked like CID. The highest rank they could ever hope to achieve was Chief Superintendent and Mal, as Deputy Chief Constable, outranked them all. As McDowell had intended, he would take the crime scene and it quickly became clear that it wasn't a popular initiative with the CID officers. An argument started, getting increasingly loud as Duncan and Lucy went to join Mal.

Anders slipped into a Microguard coverall and put on a pair of headphones before selecting an album from her phone at random. Ensuring that she hadn't used it at a previous crime scene, she grabbed a SOC kit, stepped under the yellow and black tape and started walking the site. Samson et Dalila came softly through the headphones as she trod carefully over the grass. The crucifix was roughly three hundred yards from the road and Anders saw the tyre tracks that a large vehicle had made. She guessed that it would have been large enough to carry the crucifix in one piece. Where the van had stopped, small drops of blood spatter could be seen on the grass. Careful to avoid the area, she placed a flag at the site. The victim had been pulled from the vehicle here and further abused.

Scanning the area carefully as the music played, she followed the blood to the crucifix. Ignoring the cross for now, she focused on the blood, creating a picture in her mind, seeing the dent the cross had made in the grass. The flattened plants and deep grooves in the mud also showed that something heavy had been dragged. Cord and tape had been left at the site and she flagged them as well. For something so elaborate, there seemed little care about leaving evidence. There were four large pools of dark blood soaked into the grass. Insects and flies had already converged on the site and the air was thick with them. The location of the sticky blood showed where nails had been hammered into wrists and ankles. The fourth spot looked like it would come from where she guessed the victim's head to be.

Finally looking up to the crucifix, Anders saw a sickening sight. The victim had been stripped to his briefs and the nails thrust through his limbs held him tightly to the wooden cross. It looked like it had been crafted from Red Oak and the blood had soaked into it making the wood darker still. His clothes lay in a pile at the bottom, his wallet open and some ID exposed. The victim's head was lowered, his chin resting on his chest. Careful to avoid the blood and any evidence on the floor around the crucifix, Anders looked closer and saw a wound on his torso that looked like a stab mark. Blood had coursed freely from it and covered his legs, a swarm of buzzing flies laying their eggs on the dried crust. The size of the white, tube like structures, meant that they had done so very recently. The blood also confirmed that the victim had been alive when he had been hung up.

His eyes had been gouged out by the crows that squawked and danced on the trees nearby, annoyed at the interruption to their meal as the empty sockets of the victim glowered accusingly at Anders.

His lower jaw was a ruinous mess and Anders peered closely to see what looked like thorns protruding from the mouth, savage spikes jutting from the cheeks and lips. She stood back once more and surveyed the space around her, placing every tiny detail in context. The argument at the road looked like it had come to an end and Mal was leading his team across the Common to the crucifixion, a scowl darkening his features. They moved slowly and she took heart from the professional way they walked the scene.

Behind Mal walked two others that she had not yet met. Anders guessed them to be the SOCO's that he had ordered to meet them there. One looked exceptionally young. He was lanky and walked as if he was all elbows and knees. He had an unruly mop of hair that kept falling in front of his eyes as a gentle breeze tugged at it. The other was a curvaceous woman who looked to be in her late twenties. By contrast, she walked with elegance but there was a palpable sense of restless energy about her as if she never stood still. They both struggled with boxes of kit and laid them out a distance from the scene as Mal drew near. Lucy made the sign of the cross as she stepped to the crucifix. Anders tried not to see the irony in that as she pulled the headphones from her ears and put them away.

"Looks like he was driven here in a van or some large vehicle," she said as Mal stood next to her and surveyed the area with keen eyes. "Round here you can see a struggle where he was taken from the back of the vehicle, but he was alive and certainly conscious." Duncan walked the same path as Anders had and nodded his agreement.

"Nailed him to the cross here," he muttered. "Excessive blood round the head area though." Anders pointed to the victim's mouth.

"Gag of thorns," she said. Barry give a grunt of distaste and peered closely at the spikes that jutted agonisingly from his cheeks.

"Looks like Buckthorn, but we'll get Helen to check that."

"Why a gag of thorns and not a crown?" asked Lucy as she crouched down to peer at the ID. "Matthew Peters," she said, standing up to reach for her phone so that she could get Jesse to run a search on him. Mal shook his head.

"Don't bother," he said. "Matthew Peters is a High Court Judge." He sighed heavily. "As if the press wasn't going to be all over this anyway." While he considered his options, the two SOCO's approached and brief introductions were made.

"Anders, this is Helen, she's our lead forensics manager and this is Ben. He looks twelve but he's smarter than all of us put together." Ben gave a lopsided grin and made a brief stammering sound. Helen patted him on the back affectionately.

"And he's useless around pretty women. Now, what have we here? Barry, Duncan, be a pair of dears and get the tent set up will you, keep prying eyes away from this poor chap." She had an infectious energy and a genuine warmth that made her easy to like. Her Yorkshire accent made her seem even friendlier, but Anders saw a no nonsense approach to Helen and enjoyed how quickly Duncan and Barry set to their task. Mal watched them struggle with the tent before assigning duties.

"Lucy, coordinate the CID officers and make sure the cordon is secure. Once you've done that, I want a house to house of the whole area. Duncan, you can join them after you've set up the tent. Barry, organise the sweep; I want all evidence found and bagged. Get your mic's out, I want constant communication with Jesse." He tapped his own earpiece as Anders put hers in and she heard Jesse's deep voice through the set.

"Reading you loud and clear folks, Abi is with me as well so she can start making a profile. Any tidbits you can pass to me now would be great. I can put it into HOLMES and cross reference any evidence with previous entries, see if we get a match."

"Doubt it," muttered Lucy. "Ain't ever heard of a crucifixion on these lands in a while." Mal shook his head wearily. There were relatively few murders in Britain and he'd dealt with a great many cases, but this was far beyond what any of them had thought they would encounter. The only one who'd had any real experience with this type of elaborate killing was Anders. He'd only just met her, but could already see that she was someone exceptional. A little distanced maybe, but that was to be expected after what she had gone through and the fact that, three hours into her new job, she was standing on a golf course looking at a scene from the Roman era. He could see the tension between her and Lucy, Duncan as well, but almost pitied them. If Anders' reputation was anything to go by, they'd better watch out. She looked small and diminutive, but she packed a punch. Deciding to keep them apart for now, he spoke to Anders.

"Help Helen and Ben here. The sooner we can process the evidence, the better. I'll go and see Matthew Peters' family and break the news." He checked his watch and made a quick calculation in his head. "Briefing in Scotland Yard at eighteen hundred hours." With that, he strode back to the van, removing his coverall as he approached the edge of the Common. Helen turned to Anders with a welcoming smile, instantly putting her at ease.

"Right then, let's get to work. I must say, I'm very excited to be working with you. I've been reading up on all of your cases! Ben has too." She turned to Ben, who blushed crimson. Helen winked mischievously at Anders who smiled back. She liked her already.

Chapter 4

They worked tirelessly, gathering as much evidence from the scene as possible. Anders kept a running commentary with Jesse who entered the information into HOLMES. It was a database designed to collate evidence from around the country, find matches, make links and offer suggestions as to what avenues to follow. Its first iteration had been difficult to use, but the updated HOLMES2 had proven invaluable.

Leaving Ben at the Common to coordinate a sweep of the entire area, Anders and Helen transported the body back to the Forensics lab. They'd commandeered a large van to transport the corpse still attached to the cross and Mal had ordered a squad of MET officers to help get it to the lab from the parking bay. They'd grumbled and complained, but Helen charmed the surliness from them. She spoke incessantly and flirted with everyone. Her manner hid an astuteness though, and Anders had been impressed with her work. As the cross was placed over two of the metal tables in the lab, Anders scrubbed up for the autopsy while Helen took pictures and recorded her observations. Mal and Abi came down to witness the preliminary work and Abi paled as she saw the body.

"Good heavens," she said, hand reaching to her mouth in horror.

"You don't need to see this," said Mal and she brushed him off.

"Don't be daft, I'm here to help." They stood back as Helen finished her photography and Anders wheeled over a cart of equipment. Helen, clearly nervous to be working with Mal in the room, chattered away rapidly, the words spilling out in a rush.

"Did you know, Herophilus was the first physician to dissect bodies back in three hundred BC and that…."
"Helen," said Mal, his tone soft but firm. "Your initial findings please." She clamped her mouth shut and nodded an apology before stepping to the body.

"Matthews was alive when he was nailed to the cross. Whoever did this tied him to the cross first and you can see he struggled with his bonds as the nails went in. There are perimortem burn like marks along the wrists where the bindings dug in. The nails used are six inches long, steel, generic. Thick though. Thick enough to get through the bone and the hard oak beneath." Anders switched on a UV lamp and, with a visor over her eyes, examined the nails, scraping off debris and placing them in a labelled vial.

"Torn and ripped," she said. "But pulled upwards as if he was dragging his hands down something, maybe the back of a vehicle. Plenty of blood, so I'll run it through the PCR, make a plate and see if we have more than one sample. We may get lucky." Helen moved to the mouth of the victim and clipped off one of the thorns.

"Barry says it's Buckthorn, but I'll check that out." Abi stepped closer, having placed a mask over her mouth and a coverall over her expensive clothes. Matthew Peters had been left for many hours after his death and the skin to the upper body was pale as the blood had drained downwards, making the lower limbs bloated and red. He had been handsome once, but death had robbed him of such things. She looked at the torn flesh of his mouth intently.

"Why a gag of thorns?" she muttered. "There's a practicality to the act. He put so much in there it would have muffled his screams, but there's a sadism to it that is cruel beyond the act of crucifixion."

"He wanted to replicate crucifying Jesus, right down to the stab wound to the right sternum, but there's a reluctance to putting a crown on his head. It's not just sadism," replied Anders. Abi nodded her agreement.

"It's contempt. There's a personal motive to this, but it goes beyond anger."

"There are fingerprints everywhere," said Anders. "I don't think he's worried about getting caught. Either that or he intends to reveal himself. Something this public? I'm guessing this guy wants his credit." Abi grimaced in agreement and started to speak.

"How long has he been up there?" asked Mal curtly. He was keen to move on to more practical matters. Helen had taken a buzz saw from the tray as Anders pushed down slightly on the arm so that the top of the nail could be removed. She peered closely at it and moved to the other nail to confirm her suspicions. As Anders moved, Helen turned to Mal.

"There's little putrefaction and relatively few eggs laid in the wounds or blood. Nothing more than you'd associate with this type of warm weather. The temperature of the torso, combined with the weather reports from last night and the lack of any real insect succession enabled Ben to calculate a time between three and four in the morning." Mal scribbled some notes in his pad as Anders called Helen over.

"Take a look at this," she said and bade Helen to look at the stab wound. "It looks like one deep cut, followed by another into the same area but shallower and at a steeper angle." Helen peered at the wound and lifted the ruined flesh with the tip of a tweezer before grunting her assent.

"Is this important?" asked Mal. Anders nodded and showed them the nails.

"This one has been hit right through the bone and oak in one hammer blow, maybe two. The head is straight and flatter than the others. This one," she said, moving round to the other side of the cross. "Is sloped. Less flat and the wood below shows scratches where the nail didn't go through first time but needed several attempts. The stab wound has a shallower cut inside at a narrower angle. The fingerprints have the odd smudge going across them. It could be a cloth he was carrying or simply smudges from what he was doing. Or it could be someone wearing gloves. I think we're looking at two people."

Mal gazed at the body thoughtfully, one arm folded over his broad chest and the other resting on it, one hand idly scratching his beard.

"Abi, do you think this could be two people or hesitancy?" She considered it carefully.

"There are several factors that can account for it. The perpetrator may have been hesitant with the nail if it was the first one, or could have been at an awkward angle when hammering it in. We can't be sure of that unless Ben finds something up at the Common to support it. The wound is more compelling, but it could be that the person changed position, or slipped. This killing feels personal. It's rare for two people to have such a deep grudge as to willingly commit this kind of atrocity." Mal gazed at Anders thoughtfully before nodding.

"We'll put it out there for the time being, keep an open mind," he said. "Now, let's get him off the cross. Abi, I insist that you are not part of this." She gratefully left while Helen cut the heads from the nails and the three of them lifted the corpse from the cross. Rigor mortis had set in and the blood had congealed to the wood. During the first stage of decomposition, the body's digestive enzymes start to destroy its own cells until they become too inactive from the colder body temperature. This created a layer of liquid between the muscle and skin, which now peeled off as it was lifted from the oak, the liquid draining off into steel containers below the table. Mal flinched at the tearing, sloppy sound.

Placing the corpse on one table, they were able to wheel the cross to the side. They would examine that later once the autopsy was finished. Helen and Mal lifted the corpse while Anders slid a body block under the spine so that the arms and neck fell back making it easier to make the Y-shaped incision.

The next task would be to cut from the top of each shoulder, down the chest and meet at the sternum, where the incision would continue as one down to the pubic bone. Often, there would be very little blood unless the victim had drowned. Sheers would be used to cut open the chest and a saw run through the ribs on the lateral sides of the cavity to pull up the sternum and attached ribs as one piece.

The organs would then be removed en mass and the pericardial sac of the heart would be opened and blood taken from here for toxicology and chemical analysis. The spectrometer would help with that. The stomach and intestines would be sliced open and examined before moving the thick rubber body block under the head so that the cap could be removed and the brain extracted.

Knowing what was about to happen, Mal went to leave. He'd seen enough autopsies and it wasn't something he could get used to. As he stood at the door and removed his coverall, his phone went and he raised it to his ear.

"Mal speaking." He listened for a few brief seconds before hanging up and turning to Anders. "Jesse has something to show us. Helen, you stay here and finish the autopsy, Anders, you're with me." Anders turned to Helen as she made her way to the door.

"Sorry hun, you want some help, you call any time, you hear?" Helen waved a scalpel in her direction as she leant down to start the incision.

"I'll be fine. You come down later for a drink and a chat though. I have some tequila cooling in the chiller." Anders pointed to the cabinets where any corpses would be kept until they were released back to their families.

"In there?" she said. Helen gave a nonchalant shrug as if it would be strange not to.

"Of course." Grinning at Helen, Anders promised to bring the lemon before hurrying down the corridor to catch up with Mal, his long strides making short work of the lengthy space. As they entered the Hub, something Jesse had started calling the central area, Anders saw the entire team huddled round Jesse's desk, a palpable buzz in the room. She reached into her pocket and took out a bar of chocolate that she started to demolish.

"Projector," snapped Mal as he drew near. Barry reached up to the ceiling and turned on the projector, his tall frame easily reaching the device. As it whirred into life, Lucy and Duncan cleared some desk space and sat on it as the image came up on the far wall.

"It's all over the news," said Jesse. "Gone completely viral. If they don't already, the whole country will know about this in the next hour."

On the wall, they could see a website. An artfully framed photo of Matthew Peters nailed to a cross lay beneath a banner reading "Fifty Two Weeks Of Murder." Anders read the text below and felt a chill ripple down her spine.

"Forget the UK," she said in the shocked silence. "The whole world is going to know by the end of the day."

Chapter 5

Mal stood in front of the team, his mind reeling. Gathering his thoughts, he addressed them all.

"We're in the middle of a shit storm and make no mistake. We have a member of the aristocracy, Lord Michael Buckland himself, paying folks five million pounds to cut people up in inventive ways. I guess that explains the thorns. We need to approach this from several angles. Jesse, can we shut down the website? That has to be our first priority."

Jesse held up his hands in a helpless gesture.

"Already tried that, came right back up with a new IP. This one in Russia. I shut that down, another comes right back up. Different IP, different country."

"Check Buckland's background," said Anders. "See if he has any IT training. If not, then someone is doing it for him. That may be a way to him." Mal nodded his agreement, but frowned as Anders continued.

"I still think we're looking at more than one person for the crucifixion." Lucy snorted in derision.

"He's admitted to the act himself. It's on the wall right in front of you."

"He's hardly going to say if someone helped him. It's enough to have his name out there. We look for two people. It widens the net, doubles our chances of finding him."

"And cuts in half the time we have to look for Buckland," said Lucy, standing to confront Anders. Mal intervened before the exchange could get even more heated.

"Right now, we work with what we have. Buckland has claimed responsibility, so we look for him. I'll see the Director-General, get a statement out there, make it clear that we will find him and anyone else who tries to enter his competition. Lucy, you get in touch with Europol and Interpol, get a red line set up, make sure everyone starts tracking Buckland. Jesse, get someone from GCHQ over here now. I want them to follow the traffic to and from this site, see if we can't stop any entries before it happens."

GCHQ patrolled the internet, sniffing out paedophiles, criminal activity and anything linked to terrorism. They were the elite cyber intelligence unit in the country and were based in a building fondly referred to as the "Doughnut" in Cheltenham. Since the Investigatory Powers Bill in twenty sixteen, their ability to track any and all internet activity had increased exponentially. Mal had argued strongly against such a breach of civil liberties, but welcomed its use now, reeling off more work as his mind kicked into overdrive, the thrill of the chase pushing him on.

"We need checks on everything linked to Buckland. Emails, smart phones, social media, Oyster cards, credit cards, cash cards, store loyalty cards and any other damn cards you can think of. Tap his phone, get his car plates on the system, have them tracked. Anything to do with Buckland or his family, I want scrutinised, turned over and torn apart."

Britain had become known as The Surveillance State in recent years and not without some justification. Anywhere between four and six million CCTV cameras followed your every move. Any individual will have their communications tracked several hundred times a day, with data from smart phones and computers stored in bulk, ready to be analysed at the push of a button. Combined with automatic number plate recognition technology and over seventy thousand cash machine cameras, Anders hated the fact that everyone was their own star of CCTV, making over three hundred appearances a day. Even in her profession, she didn't see the need for it. There were other ways to hunt. Basic human weakness always won out and it was something Mal was keen to exploit.

"Abi," he said, pacing furiously. "Get me a profile, Anders, you can help. The best fugitives behave unpredictably, but he'll make a mistake eventually. Buckland can hide from us, but he can't hide from himself. I want to know his pressure points. What can't he be without? Where will he retreat to when the paranoia gets to him? He'll want contact with someone he knows, so once we're done tearing his life down, I want everybody he's ever met, anyone he's ever spoken to or even looked at funny. Invade their lives so completely, you know them better than their own mother. I don't care how grubby or invasive you feel, I want every last detail. Duncan, work with MIT, I want feet anywhere he's linked to, a full search. Extend your PACE authority to each squad. Lucy, when you're done, help speak to Matthew's family, see if they might have anything that can help." He paused once more, his fingers drumming the desk in agitation.

"Anders, get his ex-wife in and his brother. Barry, go to counter-terrorism and get as much of their manpower as you can. I'm sure this comes under their remit." Though part of the NCA, they were a separate and autonomous unit to Mal's. He gazed at each member of his team intently, considering his words carefully.

"We were made for this. Each of us is outstanding in our field, the very best the Force has to offer. The country will be looking to us for decisive action. Everything we do will be scrutinised to the highest degree, but remember one thing. The NCA is exempt from the Freedom of Information Act. There will be no leaks."

He needn't have threatened the group. His tone made the consequences clear.

"Let's move. We have a killer to catch."

Chapter 6

Anders brought Buckland's ex-wife, Lady Margaret, into Abi's office and had her sit on one of the comfortable chairs. She took the sofa opposite as Abi moved from her desk and sat next to Anders, both of them facing Lady Margaret. Anders took the opportunity to scrutinise the woman as she fussed in her handbag for some tissues. She was tall and regal, carrying herself with the manner of those born into wealth and titles. Anders knew Lady Margaret to be in her mid-fifties, but she looked much younger, with red, permanently flushed cheeks and hair tied in a fierce bun behind her head. She wore an expensively tailored suit, with a pearl necklace and matching earrings. Putting her bag on the floor, she smoothed the hem of her skirt with perfectly manicured hands before clasping them together in a defensive manner.

Anders found her to be remarkably composed considering what her ex-husband was getting up to. Crossing one leg over the other and resting her hands on her knees, Anders leaned forward and gave her guest an open smile. Unthreatening but engaged.

"Lady Margaret," she started, but was interrupted by Buckland's ex-wife, her perfectly enunciated tones a sharp contracts to Anders' American accent.

"My friends call me Maggie. You may do the same." Anders nodded her thanks and continued.

"I'm Assistant Chief Constable Anders and this is Abigail Philips. She's a psychologist attached to the NCA, and is here to support the team. Please may I reassure you that we are simply here to discuss what you may know about your ex-husband's whereabouts. We wish to make this as painless for you as possible." Lady Margaret gave her a wan smile and Anders could see her mask of composure slip for a brief second. Abi reached out and took her hand, giving Lady Margaret an empathetic smile.

"I appreciate that this is very difficult for you," she said. "I'm told that you and Michael have a son together." She nodded and dabbed at her eyes with some tissue.

"Yes. Lawrence. He's in America at the moment, studying at Yale. I can't get hold of him yet. Time difference I guess."

"Would you like me to contact someone at the Bureau and see if they can get in touch?" asked Anders. Lady Margaret took a sharp breath as she noticed the scar on Anders' neck and her eyes narrowed as she searched her memory.

"You were that FBI agent," she said softly. "The one at that horrible house. That man did some terrible things dear. He fully deserved what you did to him."

"Your ex-husband ma'am," said Anders quietly, changing topic and ignoring the questioning look Abi gave her.

"Of course," Lady Margaret replied. "I've not seen Michael for several months now. We've been divorced for over a year, but he stayed close to Lawrence. Our social circles often brought us together, but it was never a problem."

"If I may, what were the reasons for your divorce?" Lady Margaret smiled sadly.

"We just grew apart. Sometimes you live with someone for many years and then see them anew one day. Realise that you simply don't love them anymore. Your love has become that for a friend or companion."

"Most successful marriages are based upon friendship," said Abi. "It's best to have that at the beginning and see if love flows from there." Lady Margaret nodded her head in agreement, her mind wandering through happier times.

"Absolutely. We started the wrong way round. We met when I had just finished my training as a nurse. Came in to A&E after he'd fallen from his horse. A whirlwind romance you might say, married by the end of the year. It caused quite a stir, I can tell you! As if my father wasn't annoyed enough at me becoming a nurse, I go and get married within a year of meeting Michael." She smiled wistfully at the memory, though it faded as she remembered those passionate times turning to cold embers. "He had such an energy and vibrancy about him, it was infectious." As she spoke, Anders and Abi let her do so uninterrupted, content to let her reveal the man they were hunting. Lady Margaret looked forlorn as though she mourned someone who had passed away.

"And then he changed. So slowly you never really notice it at the time. He lost the joy, the passion. It was his eyes. They used to sparkle. By the time we divorced, they were blank. I could never work out what he was thinking, what was going on behind that stare. We used to spend hours just talking, sharing ideas and thoughts, revelling in each other's company. But that just vanished. Slowly, piece by piece until you realise one day that it's gone and you didn't even see it slip away. Like a call in the night to tell you your husband's died in an accident. You never see it coming."

Her words married with the text on the website. Of someone who had lost their way and turned to something more dangerous and exciting to find some meaning. Anders was drawn to the idea that it was some spoilt little posh boy with too much money and too little perspective, but it was more complex than that. It always was. The words he had written were that of a zealot. Of someone who passionately believed in his cause. In his blog, he'd written that belief defiles sound thought and reason and she wondered if he'd seen the irony in his own words.

"Have you read the blog on his website?" she asked. Tears welled in Lady Margaret's eyes as she recalled the horrific text, but Anders kept pushing. "I'm sorry to ask you these things, but his ideas on mankind, about us being some kind of plague. Is this something you've heard from him before?" She shook her head.

"No, not at all. He was such a kind man. Gave so much time and resources to several charities that he set up." Anders groaned inwardly. She'd have to investigate those charities.

"Would you know where he may be hiding now? Any places he loved to frequent, anywhere he mentioned he felt safe?" Lady Margaret shook her head, closing her eyes and sighing heavily as she struggled to maintain her composure.

"I've tried so hard. I wanted to come here with something useful, but I have nothing I'm afraid. What I can tell you is that Michael is no fool. If he has set himself to this task, it will not be done haphazardly. It will be meticulously planned and executed. He will see it through."

Anders saw a chilling truth in her words and found herself startled by a loud tap on the window. She turned to see Mal on the other side and he beckoned her out.

"Excuse me Lady Margaret, I will leave you with Abi to finish the interview. If you think of anything, here's my card. Please don't hesitate to call me at any time."

Standing to leave, Anders caught Abi's eye. She nodded to say that she would be fine and ushered Anders out. Closing the door to the office behind her, Mal asked if she had anything.

"Not much," replied Anders. "Abi's finishing up, but I don't think we'll get anything of use. You?" Mal shrugged.

"McDowell's doing a press conference in an hour. As you can imagine, he's keen for us to get results. Have you set up an interview with his brother?" Anders nodded and moved to the stairs leading out, taking her jacket from the back of the chair at her desk as she did so.

"He's at Parliament now. Ten minute walk. You fancy a stroll?" Mal scratched his beard absently as he assessed what else needed doing. Realising that he couldn't do anything until his team had all checked back in, he gave her a grin.

"Why not? Always wanted to go to Parliament." His grin faded as they reached the staircase.

"We do have lifts, you know," he grumbled.

"I know," replied Anders as she hit the steps at a frightening pace. Shaking his head, Mal followed her up, careful to avoid staring at her rear and telling himself to behave.

As they left the Yard, Anders crossed the road so that they could walk along the Thames. The sun was setting and the roads were jammed with cars and vans snarling their way home. A few buses and taxies sped past, enjoying their own lane and a biting wind forced them both to bend their heads against its chill, unprepared as they were for the cold in the summer months. Hands thrust into his jean pockets, Mal raised his voice to speak above the traffic and the rambunctious wind that toyed playfully with their clothes and hair.

"Heck of a first day," he said as a boat sped past crammed with tourists taking photographs and waving. Anders waved back, grinning at their cheers.

"I've had worse," she replied.

"You come across anything like this?" asked Mal. Anders gave the question some thought before replying.

"No, but like Lord Buckland, I've seen plenty of folks justify their killings no matter how bizarre it may seem to us. Dennis Nilsen killed fifteen men and kept them at his house in various poses for company. Brenda Ann Spencer spent one morning shooting at school children. Why? She didn't like Mondays. That's where the Bob Geldof song came from. On the flip side, look at Fergus Glen. In two thousand and three he hacked his brother to death when he didn't say thank you for his meal. His defence? He just annoyed me, he said." Mal saw a gap in the pedestrian traffic and led them back across the road as Westminster Palace loomed closer, its Gothic architecture towering above them. The wind abated slightly and a warmth infused the air.

"They're the scariest ones," continued Anders as she undid her jacket and shrugged it off. "The ones with no motive, no cause. They just want to inflict suffering and pain. I think Buckland actually veers more towards that when you strip away his twisted ideology."

They took a right as they neared the iconic structure and skirted around it so that Westminster Abbey was to their right and the Houses of Parliament to their left. They had access to the St Stephen Entrance on the West side and Anders smiled as Big Ben ushered in a new hour above them. It would take a long time to shake the feeling that she was just a tourist in London. Mal frowned at her words, oblivious now to the famous landmark.

"How come?" he asked. Anders, neatly sidestepping a queue of meandering tourists, gave an exasperated sigh.

"I'm not sure. The sadism mainly. It feels too personal to be linked to a cause. There's also the public nature of it. That's what he's getting off on. Dressing it up as he's doing, gives him a following, a cult. It gives his actions legitimacy and anyone who wishes to emulate him, a justification. What's more powerful than changing the world?"

Her words sent shivers down Mal's spine and he gazed at her thoughtfully. Anders was oblivious to his stare as she looked around in wonder at the embodiment of the British Constitution. Suddenly her phone vibrated and she pulled it from her back pocket as Mal turned to find the entrance. Leading them through St Stephen's Hall, past the marble busts of Pitt and Fox, he listened in on the conversation.

"Anders here," she said and turned the volume of her phone up so that she could hear over the bustle and hubbub of tourists taking photographs and chatting away animatedly.

"Agent Anders, it's Crackers." Anders rolled her eyes as Jesse continued to push his moniker.

"You're too old for a nickname Jesse," she said and laughed at his mock indignation. "What's up?"

"You're a hard woman Agent Anders. Got the skinny on Buckland's brother for you. Turns out they're identical twins. Born in nineteen sixty five, Francis popped out first, so I guess he's the elder brother. Seems that way from his career anyways. Went to Oxford to study physics, his work led to some of the Haldron Collider stuff they do at CERN. I'm looking at the maths here, but it's not in any language I know of." Anders chuckled as Mal led them to a desk in the Central Lobby and presented their warrant cards to an officer stationed there. The room was huge, opulent and elegantly decorated. It spoke of understated wealth and prosperity, a symbol for the nation.

They were led down a long corridor to meet with Lord Buckland and Anders asked Jesse to hurry with the cliff notes.

"His brother, our little psycho, went to Cambridge instead and studied History. Has a few papers published by the looks of it. Francis married in nineteen eighty eight, did lots of charity work, MP for a few years. He then joined the House of Lords at the Queens request in two thousand and seven. Wife died last year in a car accident. DUI." They neared a large oak door and the guide knocked before entering and announcing his guests.

Anders followed Mal and found herself in a large, well lit room. On the walls hung paintings of every King and Queen since George I. Statues of gilded caen stone lined the thirty metre room, each one depicting a King who had ruled during times of war and conflict. Two large frescos, weathered by age, depicted the death of Nelson and the battle of Waterloo. The Royal Gallery was close to the debating chamber, so several large tables and chairs were placed down each side to enable conversation and work. The room was empty at this time, save two people.

One sat at a table, hands resting on his large stomach. His face was pinched and he gazed at the officers with hooded eyes over his beaked nose. The other paced the room, hands resting behind his back as he gazed at the paintings. He was tall and powerfully built. Though in his early fifties, Lord Francis Buckland seemed to have weathered like oak, getting tougher with each passing year. Grey speckled his temples, but his face was smooth and unlined. He wore a well-tailored suit that highlighted his physique and had an air of authority about him. Anders could tell that he was used to command and accepted it as his right. Mal stepped forward, suddenly incongruous in his jeans and flannel shirt, and offered his hand to Lord Buckland, who gripped it tightly.

"Good morning Lord Buckland, thank you for agreeing to meet with us. I'm…"

"I know who you are," he said, his voice deep and smooth. "I was part of the committee that agreed to McDowell's initiative." Mal gave a gracious nod of his head.

"Then we are indebted to you. I'm sure you know why we are here." Buckland indicated the man sat at the table. He hadn't moved and simply stared quietly at the group

"I do. That is why I have my solicitor present. I'm sure you won't mind." The figure gave a grunt of acknowledgement and proceeded to write notes as Anders spoke, Mal content to let her lead.

"We're only here to see if you can help us with our inquiries. This is very much an informal discussion."

"Who was he?" asked Buckland suddenly. Anders gave him a querulous look before Buckland gave an impatient gesture. "The man my brother crucified. Who was he?"

"I'm afraid that we cannot disclose that information yet." Mal leaned forward and spoke over Anders.

"It was Matthew Peters," he said, eyeing Buckland closely.

"Good God," he muttered, visibly shaken by the news. He turned from the pair and Anders saw him shake with grief. "He was a very dear friend of mine. We'd known each other our whole lives. Went to school and University together. A dear, dear friend."

That would account for the spiteful nature of the killing, thought Anders.

"Do you think his choice of victim was deliberate?" she asked. Buckland turned back to them, eyes red with grief. His voice, when he spoke was full of sorrow yet laced with bitterness.

"Most certainly. We never saw eye to eye. He hated me as only a twin could."

"His ex-wife, Lady Margaret, seemed to think he was a kind man and that this is out of character." Buckland gave a snort of derision.

"Crucifying someone is out of character to the majority of people Miss Anders. It *is* out of character for Michael, but he is not incapable of such things. He was quick to anger as a child and always taking up some crusade or other, flitting between them like a moth to flame. If he believes in his work, he will fully commit to it."

"Where is he likely to be now," asked Mal, his voice soft and gentle. "Our records show that he has land and holdings all over the country. We are searching them now, but it will take some time to conduct a proper search."

"Nowhere there," replied Lord Buckland. "He's no fool, my brother. Makes the brightest of us look dim by comparison. He'll have somewhere that your records won't show and all of his accounts offshore."

"Might I ask that we take some fingerprints and DNA samples? As a twin, it would provide vital data that may help us catch him more quickly." Lord Buckland turned back to Anders, who had asked the question.

"Twins don't have the same fingerprints Miss Anders. I'd have thought that someone with your training would know that." She gave him an easy smile and Lord Buckland found himself charmed by her.

"I am aware of that sir, but your fingerprints are not only shaped by your genes. During your time in the uterus, the maternal nutrition, blood pressure and your own position in the womb will have affected the growth of your fingers during the end of the first trimester. The whorls and ridges on your hands will have some similarities with your brother. It would help make a partial match." Lord Buckland grinned and winked at her.

"Thank you for the lesson Miss Anders, I'd be more than happy for you to take some samples." At this, Blackwell coughed politely and stood up, scraping his chair loudly on the wooden floor, the sound echoing around the chamber.

"At this point, I must intervene and recommend that my client does not provide any samples. I will not have it in the public domain that DNA and print samples have been taken. My client's reputation would be damaged beyond that which it already has."

"Not helping in our investigation is equally damning," snapped Anders. She'd taken an instant dislike to this unctuous man who used the law as a weapon, his tone and demeanour insidious and reptilian.

"Then he will provide samples when it is clearly proven that, in doing so, he will further your investigation. You have his brother's written confession, posted for the whole world to see. That is sufficient for now. You are conducting a manhunt, not a murder investigation." Anders made to reply, but Mal stepped forward, his voice calming the increasingly heated debate.

"We are not governed by the Freedom of Information Act. Lord Buckland here ensured that the NCA was exempt from that. No one will know if he has given samples. All our work is done in-house."

"Your department is less than a week old Mr Weathers. It is untested and not yet proven to be secure." Francis opened his hands in a gesture of apology.

"I'm sorry, but I need to abide by his instructions. There's little point in paying him so much otherwise. If I can help in any other way, please let me know." Mal gave him a brief smile and shook his hand as he made to leave.

"Thank you Lord Buckland," he said and strode to the exit. Anders followed, but Francis called after her.

"Miss Anders, before you leave, let me tell you a little about this Palace." He walked with her to the exit as Mal waited at the door. "It was built in the eleventh century, but in fifteen twelve, it was destroyed by fire. After that, it was rebuilt and became the House of Parliament. In eighteen thirty four, it was burnt down once more and during the Second World War, it was bombed no less that fourteen times. The statue you walked past on your way here, the one of Richard the Lionheart. It was blown from its pedestal and its sword bent. But it did not break. That became the symbol for democracy during the War. This whole building represents this nation's commitment to democracy and social justice. My brother will cause chaos and attempt to undermine the very values this society has been built on for over five hundred years. He must not be allowed to succeed."

As they reached the door, he wished them good day and turned smartly on his heels, his footsteps echoing off the Royal Gallery walls. Anders and Mal let themselves drift with the tide of humanity as it poured through the Palace and found themselves deposited on the steps of St Stephen's entrance. Mal shook his head, a dour look on his face.

"We're not going to get much help from him or his ex-wife," he said. He checked his watch and turned to Anders.

"Come on, let's get back to the Yard. We need to debrief the team."

Chapter 7

Anders opened the door to her apartment and tossed the keys into a glass bowl on a table in the hall. She hung up her jacket and made her way to the kitchen. Cassie had made dinner and decided to use every pot and pan available. It smelled good though, and her stomach rumbled at the inviting odour. Cassie had left a portion for her in the oven and she spied it through the glass. On the fridge, she saw a painting that Aaron must have done that day at school. He'd drawn Anders, snake like scar round her neck, holding a gun to a frightening monster. It was painted black, but the eyes were blue, much like his father's. The monster was tall, but Anders was taller, Cassie and Aaron standing behind her, shielded from the fury of the beast.

"Pretty sure that's going to come up at a parent-teacher meeting," she muttered as she turned the oven on to warm up her food. While she waited for that to heat up, she took a bar of chocolate from the fridge and sighed in delight at the English chocolate, so much better than the American version Aaron and Cassie preferred.

Hearing sounds coming from Aaron's bedroom, she took off her boots and padded along the corridor to his room. The door was ajar and she could see a light spilling from the crack. The shower was on in the bathroom and she could hear Cassie's soulful voice as she sang an old Christian song, "In the Pines". Cassie imbued the words with such sadness that Anders felt overwhelming sorrow for her.

Sliding Aaron's door open a little more, she saw him lying in bed, curled up under the sheets and wide awake. He smiled as he saw her and shot from his bed to give her a warm hug.

"Bumble!" he cried. She lifted him up and carried him to his bed, tiptoeing over the scattered action figures that created a prickly minefield for her bare feet. Posters of his favourite Marvel films adorned the walls and she noticed that he still wore his Captain America T-shirt.

"It's way past your bedtime little Munchkin. How was your first day at school?" As she tucked him back into his bed, he shrugged.

"It was ok. I painted you a picture."

"I saw. Thank you. I always wanted to slay big scary monsters! Grrrr!" She gave Aaron a tickle that caused him to shriek loudly and throw his sheets off in delight. Tucking him back in, she asked if he'd made any friends that day. Another nonchalant shrug.

"A few," he replied. "Can you read for me?" Anders smiled, reached over to the bedside table and plucked a book from the top before sliding back on the bed and leaning against the wall, folding her legs under her.

"Of course. We haven't finished The Hobbit yet." As she flicked to the right page, she heard a creak in the hallway and guessed that Cassie was outside, listening in. "Come on in hun," she called and Cassie gave a rueful smile as she snuggled up to her on the bed, her damp hair soaking through Anders' blouse. Though she was nineteen years old, her past had aged her in many ways but stunted her development in others. Anders cleared her throat and started to read, putting on her best dragon voice for Smaug, as Aaron and Cassie drifted off to sleep.

Later that night, Anders showered and changed into her nightwear, a strappy top and some shorts, and moved quietly around the flat as she cleaned the kitchen, took her tablets and turned off the TV that had been left on. She'd even managed to get Aaron's favourite t-shirt off him and in the wash. She'd have it dry for tomorrow. Once Anders was done, she made her way to the workroom, taking a bundle of papers with her. Closing the door quietly, she started to pin the sheets to the whiteboard that she'd screwed to the wall. Using a black marker, she drew lines, scribbled ideas and started to build a pattern of evidence. Her work done, she stepped back and appraised her notes, chewing the tip of the marker absently. Finally satisfied, she locked the door behind her and made her way to bed, easing herself under the sheets with a satisfied purr. Within seconds she was asleep.

A few hours later, Anders' phone rang, crashing through her sleep. Snapping instantly awake, she grabbed the device before it could wake Aaron and Cassie.

"Anders," she said, sleep making her voice groggy. Mal's dulcet Welsh tones came from the speaker.

"Get to Smith's Antiques opposite the Natural History Museum. We have our first entry into Buckland's competition."

Chapter 8

Throwing on a pair of jeans over her shorts, Anders moved swiftly through the flat to the kitchen. She quietly set up breakfast and left a note on the fridge before grabbing her jacket and sneakers and running down the steps of the apartment building to the basement where her car was parked. Slipping on her sneakers as she ran, she hopped into an old Ford pick-up truck and tapped in the address Mal had given her into a small sat nav tucked away in the glove box. With scant regard to the British Highway Code, Anders sped from the basement and skidded onto the street, covering the distance to the crime scene in half the time that the sat nav predicted.

As she approached Smith's Antiques, the roads narrowed. Store fronts lined the streets, selling London tourist paraphernalia or dinosaurs and other items of interest that anyone coming from the Natural History Museum might fancy. Most shops sold cheap tat, but there was the odd gem hidden among the back streets where only those who knew what they were after went. Smith's Antiques was one such gem. A small shop sandwiched between two large houses, they seemed to creak inwards, shrinking the shop yet further. The sign was old and muted, the window's dark and musty, but the shop was filled with rare finds that would sell for many thousands at auction. The whole street was filled with a flashing red and blue light as stationary patrol cars idled close by, yellow police tape strung across the road.

Anders parked near the tape and walked to the closest uniformed officer, holding out her warrant card for him to see. The three silver downturned stripes on his epaulettes showed the officer to be a Sergeant. Had she been in uniform, her insignia would have shown a circle of oak leaves with crossed tipstaffs in the centre, a call back to the fourteenth century when arrest warrants were carried in the hollow tips. It was also handy for clubbing and led to the distinctive police batons. The sergeant looked young and was visibly shaken by what he had seen, blinking rapidly as he leaned forward to look at her card. He frowned as he saw her rank and stood to attention, his training overriding his shock.

"Report, Sergeant," she said and he gulped at the recall, wiping sweat from his shaved head with a damp tissue.

"Yes ma'am," he said. "An alert was posted an hour ago. Neighbours rang us when they saw blood pouring from under the doorway. They banged on the door to see if anyone needed help, but there was no reply." Anders looked around the street and saw curtains twitch in a few windows. The locals were clearly enjoying the show, she mused, before turning her attention back to the Sergeant.

"I entered the premises by jimmying the lock and found…well…it looked like something from that website so I called it in. Been here waiting for you guys. No one but your boss has been in or out since I saw…" Anders gave him one of her dazzling smiles and thanked him for his work, giving him a comforting pat on his arm. She told him to get the rest of the uniformed officers and start knocking on doors and taking statements.

"Start with that one," she said and pointed to where she had seen a shadow through the curtains as a bored housewife watched the excitement below. She made her way to the same van that Barry had requisitioned earlier and saw Ben getting into a new set of coveralls.

"Hey Ben," she said, grinning as he spun on his heels to greet her, his lanky frame twisting to accommodate the sudden movement. He brushed a mop of hair from his eyes and smiled a welcome.

"Hi Anders," he said, his voice surprisingly deep and strong. "Enjoying your first day?" Anders gave a wry chuckle.

"Thought you'd still be at the Common, processing the Crucifixion." Ben shook his head and the mop of hair drifted back over his eyes again.

"I've got SCO on it now. I've done enough there that even they can't muck it up. Mal wanted us here." SC+O were the Specialist Crime and Operations Unit of the Met and consisted of the Major Investigations Team. Had McDowell not set up this specialist task force, then they would have been handling this case. They were an excellent unit, but Ben worked on a different plane to most of his colleagues. He turned back to the van and started unloading more equipment, Anders helping him with some of the heavier gear.

Once they'd finished, Helen walked round the corner and Ben blushed wildly as he saw her. She'd clearly been on a date and wore a figure hugging dress and heels that were even taller than her usual. Anders chuckled as Helen approached, a scowl on her face.

"On a date Helen?" she asked. "Anyone interesting?"

"It was about to get interesting," she grumbled as she sat on the back of the van and pulled off her shoes, the hem of her dress riding up to reveal the tops of her stockings. Helen noticed Ben glancing at them and winked at Anders. "I guess this case is really going to interfere with my sex life. A woman has needs you know." Ben blushed further as he reached into a box to get out his forensics kit and Helen couldn't resist teasing him further.

"If I don't get my fix regularly, I just get cranky," she said with a grin. Anders joined in gleefully.

"There's always that twixt works on batteries," she replied and Ben dropped his case, spilling powder on the street. Helen sighed theatrically.

"True, but they never last long enough!" She guffawed with laughter, but soon took pity on Ben and helped him gather up the equipment, fussing over him like a mother. Mal exited the shop as they worked and gave them a curt nod. He looked tired and obviously hadn't been home yet. Under his coverall, Anders could see the same shirt and jeans that he'd worn the day before. When he spoke, Anders could hear the tiredness in his voice.

"Sorry for calling you out at this time of night, but it looks like Crime and Punishment in there." Anders took off her jacket and tossed it into the back of the van as Mal spoke. She stepped into some coveralls and pulled them up over her legs, seemingly oblivious to the fact that her top showed the scars that ravaged her back. She was turned away from the crew and Helen gave her a smile, both sympathetic and sad. A look of sorrow crossed Mal's craggy features and he quickly averted his gaze as Anders zipped up the coverall and turned around.

"Didn't take you for a fan of Dostoevsky," she said, unaware of the stir her back had caused.

"A-level English," he said. "My teacher's favourite book." Anders smiled and put some headphones in her ears. Selecting an album at random, she gave Mal a nod and stepped into the antiques shop as "A Feather on the Breath of God" played from her phone. After she left, Helen looked to Ben, who shrugged.

"Most likely some form of strategy training to effectively recall information from a crime scene." Mal gave him a strange look, but he carried on regardless. "I'd imagine she's combining episodic free recall with cued recall using the music to stimulate the medial temporal lobes for conscious recollection coupled with the posterior midline region for imagery. She's most likely creating a state dependent recall at the same time. One that can be enhanced by replaying the music without necessitating the need for drugs."

Mal turned to Helen and opened his hands in a helpless gesture. Helen smiled and gave Ben a maternal pat on the back.

"Aww bless. What he's saying is that he really needs me to find him a woman. When was your last date love?" Mal sighed and walked off, following Anders into the shop and neatly sidestepping the congealed pool of blood on the pavement. Helen chuckled as she picked up her case and followed Mal.

"You could have just said she's a woman and remembers things better," she said. Ben, hurrying to catch up spoke animatedly.

"Well, it's interesting you say that. How different is the brain of a…" Mal stuck his head from the storefront and gave them an impatient look.

"Will you two stop faffing about and hurry up!" Scampering after him, they made their way into the crime scene that made up the first known entry to Lord Buckland's macabre game.

Chapter 9

The shop was dimly lit despite the cluster of lights that adorned the ceiling. The owner had used low wattage bulbs and they were grimy with age. The floor was lined with rows of wooden shelves and they were packed with antiques from all ages. They'd been placed together according to rarity and not location or date, so the statue of Amon Ra from Ancient Egypt found itself rubbing shoulders with a clay bowl from Macedonia. Anders spied a terracotta figurine from China and noted the Samurai Sword from Japan that had belonged to Yamada Nagamasa. A small tag was tied to each piece, though no price was listed.

As Mal entered, he saw Anders walking slowly through the shop, a look of intense focus on her face as she surveyed the room, taking in the tiniest of details before turning her attention to the corpse. The body sat on the floor slumped against the counter, a terrible mess of wreckage where its head used to be. Mal's eyes were drawn to the axe that was embedded into the floor next to it, positioned in such a way as to give the most dramatic effect when photographed correctly. Blood and chunks of gore spattered the walls, floor and ceiling. It had been a crime of unrelenting viciousness. Mal had no doubt that it was an entry into the Murder Competition as the press were dubbing it.

Helen knelt by the body, careful to avoid disturbing the pool of blood that surrounded the victim and grimaced at the pulpy carnage. Ben had set up some halogen lamps and the shadows were banished from the store as he switched them on. Gone were his awkward movements and bumbling personality, replaced by an efficient professional who knew his work. Anders removed her headphones and stood next to Helen, just as Mal asked for her thoughts.

"Repeated blows to the crown of the head with a blunt object. I'd say the blood stained axe is our culprit," she said with an arched eyebrow. "Helen?" The axe was covered in blood, but it was the back that had been used, not the blade, which was free from gore.

Streaks of blood had run from the back, down its edges and then soaked into the wood that it had been slammed into. Helen nodded her agreement.

"I'll have to check the measurements of the axe and match them to some of the compaction fractures on the skull, but it's more than likely correct. The problem is going to be finding a spot on the skull where I can get a clear enough reading. There must be more than a dozen separate impacts that have crushed the skull."

"There's a lot of rage here. In the book, the Pawnbroker's head was probably mostly intact. The author wrote of the dead eyes that watched his killer accusingly. Here, there's so much damage, the skull is crushed to below the nose."

"The attacker probably only stopped through sheer exhaustion," said Helen as Ben started photographing the body and putting flags down to mark blood spatters. Helen saw a leather wallet peeking out from a pocket and asked Ben to photograph it before removing the wallet and passing it to Anders. She took a tablet from the forensics bag and tapped in the name on the driving licence, scrolling through the details until she had what she needed.

"James Smith. Owns this shop. Married to Janice Smith and a father to Mitch, who lives at home. I'll get Abi and Lucy to go round their place." Mal nodded, his eyes drawn to the corpse. The way the arms were slumped to the sides and the legs splayed out meant that he could simply have been resting were it not for the savage damage done to his head. He let out a deep breath and his features hardened.

"This is the first entry we know of. We need to solve this quickly, before peoplefolk go thinking it's ok to enter this damn competition. Most people are killed by someone we know, so I want everyone checking and interviewing anyone that has links to him. This much blood doesn't scrub off easily, so there'll be traces. We're still searching Buckland's properties for any sign of him and I'll leave Barry on that." He pinched the bridge of his nose and lifted his head to ward off the tiredness.

"This is what we do, why we were formed. Why we're a self-contained unit that doesn't need to wait months for forensic analysis. This is also why we don't fuck up." Pep talk over, he left to coordinate the uniformed officers and get SC+O onto the site to help process the evidence more quickly. He knew that if this case went unsolved, it would give others the push to try and make their own entry. Regardless of Buckland's motives or justification, five million pounds went a long way to overcoming any moral quandary about murder.

Chapter 10

Anders put Aaron to bed and left some food in the oven for Cassie, who was on a late shift at her café. Exhausted, she poured herself a glass of red wine and made her way to the workroom, stealing some chocolate from the fridge as she passed. She mused that it was a good job she did so much exercise or she'd regret the recent lapse into chocolate binging her return to England had started.

She carried a large bag of papers that Jesse had printed off for her and sat crossed legged in the middle of the room. It had been a long day. Processing a crime took months. From finding evidence at the scene, interviewing witnesses, notifying the family, carrying out the autopsy and analysing toxicology reports, the whole process took time, not the forty minutes a TV show would take. Though they could analyse much of the data in their own lab, it was still a laborious task. Leads had to be followed, suspects interviewed, alibies checked, evidence trails followed, rechecked and new avenues pursued.

The team had worked hard, Lucy and Duncan following up on leads as Anders helped with the physical evidence. Mal had used his rank to get SC+O support and had enlisted officers from the Met into collecting more data. All told, more officers had worked on this case in the last twenty hours than had worked on all the murder investigations in the previous year combined. McDowell had called in many favours to get a resolution quickly and, as she sat on the floor, Anders started to comb through the evidence, glad that any request from her division automatically took priority in any other department. At the same time, she had "A Feather on the Breath of God" playing softly through a docking station for her phone.

Reading through the evidence, she placed the papers around her when she was done, a physical manifestation of the mental construct that she was building. Anders' laptop would chime frequently as more evidence was sent to her. She printed these off and added them to her construct.

Blood spatter analysis. The blows came directly to the top of the skull, an even arc of blood blooming around the shop floor and spurting upwards to the ceiling. First blow, centre of floor. James Smith was five seven, slightly below average. Length of axe showed killer to be roughly the same height or more to get a clear hit on top. Weight of axe, five kilo's. Average person could lift the axe, but it would take a little time. No suspects were above average size. Means blow likely came from behind if Smith wasn't to dodge such a perfect strike.

Next page. Autopsy. Nothing from toxicology. Stomach analysis showed he'd eaten at around seven the previous night, as indicated by his wife. No alcohol or drugs. Nothing unusual outside of the pulped skull, no defensive wounds. Caught unawares, or too shocked at what was happening. Either hit from behind or knew suspect well. Blood spatter inconclusive.

Witnesses. Nothing seen. One reported a noise at roughly midnight and some shouting or cheering. Security cameras in store hadn't been switched on for years and none of the local cameras showed anything useful.

Prints. Three sets. The wife, the son, Mitch and the shop assistant, Beth. All happy to have their prints taken to discount them from analysis. No other prints. Fibres on body. Hairs, same length and colour as wife, one on shoulder matching Mitch's colour. Beth's hair everywhere. Peroxide blonde with green tips. Spectrometer still in action at the lab.

Stocktaking report. Nothing missing. No evidence of theft.

Smith's background. No friends to speak of. Spent most of his time at the store. Well regarded in his field. Medical records show no major illnesses. Autopsy found no underlying ailments. A healthy fifty year old. Anders scanned the pictures of the family and Beth, committing them to memory and placing them in her construct.

The process took hours and she was mentally exhausted by the time she was done. She'd had but a few hours' sleep in the last two days.

Taking her first sip of wine since she had sat down, Anders put the music back on and slowed her breathing. Closing her eyes, she focused on the movements of her chest as it rose steadily with every breath. Slowing it down further, she used the music to return her to the scene of the crime. This time, she removed the police presence, the flashing lights and the noise created by the mass of people at a crime scene.

Walking slowly across the street, she stepped into the shop. The image in her mind was crystal clear, every detail committed to memory. Where there were gaps in her knowledge, a blur shaded across that area, a trinket on a shelf she had forgotten, blurry and indistinct. James Smith, now alive and well, stood in the middle of the floor staring at her mutely. She had no voice for him, but she would give him chance to tell his story.

She walked behind him, holding the axe in her hands and swung it in a looping arc, her full strength behind the blow. Both hands held the end of the long wooden handle as her body arched forward. The blow was sickening, the splintering crunch of bone as the back of the axe head made contact, the length of the handle and speed of the blow giving it tremendous force and momentum. Blood lanced out at shocking speed, bright in the dim light, and splattered over Anders.

She didn't flinch.

She would stare hard into the abyss and dare it to return the challenge. She was not afraid of the worst humanity had to offer. She'd endured it, the pain manifest on her body. She saw the darkness reflected in her own image each day and knew herself the embodiment of humanity, capable of both good and evil. She fought for those who had suffered and died because she was touched by darkness yet laced through with light. Just as we are capable of the foulest of deeds, we are capable of the greatest compassion. Anders chose compassion. Had been forged in fire and brimstone, been torn asunder and suffered redemption through transformation. She turned from darkness willingly and so stared hard at the evils of men knowing that she could not be tainted or sullied any further by it.

Smith's body slumped to the floor as if a marionette with the strings cut. Anders swung again, crashing the axe into his head as he lay prone on the ground. She stood straight, panting as she did so, leaning on the axe as she surveyed her work. Mentally, she lay the blood spatter analysis over the scene and muttered to herself. It wasn't right.

Focusing once more, James Smith stood up, perfectly unharmed, and walked slowly back to the middle of the floor, his eyes following her as she stood in front of him. She swung the axe once more, blood splashing the ceiling in the same spot that they'd discovered earlier. Smith's body slumped down, crashing against the counter and sitting upright as he jammed against it.

Anders swung again and again, turning his head into a bloody mess, blood splashing on the floor, covering her face and dripping from her in rivulets of gore. Skull fragments flew in all directions and lumps of brain smeared into the unit behind. An eye popped out from the skull and snaked across the floor, coming to a slithering halt beneath a shelf for Ben to find later.

Her energy spent, Anders surveyed the carnage. She turned to see a blurred shape to her left. Streaks of blood had stopped at that point and the figure watched as Smith was brutally murdered. Recalling the witness testimony, she pictured the blurred figure shouting, then cheering. Stepping backwards, she placed an image of Mitch over the blurred image. Too tall. Blood spotted the wall behind. Taking Smith's height and that of his son, the trajectory didn't match. It was travelling too fast to dip, so it had to be someone shorter. Beth, the cashier. Height matched. Did the wife wear heels? That would make her the right height if she was.

Thrusting the axe into the floor by Smith's body, Anders stepped back, blood dripping from her sleeves and hands. She paused the scene in her mind and stepped away to look back at the figure who'd bludgeoned a man to death. Though blurry, she was forming an image in her mind and it came to sharp relief. The second figure was troubling her and she moved around the scene to get a better image, looping round the left to come behind the figure on the right. She then saw a smudge of blood on the floor and frowned at the smear. The direction was all wrong. It didn't match any other splatter.

Retracing her steps, she replayed the scene, wielding the axe on Smith over and over again, using different scenarios of the two people, where they would move and how, but that smudge kept coming back. She couldn't find a reason for it, no matter how she moved the protagonists. Suddenly the answer hit Anders and she snapped her eyes open to find herself back in the workroom, paper littered around her. She gave a rueful shake of the head and muttered quietly in the silence.

"Well I'll be damned."

Chapter 11

Beth, Janice and Mitch sat in Abi's office as Anders and Jesse watched them through one of his monitors. Anders had sent two uniformed officers to bring them in and they'd arrived protesting at the early hour. Anders had wanted them unsettled and thought that a three a.m. call would be good for them. Jesse had disagreed and grumbled at Anders as she sat next to him. Despite the early hour, he was impeccably dressed and Anders thought him the best dressed Blackhat she'd ever met.

"A man like me," he said. "He needs his beauty sleep. You think looking this good comes easy? No, that would be a carefully planned routine of exercise, nutrition, positive mental attitude, women and sleep. The five pillars of life. See how they all intertwine. See how they all require each other for a stable foundation to healthy living." Anders squeezed his thigh and grinned at him. He sighed theatrically.

"It's not right you being so good looking and having such scant regard for the welfare of those around you. Makes us susceptible to manipulation."

"I'd never manipulate you Jesse," replied Anders sweetly. "Punching you in the face is much more fun." He surreptitiously moved his hand to his jaw where she had broken it all those years ago. He chuckled.

"I did deserve that. I was kinda a dick back in the day."

"Was?" asked Anders, ignoring his hurt expression and concentrating on one of the monitors on his desk. The main hub was empty save for the two of them and only the lights on his desk were on. Anders had debated whether to call Mal, but he'd looked so tired when he stumbled from the antique store, that she thought it best to let him sleep. It hadn't occurred to her to call the others. Everyone had pulled a triple shift and tempers were frayed.

In silence, they watched the three suspects, Jesse turning up the sound slightly so that they could hear the conversation. Beth's voice came through the speaker, a thin immature sound that gave lie to the adult that spoke it. She wore jeans and a baggy jumper, though Anders noted that her coat was Dolce&Gabbana and the jewellery she wore far outside her pay bracket.

"Champagne lifestyle on beer money," muttered Jesse, sensing Anders' thoughts. She nodded her agreement as they listened to Beth speak.

"Why are we here? What's going on? They can't keep us here without telling us why!"

She held Mitch's hand as she spoke and he stroked her arm reassuringly. He was a little taller than his father had been, but his shoulders were broad. His blue eyes radiated intelligence, but Anders could see that Beth had turned his head. He looked young, barely twenty, but the relationship with Beth jarred a little. Anders couldn't see the fit. As if Beth suffered him until something better came along.

"It'll be fine," he said. "They just want to ask a few questions. Solve this case quickly." She started to whine again but Janice cut her off. She was a sour faced woman, all skin and bone with greying hair tied severely behind her back. Her voice was husked by years of smoking and came out in a growl.

"Watch your tongue," she said. "Shut your trap and this will soon be over." A sullen silence settled over the group and Anders clapped her hands together.

"Right," she said. "Let's get them their own rooms shall we?"

The basement held three interrogation rooms, all grey bricks and steel pipes with one table and three chairs in each. They were dimly lit and forbidding, with large one-way mirrors covering an entire wall. Anders and Jesse invited them into each one, maintaining pleasantries and giving the impression that this was merely to wrap up a few loose ends in their investigation. Once they were seated, Anders walked back to Jesse and told him to start recording.

"Visual and audio please." He gave her a thumbs up, put some large headphones on to listen to the conversation and told Anders to switch to channel three on her earpiece so that he could communicate with her. She decided to start with the wife and opened the door to the room with an apology for keeping her waiting.

"And I must apologise for the late hour," she said. "I'm sure you understand that investigations of this nature must be dealt with swiftly. Can I get you a drink at all?" Janice pursed her lips in disapproval, her hands clasping the handbag that rested on her lap. She wore an old coat that had seen better years, let alone days, and her earrings showed the metal glinting through the gold plating as it wore off. Her clothing and shoes were functional. No heels on this lady.

"Before we start, may I offer my condolences for your loss. This must be a very difficult time for you."

"It is," she said, her gravelly voice a contrast to Anders' soft American tones. "I'm happy to answer your questions as best I can, but I've not slept. If we could get this over with, I would very much appreciate it." Anders gave an acquiescent nod of her head.

"Of course. I was wondering if you could tell me a little bit about your husband. What sort of person was he? Did he have any enemies? Anyone who might have wished him harm." Janice gave an impatient sigh.

"I told all this to the blonde detective who interviewed me. He was a wonderful man, a wonderful husband and everyone loved him."

"How long had you been struggling with debt?" Janice frowned, caught off guard by the question. It had been a guess, but Anders' suspicions were confirmed.

"Antique's is hardly a booming business. James was always after that one find. The one item that would clear our debts."

"Did he have any luck?" Janice gave a contemptuous snarl.

"No."

"Beth is well paid though. How can you afford her wages? I wouldn't imagine that the shop was busy enough for extra staff." Janice sneered at the mention of Beth and Anders probed deeper. "How long has she been dating Mitch? That's a lovely coat he's bought her. I was looking to get one myself, but I don't have two grand spare." Janice paled at that and clenched her hands tighter, gripping her handbag with a creak of leather. Anders changed tack once more.

"You said you cooked your husband a meal at seven. Why did he go back to the store after?"

"He loved his silly little shop. It made him happy to be surrounded by the past. Could never see the sense of it myself. We live in the present."

"The past informs who we arc, shows us where we may go." Janice coughed loudly as her retort was swallowed up in a fit of hacking and wheezing.

"Here, let me get you a drink." Anders stood to leave and told Jesse to get her a drink as she stepped into the next room. Beth sat at the desk, coat over her knees, scowling at Anders as she sat down in front of her.

"I'm so sorry to keep you waiting, and I must apologise for asking you to come here so early in the morning." Beth shrugged and gazed at Anders wearily.

"Do I need a lawyer?" Anders gave an easy smile.

"I'm just asking you a few questions to help with our investigation. If you want a lawyer, I'm happy to call for one. He will arrive within a few hours." Beth blanched and gave a curt shake of her head. Anders took that as a sign that she wasn't requesting a lawyer and continued.

"Mitch's mum doesn't like you very much does she?" Beth gave a rueful laugh.

"Not much. Says an airhead like me isn't good enough for him."

"You were with Mitch last night?" Beth nodded.

"Yeah, watched some TV, had a pizza. The usual. Boring really."

"Tell me about Mr Smith?" Beth gave Anders a sad look. One that seemed genuine to her.

"I liked him. He was always nice to me. Not like Janice. Paid me well and let me have the odd day off here and there." She gave a look of such sorrow that Anders almost misread it.

"Nice coat." Beth smoothed the material as she considered it.

"Yeah. Mitch likes to spoil me." Anders gave a conspiratorial grin.

"He do everything you ask?" Beth returned the grin.

"Pretty much!" Anders chuckled and leaned back in her chair.

"I'm sorry, I forgot to get you a drink. Tea? Coffee?"

"Coffee please. Black. No sugar."

"Coming right up." Anders left the room and moved to Mitch's, telling Jesse to get Beth a coffee.

"I'm not a bloody waiter," he muttered through her earpiece as Anders sat down opposite Mitch. He gave her a surly look and paced the bare room like a caged cheetah. Anders noted that his clothing looked as worn and threadbare as Janice's.

"Thank you for your patience Mitch," started Anders and indicated that he could sit. Mitch pulled back the metal chair with a screeching sound and threw himself down. He leaned forward aggressively, hoping to intimidate Anders. He wasn't successful. She continued leafing through her notes as if she wasn't even aware of his anger.

"How long are you going to keep us here?" he demanded. Anders indicated the door.

"You're not under arrest Mitch. I'm here because your father has been brutally murdered and I need you to help me find the killer." Mitch gave an immature sounding laugh and rubbed his hands through his hair. Deflated, he sat back.

"You know, according to the Peelian principles of law, you are just a citizen in uniform. You police by consent. If I don't give that consent, you wouldn't be able to legally arrest me." Anders ignored his statement, leading the conversation to where she wanted it.

"Were you and your father close?" Mitch made himself comfortable in the chair as he considered his answer.

"No more so than Socrates was with his." Anders sighed inwardly. In her ear, Jesse spoke with a wry chuckle.

"Oh yeah. He studied philosophy at Bristol University."

"Socrates was the son of his mother," she replied. "Are you close to yours?" Mitch gave her a sly look.

"I guess."

"Plato often talked about how the interests of the father correlate to how well their sons actually turn out. What exactly is it that you do?" A glare of contempt.

"I helped my father with his work."

"You don't seem that shook up about his death."

"I'm no expert in death. As a concept it is an abstract notion, hardly real."

"Loss is real."

"Loss is real. Grief isn't. How we cope with loss, how we manage that and articulate it to ourselves is what causes the pain."

"But if death isn't real, then neither is loss."

"The pain from the loss cannot be if death isn't an absolute." Jesse grunted in Anders' earpiece.

"What the hell are you two talking about?" Anders reached up and switched off the earpiece. Her mind was racing to try and tease the information she needed from Mitch.

"Death is an absolute if you believe in it," she said. "Either way, it's not an experience you'll ever have." Mitch, suddenly animated, leaned forward to exchange his ideas as he warmed to the topic.

"Exactly! So I deny the absolutism of death. It most certainly is not contingent."

"It may not be true and our perception of it may be imperfect, but the reality of nature is not imperfect despite what Spinoza would have us believe." Mitch rapped the table in delight.

"That's it! So our perception of the world is wrong. We see things as we want to. We give definite terms to death and life and meaning, but the true reality is that we cannot do so. If death is real, then it is a rebirth, a gateway to another world, temporal or otherwise. If death is not real, then it is simply the end." Anders leaned forward, drawing him in further.

"So we're led to metempsychosis. The transmigration of our souls. How can you kill someone if death is either not real or if they reincarnate if it is real? You're telling me that no one can truly die?" Mitch slapped his hand on the desk in triumph, grinning with enjoyment.

"And here's me thinking all cops were dumb!" Anders cackled with delight, seemingly attuned to Mitch's way of thinking.

"So by that rationale, how can you have killed you father when he can't die?"

"Exactly!" cried Mitch. His features dropped as he realised his mistake.

"Hang on," he said, suddenly nervous. "That wasn't a confession." Anders pushed home her advantage.

"Beth is way out of your league. You try that philosophy crap with her?" He flushed, his cheeks burning red with anger.

"She loves me," he declared.

"Sure. She loves the two thousand pound coat you bought her and the flashy jewellery. I'm pretty sure I'll find a Magistrate in the morning who'll let me look at your finances. How much debt do you have?"

"She loves me!" he repeated. Anders gave him a pitying smile.

"Aww shucks," she said. "All your highbrow talk and fancy ideas and you still need to buy her affection. Mitch Smith, I am informing you of your rights to a lawyer. You are being detained here on suspicion of murder." Mitch stood up quickly, his chair falling back as it slammed against a wall.

"I've not confessed to anything. I don't recognise your right to do that. You do not have my consent!" Anders stood up with a nonchalance that infuriated Mitch.

"That consent is given by the people of the nation, not by the individual. Get your bullcrap right before giving me the Wikipedia highlights."

She locked the door behind her and switched on her earpiece to find Jesse guffawing with laughter.

"Agent Anders!" he cried. "I fall in love with you more every day!"

"Never gonna happen Jesse. I've seen you naked, remember?"

"Ouch." Anders supressed a yawn and looked up to a camera in the corridor.

"Come on, let's wrap this up. Janice or Beth?"

"Janice is just ugly. Beth. She's prettier." Anders gave a sigh and stepped into Beth's room. She sat on the chair with her legs tucked under her, cradling a hot cup of coffee in her hands, steam rising from the dark liquid.

"Oh, hi," she said as Anders entered. She almost dropped her mug as the true questioning began.

"So, Beth. Were you the one laughing and goading Mitch on as he killed his father, or were you the one screaming and hiding behind a shelf?"

"What? You can't accuse me of that!"

"He's punching well above his weight. See, I think you're about, what, a seven? Attractive, but not enough to get the really good looking, rich guys. Mitch? He's a five, on a good day when you've had too much to drink."

Beth shrank in her chair as Anders spoke.

"But the thing about five's or less. When a pretty girl eggs them on? They'll do just about anything. Especially when they can rationalise it to themselves. And especially when there's a cool five million involved. Nice coat."

"I want a lawyer," she said. Anders ignored her.

"Did you cheer him on or stand back and let him do it? I think you put him to it then stood back and watched the show. Not quite what you were expecting was it? There's a lot of blood in a body. Smeared around the place, looks a lot more than it actually is. Then the insides start spilling out. It's so much worse than you think." Beth started to sob quietly, and Anders saw her emotions for what they were. Guilt.

"I love films. Aaron, my boy. He loves Marvel films. They're all PG-Thirteen, or Twelve-A as you say here. Lots of violence but no blood. Makes people think that getting shot or beaten up comes with no consequences, but it does. It's horrible and sticky and gory and it just won't wash off no matter how hard you scrub." Beth subconsciously wiped her hands, the sleeves of her baggy jumper lifting up to reveal arms rubbed raw from scrubbing.

"I want a lawyer!" she screamed. "I want a lawyer!" Anders stood up slowly and gazed at her coolly.

"There's one on the way. In the meantime I'm arresting you for the murder of James Smith. You do not have to say anything, but it may harm your defence if you do not mention, when questioned, something which you later rely on in court. Anything you say may be given in evidence. Do you understand?" Beth sobbed loudly, screaming in abject terror. Anders waited calmly until she had stopped her melodrama.

"Do you understand?" she repeated, her voice hard in the sudden silence.

Beth, snot dribbling from her nose, eyes puffy with tears, nodded her understanding, flinching as the door to the interrogation room slammed shut, leaving her alone.

"Strike two. One more and we're out," said Anders as she left the room and made her way to the third interrogation.

"This is messed up," said Jesse. "All three of them?" Anders grimaced as she opened the thick metal door, typing in the code and giving the door a hefty shove.

Janice looked up suddenly, startled from her reverie. She was about to protest until she saw the anger radiating from Anders as she glowered at Janice for what seemed like an age. Eventually she spoke, her voice filled with fury and scorn. She'd inhabited the darkness that had killed this woman's husband. Re-enacted the scene countless times to piece together the evidence. She hated the three of them for that. She would see them pay and eventually let go of that hate, let the light shine and allow Smith to speak through her. She'd let his light banish the darkness from her, little whispers and tendrils of his death clinging to Anders for the rest of her life. She bore that burden gladly so the dead may rest.

"You were married for thirty years. That's a long time to hate someone."

"I loved him once."

"That doesn't mean anything. You stood by and goaded Mitch. Laughed and cheered as your son caved in the skull of his father and your husband. Mitch is guilty of the act. Beth of committing him to it. But you saw to it the deed was done." Janice straightened her back and glared at Anders defiantly.

"He spent more time in that damn store of his than with his own wife. He never cared one jot about me. Just his stupid trinkets. I cheered because he neglected his own family. For that, he deserved it." Shaking her head at Janice, Anders left the room. There was nothing else to say.

Chapter 12

Anders woke to find herself curled up on the sofa in Abi's office. Every muscle ached, scrunched as she was in the confined space. She'd managed a few hours' sleep and groggily made to sit up, checking the time with a quick turn of the wrist. A voice made her startle and she shot up, hand reaching for a gun that was no longer there. Old habits died hard and she scowled at Mal as he stuck his head through the door, having seen her wake.

"I've just seen the footage. Impressive," he said, his smile cutting through her temper. He looked much refreshed and had even shaved, looking ten years younger and grinning like a cheeky school boy as Anders sat up and arched her back with a huge yawn, arms stretching to coax some blood into them.

"Would have woken you, but you needed your beauty sleep," she replied. Mal shrugged to show that he wasn't bothered and beckoned her into the hub.

"Come see the news. McDowell is extolling our virtues, telling the world that we will catch any entry to the competition before the day is through. Kinda likes the sound of his own voice." Anders followed him through to the central hub where the team was assembled. Duncan voiced his approval at her work and Barry gave her a big grin.

"Good work Anders," he said. "Loved all that philosophy crap!" Jesse had the good grace to look sheepish as Anders glared at him and he held his hands up in apology.

"I was just showing them the highlights!" he protested.

"Shower. Need shower," she said and Barry laughed.

"There's one in the back, by the training mats." Anders thanked him and headed to where the shooting range was nestled alongside the gym area. Barry called after her, a mocking tone to his voice.

"Those Eighty Second Airborne? Always thought of them as pussies." Anders turned around, eyebrows raised in surprise. She gave him a slow look, taking in his massive torso and bulging arms.

"Compensating for something there Barry? Heard something similar about the Twenty Two boys, strutting around playing soldiers." He grinned back.

"You really teach CQB at Quantico?" CQB stood for Close Quarters Combat and she'd spent several months teaching it to recruits as a favour to an old friend.

"You wanna find out?" Helen, stepping from the lift just in time to hear the banter gave a loud cheer.

"America versus Britain?" she called. "Screw that! Man versus woman!" Anders gave a light backwards jog, making "bring it on" motions with her hands and grinning broadly. Barry cricked his muscular neck and slapped his hands together.

"Don't want to hurt you little lady, but I will if you test me." His tone was good natured as Anders goaded him.

"You'll try, but this little lady will kick your butt." He followed her into the Training and Firearms room and walked to the mats set in one corner. Within moments, the entire team was cheering them on and placing bets. Lucy and Duncan supporting Barry, Jesse and Helen on Anders' side. Ben stayed quiet, happy to watch whilst Abi and Mal whispered to each other, keeping their bets to themselves, but clearly placing them. As Barry stepped to the mats, Mal's phone rang and he moved away to answer it.

"We all in?" said Anders as she made a few stretches to loosen up her stiff muscles, keen to show that she didn't want Barry to hold back. He smiled at her, the toughness that had made him part of the SAS coming through. He would be determined to win and wouldn't accept a loss. Not easily anyway.

"I'll hold back a little. Don't want to hurt you too much." He crouched low, hands raised in a defensive posture, waiting for

Anders to make her move. Barry had been taught in the Fairbairn system of close combat and it was ruthlessly efficient. Anders knew that his strength and size would eventually win out if she adopted the same system that she had taught at Quantico so switched to her favoured Wing Chun and Silat combination. She liked to mix it up with Muay Thai, so would start with the Wing Chun then switch to Muay Thai or Silat to keep him off balance. Jesse cheered at the change in stance as Anders moved in to strike.

Before they had chance to fight, Mal spoke loudly, cutting through the jovial atmosphere.

"Sorry folks, we've got another entry in Manchester and one underway right now in Greenwich. Duncan, Anders, get over there. Barry, get a van, we're moving out now." Barry lowered his guard and gave Anders a rueful smile.

"Wing Chun? No chance." He winked at her and sprinted off at a brisk pace to get a van. Anders sniffed her armpits with a grimace.

"Dammit. Never did get that shower."

The Interview

Part 2

"Tell me about this," Cooper needled in his pithy tones. Anders stared at the picture and recalled seeing the image splashed across the news and every paper in America.

"I was investigating a case and slipped up. I was tortured by the boy's father before escaping and rescuing him and his sister."

"They live with you now?" Barrett spoke, clearly intrigued. Anders smiled at her and nodded.

"They do."

"Even though you killed their father?" Cooper kept up with his aggressive questioning as Anders turned back to him, once again keeping her face and voice neutral.

"He was their captor and abuser. It was their decision. They asked."

"But you tortured their father to death." Anders' eyes flashed briefly, but she controlled her emotions as they threatened to burst out.

"I didn't turn the other cheek if that's what you mean."

"I mean you tortured the man who whipped the skin from your back."

"I was exonerated." Cooper laughed. A genuine emotion that made Anders hate him even more. Barrett and McDowell were quiet and she could see them scrutinising her closely. She'd expected some tough questions, but not to this extent.

"This isn't the Wild West. We don't tolerate that kind of behaviour in Britain. You were cleared because of the public support that picture drummed up."

"You said that picture proved I was a killer."

"Pretty, semi-naked woman covered in blood saving a poor child. People see what they want to see. You let your fiancé die that night." It was a statement of fact.

"I did," said Anders frankly. She'd never hidden from that despicable truth.

"Makes the sympathy card easier to play, I guess." Cooper was relentless and changed tack quickly, oblivious to the flash of anger that coloured Anders' cheeks. "Santa Muerta. That's what they called you in Mexico wasn't it? You were only there for nine months. Didn't take long to earn a moniker like that."

Anders was used to the technique having employed it in many interrogations and kept pace.

"Kidnappings rose by seventy percent in twenty twelve, after I left. The records are in the public domain."

"That's not what I'm saying."

"I didn't call myself Santa Muerta." Cooper gave a patronising sigh.

"Again, that's not what I'm saying."

"I followed the law as I have always done. I believe in it absolutely and without question. I've saved countless lives and upheld the American constitution as per my Oath."

"This isn't America," shot back Cooper.

"No. This is the United Kingdom, with the oldest Parliament in the world. A law with over five hundred years of moral wrangling and debate behind it. The Peelian principles of an ethical police force are those that I've followed my whole career. I'd be honoured to uphold UK law with all of the diligence and care that my reference from the Director of the FBI states." A tense silence settled across the room as Cooper glared at Anders. She kept her breathing steady and gave him a dispassionate gaze. McDowell grinned and laid his hands flat on the table in front of him. A conciliatory gesture.

"You have to understand, Miss Anders, that we need to ask these difficult questions." Anders was about to reply, when Cooper cut in once again.

"Damn right we do, so let's not stop here. You, *Miss* Anders, started off life as a man, so how can you, of all people, be expected to lead seasoned professionals?"

Chapter 13

Anders and Duncan sped through the streets in a patrol car, sirens blazing as Anders steered them through the traffic as quickly as she could. Duncan maintained a sullen silence and Anders grinned as he clutched his seat belt with one hand and kept the other on the dashboard to steady himself as she weaved around a stationary lorry, cutting the angle as close as she could.

The alert had come through half an hour previously. A neighbour had heard screaming and called the local police, who'd contacted Mal's team as soon as they arrived at the scene. A husband had taken a Samurai sword to his wife, trying to replicate James Clavell's Shogun. Luckily, the police had arrived quickly and he had fled, leaving his injured wife behind.

Coleraine Road was lined with old Victorian houses. High ceilings and large rooms with bay windows and front doors that could fit a large sofa through comfortably. Many had been converted to flats, the landlord turning the lower and upper floors into separate living areas to rent out. Spotted among the grand houses were the odd newer structures that had been erected after the Blitz. They were poorly designed, cheaply built and ill at ease next to their expensive neighbours. The Victorian houses themselves had seen their value sky rocket over the last few decades, so many of the owners had significantly less wealth than those who had bought the properties recently. Anders passed Aston Martin's parked in the street next to old Ford Cortina's.

The street was on a steep slope and, half way up, Anders spied a squad of patrol cars parked against a tatty group of flats nestled between their more illustrious neighbours. Uniformed officers stood in the road and guided in an ambulance that had just arrived. Anders and Duncan stepped from the car and showed their Warrant Cards to the senior officer on site. He gave their rank a long stare before deciding that he was happy to relinquish control of the scene to the dour man and the attractive, but intense woman. He led them up to the flat where the crime had taken place. It was on the upper floor and they climbed the concrete steps clutched to one side of the building to get there. The senior officer, a balding man in his forties chatted amicably as they made their way up the staircase.

"Marshall Johnson," he said, giving them the details. "Goes at his wife with a damn sword." He shook his head in disbelief. "People are going nuts over this website. What about you? Would you kill someone for five million?" Anders gave him a brutal gaze and he hurried up the stairs, keen to finish his escort duty.

As they walked along the concrete balcony, Anders noted the dilapidated state of the building. Paint was peeling from every window, doors were worn thin and a sour whiff of urine hung in the stairwell. For such a wealthy area, this was a tiny pocket of misery. Screams could be heard from the end of the balcony and they picked up the pace. Arriving at the door to the last flat, Anders stepped over some blood that had pooled at the entrance. The interior was dark, the only natural light coming from the open door.

Inside, Anders could see a long, rectangular room with a kitchen at the end, separated by a breakfast bar. In front of that were several old sofas, the material patchy and the cushions permanently depressed by years of use. The walls were full of shelves and books were scattered around the floor, piled in corners and stacked around the large, flat screen TV. On the sofa, a morbidly obese woman lay screaming as two paramedics worked to stabilise her before moving the poor victim down the stairwell. Dark hair was plastered to her face as blood gushed from a wound in her scalp. Her T-shirt was ripped, presumably by the sword and deep wounds could be seen under the material, covering her arms and stomach. She wailed at the pain and shock of her ordeal.

"How's she doing?" asked Anders. One of the paramedics, an achingly thin man in his early twenties, glanced around before returning back to the task of stemming the flow of blood. He had to shout to make himself heard above the screaming.

"She'll be ok if we can get her to sit still for a minute," he replied as the woman screamed even louder at his touch. Anders checked the mail that had been left on the floor.

"Jenny Johnson," she muttered and moved into the house to let Duncan through. He turned his nose up in disgust at the dirt and grime. Blood had spattered the walls, thickly dark in the dim light and his eyes roved the scene, piecing together what had happened. Moving through the flat, Anders saw a picture of the husband, Marshall, on his wedding day. Oddly enough, he wasn't with his wife, but with an older woman who looked like his mother. There were enough shared autosomal characteristics evident. She rested an arm protectively around him. He was lean and wiry with a buzz cut and piercing eyes that seemed on edge. Anders' thoughts were suddenly interrupted as Duncan lost his temper.

"Get that woman out of here and sedated!" he yelled. The paramedics gave him a wary look, but tried to lift the huge woman from the sofa, eliciting further shrieks of pain.

"Belay that order," snapped Anders, giving Duncan a challenging look as she did so. He scowled at her as she exercised her authority. "Get outside and organise the search. Check with the neighbours, see if they know anything." He made to protest, but thought better of it. Turning sharply on his heels, he stepped over the blood in the doorway and left.

Anders continued her search of the flat. Putting on some gloves, she picked up various books and sheets of papers lying around the cluttered room. Blocking out the screaming, she started piecing together a picture of Marshall. Bills with angry red lettered headings showed him to be in some considerable debt. Tax returns lying under a betting paper showed he made little from his self-employment. Some were dated from fifteen years ago. The fridge showed pizzas and pasta. One cupboard held three boxes of the same cereal. Pictures of Marshall as a child, same houses. Raised here.

Likes routine, finds comfort in the familiar, limited expansion and outlook. Lives through these books but unwilling to do anything for himself. Mummy's boy. Finally, Anders made her way back to the sofa and crouched down so that she could look at the miserable woman. Her bleeding had been staunched and one paramedic was bandaging her head and the other putting gauze around a deep cut on her arm.

"Mrs Johnson," she said. "I'm Assistant Chief Constable Anders. I'm here to find your husband and make sure he pays for what he did to you." She burst into fresh tears, throwing her head back and knocking the young paramedic aside, causing her to scream in fresh pain as her wound jerked open.

"Mrs Johnson, I need you to be very calm for me. This will be over soon and then we can get you to hospital and make sure you're well cared for. Do you have any children? Anyone we can call to come and be with you." She sniffed loudly, streams of snot dribbling from her nose. Her voice, when she spoke, was raw and scratched, her vocal chords shredded from her screaming.

"No. There's no one." Anders placed a gentle hand on Jenny's and gripped it tightly.

"I need you to answer one question for me and then I'll make sure you're looked after by these kind men. You've been very brave. Where does Marshall's mother live? Is it around here?"

Duncan was banging on the door next to the stairwell when Anders hurried from the flat and called out to him.

"Next street along. Number ninety nine. His mother's place. I'll bet we'll find him there, hoping this will all blow over." She took the steps two at a time and could hear Duncan pounding after her, tie flying behind as he sprinted after her. Anders had started the car by the time he caught up and, panting heavily, hurried to buckle his seatbelt as she swung the car round and sped down the hill, leaving behind an array of bemused police officers trying to fathom where they were going.

"I'll pull up a few houses down," she said, using the handbrake to swerve round the corner at the bottom of the hill and then starting back up the next street in third gear. Duncan, despite himself, was impressed.

"Shouldn't we be calling this in, get those officers to back us up," he asked as the houses flew past at great speed.

"I'll call it in when we've stopped. I want a few minutes before we spook Marshall away." Skidding to a halt half way up the hill, Duncan scrabbled to the boot and pulled out a stab vest and a belt with speedcuffs, CS spray and an ASP baton that would extend out at the click of a button. Anders relayed their position to Jesse and he started to coordinate a cordon around the area in case Marshall did escape. Duncan threw a set of gear to Anders and she pulled the heavy vest over her head and pulled the side straps tight before buckling the belt up. It was slightly too big for her tiny waist and hung loose.

The street was virtually identical to the last one they were on. Victorian houses lined the sides and, again, the pattern was interrupted by the odd council house that had sprung up in the gaping holes left by the Blitz. The Ninety Ninth house was smaller than its two neighbours, as if they had dominated it into submission. Where they proudly displayed their pale bricks and bay windows, this house had wooden slats over the newer bricks and small windows covered in a semi permeable membrane of filth that allowed little light into its murky interior. The front door had iron bars over its front and looked incongruous in the neighbourhood.

A side path led to the back and Anders nodded for Duncan to take it. He signalled his agreement and slunk down the path, ducking below a round window on the side, while Anders strode up to the front door and rang the bell. Mack the Knife sounded from the ringer and she heard an argument seeping through the thin wooden door. She saw the eyehole darken as the owner peered outside so she held up her warrant card.

"This is Assistant Chief Constable Anders from the NCA ma'am. Please open the door."

"What do you want?" The voice was old and distrustful. Anders imagined a frail woman on the other side, stooped with age.

"I'm here to ask a few questions about your son. He's attacked his wife with a sword."

"No he didn't," came the swift reply. "She's making it up. Always took him for granted she did."

"Ma'am, I'm going to have to insist that you open the door. Under the Police and Criminal Evidence Act, I have the power to gain entry and search your premises. I wish to enter the property and discuss with you the whereabouts of your son before he hurts anyone else." There was a long pause and Anders could almost hear the woman thinking.

"Fine," she said. Chains were unbuckled and locks unlocked as Miss Johnson made sure to take her time opening the door, acting older and more frail than she really was. She glowered at Anders before unlocking the steel gate across the entrance. Suddenly, Anders heard a shout followed by a scream from behind the house. Without thought, Anders barrelled past the old woman and sprinted through the house, unclipping her ASP as she ran. A narrow hallway led to the kitchen at the back, all immaculately maintained; a clean interior despite the grimy exterior. Anders kept moving forward, saw a door leading to the back and burst from the house into the garden.

Duncan was on the floor, blood pouring from a wound in his arm as he tried to raise his other to ward off the killing blow that was coming. Marshall stood over him, wielding his Samurai sword and screaming incoherently. Anders could see the rage in his eyes and knew he'd lost his grip on reason.

"Hey!" she yelled and he looked up, sword poised in mid-air. She used that moment to extend her baton, thrusting it outwards with a satisfying *snick*. The noise spurred him to action and he ran at her, closing the gap fast. Anders waited a brief second, letting him move closer. With lightning speed, she stepped into his swing and ducked so the sword swung behind her. As she moved, Anders swung her own weapon.

Her training in America had given her a very different approach to violent confrontation. Living in a country where it was your legal right to be armed gave a different starting point. Suicide by cop was not a term used in Britain where knives were more likely to be used and police, as a rule, were not armed with handguns. When being trained in the use of a baton, officers were given sweet spots that they could hit. The back of the leg for instance. They were also shown areas to avoid if at all possible. Skulls and joints were off limits unless in the most dire of circumstance.

Anders' swing cracked his knee cap and Marshall stumbled with a cry of pain, his leg giving way beneath him. She swung again, a backhanded blow, whippet fast, that smashed his elbow joint to a pulp and caused him to drop his sword, the wickedly curved blade spinning away wildly. He gave another snarl of pain but managed to stay upright. He glared at her in rage and fury, his voice shrieking hoarse as he screamed.

"You fucking b…" Anders' baton clubbed the side of his head with a crunching blow and his eyes rolled upwards as he collapsed to the floor, his legs buckling under him as he hit the ground with a meaty thump.

"Dammit," muttered Anders, her heart beating calmly in her chest. "There'll be a complaint about that."

The Interview

Part 3

Anders gazed at him coolly. Her voice, when she spoke, was calm yet laced with steel.

"I've led squads of men to battle and ran the lead team on serial killers in the most prestigious office of the FBI. I believe that question has already been answered."

"You don't look like a man." It was a statement and a challenging one at that.

"I'm not. That's the point of gender reassignment surgery."

"You sound like a woman. Thought you'd look and sound like those drag queen hookers at Soho."

"You have my picture on file. It's right in front of you. You know what I look like." Cooper held his hands out in a gesture meant to placate yet was anything but.

"I'm just curious, that's all."

"I was lucky enough to know what I was from an early age. There are hormone blockers you can take to inhibit the effects of testosterone." Cooper smiled at that.

"So you chemically castrated yourself and then your parents kicked you out." Anders frowned, curious as to how he knew, but quickly shut down her emotions. She'd suffered worse and had changed far too long ago to let him bother her.

"They did, yes."

"You had your op at eighteen. How did you pay for that?"

"I worked hard, got my diplomas and paid with the money I earned at that time."

"Touching. How did you pay for the op?"

"Hard work and grit. I also came into a little money."

"From a notorious crime lord who you then arrested ten years later." Anders chuckled.

"Would that my life were so interesting," she replied. "It's a little more mundane than that. Death in the family."

"The same family that disowned you."

"Not all of them." Cooper leaned back in his chair and gazed at her, his eyes roving her slender frame with distaste.

"So, you're a transsexual who does all the manly things like join the army and excel at CQB. It doesn't fit." Anders shrugged.

"As I said, I knew what I was from an early age. I also realised that I'd have to excel at everything I did so that what I was wouldn't matter."

"How do you know it doesn't matter to me?"

"I'm here aren't I?"

"As a transsexual, how can you be relied upon to be stable in this pressured environment? Aren't you too busy mincing around, pretending to be a woman?"

"I had two years of psychological analysis before making the transition. Judging by this conversation, I'm the most rational and stable person in this room." She saw Barrett supress a smile at that.

"Your parents must be proud of their fag son?" Anders stilled suddenly and the atmosphere thickened. Cooper had gone too far. Barrett quickly stepped in and banged her fist on the table.

"I like this one! She has fire!" McDowell grinned suddenly and stood up, striding to a drinks cabinet sat flush against the wall.

"I agree! Cooper?" All eyes turned to Cooper, whose demeanour suddenly changed. His patronising attitude vanished and he looked a different person as he clapped his hands suddenly and stood up, shooting round the table to offer his hand to Anders. Nonplussed she leaned back slightly, unsure of his change.

"I'm so very sorry," he said. "We had to be sure." McDowell poured some brandy into the crystal glasses and handed them out.

"Cooper loves his job Miss Anders, but he plays the role of arsehole a little too well for my liking." He raised his glass and offered a toast. "To Assistant Chief Constable Anders." As they drank their brandy, Anders eyed them all over the rim of her glass.

Mad, she thought. They're all mad.

Chapter 14

Gordon's Wine Bar was tucked away in the street behind Charing Cross and Embankment. Its entrance was a small archway that led underground and, despite the seemingly hidden entrance, the bar was always full. It sold wine in all its variants, Coca Cola and very little else. Low, stone archways forced everyone to crouch and the space was dimly lit, large kegs making up the majority of tables. It felt like some old throw back to the years of Jack the Ripper and horse drawn carriages and Anders loved it.

A ten minute walk from Scotland Yard, Mal had taken the team there to celebrate Duncan's release from hospital. He'd lost a lot of blood from his wound and had spent the night under observation. He still looked groggy but tucked into his wine with enthusiasm. They'd taken over a section at the back of the bar and were raucous company. Despite having no leads on the whereabouts of Buckland, they'd had several successes stopping those who would enter his depraved competition and they'd decided to bond over wine and food.

Abi and Helen were seated with their backs to the wall and sniggered as they shared a bottle of Riesling. Anders was surprised that Abi enjoyed Helen's filthy stories so much and smiled to see Abi throw her head back and laugh at Helen's latest sexual exploit. Duncan had thawed slightly towards Anders and even offered to buy her a drink. She sat between Mal and Barry and they dwarfed her completely, making her feel like some kind of midget. They were listening intently as Duncan told of how Anders had rescued her.

"I'm telling you Barry," he said, sloshing some wine over his white bandages and staining them red as if blood had seeped through the stitches. "She moved like lightning. I've never seen anyone move so fast, that guy never knew what hit him. Two seconds, three hits." He waved his glass around to emphasise a point and Jesse guided the glass back to the table by grabbing hold of his arm.

"Easy there soldier. Wine in mouth not on table." Barry gave a throaty chuckle and clapped a meaty paw on Anders' shoulder.

"We'll see little one. Speed isn't everything. It's about reading the situation, anticipating the moves, speed of mind, not just body." Jesse chuckled and put an arm around an increasingly drunken looking Ben, his mop of curls seeming to get wilder with every glass of wine.

"If it's about speed of thought, then you're stuffed mate! My money's on Ben here!"

"Is it bollocks!" cried Barry and winked mischievously at Ben. Helen grinned at Barry and joined in.

"That's a proper swear word there Anders. None of your American nonsense. Goddammit!" she cried banging her fist on the table and imitating an American accent. "You goddamn assholes!" Abi laughed again as Jesse spoke.

"She's right Anders Americans have no imagination when it comes to swearing. I know. I lived there for ten years." Anders held up her hands in acknowledgement.

"I will admit, it is much more fun to swear using the Queen's English. There's nowhere else I can call Jesse a dodgy, gormless git."

"Or a wanker!"

"Tosspot!"

"Prat, pillock and plonker!" Ben had shouted the last and everyone turned to him with a smile and a laugh, making him blush with the attention. Lucy sat next to him and she drank quietly from her glass, not engaging in the conversation.

"Well bugger me," said Jesse, giving Ben a look of delight. "You have to drink some more wine for that." He poured a large amount of wine into Ben's glass as he protested the large serving with imaginative use of the Queen's vernacular.

"Piss off you bell end!"

"More British swearing! I'd say Ben was on a roll." Helen looked on like a proud mother.

"I taught him everything he knows," she said with satisfaction. Abi leaned forward.

"Not everything, I hope." Helen slapped her arm and grinned. She caught Anders' eye and indicated the table behind her. There sat a group of lads and they were clearly deciding who would go up and offer Anders a drink. They were a little intimidated by the man mountain Barry and the no slouch in the brick house department Mal. Anders sighed at Helen.

"That's enough of that you," she said. Lucy took the opportunity to speak for the first time. It cut a swathe across the banter and stopped it dead.

"Can you actually have sex?" she asked. All eyes turned to Anders, the atmosphere suddenly turning cold. Anders sipped from her glass as she eyed Lucy coolly, debating how to handle it. *The usual*, she thought. *Directly*. Mal went to speak, but she lay a placating hand on his forearm.

"It's fine. I'm always happy to answer any questions you may have. How else can we lose the stigma? I'm functional down there, so yes, I can have sex." Lucy sniffed.

"Shallow though, isn't it? Down there?" Anders grinned, determined to play this lightly.

"The results vary, but I'm satisfied with what I have. I've never had any issues."

"That's because you've not met someone like me." This from Barry. He gave a wink to show he was on her side and she appraised him openly before shaking her head in sorrow.

"Sorry Barry. From what I hear, it'll be like rattling a stick in a bucket." He guffawed with laughter and the group joined in, the tension broken.

"Do you mind if I ask a question?" Helen slurred her words as she spoke, leaning on the table and soaking her sleeves in some spilled Riesling.

"Of course," said Anders, happy to do so.

"You don't look like a transsexual. You don't sound like one either. You're a stunner. How are you so different than the ones we immediately think of? We only know you weren't born a woman because we read your file before you joined us, otherwise we wouldn't have known." Anders shrugged, brushing aside the complement as they always made her feel uneasy.

"There are many transgender women who are more attractive. There's a scale, just like there is with all people. You have attractive men, like Ben and then less attractive men, like Jesse here." Ben blushed as Jesse bristled with mock indignation. "I knew what I was from a very early age. I managed to get some hormone blockers that stopped my testes producing testosterone. It stopped any secondary sexual characteristics before I could undergo surgery."

"That's vaginoplasty right?"

"Vagino-what-now?" asked Barry. Anders turned to him and gave a devilish grin.

"They slice your penis open and scoop out the flesh…" He held his hands up in horror, his tattoos seeming to recoil in fright as well. Mal laughed at his discomfort.

"It's body mutilation is what it is," said Lucy sourly. She'd put down her glass and stared at Anders with open hostility. "It's not gender correction. It's a pure fantasy of overly passionate autogynephilia. You're attracted to the thought of yourself as a woman and need to be treated psychotherapeutically as you would any mental illness."

"Here comes the militant Bible bashers," muttered Jesse as tension rose once more around the table. "Been to your Bible classes again Lucy?" he asked. She gave him a look of distain.

"I have raised it, yes. We had a very interesting discussion."

"I'm sorry you feel that way Lucy," said Anders. "My intent is to go about peaceably with my life." Lucy snorted contemptuously and Mal once again went to reprimand her. Anders kept her hand on his arm, gently reminding him that it was her fight as Lucy spat a reply, drink making her angry, blotches of red colouring her cheeks.

"God creates people as male and female. It's a divine mandate against gender variance. Your gender is determined by biological sex, not by your own perception. Your DNA is XY, not XX."

"Jesus himself discussed the need for tolerance on how to love your fellow man. Many philosophers have seen the journey of transgenderism as a journey of faith through the darkness and desert."

"Your mental disorder is a challenge to overcome, not to acquiesce to." Anders shrugged.

"I did see it as a challenge I needed to overcome and did so many years ago. Redemption through transformation. Isn't that what the bible preaches?"

"It's against God. Pope Benedict said as such when he declared that it would lead to the destruction of mankind."

"Islam, Hinduism, Buddhism, Shinto, the Shona, pre-Christian Philippines, the Wicca, even Dionysus, the patron God of intersex, born of Zeus. Loki often turned to female form. The ancient Egyptians worshipped Nile Gods who were men with breasts. Even Conservative Judaism has said that reassignment surgery is permissible. Pope Benedict retired a long time ago. His views are archaic. The Christian church welcomes transgender individuals and has done so for a long time."

Lucy changed tack, determined to win the argument.

"Feminists don't even agree with it," she said, loud enough for all in the bar to hear. Abi tried to calm her down, but Lucy was filled with wine and righteousness. A dangerous combination.

"Morgan says that you all have the mentality of a rapist. You reduce the female form to an artefact. You've bypassed the lifetime of sexual repression us real woman have had to endure." Anders laughed at that.

"I've been a woman longer than I have a man. I've had a lifetime of prejudice when feminists such as Morgan and Raymond promote a monolithic, ideologically driven representation of us, pushing transgender women and men even deeper into a repressed minority." Lucy, spurred on by Anders' calm and reasonable tone sneered at her.

"Easy for you to say when you look like that, a poster child for those too caught up in their sex addled minds."

"On the contrary, sex was never part of the equation. I was still a virgin when I underwent my reassignment. You're buying into diagnostic tools that were added to psychology in nineteen eighty and have served to stigmatise transgender individuals long after homosexuality and other such taboo's have become accepted as norm." Lucy glowered at Anders as everyone shifted uncomfortably in their seats at the exchange.

"You're no woman. After all, real women don't close up if it doesn't get any use," she said venomously. It was low blow, aimed at riling Anders, but she gave an easy shrug.

"I have to dilate, yes," she said, her voice betraying no shame or embarrassment. Abi gave a loud snort.

"Me too love, I'm pretty sure I'm all sealed up, it's been so long!" Helen coughed loudly, spluttering on her wine as she burst into peals of laughter.

"I'm not joking," cried Abi, enjoying Helen's reaction. "I reckon my hymen's grown right back!"

"Hang on a minute," said Jesse, taking the opportunity to steer the discussion further from Lucy. "Are you telling me that you took some blockers or other before you hit puberty? So you've never actually been through puberty?" He laughed at that, cracking himself up and easing the tension even more as conversation tentatively flowed back into the group. Soon the argument was forgotten and laughter rippled around the table again. Anders caught Abi's eye and gave her a brief nod of gratitude. Abi gave a cheeky wink in reply. Lucy had isolated herself with her comments and slunk off unnoticed, giving Anders a sour glance as she shared a joke with Mal.

Eventually, Anders declared that she needed some sleep, so grabbed her jacket and stood up carefully, letting her legs decide how drunk she was before saying her goodbyes and heading for the stairs.

"I'll come with you," declared Mal, standing up and banging his head on the low brick arches.

"That'll help with the hangover," declared Duncan drunkenly as the group bid the pair goodnight.

Out on the street, a chill wind harangued them both as they pulled their jackets closely around them. Charing Cross station sat opposite, but Anders fancied a walk across the river to Waterloo. It would take ten minutes and freshen her up a bit.

"Mind if I walk with you?" asked Mal. Anders slid an arm through his and let herself be guided through Embankment and up the steps to the bridge crossing the river. Though he was her boss, he had an easy, gentlemanly manner about him and she could see that he cared for his team.

"I'm sorry about Lucy," he said. "She was out of order." Anders gave a wry grin.

"Nothing for you to apologise about. It's her issue, not mine."

"Well, I'm sorry anyway." He gave a sidelong glance at her, clearly wondering whether he should ask what was on his mind. She saw his look and raised an eyebrow, daring him to ask.

"Why are you so open about it? No one would ever have to know?" She considered the question for a while as they walked through the small crowd of tourists on the bridge who were snapping pictures of the London Eye or Parliament. The bridge had large, smooth paving stones on the walkway that had large gaps between each slab. She had to mind her step or her heels would slip into the mud filled spaces and she idly walked along them as if doing hopscotch. Eventually she spoke.

"I don't shout it from the roof tops, but it's not something I'm going to hide from. Say now you just met me, what would you think?" Mal shrugged.

"I'd think there was an attractive woman." She slapped his arm playfully and continued.

"We got to know each other over several months and one day I told you I was transgender. You'd look at me differently. You'd think I was different, that I had changed, but really it was your perception that had changed. I was still very much the same. The more people realise that it's a matter of their perception, the better. Besides, it rarely comes up. It's not something I really think about any more, it was such a long time ago."

As they made their way down the steps and approached Waterloo, the grand entrance looming overhead, Mal, clearly intrigued spoke again. Anders didn't mind. This wasn't the aggressive questioning of Lucy, but someone who wanted to get to know her some more.

"Do your wards know? What were their names?" Anders smiled at the thought of them.

"Aaron and Cassie. They know. Hard not to considering the publicity at the time."

"They know you killed their father?"

"They do. They also know what he did to them."

"They'll forget. Time will distort things and maybe one day they'll want a reckoning." Drink had made him maudlin, a great sadness in his eyes. Anders wanted to know what was behind such deep sorrow, but let it go for now.

"When that time comes, they can have their reckoning," she replied. "It's the least they deserve. Speaking of which, Buckland will get his too. We'll find him." He sighed abruptly.

"He's a ghost. No trace anywhere." It was frustrating that, with all of the technology available to them, it was still possible to hide in the UK. Anders had warned him that the excessive data compiled by the British surveillance network would swamp the system, and so it had proved. They simply had too much, so Mal had the team break it up and focus on key areas, but it was still overwhelming. It didn't help that Francis, Buckland's twin brother kept showing up on the facial recognition software and that calls to the helpline had all tagged him. It was an arduous task to eliminate him each time and he had been reluctant to curtail his activities. There had even been a fight outside parliament when a tourist mistook him for Michael and Francis had to be ushered away with a police escort. Mal interrupted her thoughts.

"You think many people will rally to his cause beyond getting the five million quid?" Anders gave it some consideration as they entered Waterloo Station through the impressive, carved stonework gilding the flight of steps. Inside the station, armed police patrolled silently and with an air of slight menace. Of the one hundred and thirty thousand police officers in Britain, six thousand were now trained in firearms – a number that had doubled over the last few years, notably since the Paris attacks. Anders, used to such sights in the States, found it jarring and watched them as she replied.

"There's always those who are looking for something to latch on to, something to be part of that gives them hope. It's easy to be down on humanity. We kill and maim and torture and we see the worst of it, but there is grace in our failings, hope in our triumphs. There is much good in us, but it's easier not to be. Buckland's tapping into our fears and using greed and avarice as back up. It's a potent cocktail." She turned to see Mal gazing at her strangely as she mused out loud.

"What?" she asked. He chuckled at her defensive tone.

"Nothing," he protested. "It's nice to see you open up a little is all."

"So I'm buttoned up am I?" Mal's eyes sparkled with mischief.

"A little intense perhaps," he said and neatly sidestepped her backhanded swipe. Anders checked her train times on the billboard and saw that she had half an hour to wait. Sighing, she spotted a bar at the back of the station at the top of a flight of steps and asked Mal if he fancied another drink.

"Sure," he replied and led her to the bar, weaving through the throng of people with practised ease and grace despite his bulk. "So tell me about Jesse," he asked. "You two clearly know each other well." Anders gave him a guarded look.

"What do you know?" She wasn't about to give away any details of him that Mal didn't know. He saw her weariness and smiled, glad that she had such protective instincts over those she cared about.

"Spent time in America and some of that in a prison for hacking into the NSA. Something about making every computer screen show Solskjaer's winning goal in the Champions League final on repeat." Anders smiled at the memory as they entered the small bar and sat overlooking the crowded station floor. Anders enjoyed people watching and had her back against the wall looking down below.

"I was his arresting officer. Dragged him naked as the day he was born from his bed. He made quite the scene." As they ordered more wine, Anders continued the story. "Anyways, a year into his sentence, I pulled him out to help me break into a paedophile ring down South. He got a taste for the right side of the law and I convinced the judge to suspend his sentence." Mal chuckled as the drinks were served and chinked her glass with his.

"I knew there was a big softie in there somewhere," he said and laughed as she gave him a mock scowl and lifted her own glass to salute him.

The next morning, Anders took her time with her run. The drink had fuddled her mind and body, so she let the alcohol sweat itself out before pushing herself. The Richmond Hill Gate was already open when she arrived and the Warden grinned at her as she passed.

"Little late this morning," he called as she waved good morning.

Returning to the flat, she found Aaron and Cassie already up and making breakfast. It was the weekend and they were all at home together that day. They grinned as she came through the door, visibly sweating and tired.

"Morning," said Cassie. She was dressed in a short skirt and loose t-shirt that hung lower than the skirt itself, eyes heavily made up and sporting a new ear piercing. "Heard you banging your way in nice and early this morning. Few drinks last night?" Anders slumped down in a chair at the table and helped herself to some toast. Cassie passed her a large mug of coffee, which Anders took gratefully.

"A few," she replied. Tucking into her toast, she asked what they would like to do today. She had the day off and was determined to spend it with the two of them.

"The IMAX is showing a quadruple bill of the Avengers films," declared Aaron. Cassie rolled her eyes.

"If I'm going, I want popcorn. Lots of it. And candy. And soda."
Anders grinned.

"Sounds good," she declared. "Anyone who doesn't have diabetes
by the end of the day has failed miserably.

"What's diabetes?" asked Aaron. Cassie gave Anders a look that
suggested she could deal with that one. Grabbing another slice of
toast and sticking it in her mouth, she ushered Aaron into his
bedroom to get changed and tame his wild mane of blonde hair while
she explained all about blood glucose levels. It made little
difference. He still wanted a giant bag of popcorn at the cinema.

Week 2

And so our first week concludes. It's been a wonderful week, with so much support for our cause. You have taken my teachings and owned them. There were so many entries, it was overwhelming and I have decided that next week, I shall choose two winners. For the first week of our revolution, I chose an entry from Spain. A re-enactment from A Game of Thrones. The Red Wedding. You have to love a man willing to chop the head from his fellow man and stitch it to the body of the family pet and vice versa. I was quite taken aback and only too pleased to grant this the winning entry. I have posted the pictures below for your delectation.

The winner proves one thing. That this is now an international revolution, though we mustn't lose sight of the ultimate goal; a revolution of the species. It is time to break the shackles, destroy democracy and crush antiquated notions of civilisation. As a species, we have castrated ourselves and lost sight of what we can truly be, what our role on this planet should be.

We think ourselves perfect, yet it is our imperfections that make us beautiful. Every mutation, every defect is essential to our very existence, the fundamental driving force behind the survival of every species. Each of us carries thousands of millions of anomalies and outliers, written into our very code. That is our strength. Non-conformity to a norm determined by whom? We have become bland, driven to an idealised image that we should reject, not embrace.

That is why, this week, the theme is that of your own fantasies. Live them out. Be bold. Be creative and express your innermost desires. Don't let society tell you it is a fantasy when society should be encouraging you to embrace your deepest desires, to turn them into reality and allow your true expression. Omnia romae vernalia sunt.

My fantasy is complete liberation in the true sense of the word. Our souls free to express, to lose their temporal chains and unite completely with its pastoral self. Only then can this planet and humanity be saved.

I present my entry for the week. A policeman. Someone we allow to enforce the rules we agree to abide by. Passively realising that we created our own prison by the acceptance of laws that rely completely on our acquiescence. What happens when you realise that this acceptance is no longer permissible?

Taking him is easy. When I do, he hits the news and his family speak tearfully of how worried they are for him. He knows none of this, none of the search for him in the outside world for I am setting him free from his physical being. It takes a long time. Many, many weeks, but Sergeant Boyle is strong. He holds on to his form, even when I take it from him.

Day one, I remove a finger. The little one. He screams. He begs. He threatens, but I ignore him. He is trapped in this box, chained to a chair in front of a large mirror so he can see what I do to him.

The next day, I take my sheers to him once more. Another finger. I do this for many days until he has no fingers and toes. He's given up screaming. He just sobs. His spirit is broken and he does not see that I am making it anew. I preserve his fingers and put them on display in his prison. I hang some by wires, I glue some to the walls, an effigy of Boyle so he may know what he loses as I help him gain immortality.

I then move onto his hands, bloody fingerless stumps that I hack my way through. He starts screaming again. I tire of this, so I take his tongue, scissors slicing through the flesh with a delicious cutting sound. His teeth next, one by one with pliers, a clamp to hold his jaw open.

My project requires work and dedication. It is not easy. I walk among you, brushing myself against the disease that we have become and know that I am setting one of you free. That I am creating art from his temporal spirit. I wanted to scream, to shout, to show you all, but the time was not right. I needed to remove a limb. Then another. Piece by piece. A drip to keep him alive, drugs to stave off infection. He wishes to die, but I fight for him. I fight to keep him alive, so that he may see. He turns away, so I clamp his head in place, remove the eyelids. He sees then and suffers cardiac arrest. His appendages displayed in wondrous fashion around him, he gives up.

But I save him once more. He is alive. He is waiting for you. I have succeeded in my task. It is time for you all to follow.

Chapter 1

Anders sipped her coffee as she watched Aaron pour himself some cereal into a bowl. He looked smug as he poured his milk over the flakes and scooped out a large mouthful with his fist wrapped around a spoon too large for his small hands. He looked triumphant and rammed it into his mouth, his face turning to despair as he realised that Anders had swapped back the inner packet of cereals that morning.

"That's not my Frosties," he moaned through a mouthful of Corn Flakes. Cassie laughed delightedly and gave Anders a high five, wooden bangles banging loudly as she raised her arm.

"New joke," she declared causing Anders to groan loudly.

"Enough with the jokes already," she said but Cassie ignored her.

"Why can't you have a twelve inch nose?" she asked. Aaron crinkled his forehead in thought, absently chewing his cereal as he did so.

"Dunno."

"Because then it would be a foot." Anders snorted with laughter, coffee spilling from her nose as she fought to control her fit of giggles.

"That's terrible," she declared as she wiped coffee from her chin. Aaron shrugged.

"I don't get it." Cassie started to explain the joke when Anders' phone rang. Still cleaning her spilt coffee, she tapped the phone and Mal's voice came through the speaker.

"He's posted a new blog. Just come up. Get to the Isle of Dogs now." Switching the phone off the speaker with an apologetic glance at Cassie, she stood up and walked away from the table.

"What's going on?"

"Jesse will explain as you go, just get moving. We may have time to save him. Barry's on the way." With a click, he was gone. Anders paused for a moment, gathered her thoughts and grabbed a rucksack from her room, putting her keys, phone and wallet in there. She wedged a blue tooth device into her ear and set her phone as she reached deeper into her cupboard and pulled out a Kevlar vest with the word Police emblazoned on it. She then buckled a belt around her waist with her cuffs, spray and ASP baton attached, yelling through to the kitchen as she secured the straps.

"Cassie, I need your bike. You can take the truck." Cassie rolled her eyes as Anders swept past, giving Aaron a kiss on the forehead and Cassie one on the cheek.

"That rust bucket! Something breaks every time I look at it!" Grabbing Cassie's helmet and leathers, Anders ran out of the flat, calling Jesse and sprinting down the steps three at a time, struggling into the helmet and jacket whilst trying not to trip. Jesse picked up immediately.

"We got some screwed up shit here," he said, not bothering with pleasantries. Anders knew him well enough to know that he was shaken by what he'd seen online. Anders burst through the door at the bottom of the stairwell and ran to Cassie's bike, a BMW S 1000 RR that she'd bought for Cassie on her eighteenth birthday. Revving the engine, she spun the bike around and raced out of the building, leaning low into the turn as she sped through the early morning traffic.

"Where am I going?" she asked.

"Docklands Museum, I'll guide you."

"Why the rush?" Anders sped through traffic lights, used the bus lanes and ignored basic traffic courtesies as she rode. Were it not for Jesse's description of events, she'd have been grinning with joy.

"Read the blog to me," she said while several cars beeped loudly as she cut them up in her haste.

"No way man. It's too disturbing. I read it once and I feel all dirty. Like I need to take a shower."

"Get Abi to read it to me then, just let me know what I'm heading into." As she neared the location, Abi read the blog. Anders frowned as she listened.

"It's a different tone to the last one. He seems more unhinged here. The message is different, yet close enough that most folks won't discern the difference."

"I agree," said Abi. "I don't think he means what he says at all. He's just getting kicks from what he does and is trying to legitimise it, get others to join his sick fantasy and exonerate him. I've checked the web and he's building quite a cult in just a week. This goes on any longer and the disaffected will flock to him even more." Anders grimaced inside her helmet as Abi passed over to Jesse.

"Just around the corner now. Should be a building next door to the museum," said Jesse who paused briefly as he scanned the news channels on one of his screens. "Heads up, it's on TV. Camera crew just pulling up ahead of you now. There's a few folks around the door trying to get in. They look...er..."

"Fanatical," said Abi in the background.

"Yeah, fanatical. Or bat shit crazy. Take your pick. Barry's a few minutes behind with a van full of Met's, got caught up in traffic. Mal is another ten. I'd wait if I were you." Anders shook her head as she rounded the corner and slowed to a halt by a statue of Robert Milligan, who stood proudly outside the museum.

"Can't let them compromise the scene," replied Anders as she stepped from the bike and strode across the cobbled paving towards a posse of men and women who were beating at a large wooden door on the building next to the museum. To her right, the sun sparkled off the Thames in glittering beams that reflected sharply off the large windows that adorned the old fashioned warehouses that lined the dockyard. They'd been renovated and the ships removed, but the upscale vibe to the area couldn't disguise its heritage. Anders would have loved to have spent a peaceful day here with the kids, but had rather more pressing matters at hand. She unzipped her jacket and let it drop to the floor to give herself more freedom of movement and show her Police Vest.

There were around fifteen of them and they'd read the blog. It was the mix of people that surprised her. A business man in a suit there, a spotty looking teen here and a housewife among the crowd. They were cheering as a large man in a denim jacket succeeded in pulling the lock from the massive doors. Aware that a film crew was watching her, Anders shouted over the crowd.

"Police! This is a crime scene and you are now trespassing on it. Back off and leave this area immediately." The large guy turned at her shout and stared at Anders belligerently through beady eyes, his neck and shoulders thickly muscled but his belly large and round. He swatted an elderly man aside as he moved towards Anders, narrowing the gap quickly.

"We don't recognise your authority to govern," he snarled. "Haven't you heard love, we're in the middle of a revolution." Anders sighed inwardly as she approached the group. They had fanned out as she drew near, flanking her sides and giving her little room to move except backwards. She stopped a few feet from Beady Eyes and unclipped her baton. She was acutely aware of the news crew filming the scene from a safe distance and kept her voice low.

"There's no revolution," she said. "Not today." He stepped forwards threateningly and clenched his fists.

"There's a change coming. You won't be able to oppress us for much longer. He's done this for us to see. We need to see what he's done."

His words emboldened the crowd and they advanced on her. In the background she could hear sirens as her colleagues raced to catch up, stuck as they were in the morning traffic. She didn't think they'd get here in time. Shifting her stance and lowering her centre of gravity, she thrust out her hand and the baton extended itself with a threatening sound, full of menace and ill intent.

The crowd paused as Anders, silent and still, stared hard at Beady Eyes, daring him to step forward. Jesse's panicked voice burst through her headset.

"I'm watching you live on TV! Be nice, be nice, be nice."

To the sides, Anders saw some of the bolder fanatics close in on her. Still staring at the large man, she assessed her options calmly. Choosing her course of action, she took a steadying breath and prepared to move.

Before she could act, the dockyard front was bathed in flashing lights and a cacophony of sound as Barry skidded round the corner in a large van. As he screeched to a halt, the back doors flew open and a squad of officers in riot gear poured out, advancing on the crowd who dispersed rapidly. Barry leapt from the vehicle and sprinted to Anders as the large guy turned to run. Anders was faster and stuck out her baton. It tangled his legs together and sent him crashing to the floor, his forehead taking the brunt of the impact.

Too groggy to get up quickly, she knelt on his back and immobilised him with her speedcuffs. They had a thick plastic handle instead of a chain and she used that to lift his arms and force him to his feet, pushing him towards some officers who'd arrived to help. The rest of the group had been rounded up and were being loaded into the back of another van for questioning. Barry gave her a wry look.

"Making friends I see," he said and passed her a Glock 26. She checked the clip and chambered a round. Though police officers weren't armed in the UK, there were armed units and McDowell had made sure that both Barry and Anders' credentials and training made them eligible in specific circumstances.

"You know me," replied Anders. "I'm a party a minute gal." Barry chuckled before sobering up quickly as he eyed the door. He'd also read the blog.

"Ready?" he asked. Anders gave a curt nod and they moved quickly to the entrance, Anders switching off her blue tooth as they moved. The door was set deep into a stone arch and there were no visible windows on the building. It hung ajar slightly and Barry nudged it open further with the tip of his pistol, flashlight held in the other hand, weapon resting gently on it. The interior of the building was dark, the gloom sucking the light from their torches. Anders, clicked the safety off her Glock, the noise gleefully signalling malicious promise.

She moved in and slid to the right, giving Barry free space to enter while she offered covering fire. He tucked left so that they were no longer framed by the light from the door. Using their flashlights, they could see that they were in a large warehouse that was completely empty apart from a large metal shipping container in the middle. An unnerving silence smothered the large space and Barry felt a chill as he eyed the container. Looking to Anders, he saw a focused expression on her face and drew comfort from her professionalism.

Flanking the metal box, they circled it before coming back round to the front. It was roughly twenty metres long and ten wide. Anders gave the nod to Barry and he pulled the large lever on the door, tugging it open silently. He stepped back as a red glow ebbed from the container, allowing Anders to quickly move in. She stopped short at the macabre scene inside.

Sergeant Boyle was still alive.

Pieces of him hung from the ceiling like some twisted mobile, swinging gently in a breeze the door had created as it opened. Boyle's fingers had been glued to the walls in a criss-cross pattern and his feet had been stapled to the floor in a penguin stance. Boyle was shackled to a metal chair by his neck. His limbs had been removed and he was propped against the chair by steel wire sown through his torso. His eyelids had been sliced off as had his nose and lips. Several drips hung beside Boyle, litres of fluids and antibiotics pumping through him.

The smell was horrendous and Anders wondered at how he still lived, mewling noises coming from his ruined body. The odour was that of rotting flesh but one that had been dipped in formaldehyde to slow the decaying process. Barry came in behind her, weapon held high, but he lowered it as soon as he saw Buckland's work. He stood silent for several heartbeats, both of them too shocked to move. Anders had seen the worst that humanity had to offer and still had the capacity to be horrified by it.

As Barry moved towards Boyle, he holstered his weapon and stepped around him, placing a gentle hand on his shoulder. In the red light, the tattoos on his arm seemed to writhe with a life of their own. A silent tear fell unknowingly from Anders as Barry gave her a hard stare.

She knew what he was saying.

"I'll do it," she said softly. Barry shook his head sadly. Neither wanted to be the one to abdicate responsibility. In that moment a bond was forged between the pair as deeply as if they had fought together on a battlefield. Placing his hands softly around Boyle's head, he gave a sudden jerk and a loud snap echoed around the container. Barry stepped away from Boyle's corpse and walked out of the container. He spoke to her as he passed.

"It'll be a few minutes before Mal gets here. You do your thing." As he left, Anders took out her headphones and placed them in her ears. She hesitated before pressing play, knowing what it meant. She would not turn from it though. She would gather the evidence, build a picture and relive the scene. She would do to Boyle what Buckland had done to him again and again in a twisted time loop until she had what she needed. As she moved around the room, a part of her wondered at the cost to her own soul.

Chapter 2

A grim silence smothered the warehouse as Helen and Ben stepped into the container. Anders was already inside and she lay a comforting hand on Ben's shoulder as he paused in the doorway, too shocked to fully process what he saw. Helen, experienced as she was, also paled and suddenly looked vulnerable. They'd all seen death and horror in their work, but sometimes they saw things that they knew they'd never forget, that would haunt their dreams for the rest of their lives. They worked knowing this and accepted the consequences because they knew that what they did mattered. They were driven to uphold the moral values of the law regardless of the cost to them. They knew all too well that its function was to enable free expression whilst providing protection for everyone. It was its fundamental and guiding principle and Buckland had warped and twisted its purpose to legitimise his barbarism.

"How long's he been here?" asked Mal, looking ill as he gazed around the container in shock. It was everyone's worst nightmare made real.

"There's forty body parts glued to walls and hanging down from the ceiling," replied Anders. "If his blog is correct, then that's forty days. And nights I guess. Seems he has a messiah complex, which fits in with the more religious aspect his last blog took." Abi had taken one look and blanched, turning around unsteadily and going to sit in a van outside. Her voice cackled through the coms.

"He's taken too much pleasure in this act. The first killing was brutal, but served a very specific purpose. Almost a necessity in his eyes. This act is more polarising. It'll turn those intrigued by his ideology away from him, but make those rallying to his cause more fanatical. I don't get it."

"Were assuming there's a rational mind behind this," warned Mal as he watched Helen step gingerly to the body on the seat, grimacing at the ruined mess. Ben, unsure of where to start, began by taking photographs of each body part from several angles, the flash of the camera bright in the poorly lit container and reflecting off the mirror that Buckland had placed in front of Boyle.

"What I don't get," said Jesse through their headpieces. "Is why we're processing this scene. We all know *Dick*land did it. We should be finding him."

"He may have been careless," replied Mal. "Left something of use."

"What? Like a note he's written to himself of where he's hiding because he's so damn crazy?"

"Something like that. Why don't you find out why this building isn't on record as belonging to Buckland. I want to know who or what owns it. Hopefully, that'll give us something useful." Staring at the body parts dangling from the ceiling, he shook his head sadly. He couldn't fathom the mind that could do this.

"How did he live for so long?" he wondered aloud, turning his attention to the corpse itself.

"Drugs and antibiotics, probably mixed in with coagulants as well," answered Helen as she moved around Boyle's corpse. "Buckland was careful too. Sawed through the bone, then cauterised the arteries. I'm guessing I won't find any painkillers in that cocktail either," she said sadly, peering at the drip bags. As Helen examined the torso, her eyes narrowed and flickered to Anders, then Mal.

"Neck's broken," she said. She put a hand on his torso briefly. "Still warm. Inexact, but I'd say it was recent." Mal gave the body a thoughtful look before turning to Anders.

"Let's give these guys some space. We'll head back to Scotland Yard and I'll liaise with McDowell, while you and Barry chase up the ownership of this place." As they left the container, Mal paused in the open space between that and the door leading outside. Switching off his headset, he bade Anders do the same. He looked hard at her, close, so he had to look down.

"If Boyle is recently dead from a broken neck, then I can only assume that Buckland was here moments before you. That would mean that I would need to send out search parties from this location and scour the area. That would require a lot of manpower and time, which is something we don't have enough of." His eyes searched her face, trying to read Anders' passive expression, but she gave him nothing as the silence stretched out. He turned to the container and considered it for some time as the flashes from Ben's camera spilled out, a white light to chase away the ebbing red that seeped insidiously from the door. Eventually, he nodded to himself and turned back to Anders.

"I'd have done the same." He spoke so quietly, that Anders wasn't sure that she heard it. He gave her arm a gentle squeeze and strode towards the door, his masculine scent lingering in the still air as she watched him go. When he'd left, she let out the deep breath she didn't know she'd been holding.

Chapter 3

Anders parked the bike next to the squad cars in the underground bay, ignoring the salacious stares from the Met officers as she took off her helmet and strode towards the stairwell nestling in the corner.

Down in the Hub, Jesse greeted her with a cheer.

"Well look who it is! It's the sexiest, most famous police officer in the country!" She grinned broadly at his good cheer and sat on Jesse's table, facing him. He pointed at the screens behind her and she swivelled to see that he was watching Sky News, BBC News and the ITV News on several different screens. They were all showing her stand-off with the crowd and subsequent tackling of Beady Eyes.

"They're loving you," said Jesse, chuckling as they asked who this mystery officer was. Anders sighed. She hadn't wanted a high profile in the UK. It was one of the reasons she'd had to leave the FBI as it had affected her ability to work.

"Dammit," she said and slid from the desk. "That's the last thing I need." She snaked her way through the tables and pushed open the door to the ladies toilets, her temper grim. It was well lit and clean, with several cubicles lining the side. Opposite, there was a large mirror above the wash basins and Anders found Lucy there, dabbing tears from her eyes. A stillness came over Lucy and Anders made to leave.

"I'll come back another time," she said, knowing that Lucy wouldn't like her presence in the female toilets. Normally, she'd have had little time for such insecurities in others, but Anders was still shaken by what she had seen this morning and wasn't in the mood for confrontation.

"No, it's ok. Please stay." Lucy's voice caught as she spoke, the desperation clear. Anders moved closer and leaned against a sink, back to the mirror and facing Lucy. Her blonde hair was covering her face as if she was ashamed, so Anders gently tucked it over an ear as she spoke.

"What's up? Anything I can help with?" Lucy shook her head and dabbed at her tears. She'd been so horrible to Anders, but now looked like a lost child. It was difficult to feel any anger towards her.

"No, it's ok. I'm just a little shook up by what we saw back there. I never imagined we'd be doing things like this when I joined. It's all so…" She wrung her hands in frustration, lost for words, unable to articulate how she felt.

"It feels like you're being sullied simply by being there. Like you become a participant." Lucy stared at Anders thoughtfully.

"Yes. I suppose it does. How do you cope? The things you've seen in America and now here? It's a wonder you're functioning." Anders reflected for a moment, contemplating her words.

"I look at the worst of us so others don't have to. Doing what we do makes a difference. It comes at a cost, but I pay that willingly If it means justice. Take a walk down the street. Watch the kids on their phones, the couples arguing about the tiniest things or mothers mollycoddling their children. We do what we do so they can go about their lives free from fear and oppression. Buckland seeks to undermine those very values and that is why we must stare hard at his work and not flinch."

As she spoke, Lucy watched her intently. She saw the passion and fire in Anders' eyes and knew that she believed every word. This was a calling for her and no matter how difficult the task, how ruinous the burden, she would suffer it stoically.

"I'm sorry about what I said the other night. It wasn't fair to attack you like that." Anders gave an easy shrug.

"I've had worse and I'll have worse again. It makes no nay never how to me." Lucy started picking some varnish from her nails, uncomfortable with what she had to say, but determined to do so.

"I just…it's just that…I was raised Catholic. My family were very clear in their scriptures. When I heard you were coming, it was so easy to believe every word my group said. My mother even lent me some books on the matter and I soaked it all up." She looked at Anders, guilt plain on her face.

"But you're so…well, normal." She let out a short bark of bitterness. "Actually, you're not normal. You put most women to shame." Anders shuffled her feet. She hated compliments. Too often they served some purpose for whoever was saying it, but she felt that Lucy was being genuine.

"That's untrue," she replied. "I look to every woman as a role model. You're pretty kick ass yourself, you know." Lucy chuckled, wiping at her drying tears as she did so.

"Not on your level. I can't stand all that shooting and fighting." Anders gave a throaty laugh, leaning in conspiratorially as she did so.

"I'll tell you a secret and you're not allowed to laugh." Lucy leaned closer as Anders made a show of looking around to see that they were alone. "There was a Muay Thai boxer called Parinya Charoenphol. She was transgender and kicked butt. I figured if she could do it, then why should anyone tell me what I couldn't do? I also watched far too much *Buffy the Vampire Slayer* during my transition!" Lucy gave Anders a strange look before bursting into peals of laughter, Anders joining in with her infectious laugh. Lucy quickly sobered and looked thoughtfully at herself in the mirror.

"My parents will hate me," she said. "If you're so real, how can it be a sin? You said that it was redemption through transformation and it's hard to disagree."

"The Catholic Church is a tolerant place now Lucy. There is even a transgender priest. Sure, there are groups that are less tolerant than others, but you find that everywhere. At the end of the day, we're not here to judge. That will come later." Lucy took her hand and gave it a squeeze.

"Thank you," she said. "You could have been a real bitch to me, you know that?" Anders gave her a hug.

"Hugging it out is better," she replied as Lucy returned the embrace. "Besides, the Gospel of Luke teaches us not to condemn or judge, but offer forgiveness without measure." Lucy gave her a startled look.

"Chapter six, verse thirty seven, how did…?" Anders gave a sad smile.

"My father was a devout Christian. Some of it rubbed off I guess. He used to tell me that there wasn't anything bound in thought that you couldn't change. I thought he meant that in a positive way until he found out what I was." Lucy whistled in disbelief.

"You're full of surprises, you know that?" Anders smiled.

"It's been mentioned on occasion," she replied. "Come on, let's freshen up and get out of here."

A short while later, Anders left the toilets and strolled over to Jesse. He gave her a knowing look.

"You left Lucy in one piece or do I need to call an ambulance?" he asked. Lucy came out from the toilets and gave them both a big smile. She'd fixed her make-up and looked her normal self once more, if a little less sour.

"Okay," said Jesse nervously. "What happened in there?"

"Never you mind," said Lucy and sat next to Anders as they appraised his work on the screens. He'd put the projector on and showed them his research.

"So the warehouse belongs to a company called MB, Michael Buckland obviously, but it's not registered to his name, rather an offshore company that doesn't actually exist."

"Try variations on his name and initials, see how many we come up with," ordered Lucy and Jesse tapped away at the board furiously. Meanwhile, Mal and Abi joined them. Abi looked at Anders and Lucy side by side and smiled to herself. Mal pulled out a chair for her and she sat with an appreciative nod while he leant on the table next to Anders.

"How was McDowell?" she asked. He grimaced.

"Not happy. He's getting a lot of pressure from above. Not best pleased with you either."

"Me? What did I do?"

"You were filmed speeding around on that damn bike and then confronting an angry mob. You were supposed to lay low, not tackle a man three times your size live on TV."

"I barely touched him," retorted Anders.

"He did kinda fall on his face," said Jesse, looking up from his keyboard with a grin. Lucy grinned as well.

"It was a little bit funny." Mal gave them both a strange looked and turned to Abi who gave a nonchalant shrug. Before he could say anything, Jesse gave a cry of delight.

"Ladies and gentleman, I give you Lord Michael Buckland's thirty two brand spanking new buildings and land deeds. He's been a busy little boy."

"You have a warrant to look at these records?" asked Mal.

"Um. Can you get me one?" Mal sighed and made to pick up the phone, but it rang before he had a chance. He grabbed it and listened, a horrified expression crossing his face. Dropping the phone, he sprinted to the elevator, yelling over his shoulder as he ran.

"Armed individual on the street outside, calling for the NCA taskforce." Barry stepped from the lift just as Mal arrived and he hustled him back in. "You have your weapon?" he asked. Barry nodded as Lucy caught up with them and slid through the closing doors. Anders headed for the stairwell as Jesse tossed her an earpiece. Taking the steps two at a time she barrelled up them, bursting from the door to the ground floor as Mal stepped from the lift. Barry tossed her the same Glock she had used earlier and they made their way to the street outside.

Chapter 4

The road along the Thames was filled with traffic, but it ground to a halt at the sight of an armed man walking towards the Scotland Yard entrance. Tourists and locals alike scrambled for cover as a squad of armed police officers swarmed from the Yard and flanked him, taking cover behind walls and cars. Mal told them to back off and clear the site and they reluctantly shepherded civilians from the area.

The gunman was covered in blood. Cloying and sticky, it clung to his clothes, his skin and his hair, plastering it flat. Anders could see clumps of gristle clotting his tie and levelled her gun as she moved left and Barry circled the other side, careful not to place himself in line of Anders' weapon and her to his. The gunman was plump and looked as if he'd never done a hard day's work in his life, his chubby hands soft and manicured, his suit perfectly cut and his shoes unscuffed, gleaming in the midday sun.

He looked terrified as he stumbled towards Mal who strode confidently in his direction. The gunman held his weapon loosely by his side and it looked like an old handgun from the Second World War. Anders readied to shoot if he raised it, but she wasn't sure the gun would even fire, it looked so old. She saw Barry prepare to do the same from her peripheral vision and scanned the area quickly. It was clear of civilians, the armed response team having hurried them from the area and secured it. There were at least a dozen guns aimed on the man, though only Anders and Barry were out in the open. She wasn't worried. She knew that either herself or Barry could shoot him before he raised his weapon high enough to hurt someone.

"I'm Deputy Chief Constable Mal Weathers," he said, his voice carrying clear across the suddenly silent street, a cool breeze wafting off the Thames and snapping at the flags above the Scotland Yard building. "I'm leading the taskforce currently assigned to catching Lord Buckland. I'm told that you have requested my team. What's your name?" The gunman looked confused for a moment, clearly distressed, before focusing his attention on Mal.

"Why are they armed? Will they shoot me?" he asked. His voice was raw and strangely childlike, his chords scratched to ruin from shouting and screaming as he'd walked along the river. Mal raised his hands in a placatory gesture.

"You *are* carrying a gun. How about you drop that so we can have a chat?"

"They're pointing their guns at me. I'm not pointing mine at anyone." Mal indicated for Barry and Anders to lower their weapons and they did so reluctantly. He yelled for the armed response unit to stand down and there was a tense moment as their sergeant weighed up overruling a superior officer. Eventually, he nodded and they slunk into the shadows, their presence felt but not seen.

"There," said Mal softly, his gentle Welsh accent soothing and full of kindness. "They've lowered their guns. What's your name?"

"Steve," he said. "Steven Kelly. I didn't want to do it. I thought I did. I thought that what Buckland said was true. That we had to start a revolution. That life didn't matter. It was cheap. Isn't that what he said? There's too many of us."

As he spoke, Jesse relayed information into Anders' earpiece.

"Steven Kelly, lives in Brixton, works in the PM offices, a few hundred metres from where you are now. Recently divorced. I'm sending a car to his work and his home, see what he's done."

"And his ex-wife's place," called Abi in the background as Mal inched closer to Steven.

"There are plenty of us Steve," he said. "That doesn't make life any less sacred does it? We value life, we treasure it and we fight to survive. We celebrate every birth and mourn deeply every loss." Anders heard his voice catch, as if he recalled some great tragedy in his life. He spoke from the heart and Steve saw it too.

"That makes it worse then doesn't it? What I've done." Mal moved closer, almost close enough to reach out. Steve's hand twitched and

133

Mal stopped, Barry and Anders raising their weapons in response. Steve hadn't noticed, focused as he was on Mal.

"I don't know what you've done Steve. Whatever it is, I'm sure that you are deeply sorry. That you didn't mean to. That's why you're here. To turn yourself in." Jesse's voice burst through Anders' earpiece, startling her. Keeping her breathing steady and calm, she listened to Jesse as Mal talked quietly with Steve.

"Shooting at his workplace. Seems his fantasy involved blowing his boss' brains out and throwing him from a window. Then he shot the secretary, his ex-wife, and apparently spent five minutes sobbing over her corpse. I'm listening to a recording of the nine, nine, nine call from the building. Sounds like several more shots were fired, but it's garbled and panicky."

Gun works then, thought Anders to herself as Mal spoke, failing to calm Steve who started pounding his skull with a clenched fist.

"It was supposed to make things better," he shouted, frustration coursing through him, his body shaking with rage. "I was helping us all, making things better."

"That's the thing about fantasies Steve. Oftentimes, it's best that they stay that way. We don't always act out our fantasies because we know the hurt they'll cause. Having them and feeling them makes us cope with the world as it is, not as we want it to be."

Steve calmed at that and gave Mal a listless look.

"Is five million pounds worth it?" he asked. Mal gave the question some thought.

"That's not for me to say. Hand me your gun and I'd love to talk it through. You and me." Steve gave a long sigh and shook his head sadly.

"It's not, you know. It really isn't." He gave a short, bitter bark of a laugh. "Heck, I don't even know if I won." A sudden thought hit him. "I forgot to take a picture."

With that, he raised his gun. Mal lurched forwards, but was unable to cover the distance to wrestle the weapon from Steve as he lifted it to his own head. Two shots rang out, loud in the street, echoing off the concrete buildings and rolling away, screams of shock and fear in its wake.

The first bullet hit Steve in his shoulder and the second his arm. He spun to the floor, gun spinning away and blood gouting from his wounds. A silence smothered the street then as Mal turned to see that Barry and Anders had both fired. The sudden calm was punctured by screaming as the shock of Steve's wounds wore off and the excruciating pain set in. He writhed on the floor, clutching his injuries as Mal ran to him, taking off his shirt and pressing it to the bullet wounds to stem the bleeding.

"Ambulance on the way," said Jesse over Anders' earpiece. She went to help Mal as the sounds of London slowly seeped back to the blocked off street, the city no longer holding its breath. He shook his head at her as she knelt down, removing her jacket and stuffing it hard against the second wound.

"This has got to stop," he said. As the blood pooled around Steve, she looked down and knew that as each week went on, it would escalate further. They were only in the second week and there were another fifty to go.

Chapter 5

As Barry filled in the weapon discharge forms, Anders and Mal completed the incident report. Steve had been taken to hospital and they'd managed to stop the bleeding. The paramedics couldn't say whether he'd survive or not.

"Should have let him bleed out in the street," muttered Duncan as he sat down next to Anders. The team were all in the central Hub, working at their desks and filing paperwork. Since the NCA had been labelled ignorant and ill-informed by a High Court judge over their work practises in twenty fifteen, they'd had to be more diligent with their paperwork. Barry looked up as he typed on his computer, massive hands dwarfing the keyboard as he poked each key with a forceful thump.

"No way. Suicide's too easy for that guy. He needs to pay his dues in the here and now." He glanced at Lucy. "If there is a Heaven and Hell, he can damn well wait until we're done with him first."

As he spoke, Jesse switched on the projector, the whirring noise from the machine loud in the confined space. While it warmed up, he turned on the speakers and they all heard Lord Francis Buckland's voice before the picture came on screen. He was standing outside the MP's offices and speaking to the press.

"It is a truly tragic event that has happened here. As I have said many times in the past week, I cannot in any way condone my brother's actions. They are a despicable affront to humanity. We were raised as children of Christ, promoting charity and Serviam above all else. I have initiated several new projects with the sole purpose of..." Anders tuned him out as she finished her report. A chime on her computer showed an email had come through and she opened it up to find Ben's crime scene report from the Docks. Swiping the screen, she sent it to Jesse who put it up on the projector.

"It's only preliminary," said Anders as the team looked at the report. She stood up and switched the lights off. By now, the team had learnt to sit back and let her work when she wore this look of intense concentration. It was as if nothing else but the crime existed.

"Jesse, can you get Helen on loudspeaker please?" she said as she walked to the projection image on the wall. "Show me picture three. Zoom in." A close up of Boyle's decapitated limb filled the screen and the team shifted in discomfort. Abi didn't, intent as she was on watching Anders.

I could write a paper on this woman, she thought as Anders had Jesse zoom in and out of several photographs, scanning back to previous ones, laying the images over each other and placing them in columns on the screen.

"Helen, you there?" asked Anders as a fuzzy noise came over the speakers.

"I'm here love," replied Helen. Her voice was muffled by the mask she wore for Boyle's autopsy in the pathology lab. "What's up?"

"Take a look at the left Ulna, right Tibia and right Patella. Tell me what you see." A scuffling could be heard over the speaker as Helen sifted through body parts until she found the right ones. Eventually she spoke.

"You could be right. I'm not going to bet my career on it, but I think there is a possibility. That's as far as I'll go."

"Thanks Helen, I'll leave you to it." As Helen hung up, Anders turned to the team who had been waiting patiently. She pointed to the photographs that she'd had Jesse sort. "What you're looking at are the saw marks made by whatever device Buckland used to hack Boyle's limbs off. This one here, three strong thrusts of a saw, this one, shallow cuts, followed by deep strong ones. This last one, smooth and steady, but not as deep with each cut."

"Oh," said Abi as realisation dawned. "You think there's three people. First one is Buckland, strapping lad that he is, the second, someone new to this. Hesitant at first then getting into it, but strong too and then someone weaker, but not hesitant." She gave a triumphant look. "And here's me thinking you lot were policemen of the highest calibre," she gloated. Mal gave her a sardonic look.

"So the crucifixion, you say we have two people and now you say we have three?" he asked. He'd changed into a new flannel shirt, causing Anders to wonder if he had a supply of them tucked away somewhere. Her own jacket had been ruined by Steve's blood and she'd thrown it away with some regret. She had loved that jacket.

"You heard Helen," she answered. "There's not enough evidence. Buckland could be at an awkward angle, or he could have slipped. There could be any number of variables. Having said that, with the evidence from the first crime scene, I'm certain he is not working alone."

"I agree," chipped in Barry. "He's not working alone. For starters he doesn't have the technical knowhow to outsmart our own little hacker boy here." Jesse gave him a pained look and Barry winked at him.

"I'm with Anders too," said Duncan. "How else did someone without any medical training keep Boyle alive for so long?" He still had a thick bandage around his arm, but had removed the sling. His normally pale complexion had become slightly less grey and he was recovering well.

"I agree with Anders and Duncan," said Lucy, causing Mal to give her a strange look.

"Seems we have some harmony on the team," he said. "Good. Let's expand the search. Work over the crime scene again. Eliminate everything we know to be Buckland's and work on what's left, see where it leads us." He indicated the screen where Francis Buckland was still talking to the press. "I'll see if I can get his DNA sample again. He seems willing, but the lawyer isn't. At the very least, it will help us eliminate his brother from the crime scene. Barry, I want you to coordinate the search of the new buildings Jesse has found. Anders, you can…"

He stopped as the phone rang and Jesse answered it. Mal waited patiently for him to finish and hang up. Before Jesse could speak, the phone rang again. Another conversation.

"Ok boss," Jesse said when he was done. "Interpol called, says the Spanish have caught the winner of week one, a Devonte De La Cruz. They're on the way now."

"That was quick!" exclaimed Duncan. Jesse laughed as he recounted how the winner had been caught trying to buy a new Ferrari with his Debit card.

"And the first call?" asked Mal impatiently. Jesse grimaced.

"Another entry. Up in Liverpool, next to the Kop. Something about a Blood Eagle?" Duncan spoke, earning a few shocked looks from the team.

"It's an old Norse ritual, a sacrifice to Odin. You cut the ribs from the backbone and then pull out the lungs. Make's an Eagle's wing. What? I do read, you know."

"Oh sure, when we were growing up, he read Dandy, Beano, all the classics," said Abi sarcastically. Jesse gazed at the pair and shook his head. Duncan was a scruffy layabout, whilst Abi was prim and proper.

"How you two are related is beyond me." Ignoring Jesse, Mal turned to Duncan and Lucy.

"You two get up there and take the scene. Seems like someone's fantasy is to become a Viking or some such. Anders, you can meet and greet with the Spanish folks. Until they get here, help Barry but make sure Helen and Ben don't need you first. Abi, I need an updated profile on Buckland and something on what his disciples might be like. I've a feeling they'll be popping up everywhere."

There was a brief pause as his words sunk in. He clapped his hands together loudly in the silence.

"Let's go!" Chairs scraped and tables shifted backwards as everyone moved to their tasks, galvanised into action. Anders and Barry turned to Jesse as he printed out a list of new properties they could search. Taking the list from the printer, Barry scanned down the sheet before turning to Anders.

"I got this," he said. "You go help Helen out, get us some more evidence."

"You sure?" He waved her away.

"Yeah. It'll take me a while to draw up some warrants and coordinate the different boroughs anyway."

Anders made her way to the lab to find Helen surrounded by bags of body parts, each one labelled and sealed tight. She was just opening one as Anders entered.

"Need a hand?" Helen gave a sigh of relief and nodded to the sink.

"Scrub up love, you're a life saver. I need to reassemble poor Boyle here and see if there's anything missing before scanning him into the computer." Anders moved to the sink and grabbed a lab coat before scrubbing her hands and forearms.

"Where's Ben?" she asked, turning the tap off with her elbow and slipping on some latex gloves and a face mask.

"At the Dockyard, making sure SCO don't screw up," replied Helen as she removed a toeless foot from a bag and laid it on the metal gurney in an approximation of where Boyle's foot would be. Anders opened another bag and grimaced at the toes that greeted her. She started matching them up as Helen placed the second foot down.

"Have you seen the way he looks at you?" asked Anders mischievously. She knew Helen had been shaken by what she had seen and guessed, correctly, that levity was a good coping mechanism for her.

"No different to how he looks at you," she replied, arching a perfectly manicured eyebrow at Anders.

"It's different with you, like he's imagining the two of you as a couple. It's more thoughtful when he sees you." Helen chuckled, the sound at odds with the severed hand she was holding.

"Bless him. You just want to mother him, sort that mop of hair out and feed him up a bit. I hear you and Lucy are best buds now. What brought that on?"

"Nothing like seeing a fellow police officer chopped up to give you some perspective I guess. She invited me to her church group. Said she wanted to show them how narrow minded they were." Helen almost dropped the bag she was lifting.

"Bloody hell," she exclaimed. "I hope you told her to shove it." Anders smiled and shook her head.

"I gave up justifying my existence a long time ago, but if it makes things easier here, then it may be worth it. She's quite sweet when she's not scowling."

"I'm not sure her face even knows how to not scowl." They worked in companionable silence for a while as Boyle's form slowly took shape. Helen had taken her shoes off to work, padding softly around the table, but Anders had left hers on and the sound of her heels echoed around the room. Helen gave an approving look at the court shoes she wore with a red undersole.

"I have to ask. How can you afford those Louboutin's on your wages?"

"I was famous for five minutes in America. Made enough for us to live comfortably." Helen gazed at her thoughtfully.

"That photo right? That serial killer you tracked down?" Anders focused on her job, not looking at Helen as she spoke, working on reassembling Boyle and not really wanting to engage in recalling that ordeal.

"That's it," she said absently.

"I read you lost your fiancé at the same time. I'm sorry to hear that. It must have been hard." Anders gave her a ghost of a smile.

"It was." She held her gaze a short moment and Helen could see the grief etched in her soul. Then it was gone and Anders went back to work, engrossed in her task. Helen looked at her a moment longer before probing further. She loved people and wanted to know everything there was about someone. There were so many facets to Anders that Helen found her to be an enigma she wanted to unravel and get to know.

"The way Jesse tells it, you made a truckload of cash helping a crime lord in New York and used that money to win big at an illegal poker game." Helen kept her eye on Anders, but she was giving nothing away.

"Don't believe everything that man says. He likes a good story." Knowing she wasn't getting anywhere, she changed her approach.

"Drinks tonight?" she asked.

"I'd love to, but I'm taking Aaron to a soccer game. Tomorrow night? I'd love you to show me around." Helen gave her a cheeky grin.

"I think you and I will have some fun," she declared. They worked well together and soon had the corpse reassembled. As Helen scanned the body into the computer so they could analyse the cuts and breaks that Buckland had made, Anders checked the body for any further evidence. It was a painstaking task and it was many hours before they were done.

The moment they finished, Mal entered, looking slightly nervous.

"Anything?" he asked. Helen grimaced.

"Not much beyond our preliminary findings. We're just waiting for the spectrometer and the electrophoresis to finish up, see if they yield anything." Mal grunted and turned to Anders.

"A word?" He walked out, leaving Anders to remove her gear and follow him into the corridor. He paced nervously as she drew near and looked around to check they were alone.

"I was. Well, I was wondering if you'd like to... Um." Anders had never imagined that he could be nervous and was taken aback.

"Go out for a drink?" she said, helping him out. Mainly through pity.

"Sorry," he said. "I'm not normally nervous."

"You're my boss," replied Anders. "Won't that be a conflict of interest?"

"We're adults," he replied. "And professionals. We can keep them separate. Besides, nothing's happened yet."

"You know what I am," said Anders, a little more bluntly than she meant to. Mal frowned and lifted his hands up in consternation.

"No, it's nothing like that," he said quickly. "When I look at you, I see nothing more than a beautiful woman, inside and out. What you are, or were, never occurred to me until you raised it now." Anders softened somewhat. She saw the truth in his words.

"You like soccer? Or football as you call it?" she asked. "I have some tickets for the game tonight. Cassie will be delighted to give her ticket to you." She smiled at him as he grinned at her.

"I'll see you at seven," she said and turned to go back to the forensic lab, glad that she had worn her favourite shoes as he watched her leave.

Chapter 6

Fulham Broadway Station was packed with revellers as fans from Manchester and Chelsea converged. Forty thousand ticket holders, many thousands coming home from work and those wishing to enjoy the atmosphere and watch the game in a local pub, all descended on Stamford Bridge.

Anders guided Aaron through the crowd, gripping his shoulders as he gawped at the broiling mass of humanity. It was his first football game and he was savouring the thrilling atmosphere, decked head to toe in Manchester United colours. Anders spied Mal at the bottom of the stairs leading onto the street. He was leaning against the wall and stood head and shoulders over the crowd. Seeing her at the same time, he raised a hand and the crowd parted from him as he made his way to her.

When he came near, Aaron had to tilt his head back fully to make eye contact. The first thing he noted was Mal's blue scarf.

"You're not a Man U fan," he declared. Mal winked at Anders and knelt down to Aaron.

"Hello," he said. "I'm Mal and I'm very pleased to meet you." Aaron took the proffered hand and stared at him frankly.

"You're very tall," he said and Mal gave a mischievous laugh.

"I am indeed, but I work with someone even taller than me!" Aaron gave him a look of wide eyed wonder.

"He must be as big as the Hulk!" Anders watched the exchange and saw how comfortable Mal was with Aaron. *He's been a father*, she thought as he talked animatedly with Aaron. The boy had suffered such abuse at the hand of another man, yet seemed comfortable talking with Mal. He guided them through the crowd and asked where they'd like to eat.

"Sushi," declared Aaron and Mal gave Anders a strange look. She shrugged.

"He likes sushi," she said and he smiled. His size meant that people tended to give him a wide berth, so he pushed through the seething mass of humanity and they found themselves on the street within moments. Mal took a few seconds to orientate himself before leading them to a sushi bar he knew of nearby. Aaron had taken a liking to Mal, as did most people. He was gregarious and charismatic. Occasionally grumpy, but always considerate. A people person, which was almost the opposite of Anders. She could be outgoing, charming and witty, but often withdrawn and distant as she focused on her work.

Aaron talked freely with him but had to deduct points because he liked DC over Marvel.

"Thor would kick Batman's butt," he declared.

"Superman would kick Thor's butt," retorted Mal.

"What do you think, Bumble?" asked Aaron as they sat at the sushi bar. Anders wore a short sleeved polo neck top, acutely aware that her scars would show if she didn't. It didn't bother her, but she didn't want any focus on Aaron. It was Mal's first time in public with her outside of work and she still wasn't sure what was happening. She had decided on skinny jeans and knee high boots, not wanting to make too much effort, but not wanting to be too scruffy either.

While she gave Aaron's question the appropriate consideration, Mal eyed her over his menu. He often had a hard time working her out, she was so enigmatic. She was full of contradictions. Driving around in a rusty beat up old pick-up truck, her clothes looked like they cost more than the truck did. She was feminine yet excelled at combat, a heady mix of satin and steel. She flitted between intense and serious to flirtatious and full of humour within seconds and he often found himself twisted and turned emotionally whenever he spent time with her, as did most people. She was a force of nature. Intelligent enough to intimidate, she never used it as a shield like most intellectuals, yet would wield it to cutting effect in an argument, her IQ of a hundred and seventy three tearing opponents apart. Mal knew that, with her experience, she should be leading his team. Of that, he had no doubt. She seemed content to take his lead and he was grateful for her dedication to the role. Reading her profile had made him nervous about working with her, yet she was nothing like he expected.

She was stunning, yet seemed oblivious to it, her scars giving her an air of mystery. She could recall every detail of a crime scene, draw together all of the evidence and see patterns in a way only HOLMES could. She read people as if an open book and noticed the minute details that most people would never see, yet missed every sign and gesture that someone made when courting her. In that, she was the equivalent of a clumsy teenager. Mal guessed that it was because she was a contradiction by her very nature. Her DNA was male, yet he could only see a female sat in front of him, could only think of her as such. He'd always thought that you could know someone before you knew about them, but with Anders, the more he knew about her, the less he felt he knew her. It gave him much to think about as she announced her decision to Aaron.

"I think that they would battle until they were both too tired to fight any more and then Thor would invite Superman for a drink of Meade." Aaron wasn't too sure about the proposition of a draw so argued his point as they ordered food and drink.

They ate sushi and laughed and joked. Mal chuckled to see Anders drink beer from a bottle and then insist they stop for a Ben and Jerry's afterwards, cajoling the smitten server to add more scoops of ice cream to an already generous portion. As they approached the stadium, Mal asked Aaron if he knew about Stamford Bridge and its history.

"Of course," said Aaron simply. "It's the battle between King Godwinson and King Harald in ten sixty six." He scooped some ice cream into his mouth as Anders gave Mal a sly smile. Aaron had long since given up on children's TV and they frequently watched

National Geographic or The History Channel together. He also loved Bear Grylls and his survival shows, delighting when he ate all manner of disgusting things.

"Godwinson won, but then lost at Hastings so it didn't matter." Mal struggled to respond and lamely said that he meant the stadium, not the historical event.

"If Thor was with Godwinson, he would have won at Hastings as well. Maybe he was busy then." Anders put an arm around Aaron and kissed the top of his head.

"Definitely busy that day hun. Loki was causing mischief probably."

Mal stood happily in a sea of red as they took their seats in the away stand. He scowled at the goals his team conceded and kept his celebrations quiet as Chelsea mounted a late rally to bring the score level. He then bowed his head in shame as Manchester United scored a winner in the dying seconds, the away fans not giving him too much grief, put off as they were by his size. After the final whistle, Mal's phone rang and he stuck a finger against his opposite ear to hear the call. Listening for a few moments, he turned to Anders.

"The Spanish Inspectors have arrived. De La Cruz is in our holding cells waiting for you. When do you want to see him?" Anders leaned in, making sure Aaron couldn't hear.

"Let him stew for the night. I'll see him first thing. Tell Jesse to make sure he stays awake." Mal turned away, spoke briefly and then tucked the phone into his pocket. He led them back to the District Line tube station, guiding them away from any potential flashpoints between the home and away fans. There was a brief awkward moment when Mal said goodbye to Aaron and then stood up to say goodnight to Anders. He made to take her hand, but she leaned forward to kiss his cheek. They shared an embarrassed laugh and Mal gave a mock formal bow.

"Good night," he said. "I had a great time." Anders smiled back.

"I did too. Perhaps we could do it again sometime." Mal made to respond but blushed heavily when Aaron spoke, loud enough for everyone in the packed station to hear.

"You two should be boyfriend and girlfriend." Mortified, Mal beat a hasty retreat, leaving Anders to deal with Aaron. Sliding their tickets through the turnstiles, Aaron yawned and stumbled as the excitement of the evening caught up with him. He reached out to Anders and she picked him up, carrying him down the stairs and onto the train. She gave a grateful smile at the man who gave up his seat to the pretty lady and leaned back in her seat as Aaron drifted off to sleep in her arms.

On the train to Richmond, she reflected on Mal and what she should do. She liked him, but the pain of her fiancé's death was still raw, a ghostly pall that was a constant companion, at times leaching the colour from the world. He was also her senior officer. There were so many things that could go wrong. Then her mind flashed to an image of Mal laughing with Aaron and she realised that he needed a male role model as much as she needed to live a normal life. That was why they had fled America and come to Britain. She decided she'd give it a try and see where it led to.

Inevitably, her mind drifted to the case and she started thinking about her prisoner, stuck in a holding cell at Scotland Yard. She started working through her interrogation and barely noticed as the train pulled into Richmond and she had to carry Aaron back to the flat and up the long flight of stairs, muscles sore with the effort.

Having put him to bed, it took moments for her to collapse on her own mattress and fall asleep.

Chapter 7

Jesse handed Anders a file as she stepped from the stairwell. It was early, but he seemed fresh and awake.

"I like this new Jesse," she said. "It's good to see you with a purpose." He glowed with pride and led her back to his desk, showing Anders a squat figure sat on his bed in the holding cell on his screen.

"Devonte De La Cruz," he said. "I set up a team to knock on his door and wake him up every twenty minutes for the last seven hours. He should be nicely baked for you." Anders gave him a sweet smile and lay a hand on his arm.

"You give me the best presents," she said. "The inspectors?"

"On their way now. First up is Inspector Barco, who's decided to enjoy her stay as much as possible whilst she is here." Anders caught the triumphant glint in his eye.

"You didn't?" she asked, grinning. Jesse sniffed haughtily.

"I don't kiss and tell," he said, though his triumphant grin spoke volumes.

"You're insatiable, you know that? I take it back. You haven't changed." Jesse laughed and gave a mock bow.

"Guilty as charged Agent. Anyways, the other inspector is called something or other Molina. He's a bit dour, but was pleased with the hotel we gave him for the night." A chime from the lift sounded and Barry and Mal stepped out, striding towards them. Barry gave his usual gruff greeting and Mal smiled at them both, no trace of awkwardness at all, which made Anders glad. She was useless at things like that. He started to speak, but the internal line rang to let them know that the inspectors had arrived.

"Right. Let's go and greet our guests shall we?" Anders moved with Mal to the lift as the light above showed the cart to be moving down. He glanced sideways at her and muttered under his breath.

"I had a nice time last night." Anders smiled, still facing the lift.

"Me too," she replied and the lift pinged to let them know it had arrived. The doors opened and Duncan stepped out, followed by the two Spanish inspectors. Barco was short and pretty, dressed in a suit that highlighted her curvaceous figure. She caught Jesse's eye and gave him a cheeky wink. Molina was tall and lean. His balding head seemed slightly too large for his body and he hunched forward as if ashamed of his height. His suit was crumpled and looked as if he had slept in it.

Anders stepped forward and greeted them in Spanish.

"Buenos días inspector, me imagino que habrá hecho un buen viaje. Soy el agente de policía…" Barco cut her off with a raised hand and a sheepish smile.

"Sabemos quién usted es Santa Muerte, es un honor de conocerle" Anders blushed and waved her greeting away.

As they conversed in Spanish, Mal exchanged a puzzled look with Barry who indicated that he had no clue either. He caught the word *legend* and noticed Barco's wide-eyed wonder at meeting Anders. Making an educated guess as to what she was saying, he supressed a smile as he watched his Assistant Chief Constable squirm. She clearly hated compliments and he filed that information away for future reference. Information he would later forget. Eventually, Anders indicated Mal and Barco turned her attention to him.

"I am delighted to meet you Mr Weathers," she said, her Spanish accent thick. "This is my associate, Inspector Molina." Mal shook his hand and was given a limp squeeze in return.

"Please call me Mal. I prefer not to stand on ceremony here. Shall we go and speak to De La Cruz? He should be ready now." Barco smiled and clapped her hands together in delight.

"We'd love to," she said and Mal led them from the Hub. As they left to go to the interrogation room, Barry gave an impressed grunt.

"She speaks Spanish as well? A big surprise in a very small package that one." Jesse leaned back in his seat, interlocking his fingers over his flat stomach.

"She spent a year in Mexico, supporting the local police with their investigations. Some kind of diplomatic relationship stuff." Barry scratched the stubble on his cheek and frowned.

"That cute girl said Santa Muerta. I've heard that before somewhere. What's it mean?" Jesse leaned forward conspiratorially and ushered Barry and Duncan closer.

"It means Holy Death. That's what she was called when she was in Mexico. See, she was there to help them resolve kidnappings and the first one she was on went tits up." They leaned closer, intrigued to hear more. Jesse lowered his voice even though they were alone in the Hub.

"This young kid, son of a wealthy businessman, was kidnapped by a local drug lord. Parents super rich. This drug guy, gets the money, but kills the kid anyway. Anders is first on the scene. Snaps." Jesse had their attention and revelled in the story, fingers snapping loud in the room as he spoke.

"It's local knowledge that this drug guy goes to church every Sunday afternoon. He gets his goons to clear it out so it's just him. Anders goes to arrest him, or so she says. All we know is, she goes in alone and is the only one who walks out." He shakes a finger at them.

"She does this on holy ground. Kills fifteen men, all armed, and leaves without a scratch." Barry rolled his eyes and stood up.

"That's bullshit. I call bullshit on that." Jesse raised his hands defensively.

"Read the reports! It's all there."

"Have you read them?" Jesse looked guilty for a moment.

"No, but I have a friend who did. He swears by it." Barry snorted with derision.

"It's not like the movies Jesse. Crap like that just doesn't happen. A few men, maybe five, I'll buy that, but not fifteen."

As he spoke, he remembered the moment he had arrived at the docks the previous day. She was alone against a large and aggressive crowd, but her breathing was steady, her actions smooth and unhurried. He'd seen her move in the warehouse, calm and efficient. He'd met many different types of men in the army. He'd worked with the best in the SAS and one thing always rang true. The most dangerous, the ones you watched out for were the ones who had a stillness about them in battle. Not in movement, but in presence. The invisible men they were called. Anders had that quality. He knew in his bones that she was a warrior, much like himself.

They'd received similar challenges in the military, fear training a primary focus in both Armed Forces. Research had shown that the amygdala, a section of the brain, controlled the fear response, so their training had sought to initiate a different reflex to fear and danger. The worst of this was pool comp, where the feelings of helplessness and drowning were replicated under water for twenty terrifying minutes. More soldiers dropped out after failing this than anything else in America, but he fancied Anders would have passed first time. It had taken him two attempts.

"We should all be grateful she's on our side is all I'm saying," said Jesse. "She's an angel in the truest sense of the word." Duncan frowned, contemplating Jesse's words. They were unused to seeing him so thoughtful.

"I don't get it. Angels are pure and good. You're saying Anders is a stone cold killer." Jesse spoke softly, choosing his words carefully.

"She's no stone cold killer, Duncan," he admonished. "She feels too deeply for that. Angels are not pure and good if you go Old

Testament. They're warriors of Heaven. Lucifer himself is a fallen angel. They are not good as we understand the word, but they are righteous and that is something very different. They pass judgement and deliver it." He nodded at the direction Anders went.

"Whatever happened in that church? However many she killed? What she did was righteous in the Biblical sense. If she fell, like Lucifer did, we'd all be royally screwed. Every one of us. She walks in darkness every day and her light burns it away." His next words chilled them all. "What happens when that fades and the darkness consumes her?"

Chapter 8

De La Cruz looked shattered. He sat groggily in front of Barco and Molina, Anders and Mal leaning on the wall to one side. He was a squat figure with dark hair that had receded to a sharp widow's peak. His eyes were deep set and dark from lack of sleep. He had thick, muscular arms that lay on the table, cuffed with a chain to a hoop set into the metal of the table top. A light blinked on above the door to indicate that the interview was now being filmed.

"Devonte De La Cruz," said Barco, her Spanish accent thick, yet clear. "You have been arrested for the murder of..." De La Cruz spoke rapidly and angrily, cutting off Barco with a stream of expletives, questioning his rights to be deported to Britain.

"Soy nativo de España. Y no puedo ser interrogado en este país."

Anders answered him in Spanish, reminding him that he'd murdered his brother for a prize offered by a British citizen. She finished by reminding him to speak in English. He glowered at her sullenly as Molina leant forward. He'd transformed in the interrogation room and no longer looked surly and dour. He spoke with intensity and anger.

"She's right. You chopped the head off your own brother and his dog, then stitched the dog's head to your brother's torso." He laid out the pictures on the table in front of him, horrific images of his work, a human, dog hybrid like some modern day Chimera of myth. He then laid out several sheets of paper, all the assiduously collected evidence. "We have prints, we have witnesses putting you at the scene of the crime and we have your own weapon at the site." He put one last piece of paper on the table. His bank records.

"And we have a deposit of almost seven million Euro's in your account." Mal gave a mirthless chuckle.

"And you went straight to a Ferrari dealer to buy a new car. You really are stupid." De La Cruz glared angrily at him, his dark eyes full of hatred.

"I hated my brother. Why not make some profit from his death?"

"Well that money now belongs to Spain," said Barco and De La Cruz paled, visibly deflating in his chair. "We need to know how you received your winnings. Did Lord Buckland contact you in any way?

De La Cruz was a reluctant witness, refusing to give many details, but that was mainly because he knew very little. He'd posted his picture and description on the Fifty Two Weeks of Murder site and found the money deposited straight into his account.

"How did he get your bank details?" asked Molina. De La Cruz gave an apathetic look.

"I never gave them. The money just turned up."

The questioning continued for an hour, but De La Cruz had nothing to offer. They wrapped up the interview and Mal brought them back to the Hub, signing the papers to keep him in London in case something of use could be obtained in the future. He looked dejected at the lack of evidence De La Cruz had provided but wished them farewell and safe journey.

Barco turned to Anders and gave her a hug, speaking rapidly in Spanish as she did so. Mal felt his sour mood lift slightly at this display of hero worship that was making Anders so awkward. She returned the hug, leaning forward to embrace Barco and responding in Spanish, her tone clearly glad to be saying farewell. Molina gave her a limp handshake and set off for the lift, muttering as he left, obviously annoyed at Barco and unimpressed with Anders.

Ignoring Molina, Barco took Mal's hand and bade him farewell. As they returned to the lift, Jesse waving at Barco as the doors closed and miming a "call me" sign, Lucy and Duncan approached Mal.

"Blood Eagle case in Liverpool?" said Lucy. "We've got some good news. Debrief?" Mal grunted an affirmation, worry etching his face.

"Good news would be most welcome." Duncan bade Jesse switch on the projector and the team sat on chairs and leaned on desks as it whirred to life. There was a companionable silence and Mal could see that the group was becoming close. He'd seen pressure break several teams in his career, but these guys were the best in their areas and he realised that McDowell had selected well. As the projector shone on the wall, the crime scene photo's flashed up. Abi gave a gentle sigh.

"This case is giving me nightmares. I don't think I'll ever sleep again." The photographs showed a woman who had once been beautiful in life. Her eyes were closed and her face almost peaceful. Her naked body was curled up in a fetal position, head resting on her hands, arms covering her breasts. Her back, however, was a bloody mess and the image made Anders' own twitch, every scar pulsing in sympathy. The victim's front was clean and pure, the back bloody. Chunks of gore had splashed out, spilling to the concrete floor on which she lay, her ribs torn and shredded, sticking out in visceral white against cloying darkness. Her lungs were splayed behind her, artfully layering the superior, middle and inferior lobes like feathery wings. The picture was fascinating and beguiling, appalling and horrific all at once.

On the wall above her, written in blood, someone had written words to chill the team.

"I set you free so you may fly."

Lucy spoke as Jesse slid through the photographs. Sarah Baldwin had been a secretary in a small law firm. Lived at home. Parents had reported her missing the night before. Call had come in the next day from a dog walker who had found the body in the park, displayed on the concrete basketball pitch. On site, Duncan had noticed a tracking camera.

"One of those ones naturalists like to use. They come on at night when they sense movement. Films foxes and badgers, stuff like that." Lucy flicked through her notes.

"We traced the camera back to a retired couple a few streets down. They hadn't collected it yet, so gave us permission to download the footage. Caught everything. A Johnathan Sanders. Known to the police for stalking women but always considered harmless."

"Every stalker should be given a full assessment before that decision is made," said Abi sadly, pointing to the Blood Eagle effigy on the wall. Lucy grimaced and turned to Mal.

"We've put a warrant out for his arrest. Should be any time now."

"Cancel the warrant," said Anders and everyone turned to her. Barry saw her plan quickly and nodded his agreement.

"She's right. That picture there? That's a winner. We keep our distance, see if he wins and check if Buckland makes contact." Abi shook her head, lifting a wagging finger and speaking quickly.

"No, no, no. That poor girl's family deserve closure. We cannot do that to them." Duncan chipped in.

"I think it's a good idea. I'm not sure it'll fly in court though. Mal?" All eyes turned to Mal and Abi used his pause to carry her argument.

"We don't get to make decisions like this. The suffering of one for the good of all? We uphold the law and that's clear in its morality. No judge or magistrate would allow this." Mal stared at Anders. He'd made his decision as soon as she'd spoken, but he needed to be clear with himself whether he was making a decision based upon the idea itself or who had suggested it. He turned to Abi and gave her an apologetic look.

"I'm sorry Abi. I'll speak to McDowell and if he clears it, I'll have him tailed." Abi threw her hands up in frustration.

"De La Cruz yielded nothing. You said yourself he was a dead end."

"Buckland is in Britain. That much we do know based upon Boyle's death. He's stuck here unless he swims the channel himself. We don't know whether he gave De La Cruz the money straight to his account because he couldn't meet him personally. We traced the wire that deposited the money. It's a dead end. We have very few choices left to us." Abi stood and spoke fiercely yet quietly.

"There's always a choice. We have chosen to inflict pain and misery on her family and you can't tell me they'd be okay with what you are doing." She walked elegantly from the room to her office, closing the door firmly behind her. A thoughtful silence descended as everyone focused on Mal. He seemed to be reconsidering his choice. Eventually he nodded.

"Lucy, contact Liverpool. Tell them Duncan is on the way up to coordinate a sting." They both got up to leave and Mal turned to Jesse. "Pull up the last Interpol report." Jesse did so, overlaying the reports onto a world map. Last week, there had been a few red spots where entries to the competition had taken place. They were only a couple of days into week two and the number had increased tenfold. Red spots glared angrily over poor, deprived areas, affluent places of influence and many more in between. There's no demographic when five million pounds are on the table. Barry spoke softly as Jesse added more and more spots to the map.

"You think he can do it?" Anders gave him a sidelong look and put a gentle hand on his arm. They'd formed a strong kinship in a short space of time.

"Destabilise societies to the extent that chaos takes over? No, not at all. But he is creating enough havoc to make it seem as if he will. We have the largest manhunt ever conducted in the UK underway and a big reward for any information. We'll catch him." Mal stood up and walked to the map, arms folded across his chest as he spoke.

"McDowell is under a lot of pressure. The press, the government, agencies from every country affected. All of them are putting sustained pressure on him to deliver. He's doing well to shield us from it, but he can only do so much. If we don't find Buckland soon, things are going to get much tougher. Our operational independence will be rescinded and our ranks demoted so that SCO can direct operations." Lucy returned, having spoken to the Force in Liverpool and caught his last words. She sat next to Barry and looked at the map in shock.

"We could do with more men," she said. "It's all very well giving us power to employ local officers to our needs, but we need more in the Hub. Helen and Ben have more evidence than they can handle and if you have Anders working with them, it's one less working with us."

"You're right," agreed Mal. "We do need more people." Jesse's phone rang loudly, puncturing the solemn atmosphere. He answered it, scribbling notes on a sheet of paper as he talked and abruptly hanging up.

"Got a tip folks. Buckland's been seen entering a building near Soho. Five minutes ago." Mal shot forward and grabbed the paper.

"Barry, get a van. Anders, firearms. Let's move!" Spurred to action, Barry sprinted to the car depot, Mal and Lucy following. Anders ran to the firearms cabinet and tapped in a code, unlocking the cage and taking two Glock's and two Heckler & Koch's with spare magazines.

As she sprinted past Jesse, Abi came from her office, the sudden noise piquing her interest.

"What's going on?" she asked.

"Buckland's been sighted," shouted Anders as she ran past, following Lucy and Mal to the car depot. She reckoned they could be at the building in ten minutes and prayed that Buckland would be there so they could put a stop to his madness. She should have known better than to hope that Fifty Two Weeks of Murder would finish after only two.

Chapter 9

Barry sped through the streets, siren blaring from the police van as he covered the short distance to Soho in minutes. Slowing down, he switched off the siren and Lucy put Jesse on loudspeaker.

"Ok folks," he said. "Shop keeper on Greek Street just off Soho Square called this in. Claims he saw Buckland making his way into the building next to the Prince Edward Theatre. Barry, stop by Soho Square at the other end of the street and make your way down."

"Who owns the building?" asked Mal. There was a pause and the sound of tapping as Jesse searched the borough records. He muttered under his breath and Mal gave an impatient sigh. Anders shot him a calming look as she fitted a Kevlar vest round her waist and holstered her Glock, checking the Heckler & Koch for Barry once she was done. Eventually Jesse spoke.

"I can't find any records of the building actually existing."

"What the Hell does that mean?" asked Mal.

"It means I can find every building on Greek Street but there's a gap where number three should be. It's like it's been wiped." Lucy spoke, clearly nervous in the tense atmosphere.

"This why we can't find Buckland? He's hiding in a building that doesn't exist?" Mal gave a thoughtful look.

"Could be. He's shown enough skill with a computer so far. Jesse, you'll need to start matching up physical records with IT ones, find out where the gaps are. Could be there's more than one."

Barry parked the van, Mal sliding the door open before it had stopped and leaping out. Lucy called after him, struggling to get her vest on as Duncan tried to put one over his bandaged arm.

"Wait," she said. Mal pulled up impatiently, turning to her aggressively. "We're not equipped for this. We need to wait for the tactical response unit." Mal gestured to Barry who was wrapping the strap of the Heckler & Koch round his forearm and extending the stock to fit his large frame.

"That's why we have Barry and Anders. They're our tactical unit."

"There's two of them."

"And one of him," cut in Duncan, clearly nervous as well.

"That we know of. He's forming a cult pretty quick. We've no idea if it's even him and if he's alone. I'm not trained for this and neither are you two." Mal turned to Barry, expecting his support. He responded with an easy shrug.

"You're the boss Mal, but she's right. This isn't America. We're not the FBI. You, Lucy, Duncan, you're detectives by training and practise, not soldiers. I'll take Anders in and we'll sweep the building. Call the tactical response unit and they can back us up when they get here. You guys can cordon off the street in the meantime."

They stood on the road by Soho Gardens where people lazily watched them as they enjoyed the midday sun on the grass. A few had taken out their phones to film the Police Officers arguing in a semi-circle as Anders helped Lucy to put her vest on properly. A cold breeze tousled her hair and she pulled it back in a tight pony tail to stop it getting in her face. She lifted her wrist slightly to check the time. Fifteen minutes since the call. Mal stared down the street, frustration twisting his features.

"I'll call back up, but we're going in now. Lucy, Duncan you stay here." Lucy glanced at Anders, seeing how calm and collected she was. She remembered the conversation in the bathroom they'd had and knew that she needed to do this.

"I'm in, but it's a bad idea." Mal nodded, clearly pleased. He looked at Duncan who sighed heavily then gave a begrudging nod. Mal clapped a hand on Duncan's shoulder.

"Stay behind us," he said. "Theatre is at the very end of the street on the right, about eight hundred yards. We'll stick to the sides, try and remain out of sight." Barry spoke then, his voice low and firm.

"You three listen to Anders and me. We're in charge now. We clear?" Mal nodded and bade them lead the way.

Keeping their weapons holstered, they scrambled quickly down the street. The sun shone brightly on the opposite side, but they were in the shade as they passed a bank of cash machines and a few trendy clothes stores. The theatre was a large brick affair that stretched higher than the other buildings on the street, dominating the view. When people stepped out onto the street, they quickly rushed back into the shops at the sight of the five police officers storming towards an old, nondescript building that seemed to grow out of the theatre, almost as if it had been tacked on as an afterthought.

There were few windows on the building and one entrance, an old wooden door, painted a dull grey that now flaked to show a bright red undercoat.

Anders nodded to Barry and she drew her gun in one smooth movement as he knelt down by the door and picked the lock. Mal waited behind impatiently, Duncan gesturing to passers-by to clear the area. Eventually Barry had the lock picked and he turned to Anders. She stepped forward as he opened the door, sliding to the side to let her through. The interior was dark and Anders was lost from sight as the gloom engulfed her. Barry followed without hesitation and Lucy felt a ripple of fear tremor through her. Not only at what she may encounter inside, but at the way Anders and Barry moved. Sinuous and with a grace that reminded her of a lion stalking its prey. In that moment, they both scared her.

Mal, impatience making him jittery, gave them seconds before following in himself. Duncan gave Lucy a supportive look and slunk through the doorway, leaving her alone on the street with her fears. She'd entered countless buildings, been at the front line when doors were smashed in, but this was something different. She'd entered a new world and felt out of her depth, not realising that Duncan and Mal both had the same fears. They were just better at hiding it. Steeling herself, she glanced nervously around the street and scurried into the building.

She found herself in a decrepit old shop, long abandoned. A thick layer of dust carpeted both the floor and rows of tatty shelves. Footprints could be seen tracing a path from the door to the staircase and then to a room off to one side, both sets smudged by the team ahead of her. Mal and Duncan were immediately ahead, waiting on Anders and Barry, the atmosphere tense, the light dim and foreboding. Barry was at the foot of the staircase and nodded to her as she entered the building. Anders came from the side room and skirted the shop floor to Barry, her footsteps a whisper on the old wooden floor. They conversed with hand signals that she couldn't decipher, so Lucy, assuming the side room was clear, made her way into what looked like an old storage room.

She saw a battered table and matching chair in the centre, a laptop nestled on the surface. Scratch marks on the floor showed where the furniture had been dragged from; a cluttered pile of shelving, stools and tables in the corner. The room looked empty apart from that. The laptop glowered at her and she moved towards it, hoping that Jesse would be able to access it remotely and shut down the website. As she reached out to the laptop, she heard a creaking noise above them.

Looking through the doorway, she saw Mal sprint across the shop floor, his footsteps suddenly loud in the confined space. Anders looked to him, raising her hand to stop Mal, when she saw Lucy from the corner of her eye. Her eyes widened in sudden realisation, but it was too late. She knew the pile of junk was too staged and called her warning, surprised to see Lucy in the storage room and reaching for the laptop. She gave the computer the faintest of touches but it was enough.

Her touch cut a razor thin wire that held in place a chair in the pile of junk. It slipped a fraction of an inch and hit the charge on an M18A1 mine. The claymore detonated, ravaging the pile of junk and sending out hundreds of steel balls and splintered wood in a sixty degree arc. Lucy knew none of this. Her world was filled with sudden, agonising and tormenting pain that lasted seconds, but felt like hours, as her body bore the brunt of the explosion. She didn't hear the concussive noise as she gratefully embraced oblivion.

The detonation knocked Anders from her feet, sending her skidding across the foyer as a broiling wave of heat erupted from the side room. She dimly registered Mal and Duncan being tossed across the space with her before they were enveloped in dust, heat and a deafening noise. Air was forced from her lungs and she struggled for breath in the dust and rubble. Glass shattered with a shrieking wail, blasting onto the street. Getting to her knees, Anders forced herself to her feet, gagging and choking, the world ringing and stars fugging her vision.

"Report!" she yelled, her throat hoarse and acrid. Barry was the first to respond, followed by Mal.

"I'm okay."

"Me too." Anders tried to see through the dust to where she'd last seen Lucy but could only see shadow. A hand reached to her and she pulled it towards herself, gun raising to the target. It was Mal. His face was covered in grime, eyes streaked with tears and red raw. She passed her gun to him.

"Upstairs now. Barry?"

"On it," he called and stormed up the stairs, all pretence at quiet gone. Mal, coughing wildly, followed, holding the gun as if for the first time.

"Duncan?" called Anders. She was greeted with a groan as he stumbled from the smoke, clutching his wounded arm that had started to bleed again. She dragged him into the side room and was greeted with a horrific sight. Lucy lay in a crumpled heap on the floor. The mine that had been hidden in the pile of junk had sent needles of wood, metal and plastic flying towards Lucy and her arm was a ragged stump from just above the elbow. Shards of debris and steel balls had peppered her vest and it had borne the brunt of the battering stoically, with only a few jagged pieces piercing the Kevlar. The explosion had still caused terrible damage and she was bleeding profusely.

Anders rushed to Lucy, quickly assessing the carnage. Blood was pouring from her severed brachial artery and she knew that Lucy had moments to live. Mercifully, she was unconscious, which would make her task easier.

"Duncan," she called, trying not to cough as she knelt beside Lucy, her own body bruised and sore. Getting no reply, she tried again, her voice cracking with the effort.

"Yes?" he replied, still dazed. Anders took a knife from her belt and lifted Lucy's ruined arm onto her lap. A sickening shard of bone stuck out from a loose flap of skin and shredded muscle stuck to her trousers.

"I need water and get Jesse on the phone. Get me the first aid kit from the van and some tubing. Fast. You hear me?" She didn't turn to him, focused on what she was about to do. The brachial artery, once severed had sunk back into the flesh, the elastic tissue springing back with the sudden release of tension. Using her knife, Anders sliced upwards, quickly exposing more flesh. Digging her fingers in, Lucy rushed back to consciousness with an ear splitting scream.

She struggled as Anders burrowed her fingers further into the muscle, trying to find the severed artery.

"It's ok," she called soothingly, laying one hand on Lucy's chest. She could feel her heart beating rapidly, the action pumping more blood from the artery. Anders had seconds to find the vessel and she could feel Lucy weakening as she bled out.

"I've got you, you're gonna be ok, keep listening to my voice," she said reassuringly, finally grabbing the artery and squeezing the end tightly, her fist still embedded within Lucy's arm. With her other hand, she took Lucy's remaining hand and gripped it, talking softly, not really saying much as she tried to stem the flow of blood.

Chapter 10

Barrelling up the stairs, feet pounding loudly, Barry registered the sound of glass smashing ahead. The stairwell led to a long corridor that skirted the side of the theatre. It was bare, with wooden floors and a couple of rooms off to the side. At the end, a large window had been broken and Barry made for that, gun raised, quickly checking each room as he stormed by.

Mal followed closely behind, blood pumping through his head in a pulsating rhythm as he focused on staying upright and keeping up with Barry. As he passed the first room, he didn't notice a cupboard door open and a figure step out. He was tall and wore a hoodie jumper with the hood up. Grabbing a wooden stool as he entered the corridor, the figure swung it at Mal, knocking him into the wall with a meaty thump.

Barry, hearing the noise behind him, turned just as the stool was swung towards his skull. Cursing himself at falling for such an old trick, he punched outwards with his forearms, the old stool shattering against them. At this range, his gun was more likely to kill his opponent, so he used it as a club instead. His training kicked in and he smothered the figure with heavy blows, not giving him a chance to defend himself. The assailant gave several satisfying cries of pain and Barry put all of his power into a thump across the temple, sending the hooded figure crashing into the wall.

Without pause, Barry slammed into him, his full weight driving the air from the man's lungs. Pulling his arms backwards, Barry used his speedcuffs to immobilise the attacker. Using the plastic bar across the cuffs, Barry swung the figure round to face him as Mal groggily got to his feet, using the walls to help him stand.

"You ok?" asked Barry. Mal shook his head.

"No," he replied and staggered forwards, pulling the hood off the figure. His addled brain took some time to work out who he was. The figure looked like Buckland, but much younger, the cheeks not as sharp and the jaw slightly wider, but the Buckland genes were prominent in his features.

"Buckland junior," he said, his voice rasping from the explosion. "And here's us thinking you were still in America."

Chapter 11

Duncan looked like he was going to vomit as he lay his findings on the floor. He'd had the foresight to take some vodka from the shop opposite and followed Anders' directions. She had one hand dug inside Lucy, the other pressed against a seeping wound above her waist, just below where the vest reached. Lucy had slipped into a coma and Anders could see she was dying. Duncan had borrowed a phone as well and propped it on the floor of the shop, rubble and debris everywhere. Jesse's voice came through the speaker.

"Blood group Jesse," Anders said as she instructed Duncan to sterilise the tubing and open the first aid kit.

"Ambulance will be there in ten," Jesse was saying.

"She's got minutes Jesse, get me her blood group."

"Doesn't matter," said Duncan. "I'm type O." Anders shook her head.

"You've lost too much blood recently. You'll be in danger too." Duncan gave her a forceful stare.

"Do it," he said. Anders reassessed him. He was far braver than she'd given him credit for.

"See that syringe there? Pull the needle off. Use the lighter, melt that end. Stick it in the vodka, let it cool. Take the plunger from that syringe." She directed him with a firm touch, and, even though his hands were shaking, he cobbled together a way to get some blood into Lucy, cutting the plunger and tube and using a lighter to melt the rubber to the sides. It was the same method developed by a Canadian in the First World War and Duncan hoped it would work.

"You'll need to find a vein in her right arm." Duncan scrabbled to find a vein. Lucy's vital signs had receded and Anders was unable to help. Eventually, he found it and plunged the needle in.

"Artery in your left hand. See the one I'm holding? Imagine that running down your own arm." Anders took her hand from Lucy's stomach wound and, still holding her brachial artery tightly, showed Duncan how to put the needle in and lift the plunger to start blood flowing into her. Duncan waited with baited breath, feeling faint as his blood was directed into Lucy. He wasn't sure what to expect and was disappointed when nothing seemed to change in her. Leaning back against a wall, he slurred his words as he spoke.

"Will she be ok?" Anders looked at the ruined stump of her arm and the side of her body that had been shredded and shook her head.

"I don't know." In the distance, they could hear the sirens of an ambulance and a tactical support unit. The very same one Lucy had insisted go with them. "Where did you get the tubing from?" she asked. More to keep Duncan awake and focused than anything.

"Bikes," he replied. "There's a few bikes outside missing some tyres. How did you learn how to do this?" he asked.

"History channel," she said as red and blue lights bathed the area. She found them comforting and breathed a sigh of relief as Mal and Barry came downstairs pushing their prisoner in front of them. Lord Buckland's son. They'd paid a heavy price for him. She hoped it was worth it.

Chapter 12

Several hours later, Mal assembled everyone in the Hub. He stood before them, covered in grime and dirt, crusty blood clotting the back of his head where Lawrence Buckland had hit him with a stool. He put his hands on the back of a chair, holding himself steady as he gathered his thoughts. Everyone sat facing him in a semi-circle, a strange mixture of the clean and the filthy. When Mal spoke, his voice was filled with regret and sorrow.

"I need to apologise to you all. It's my fault Lucy's in surgery right now. We don't know how it'll go, but it doesn't look good. They lost her for a couple of minutes in the ambulance but managed to revive her. If it weren't for Anders and Duncan, we'd already be mourning her loss." Barry clapped a congratulatory slap on Duncan's back and he almost keeled over, pale as he was with blood loss. He gave a weak grin, having refused to go home after a check-up at the hospital, wanting instead to be here. Mal had skipped treatment as well, rushing Lawrence back to the Hub for questioning.

"Lucy is strong. She will pull through," declared Mal, more in hope than expectation. He turned to Abi. Both she and Helen clasped hands, tears streaking down their cheeks. They'd been shaken badly by events and Mal knew that this had pushed the team to breaking point.

"Abi, can you interview Lawrence. I want a basic profile before Anders and I question him. See if he's a stable, rational human being or his fathers' son. Are you okay to do that or do you want someone in there with you?" Abi shook her head.

"No. I'll go in alone. Jesse will keep an eye out, won't you?" Jesse, unusually sombre gave her the thumbs up.

"Of course Mrs A. Always got your back."

"While Abi is doing that, we need to see if we can get hold of physical records from every county in the UK. Have each of the counties scan them in and email them to Jesse. We can then match them up with the IT records and see if there are any blanks. Could be that Buckland is hiding in one of those black spots he's created." It was a huge job and would require many hours of work, but this was the basic foundations of any investigation. Painstakingly gathering evidence and hoping it would reveal something useful. Jesse stood up and moved to his desk, speaking as he went.

"I'll check previous IT records as well. If these buildings have recently been deleted from the system, I can see if any back up records show discrepancies."

He set to work, fingers tapping furiously on his keyboard. After a brief pause, Mal turned back to the group.

"Helen, Ben. Have you got all the evidence you need from the Boyle site?" Helen nodded that they had.

"Okay, good. You guys get over to Soho and take the scene. See if Buckland senior has been there and find out what you can about the explosive device." Barry spoke up, his background giving him some experience in explosives.

"Fragments I saw before we left looked like a mine, most likely an M18A1, take out the clacker, put in an M5 Pressure Release Device. Simple trip wire to set it off. Lucy moves the laptop a millimetre and..." He held his hands out in a helpless gesture, unwilling to explain further.

"Where the hell is he getting explosives from? Barry, see if you can trace that. It might help." Mal sighed heavily and ran his hands through his hair, frowning as he noticed the sticky blood that smeared the back of his head. He stared at the dark flakes of blood in his hand for an age before speaking again.

"How did we miss Lawrence? He was supposed to be in America."

"We were looking for Michael Buckland, not his son. We were also looking for a Buckland leaving, not coming in. He's been here for three weeks." Whilst Lawrence had been processed, Barry had run a search and found a Business Class flight from Washington with his name on it.

Just then, the lift chimed and Lady Margaret and Francis Buckland's lawyer, Blackwell, stepped into the Hub. He looked as fastidious as ever, but Lady Margaret looked shaken. Her normally cool and polished demeanour cracked and tears of worry smeared her make-up. Mal growled as he saw the lawyer.

"Jesse, pull Abi from the room. Barry, take Blackwell to Lawrence." He turned on his heel and walked into his office. He rarely went in there, preferring to work outside in the Hub and it was strange to see him in it with the doors closed. He moved to his chair behind the desk and sat on it heavily, head pounding from both the explosion and the wooden stool that Lawrence had introduced him to. Turning the chair on its swivel, he faced the wall behind him and closed his eyes, the day's events resting heavily upon him.

A few minutes later, there was a soft knock on the door.

"Come in," he called and turned to see Anders entering the room, holding a large medical kit. She was caked in dirt and dust, Lucy's blood staining her clothes a darker hue.

"Let's clean up that wound of yours shall we," she said and shut the blinds as she made her way down the narrow office. She put the kit on the empty desk and leant against the table, facing Mal. Seated, he looked up at her as she gave him a comforting smile.

"It's my fault," he said. "She wanted us to wait. I just wanted it over with." Anders reached into the bag and pulled out some saline tubes and gauze, turning Mal round with her foot on the chair so that she could clean his wound.

"It is, you should have and I know," she said, dabbing the dried blood from his scalp and making him wince. Not just with the pain either. Her matter of fact tone held no judgement and he found himself comforted by her honesty. He thought back to the moment he had brought Lawrence down the stairs, seeing the mangled shop floor for the first time as the dust had cleared. He'd never forget the image of Duncan leaning against a wall, tubing running from his arm to Lucy's, Anders with her hand inside Lucy holding some blood vessel to stop her bleeding out.

"That was some work you did back there," he said. Anders took out some disinfectant and started to apply it to the wound itself. Mal gave a short cry of pain and she yanked him back by his collar as he tried to move away.

"Stop being a baby," she said and he grudgingly held still as she applied what felt like acid to the back of his head. As she worked, her face a mask of concentration, she told him of her time in Iraq.

"I saw the damage land mines can do on my first tour. Stuff like that sticks with you. I'm going to have to glue this I'm afraid." A flap of skin was still loose and had shrivelled because Mal had not sought attention sooner. It was too late to get stitches, but some glue would at least help it heal more quickly. Reaching into the medical bag, she pulled some out and applied it to the back of Mal's head. She spoke softly as she worked.

"The team looks to you Mal. They need you. Yes, you screwed up, but they've not lost faith in you." Her job done, Mal turned to her, their faces close, breath mingling and sexual tension rising.

"What about you?" he asked. "Have you lost faith in me?" Anders leaned forward and kissed him. A brief kiss, no more than a second, but it was enough to answer his question.

"Where do you keep them?" she asked. Mal looked confused, caught off guard by the sudden change in conversation.

"What?"

"Your range of high quality shirts?" She gave him a cheeky grin as he indicated a cupboard set into the wall. She walked over and opened the door, chuckling at the range of shirts and jeans in there. She wondered if he actually slept here. Taking a clean shirt and trousers from the cupboard, she walked back to Mal and held out a hand, the clothes clutched in the other. It took Mal a second to work out what she wanted.

"Oh," he said and stood up to unbutton his shirt, dust and flakes of blood falling off as he struggled to get out of the grime infused material. He then unbuckled his jeans and stood in front of Anders in just his boxer shorts and socks. His chest was flat and firm, not muscled like the pretty boys down the gym, but lean and trim, his legs long and toned. He stood in front of Anders and folded his arms across his chest as she appraised him slowly, a sly grin on her face.

"Your turn," said Mal mischievously. Anders raised an eyebrow at him, pausing long enough to let the tension rise, before tossing Mal his clothes and leaving the room.

"Get dressed," she said on her way out. "We've an interview to conduct."

Thomas Blackwell was a fifth generation lawyer. He took little joy from his work, but knew nothing else. An unctuous man who was hard to like, his sharp intellect and unparalleled understanding of the law kept him in gainful employment with the very select few who could afford his rates. As Deputy Chief Constable Weathers and Assistant Chief Constable Anders entered the room he eyed them carefully. They both looked tired and in need of a shower.

Weathers was easy to read. He had an open, honest face that, he supposed, women were attracted to. A rough, outdoorsy type. Blackwell had met many like him, policemen to the core. Stubborn and committed, a leader of men, but not especially bright and easy to work around. Anders was a different proposition. He couldn't work her out. She was a closed book, enigmatic and alluring with that scar running up her neck. He'd read that they covered her back and, as she sat down, she gave him a cool gaze as if she'd been reading his thoughts.

Putting his musings aside for a moment, he turned to Weathers as he spoke. He didn't care whether Buckland's son was innocent or guilty. The boy looked like his father and seemed like any normal kid, apart from the bruising on his face where the police officer had assaulted him. He was charming and quick to smile, easily answering Blackwell's questions. He didn't take him at face value though. Not with that family.

"Lawrence Buckland, I'm Deputy Chief Constable Weathers and this is Assistant Chief Constable Anders. We're holding you here in connection with…"

Blackwell interrupted him, earning a reproving look from Weathers.

"You need to actually charge him with something Mr Weathers. That, or provide some clear reason as to why you will be holding him here for questioning."

"Why were you in that building Lawrence?" asked Weathers. Blackwell had instructed him not to speak and so answered for him.

"His family own the property. Lawrence was looking for his father."

"He assaulted a police officer." Blackwell supressed a smile at the thought of his client hitting Weathers with a stool.

"My client feared for his life. He thought he was being attacked after an explosion had rocked the building."

"Why was he there?"

"I've told you. He was looking for his father." Weathers laid out several sheets of paper on the desk, sliding them to Blackwell. He skimmed through them and found nothing of consequence.

"There are no records this building exists. So why were you there Lawrence?" The kid made to speak, but Blackwell lay a hand on his arm, telling him to be quiet.

"An admin error by some temping office worker isn't going to be enough to convict my client Mr Weathers." Blackwell could see that he was getting frustrated by the kid's silence and his answers, reflecting that he did actually enjoy this part of the job. Winding up police officers was ever such fun.

"Your client has the skills to run this website, hack into bank accounts and edit borough records on land registry." Blackwell gave a mirthless chuckle.

"Mr Weathers, I'm fairly certain that those skills are not part of the syllabus at Harvard. Please feel free to check though. I know the NCA likes to do things by the book." Weathers changed tack, knowing that he was getting nowhere and looking increasingly uncomfortable.

"Your mother was here last week Lawrence, saying she didn't know where you were, yet our records show that you entered the country three weeks ago."

"My client entered the country three week ago with friends and stayed with them as he often does before seeing his family. I will provide you with witnesses of course. Once he'd heard of the distressing news of his father, he set out to look for him to make him stop this nonsense." Weathers jabbed a finger in Lawrence's direction. The kid kept his face blank, looking at the desk the whole time and refusing to make eye contact. Good boy. He was far too easy to read.

"Why can't he tell me that?" asked Weathers.

"He's instructed me to speak on his behalf."

"Why was there a bomb rigged to go off?"

"You'll need to ask Lord Buckland, *if* you find him."

"One of my team almost died." Blackwell gave a gracious nod of his head.

"My sincere condolences." Weathers gave an irritated snort of derision.

"She's not dead yet," he replied testily, losing his temper. "Why didn't your client set it off when he entered the building?" Blackwell decided that it was time to wrap up this conversation.

"Did you identify yourself Mr Weathers?" He looked confused and Blackwell knew he hadn't.

"What?"

"It's a reasonable question and one I'm quite sure will be raised in any investigation into this matter. Did you identify yourself? When you entered the building, did you identify yourself and give clear reason for your entry?"

"I had a sighting of Buckland at the building. That is sufficient evidence for me to search the premises."

"It is Mr Weathers, but the moment you entered a quiet building and realised that there was no immediate danger, you should have identified yourself and your station or anything you do is unlawful according to the Police and Criminal Evidence Act." Weathers went a peculiar shade of red at that.

"I had yet to determine that we were in no immediate danger and that the building was occupied. You're dealing with semantics here."

"You can't prove that either way. If you heard any sound that the building was occupied, you needed to state your presence. This interview is done. My client will happily stay on British soil and let you know of his whereabouts should you ask. All you have is that he was in a building his family owned. Everything else that happened after is down to you. Good day Mr Weathers. Miss Anders."

Blackwell made to leave and indicated that his client should do so as well. Anders had been watching Lawrence throughout the interview, letting Weathers talk. As they stood, she spoke softly, but her words were laced with steel and sent a chill down his spine.

"Your father wasn't alone Lawrence. Two people crucified that man. Three people hacked Boyle to death." She stood up as Lawrence looked at her and she seemed to grow in stature, filling the room with her presence. "There's a reckoning coming for your father. I know you helped him and I know you're sloppy. You'll make another mistake and Mr Blackwell won't be here to bail you out." She leaned forward.

"When you make that mistake? I'll be there. And then you and I will have that reckoning."

Chapter 14

McDowell was waiting in the Hub as the pair entered the room. His gruff Scottish accent boomed in the concrete space, amplifying the anger in his voice. He'd watched the interview on the monitor.

"Mal. A word please. In your office." Mal led him in, McDowell slamming the door behind them and raising his voice immediately. The glass barely muffled the sounds as he tore into Mal. Anders walked to where Jesse and Barry worked on tracking the black holes in the land and buildings registry as Abi's door opened and Lady Margaret walked out. She looked much comforted and hugged Lawrence as he came from the holding cells, Blackwell following behind. He gave Anders a strange look before heading for the lift, holding it open as Lady Margaret ushered Lawrence in. He turned as the doors closed and winked at Anders.

"You believe him?" asked Barry, clearly doubting his testimony. Anders shook her head.

"Not a word. He's neck deep in it and we've got nothing. No magistrate will give us a warrant to tail him either, not after today anyway. Poor victim Lawrence, picked on because of his daddy."

On Jesse's screens, news footage from mobile phones showed the glass of the abandoned shop blowing out onto the street, followed by a thunderous boom. Luckily no civilians had been hurt, but the tag line made for grim reading.

"Police woman seriously injured as they fail, again, to catch Buckland."

The door to Mal's office swung open and McDowell walked out. He gave the group a curt nod and headed for the lift. Mal came out a few seconds later, looking suitably browbeaten.

"That sounded fun," said Barry. He'd been to the canteen to get some food for everyone and shovelled a large baguette stuffed with meats and salad into his mouth, sauce dripping from it in sticky lumps. Mal leaned over and took some tissues from Duncan's desk and passed them to Barry so he could clean himself up.

"Could have been worse," he said.

"We off the case?" asked Barry, his mouth full of food.

"No, but it was close." He sat down on the desk and helped himself to some crisps and a cheese sandwich. "To be fair, he's been pretty good. Today aside, we've been doing well. He's keeping the Home Office off our backs and given us more resources. This place is going to get mighty full."

"Not that he has much choice," opined Anders. "We've got to dredge through a mountain of evidence that keeps getting bigger every day. He should have given us more bodies the moment this all started." They ate in companionable silence for a while. Abi came to join them and they finished their meal, each deep in thought. Once they were done, Mal turned to Abi.

"Right, shall we go and see how Lucy is doing?" She gave him a wan smile and went to collect her bag and coat, worry etched on her face. Mal gave instructions to the team and took Abi to their vigil.

Lucy's heart had stopped on the operating table. The surgeons were unable to stem the bleeding. They started her heart again, paddles loud in the chaos of the theatre. Finally getting to the source of the internal bleeding, they were able to cauterise that and then work on her arm, removing dead tissue and sowing loose skin over the stump. It was many hours before she was taken from the theatre to intensive care and several days until anyone was allowed to see her. She had been taken to St Thomas', almost directly opposite Scotland Yard on the other side of the river, which gave Anders ample opportunity to see her on the way back from work each evening.

She brought grapes, chocolate and flowers, but had eaten one of the bars and so had to stop to buy another. She had a weakness for Cadbury's chocolate having not eaten it since she was six. It brought back memories of happy days and she was fairly certain she was developing a dependency on it.

As she made her way through the wards to Lucy's room, Anders felt a deep rooted unease inveigle its way into her. She'd spent a long time in hospital during her transition and also after her back had been whipped to a pulp. She'd endured, but the torment and pain lingered, tendrils of memory insidiously coiling round her emotions, forcing her to take a calming breath. Every hospital tended to look the same inside. Long corridors, drab walls, rooms and wards branching off and an air of depression coupled with a sour tang in the atmosphere. Arriving at Lucy's room, she sat on a deceptively hard comfy chair as she waited for Lucy to wake from her slumber. She'd regained some colour to her skin, but still looked grey and sallow, her blonde hair making her looker paler still. Her cheeks were gaunt and she'd lost a lot of weight. Her left arm was heavily bandaged and she could see the stump ending half way down to the elbow.

Anders waited a while, not wanting to leave Lucy alone and eyeing the chocolate bar she'd left on the bedside table. She saw several Get Well cards and a balloon floating above her, tethered to the chair by a silk ribbon. Deciding she'd waited long enough for Lucy to wake and claim her bar of chocolate, Anders reached over and slid the bar from the table top, gliding her fingernail under the paper wrapper and tearing the foil. The sound woke Lucy who turned to see Anders looking guilty as she popped a section of chocolate into her mouth.

"Busted," she said, and offered Lucy the chocolate. She shook her head.

"You have it, I'm all chocolated out." Her voice was dry and cracked, pain etched on her face as she moved. Her Morphine must be wearing off thought Anders as she took a small piece of chocolate and left the rest on the table.

"How you holding up?" Lucy moved to sit, struggling to do so one handed. Anders helped her up and plumped some pillows behind her so that Lucy could sit comfortably.

"I'm here and I thank God for that, but it's painful." She held back tears as Anders sat on the bed and took her hand. She'd suffered terribly from the shrapnel. It had pierced her intestines and damaged a kidney. One large piece had nicked her spine and no one could say if she'd be able to walk properly again. She'd have to recover the hard way and do so with one functioning arm.

"We're here to help. All of us. Duncan is on his way now and Barry was going to pop by after he'd followed some leads."

"How's it going?" Anders was reluctant to talk about it but knew Lucy wanted the distraction, even if only for a few minutes.

"We're swamped. New murders happening every day all over the world and the press getting into a tizz. Even the President is talking about it. Our team is huge now and the Hub is packed. Law enforcement agencies have flown in from all over the world to liaise and offer support." Lucy gave a sad smile.

"Sounds kinda exciting," she said. Anders laughed for what felt like the first time in a while.

"Not according to Mal it isn't," she said. "He looks pretty stressed." Lucy gave her a tired smile.

"No more dates for you two then?" Anders gave her a shocked look. "Oh, come on," said Lucy, delighting at seeing Anders so uncomfortable. "We can all see the connection between you two. Besides, Helen was listening at the door when he asked you out!"

"The little swine," cried Anders good naturedly. "I thought she looked too innocent when I got back." Lucy suddenly looked sad, glancing at her arm as she did so.

"I guess I won't be dating anytime soon," she said morosely. She turned to Anders, her eyes tracing the scar on her neck and across the shoulders. The weather was hot, so Anders wore a sleeveless top that showed more of her scar tissue than usual. She gave a thoughtful look.

"How do you live with it?" she asked, so quietly Anders barely heard her.

"I don't let it define me. Others will use it to put you in a bracket, find a nice easy label for you. They'll stare and judge and use it to determine your place in the world. But that only happens if you let them. I learnt that a long time ago," she said, talking about more than just her scars.

"What was it like when you changed?" Anders was taken aback by the question coming as it was from Lucy.

"Hard and painful. Brutal at times. But worth every second. It doesn't define me anymore." Lucy gave a ghost of a smile.

"I'm not sure I can do that," she said. Anders gripped her hand fiercely, imbuing Lucy with her strength

"I'll help you," she replied.

Week 3

I ponder on the nature of humanity. We muddle humane, human and humanity together, but they mean such different things. To be human is to simply exist. To have feelings or emotions is described as being human and we bestow ourselves with such honours, arrogance seeping from every pore. A dog can feel angry, happy or sad, much as we do. Is it not then human? Has it not transcended itself as we believe ourselves to have done? We strut and preen, obsessed with our own standing. Has not a simple Prokaryote conquered this Earth, its single celled existence evolving quicker and more deadly than we. Our arrogance is our undoing. Our belief in our divine right to rule, to bend the planet to our will is our undoing. There is no single living organism on this planet more destructive than Homo sapiens. Earth will revolt. It will turn on us and forsake us. As well it should.

We must act. If we don't return to our base state, learn to occupy our niche as we should, mankind will not survive. Our civilisation. Our laws. Our society. These are the ideals we worship as the epitome of humanity. They must be undone and the work has started. It is a long, arduous journey. There will be those who seek to stop us. Those who will seek to use the law of man against us. I say to them one thing.

This is the time for a different law. A law as old as the planet itself. Righteous and blind in the purest sense. The law of nature.

You are embracing this new law. All those who enter this competition do so not for the money alone, but for the greater good of mankind. For humanity. And this week, you have truly excelled. The slides below show some notable entries from across the globe as we unite to cast off the shackles of civilisation. You tear down order and show the chaos underneath. In that, we will find a new order. One that unites us all. That isn't subservient to class, creed or wealth. You have risen in your hundreds and we will only get more powerful each day.

I promised two winners this week. From the UK we have the Blood Eagle. Beautifully done, this image stands as the banner for us all.

We shall be set free. That is my fantasy and this entrant captures the essence of that perfectly. The second winner comes from North America. His fantasy was to endure his own transcendence and that of his family. Bravo.

The next theme highlights how we have moved away from our true natures. Fairy tales. I've watched the Disneyfication of our beloved stories for too long. These stories we tell our children used to be brutal and bloody. A message to every child that the world is harsh, cruel and unforgiving. These stories were a warning, not an aspiration. Not an ideal to be idolised. Change must come from the ground up. From the moment we are born, all indoctrination must cease.

I present my example.

I choose a Vicar. A man of the cloth. His ideals steer us away from the fact that we are animals by nature. They have us believe in a higher power. That our souls would suffer in Hell or revel in Heaven. Our souls belong to the Earth. We are of this planet.

He is easy to take, trusting his fellow man and welcoming me into his house. I take his wife too. I have special plans.

Snow White. The beginning of the corruption. The Wicked Queen suffers a quick death in the modern retelling. Not for those who know the true works. I take my time. The iron needs to be hot. She is strapped to a lattice wheel, arms tightly bound above her head. She is unconscious but I don't worry about that. I stoke the furnace, bellowing heat into its very heart. When it is hot enough, I place the iron boots into the furnace. The Vicar begs and pleads. He asks me for God's grace and mercy.

Our species has neither.

When the boots are hot enough, I pull them out. This is the hard part. She wakes as I start to slide her foot into a boot. She screams and struggles and cries. The smell of cooked pork fills the room, her flesh sliding from her bones.

I get both shoes on and cut her shackles loose. She must dance. That was the Wicked Queen's punishment. To dance until her feet burnt off and she died. The Vicar's wife disappoints. She does not dance, but she does try to remove the boots, hands melting to the iron as she pushes, screaming ever more loudly. She didn't dance, but she did die, clothes bursting to flame and engulfing her body.

The Vicar next. He is strapped to a giant wheel also, spread-eagled out, but his fate is very different. I choose an old nursery rhyme. These too, tell of the harsh brutalities of life, the constant struggle for survival. I choose the one that was most fascinating to me as a child. The Crooked Man. A tale of the divide between Scotland and England. I wish to create my own Crooked Man.

He screams and sobs and wails as I take a bat ever so carefully to each limb. I start with the feet, the appendages bending at an unnatural angle as I slam the heavy weapon to them. Then the knees, loud crunching sounds as I shatter the bone. I carefully break each bone in his legs. He faints so I wait patiently until he wakes screaming. Then I start on the arms. Then the ribs and the spine. But not the skull. He needs to know that he's crooked.

I unbuckle my crooked man, but he disappoints also. He will not be walking any crooked paths. He certainly won't be living in a crooked house.

This is the truth of our stories and myths. There is no happy ending. There is only the law of nature. Natural selection in its purest form. We shall cull the soft, weed out those who've shrugged away their humanity and embraced civilisation.

We have another fifty weeks of murder. Next week, there will be five prizes.

The revolution of the species continues.

Chapter 1

The United Kingdom felt restless and uneasy. Domestic violence had increased, common assault was commonplace and the murder rate was the highest ever recorded, even outside of the entries to the competition. People who had only previously thought about killing someone now found their darkest desires legitimised. Fantasies turned to reality, morality deteriorated by the allure of money and perceived freedom from censure and judgement as offered by Buckland, his words finding physical voice as a higher purpose was attached to the most base of instincts.

Anders reflected on this as she stood outside the impressive walls of the Tower of London. Buckland had driven a lorry to the square at the front entrance and parked parallel to the moat, lowering the tarpaulin sides of the trailer and revealing his work. All of the security cameras had been switched off by some virus the previous evening so there was no way of knowing where he had gone. Mal had a separate team scouring traffic cameras and feeds from every CCTV point in a two mile radius to try and work out his direction of travel at least.

The square was chaos. A glorious sun had risen early and the weather was hot already, the sky a pale blue. Though the area was cordoned off, crowds of people had come to witness Buckland's work and they were pushed back by increasingly angry officers. TV crews lined the perimeter, their lenses picking out every detail from afar. Anders closed her eyes, focused on the music, found her centre and breathed slowly before opening her eyes once more.

The Vicar and his wife had been tied back to their posts and she felt such sorrow at their suffering. The Vicar was soaked in blood, bones sticking from beaten flesh, snapped like twigs under Buckland's brutal assault. His head was untouched, face etched in a never ending scream, but the rest of the body was contorted and unnaturally twisted. She could see that Buckland had been careful with the legs. They were horrifically misshapen but the skin was unbroken. Either he'd lost control with the rest of the torso or someone else had joined in. Someone with less control.

His wife was a smouldering effigy of charred humanity and the smell of seared skin and burnt hair was acrid in Anders' nostrils. The victim's skin had burnt and peeled in places, cracking under the heat. The bones were also bent and twisted as they buckled under stress fractures from the fire. Though her clothes had burnt off, apart from the shirt which had melted to her body, Anders could see the boots she wore. They came to the knees, wide at the top to make it easier to slide her feet in and narrowing at the ankle to make it harder to shake them off. They looked roughshod and poorly made, thick rivets sticking out and hammer marks evident where someone had bashed them into shape. The metal was thick and would have required some strength to hold them with long tongs. The victim's skin had melted to the boots like some vile inner lining.

She took in every detail, walking slowly around the lorry before stepping onto it and peering closely at every wound, every horrifying detail. She blocked out everything extraneous; the people, the noise, the bustle of a crime scene and the utter sadness of their brutal murders. She would give them voice soon enough.

Eventually, she was done. Taking her headphones out, she tucked them into the pocket of her leather jacket and stepped back from the scene. Helen and Ben worked the site, leading a large support team. Anders was pleased to see Ben taking charge of a team consisting of seasoned professionals and leading them effectively.

"Have you spoken to your old boss yet?" Mal spoke as he approached her, worry lines furrowing his brow. Anders nodded. She'd contacted the FBI to discuss the winner of last week's prize, but they had nothing yet. They weren't even aware of the crime.

"They'll pass on anything they get once they find the crime scene. We know where these killings took place yet?" she asked, pointing at the vicar and his wife. Abi joined them as Mal shook his head.

"Not yet, but we'll find it. Abi, you found inconsistencies with his first and second blog. Same again? Seemed the same hatred and bile to me." Abi thought for a moment before replying, watching Duncan coordinate the team that would put a large tent over the lorry, both to preserve the evidence and give the poor couple some dignity.

"It's the same, but slightly different. It hews closer to the first blog, certainly." She looked at Mal as she spoke, a gentle breeze from the Thames tousling her normally perfectly coifed hair. "I know what you're asking though and I'd hesitate to stand in court and say it, but I do think it was written by two different people. Either that or Buckland's grip on sanity is slipping." Mal gave a short chuckle.

"I think he's lost all grip on sanity," he replied. "If he ever had it, that is." Anders turned to Abi.

"You think the blog itself was written by two different people?" she asked. "The first part seems full of rage and anger at our species, but the second part was more sadistic, full of glee for what he was doing. Less someone on a mission to change the world, more excited child torturing a fly."

"It's a fair point, but it could also be that the first part is him rationalising his killing to himself. Another psychologist could argue both sides in court."

The tent finally erected, they stepped under the entrance flap, the sounds of the crowded square smothered by the thick canvas. It had only been up a few moments, but the sun was already heating it to furnace like levels. In their coveralls, they were starting to sweat. Mal grimaced as he saw the bodies up close, their horrific injuries brought into sharp focus by the bright lights Ben had set up.

"What pushes a man to do this?" he asked softly as he climbed onto the trailer and helped Abi up. Anders refused his hand, preferring to get up herself.

"That's the one question we'll never know the answer to. Was he born like this or did something in his upbringing make him this way," said Abi, holding her hand over her nose to block the putrid smell.

"It's a little of both, I think," said Anders as she used a bright penlight to look for evidence on the corpses.

"You would argue you were born that way would you not?" asked Abi. She'd had several similar conversations with Anders and knew that she wouldn't mind such a blunt question in search of understanding. A few of the support team glanced at each other, not fully understanding what Abi meant as they listened in.

"Slightly different Abi," replied Anders absently as she worked. "In the uterus, there was a female differentiation in the BSTc part of my hypothalamus, so my limbic nucleus contains female levels of neurones. The brain of a serial killer shows no abnormalities compared to your average non serial killing person." Mal grinned at Abi.

"You did ask," he said. Abi, warming to her theme, challenged Anders further.

"Dr Kiehl found reduced density in the para-limbic systems of convicted serial killers. Maybe then it's nature not nurture for serial killers as well." Anders gave a tutting sound.

"Only in those who displayed low levels of emotion towards the suffering they caused. Yes, they may have a disease, but we still abide by a moral code of right and wrong, such that a ten year old could use it."

"If it's a disease, then we should apply a neuro-law. Criminal behaviour may be a disease that needs to be treated in some individuals." Anders indicated the horrifying brutality Buckland had put on display.

"Buckland's no sociopath. He enjoyed this suffering too much to be one." Abi looked at Buckland's work and gave a troubled sigh.

"I agree," she said as Barry shuffled under the tent, looking anxiously for Mal. As he climbed onto the lorry, Helen hurled a string of expletives at him as the vehicle shook under his weight.

"Sorry Helen," he said, clearly shocked at how the normally bubbly character knew swear words that would make a sailor blush. "Mal, we've a problem. Sanders, the Blood Eagle guy? He's disappeared." Blood drained from Mal's face and an air of shock settled over the team.

"How the Hell has he managed that?" he cried, his anger loud in the tent.

"Apparently the squad car parked near his house saw him enter and didn't see him leave. They checked this morning and it's empty."

"I'm not going to say I told you so," said Abi, her voice cold. "But whatever he does next is on us all."

Chapter 2

Anders arrived home late that evening, weary from the day's work. They'd managed to transport the bodies back to the Hub for autopsy, the police van moving slowly through the crowd gathered at the Tower. The atmosphere among the throng of people was largely hostile, anger at the lack of progress but also anger at the police themselves as Buckland's writings preyed on those who lacked purpose or direction, finding some meaning in his vitriol. The preliminary findings had yielded nothing useful. The lorry had been reported as stolen two weeks ago, the interior bleached clean and no useful evidence on the Vicar and his wife so far. It was frustrating that modern technology could only do so much if there was so little evidence.

As she closed the front door behind her, she heard the sounds of the TV, a flashing light sneaking out from under the door that led to the kitchen and living room area. She took off her boots and hung her jacket on the wall before opening the door. Cassie was curled up on the sofa, a large bowl of popcorn beside her as she hugged a pillow, her back to Anders as she faced the large screen. Cassie was watching Ju On, a Japanese horror film and jumped as Anders gave her a greeting.

"You nearly gave me a heart attack!" she exclaimed. Anders smiled and caught some popcorn thrown at her in protest.

"Sorry," she said in a tone that suggested she didn't mean it. "How's your day?"

"Not as bad as yours," she replied. "News footage looked grim." They talked briefly before Anders left her to the film and made her way to the bathroom. As she passed Aaron's door, he called her name, his voice coming through the narrow gap Cassie had left.

"Bumble?" he said sleepily. Anders pushed the door open and crept in as Aaron sat up groggily.

"You should be asleep," admonished Anders as she sat next to him on the bed.

"I wasn't tired," he said, rubbing his eyes in tiredness.

"How was school?" Aaron shrugged and leaned into Anders, finding comfort in her embrace.

"It was ok. We have to make a Roman fort for our project."

"Wow. That sounds cool. You wanna build it this weekend?" Aaron nodded. Anders sensed he wanted to say something, so gave him time to find the right words. After she had rescued him, he'd clung to her tightly, never letting her out of his sight for more than a few moments, but it had taken months before he spoke to anyone other than Cassie.

"Why is that man paying people to hurt other people?" he asked. Anders stroked his hair softly as she answered.

"He's not very well. Sometimes, when folks are not well, they do things they don't realise cause a lot of hurt.

"Like my dad did?" Anders winced inwardly at that but gave him a gentle smile

"I guess. Did you want to talk about your dad?" He shook his head.

"Not really. Are you going to catch the bad man?"

"I hope so," replied Anders. Aaron's response caught her off guard and she fought to control her emotions as he spoke.

"Will you do to him what you did to my dad?" he asked.

"No, honey," she said, keeping her voice low and soft. "What I did was wrong too." Aaron stared at her for a long time. Eventually he spoke.

"He deserves it," he said, anger making his voice harsh. In that moment, Anders knew that she was failing him. She wanted to show him a life filled with love and happiness. One where he could feel safe, away from anyone who knew him and what he had endured. Abi's words from earlier that day came unbidden to her mind and she pushed them away. Aaron would be the product of his environment, and that environment would be a happy, loving one, filled with affection. She kissed the top of his head and had him lie down so she could read some more of The Hobbit to him. By the time she had finished the first page of her chapter, Aaron was fast asleep.

A minute later, she walked into the kitchen and poured a glass of red wine, topping it up a little more as she brooded over what she could do to help Aaron. She poured a glass for Cassie and passed it to her as she sat down on the sofa, Cassie moving the pillow aside so that she could cuddle up against Anders.

"This is the scariest film ever," she said, scooping some more popcorn into her mouth. As the film progressed, they both became increasingly fearful, hiding behind their hands as the vengeful spirit took its revenge. Anders would happily face an angry mob and not flinch, but ghost stories always scared her silly.

Afterwards, Anders let Cassie go to bed, saying she'd tidy up. As she washed out the popcorn bowl and rinsed the glasses, her phone rang. Looking over, she saw that it was Mal.

"I've got an idea," he said as soon as she answered it. "Meet me in the Hub." He hung up leaving a bemused Anders to stare at her phone. With a sorrowful sigh at the thought of her bed going empty tonight, she grabbed the keys to her truck and headed out.

Chapter 3

Mal paced around the Hub with a restless energy. Barry and Jesse arrived first, having stopped nearby for drinks on the way home. As they exited the lift, Helen and Ben walked through from the forensics lab. They looked shattered and, as Anders came from the stairwell and saw how tired they were, she felt a pang of guilt that she hadn't stayed longer, despite having had mere hours of sleep over the last few days.

Duncan and Abi were the last to arrive. Duncan had collected Abi on his way in and she had been unwilling to come to work unless she looked pristine and smart. Duncan was his usual crumpled self, though his appearance hid a mind as sharp as his sister. Mal ushered them to their seats and they looked expectantly at him, none particularly pleased to be there. The Hub had become a claustrophobic pit of humanity as McDowell poured more resources into finding Buckland. Now it was quiet, sullen almost, as if the Hub resented the mess and clutter the extra people left behind.

"Thank you all for coming back here," said Mal, his voice quiet as if he didn't want to be overheard. "I know we're all tired and in need of some sleep." Jesse rapped his knuckles on the desk in agreement.

"Staying this handsome takes effort and no small amount of sleep," he said. "I've not been on a date for a week!" Barry gave him a sombre stare.

"You can shut right up. I've not been on a date for three months." Helen gave him a gentle pat on the arm.

"Bless," she said, giving him a cheeky wink. "You can take me out any time." Barry had the grace to blush and Mal gave an irritated sigh.

"On task folks," he said, wanting to get things moving. "Sanders has gone. We've no idea if Buckland made contact or if he simply realised he was being tailed and slipped the net." He hesitated, suddenly nervous. "I've only asked you guys here because we can't afford this leaking out, but I want to stage an entry to the competition."

A stunned silence washed over the group as Mal stared at them expectantly. Abi stood up suddenly, her cheeks colouring in anger.

"No. Absolutely not. How could you even think of such a thing?" Mal wrung his hands in despair, his frustration obvious. Before he could answer, Duncan spoke.

"I'm pretty sure it's not legal, but if you get a Magistrate, preferably a High Court Judge to sign off on it, then I'm in." Abi gave him a stunned look, clearly feeling betrayed by her brother. She turned back to Mal.

"First you lose Sanders after knowing he'd committed the most heinous of crimes and you want to compound this by, what? Digging up some corpses, stealing from a morgue? When did you become so amoral?" Mal, clearly stung by her words, stepped closer, his voice raising to match Abi's.

"When a madman started killing people and inciting others to do the same. Almost four hundred people around the world are dead because of him and we're sitting here helpless to find wherever the Hell he is." Abi jabbed a finger at his chest.

"We cannot stoop to his level. The cost we'd pay and the families of those bodies you'd set up does not weigh less than all those poor souls. The law is clear on this."

"So if a Magistrate signs it off, then the law is on our side, which makes it moral. That okay for you?"

"Don't patronise me." Abi and Mal glowered at each other, the rest of the group too shocked at the sudden outburst between two old friends.

"I can do it," said a voice in the silence. Everyone turned to Ben who looked nervous at the sudden attention. "My old professor can supply me with the bodies. Donated to science. Medical students use them. I can make sure they have no families." Abi deflated at that. She knew that once the practicalities of something was discussed, then reasoning was left behind. She walked away and left quietly as the group turned to Ben. Helen put a maternal arm around him.

"We'll both do it, but we'll need the Man Mountain to help us move the bodies." Barry grunted his assent and made to stand. Mal clapped his hands together in delight, pleased to finally be able to do something proactive rather than react to Buckland's killings or try and find his whereabouts in a mass of paperwork and computers.

"Excellent. I'll call McDowell, tell him to go wake a judge." Anders stood up as well, a grin on her face.

"I'm coming too. I have an idea."

Chapter 4

While Barry signed out two vehicles, Anders went through her plan. Jesse shook his head and Duncan paled slightly but gave her an impressed look.

"You're twisted," he said. "Call us when you're done and we'll start the investigation, make sure it all looks official." They left quickly, Anders and Helen in one vehicle and Barry taking an excited Ben to Oxford to wake up his old professor.

Anders tore down the empty streets in the requisitioned Ford Focus, her mind still adjusting to driving on the left. The hour was late and the traffic had thinned to a level where Anders could actually hit third gear. Helen spoke to Jesse on the phone as he guided them to an abattoir in Surrey that would have what they needed. She hung up once they were in the right direction and Helen settled down into the seat, her head resting on the seatbelt.

"Bet you thought you'd have the quiet life coming to work in Britain," she said, turning the radio on and finding a channel with music she liked.

"I never was any good at standing still," replied Anders, her eyes focused on the road ahead. "I get bored too easily."

"So why did you come over here then? You said you had no real family left in London."

"I guess it's where I was born. After I made the news in the States, it became harder to do my job effectively. The Director wanted me to take a sabbatical, come back when the fuss had died down, but I quit and came home."

"You think you'll ever go back?" Anders was silent for a long time. So much so that Helen thought she hadn't heard.

"Maybe," she eventually said. "I do miss it sometimes and I know Cassie and Aaron do, but for now, this is the right thing. My skillset means I'll always have work in America if I go back." Helen chortled quietly.

"We were all pretty intimidated by your file," she said. "Jesse kept reading out sections in his big dramatic voice, mostly to piss Duncan and Lucy off. Left here." She indicated a turning from the A3 and led them away from the city lights to the countryside, Anders seeing stars for the first time in months as the glow from London ebbed and flowed truculently behind them. Anders felt it a brooding presence in the rear view mirror as if recent events had sullied the old city.

"How about now?" asked Anders. "Having met me, I hope you're not intimidated anymore." Helen leaned over and patted her leg.

"Oh, now that we've met you, we're more intimidated than ever, but the file didn't mention that you're a real sweetheart, so that's okay. When you're not cutting people open to grab their arteries or taking on sword wielding maniacs. Then you're just plain scary."

"Thanks!" Anders feigned hurt as Helen ribbed her some more, laughter filling the car. The conversation eventually turned to Helen's favourite topic. Men.

"So tell me about you and Mal," she asked in her typically blunt fashion. "How was your date last week?" Anders gave her a back handed slap on the arm.

"That's for listening in by the way," she said. "Anyways, I'm not one to kiss and tell."

"So you did kiss!" Anders rolled her eyes and laughed.

"Nope! We had one of those awkward moments where he went to hug me and I went to kiss. Ended up doing neither."

"Ah," said Helen, knowingly. "A kug. We've all suffered them love. So when are you seeing him again?" Anders flicked the indicator on and turned into an abattoir, the headlights from the unmarked car showing a large barn with a glowing light coming from large metal doors, barred shut. Anders parked next to a battered animal transport lorry and killed the lights.

"We've not really had much time to talk about it. He wants to go out Saturday night, but we'll see. It's not as if we have much free time at the moment." Helen waved an admonishing finger as she unbuckled her seatbelt and opened the door.

"Always time for love hun, always time." Anders gave her a cheeky grin.

"What if it's not love I'm after?" she asked innocently. Helen smiled back.

"Then there's definitely time for that!" she said, striding up to the door and banging loudly on it.

They were greeted by two men, both wearing blood stained overalls and shoulder length gloves. Both were pleased to help out these two pretty women and happily sold them three pigs off the books. They were a little intrigued by their request to use the saw and be left alone, but they acquiesced. Helen was charming and flirtatious, Anders quiet and mysterious. The men were quite smitten.

Their work done, Anders and Helen had the men drag large sacks of their work into the boot of the car. They waved farewell and divvied up the cash Anders had given them, delighted at their unexpected bounty.

As they drove back to London, Helen put Barry on loudspeaker.

"How you getting on big man?" she asked. Barry's deep voice boomed through the speaker.

"Got three of the finest in the boot. Ben's professor was happy to help and promised to keep his mouth shut if Ben helped him out with a paper he was working on. Fair deal all round."

"On your way back, get some straw," called Anders. She could sense the confusion over the phone line.

"Where am I going to get straw?" asked Barry.

"You're in Oxford," replied Helen. "Find a field and go steal some from the horses!" She hung up and turned to Anders.

"Now then, don't think you're getting off the hook that easily. You and Mal. I want all the juicy details." Anders gave a theatrical sigh.

"Tit for tat. You tell me about your latest beau and I'll tell you about mine."

"Sold to the woman in black," said Helen and they spent the rest of the journey happily chatting away about nonsense. It was good to talk about something other than murder and Helen was happy company, open and honest, but strong and forthright. The journey took an hour, but felt like minutes as they arrived at their destination.

Chapter 5

Greenwich Park was closed at night, large gates blocking the main entrance to the road that wound through the park. They waited at the gates furthest from Greenwich centre and chatted until Barry arrived and flashed his lights. The street was empty, lines of houses far enough away to allow the night to shield them from prying eyes. Anders stepped from the Focus and walked over, her shoes loud in the still air. She leaned into the car as Barry lowered the window. He was calm and efficient, years of military experience making his actions measured and precise. Ben, by contrast, was a bundle of nervous energy, legs shaking up and down in excitement.

"Anders," greeted Barry. "We all good?" She grinned as he passed her a small black purse. Taking it from him and walking to the gate, she unzipped the purse to reveal lock picking tools. Kneeling on the floor and shining a flashlight on the lock using her mouth, she quickly picked it and pulled the chain out. Opening the gates, she waved Barry and Helen through and pulled the chains back around as she locked the gates again.

Running to the car, she got in and directed Helen to the spot she had in mind. Aaron had wanted to see the Royal Observatory last month and they'd spent a happy day there. It would now serve a much more sinister purpose. Helen switched off the headlights and enough light seeped from the city for them to see where they were heading. The observatory was up a short hill and they parked at the bottom and carried their items to the top, Ben panting with exertion as he helped Barry with three bodies. Once at the top, Helen could see why Anders had chosen this spot.

London was laid out before them, a stunning vista in the night as the city twinkled like star dust. The Greenwich Mean Time laser pierced the sky above them and famous landscapes such as St Pauls Cathedral could be seen towering into the sky. Complementing this was the Maritime Museum below them. It was a sight to behold.

As the last of the equipment was brought to the top of the stairs, the observatory glowering above them, Anders started directing the group. Barry laid out straw in a pile in one corner and sticks collected from the trees below in another. He then helped Helen and Ben to saw the forearms off each corpse, making sure to leave a loose flap of skin. They did the same to the legs of one corpse, cutting it off to just below the knee. Barry grimaced at the work as Anders pulled out the pig legs from the sack and started to sew them to the desecrated bodies.

"This is some twisted shit," he muttered as Helen helped Ben with the next task. Anders had sliced the skulls from the pigs at such an angle that they could be sewn to the faces of the corpses, creating a bizarre hybrid of man and pig. A human torso with pig limbs and pig faces.

"How the hell you come up with this?" hissed Barry as he dragged a completed corpse to the straw. The second was dragged to the sticks and the third tucked behind a low brick wall.

"Now we need to kill them," muttered Ben darkly and set to the bodies with a knife. Barry sighed at his efforts and snatched it from him.

"You said kill them, not tickle them." He gave several quick stabs to the bodics, opening wounds that did not bleed. Helen started spraying blood around the area, Anders guiding her.

"It's not Picasso," she muttered as Anders showed her how she wanted the blood spread.

"The Blood Eagle won because it was art. We need this to look like art." She then positioned the bodies until she was happy and fussed some more over the blood, insisting it look lifelike. Satisfied with the work, she had Ben stand behind the scene and take a picture, framing the macabre imagery with the beauty of London at night. They crowded round the camera to see the picture and there were murmurs of approval.

"Tell you what," said Helen. "I'm going to be disappointed if we don't win." They gathered up their gear, checked quickly that they hadn't left any signs that the scene was fake and made their way back to the car. A stagnant silence smothered the grounds, as if the land itself was shocked into stillness by their obscene act.

One they'd left the park, Anders stopped by a pay phone and they gathered round as she spoke, all trace of her American accent gone, replaced by a drunk, possibly stoned, teenager.

"Hey man, you gotta get over there now. I was in the park and I saw something. I don't know what it was, man, but they were dead. All of them. Which park? Greenwich bruv, where else? By the observatory. It's some freaky shit, like that competition from the web. My name?" She hung up and gave Barry the nod. He dialled a number on his mobile and waited for Jesse to pick up.

"Call should be coming through soon. Send Duncan to the scene. We'll get changed and meet him there once Mal gives us the word. You do your end. Make it look real." He clicked the phone off and patted Ben and Helen on the backs, bringing them into his giant embrace.

"Good work folks. Go home, get changed, maybe get some sleep, coz tomorrow we're investigating who could possibly recreate the three little piggies after a visit from the big bad wolf."

Chapter 6

Jonathan Sanders saw things. Flitting in the shadows, ethereal shapes that broiled and raged in the night. He saw the darkness that enveloped Man. He hadn't killed Sarah Baldwin to punish her. How could he? Jonathan loved her. He would watch her, sometimes from afar, sometimes so close that he could smell her. She would never see him. Never sense his presence, but he was always there. Always watching. He loved her.

As he watched Sarah, he saw the darkness insidiously creep into her soul, saw the shadowy figures slither into her as she lived her life. He needed to protect Sarah. To stop the darkness from taking her. He'd loved so many women. Deep in the recesses of his mind, a small part of him had always held him back, stopped him turning his fantasies into the reality of providing each love with the ultimate gift of freedom. He'd ponder on that as he watched and skulked. He'd thought himself weak. A coward. Too afraid to release their souls until Buckland's words had given him the courage and strength to act. To finally set Sarah free. She was so lovely. So full of life and vigour. He hated to see the darkness infect her, to sully her spirit.

He didn't do it for the money. It meant little to him. He saw the truth in Buckland's words, as if a veil had been lifted and he saw the world for what it was. Releasing Sarah had provided an emotional catharsis that left him a sobbing wreck. The shadows drew closer, shapes and demons flitted in his periphery as he realised that he himself was infected with darkness. As he sank deeper into despair, his daily tablets long since forgotten, madness slithered its way deeper into his mind. Without thought, he uploaded the image of the blood eagle to that website and sat in the dark, staring at nothing, his mind a whirlwind of conflicting emotions.

After many hours, his phone beeped silently. Unused to the sound of contact, he stared at the phone for a long time before reaching out and picking it up.

He'd received a text.

Jonathan. I was stunned by your beautiful image. Your work is truly extraordinary

He continued to stare as another message popped up.

You have set her free indeed. Your selfless fantasy was to ensure that she was released from this terrible world. You have found your calling.

Jonathan sat up straight in his chair. *You have found your calling.*

You cannot stop now. It is time to be strong. We need to set them all free.

He made to respond, but another message popped up.

You loved her very much didn't you.

It was a statement. Jonathan found himself nodding in agreement.

"I did," he whispered in the dark

Did you love anyone else?

He send a swift reply. *I've loved so many…*

Anyone special?

Jonathan gave it some thought, his thumb hovering over the keypad of his battered phone.

There was one. His first. The one who had started it all those years ago. She had left. When they see him, they always leave. *Melissa Adams*, he typed. He felt a thrill as he hit send, his heart beating loudly in his chest. The reply was swift.

Details

He knew all the details. How tall she was, where she used to live, where she worked, when she was born. He wrote of her favourite food, how the smell of fresh cut grass was her favourite and how she loved croissants every Saturday. The way she chewed her lip when nervous or played with her long, blonde hair when she watched TV. Her bra size and her favourite lingerie. What she always wore on a first date and how she applied her make-up. What he didn't know was why she used to cry into a pillow every night. Even after he would leave her gifts.

He took a long time to pass this information on, his fingers unfamiliar with the keypad.

He waited then. Alone in the dark. He could hear the sounds of rats as they scurried under the floor, the arguing of neighbours through the thin walls and the constant hum of distant traffic. Below all that, he could hear the gentle, insistent susurrations of the darkness. Eventually the phone beeped, startling him. He looked at the screen, the faint glow illuminating his face.

Found her. She lives in London now. Show her how much you love her. Set her free

He didn't need to think about his response. *I will.*

You are being watched.

Jonathan knew that. The shadows had told him, their voices a snarl. *Leave that to me.*

The conversation finished, Jonathan embraced the shadows, folded them around himself and stole away.

It was a surreal experience working on a crime scene you had created the previous night. Helen and Ben looked to be working diligently, but they were actually wiping away any traces that it may have been them. Duncan and Mal spoke to the Wardens, though the camera's had mysteriously been erased of all data. The investigation was thorough but no evidence of any use could be found. Mal gave Anders a strange look as he approached the scene.

"This looks messed up," he said. Anders nodded in agreement.

"Yup. Some twisted mind came up with this." She handed him a USB with the photographs on it. He pocketed the slim memory stick and walked with her down the steps from the observatory. London was in the middle of a glorious heat wave and a bright sun banished the shadows from the park, the verdant green of the grassy space bright and inviting. The park had been closed by the borough police and there was a quietness to the area that was comforting despite the macabre scene they walked from. Though they had slept little, the beautiful setting and weather invigorated their spirits.

"What did McDowell say?" asked Anders, pulling her shades down from her hair and resting them on her nose. Mal gave her a sideways look that Anders was becoming used to. One where he thought she didn't notice how his gaze lingered on her long legs or slim figure. It gave her a little thrill but she pretended not to notice it.

"He was okay with it until the call came in and he heard what you'd done. Might have lost his temper a little bit. Got to say it myself, but those pig, man hybrid things you've made creep me the hell out."

"Gotta stand out if you want to win," said Anders. Mal gave her a thoughtful look and stopped midway down the hill. Above them, the crime scene was diligently being worked. Below, more officers were walking the park, searching for further evidence. They'd find nothing, but Mal had them working anyway.

"Speaking of winning. You still up for Saturday?" Anders arched an eyebrow at him.

"Winning? I'm not some prize," she said dangerously. He danced backwards, laughing at her tone.

"Wouldn't dream of it," he said, a twinkle in his eye as she scowled at him.

Several hours later, Anders made her way through the now familiar hospital corridors to see Lucy. She had improved considerably since the surgery, but still looked wan and pale. Entering the room, Lucy gave Anders a smile as she accepted the flowers and chocolate, opening the wrapper with one hand and offering Anders a chunk.

"How you doing?" asked Anders as Lucy held up the opened bar of chocolate.

"Getting used to doing things with one hand. It's not easy, but I'll keep trying. Barry put me in touch with some of his old buddies who've been injured and they've been really inspirational." She looked determined to overcome her disability and was imbued with purpose. Anders could see that, though it would be a long struggle, she would overcome her challenges. She was a far cry from the sour transgendcrphobe that Anders had first met and she could see that, in many ways, the horror of the last few weeks had made Lucy realise that her fears and prejudices were petty and insignificant. Anders wished that more people would use challenge and adversity in a positive way. She always felt that how you chose to react to adversity was the true measure of your worth.

"I'm pleased to see you doing so well," she said as she unzipped her handbag and took out a sheath of rolled up papers, spreading them out on the bed for Lucy to read. "Here's the stuff you wanted. We're no closer to finding Buckland to be honest, but we're narrowing the search. We found three more holes in the land registry, but there was nothing in any of them. We're only half way through the check though, so there's time yet."

Lucy had asked to be kept up to date with the case. Anders was only too happy to oblige, knowing that it kept her mind from atrophying when stuck in hospital bed. She spent the next hour going through new evidence until she could see Lucy tiring.

"I'll leave this with you," she said and fetched her dinner from the cart in the corridor and helped her to open the fiddly packaging on the pudding. Once Lucy had finished her meal, she tired quickly and was asleep within moments. Anders waited a minute or two and then tip toed out so that her heels wouldn't make too much noise. Out in the corridor, Helen called, Anders' phone blaring out *It's Raining Men.* Helen enjoyed tampering with the phone every time Anders helped her out, taking delight in choosing embarrassing songs as a ringtone. Anders sighed and rolled her eyes as she got several curious stares in the corridor.

"Last week, it was "The Lady is a Tramp", I'm pretty sure I preferred that," she said as Helen gave a throaty chuckle down the phone.

"Just keeping you on your toes. My lab. Now." With a click, she hung up, leaving Anders puzzled as to what she wanted.

It turned out to be Tequila.

"We need to finish the bottle off," she declared as Anders entered the lab. The unit previously occupied by the bottle now held a cadaver and Helen was loath to have it lying around unused. "It's a waste otherwise." She poured Anders a large measure in a glass beaker and kicked a chair in her direction. Sixties music blasted from her docking station. Helen refused to listen to anything written this century and cherished the sixties and seventies even though she wasn't born until the eighties.

She removed her lab coat and danced to the music as Ben hurriedly packed his bags and tried to leave, despite the protestations of both Anders and Helen.

"Have one drink," cajoled Helen. She put an arm around him and he dithered as he realised he wasn't going to get out easily.

"Just one," he said and gulped nervously as she took out a six hundred millilitre beaker and started filling it with the golden liquor. Anders patted his arm and had him sit as Helen shoved the beaker into his hand.

"Aaron's looking forward to Game Night," she said as he sipped the tequila, grimacing at the taste. He managed a smile.

"Don't worry, I'll let him win," he said and Anders gave him a mock frown.

"You'll do no such thing. Besides, I'm pretty sure we'll all kick your arse."

"What's this?" Helen asked, sitting on the dissection table, feet swinging as she tossed back a shot. "Ben got you playing his geeky board games." Ben blushed at her ribbing, so Anders leapt to his defence.

"Can't wait!" she said. "Ben's going to show us how to play Descent. Apparently, he thinks his dungeon master is going to take us all on. You in?" Helen pursed her lips as she considered it.

"Will there be alcohol?"

"Of course."

"Then I'm in. As long as I can be a kick arse warrior with a big sword."

"You'd like that wouldn't you?" jessed Anders with a knowing look and Helen gave a filthy laugh. The conversation became even filthier as they drank the tequila. Ben, despite his best efforts, ended up quite drunk, but Anders managed to remain sober. She sipped her drink, knowing she had too much on to get drunk. Ben was starting to open up and they found his company engaging as they got to know him better. Beneath the cripplingly shy exterior, there was a charming, witty and thoughtful man underneath.

"We need to sort you out," announced Helen, a tinge of a slur to her voice. "A haircut perhaps, definitely some new clothes. I shall help you find a woman!" She poured some more tequila, the liquid sloshing around the nearly empty bottle. "Or a man, whichever," she said and he blushed.

"Um…woman," he stammered, his nerves suddenly returning.

"Well that's good, because you have two gorgeous women here," she declared and winked at him. "Two Miss Universe winners right here!" Helen giggled as she did an impression of a contestant declaring that she wished for world peace and they fell about laughing. Ben gave Anders a strange look, unsure of whether to speak, but the alcohol dulled his reserve.

"Can transsexuals enter Miss Universe?" Anders had always been open with them and didn't mind their questions. She felt that it was better to engage with people rather than stigmatising transgender issues further by hiding or being defensive. She sipped her tequila, enjoying the tingling it gave her lips.

"Someone tried in twenty twelve, Jenna Talackova, but she was disqualified when they found out."

"Bit harsh," said Ben as he quickly Googled her. "She's better looking than most of the entrants." Helen grinned.

"Purely research there Ben?" she said as he swiped through some more pictures. He blushed.

"We're allowed entry now though," said Anders. "There was a bit of a stink at the time."

"You should go on it," said Ben drunkenly. "You could be like Miss Congeniality." Anders gave him a playful punch on the arm as both he and Helen laughed. She pointed to the scar that coiled around her neck.

"Think my back might make them run screaming." Helen poured some more tequila and turned the music down slightly as she spoke.

"They ever bother you? The scars?" Anders gave it a moment's thought.

"They did at the time. So much of being transgender is about appearance. It's important because it puts people at ease around you. It took years for me to stop worrying about how I looked and then this happened." She traced a finger over the lumpen ridge by her ear. "Doesn't bother me now though. Anyone who sees me sees a woman and that's all that ever mattered to me; that the exterior matches the interior."

"Was it hard?" asked Ben, putting his beaker aside and giving Anders his full attention.

"Mentally, changing wasn't hard. I'd always known what I was, so the change was inevitable for me. I knew I was becoming a better person because I wasn't living a lie any more. Some find it much harder because they become so entrenched in their male lives. The longer you leave it, the harder it gets. Especially when you start getting the secondary sexual characteristics of a male." She gave a mock shudder. "I'm glad I never went through that!"

"Oh, it's not so bad," said Ben. Helen chuckled wryly.

"Speak for yourself hon. I'm with Anders on that one." She turned to Anders and offered her some more tequila.

"You find people less prejudiced now than twenty years ago?" she asked as Anders accepted a small amount.

"Yes and no. We're more prevalent, but only in certain areas. Modelling work, TV, things like that. People are fine with it in some aspects, but it's different in the day to day world. Bruce Jenner coming out as Caitlyn went global and the more positive press we get, the more barriers we'll break down, but old prejudices will always be there." Ben nodded his head in agreement.

"That's because we're used to seeing models and celebrities as objects, not strictly real things. You can look at a model and think that they've been made that way with surgery and Photo Shop, the same with transsexual models. You can objectify them as much as you would any other model. People overlook their natural beauty, but also fail to accept them for what they really are." Helen gave him an impressed look.

"You've been thinking about this haven't you?" she said. He shrugged.

"I'd never met a transgender person until Anders. Makes you think." Anders smiled proudly at him.

"There's more to you than meets the eye isn't there?" she declared. "Don't forget that there are many transgender men and women in all walks of life. We're not all lucky enough to have glamour model looks, but we get by and the more of us there are that simply live a full life and become part of society in a positive way, the more we'll be accepted. There are still prejudices when a transgender person does a job seen as important. That's the real barrier."

"I read the parliamentary enquiry into trans discrimination that came out at the beginning of twenty sixteen," said Ben, reciting the text from his near photographic memory. "It said that the casual everyday prejudice towards trans people is the last bastion of acceptable institutional discrimination in Britain, with transgender people suffering the same kind of discrimination that was faced by gays and lesbians decades ago."

"Sounds about right," replied Anders grimly, though with a twinkle in her eye as she finished her thought. "I'm lucky; I always got to carry a gun back in the States. Makes peoplefolk think twice about saying anything. Anyways, enough about me. I barely know you guys, it's been so busy around here. Tell me some more about you."

Helen took the lead, necking her tequila with a gulp and a coquettish burp.

"Nothing interesting about me I'm afraid," she said as she swung herself off the table and helped herself to more drink. "Born normal, raised normal, grew up normal. Regular two point four child. Probably conceived normally too," she said in a maudlin voice.

"Damn, girl. There ain't nothing normal about you," replied Anders, grinning at Helen. "The way you are, your parents probably conceived you in the kinkiest way possible." Helen laughed and raised her glass in salute.

"Bless. You say the sweetest things," she said, before turning to Ben. "What about you hun? Apart from board games and Miss World pictures, what gets you up in the morning to fight crime?" Ben looked suddenly nervous before seeming to come to a decision.

"My parents were killed in a fire," he said, gazing at his drink and not wishing to meet anyone's eye. Helen sobered up quickly and lay a gentle hand on his arm.

"I'm sorry to hear that love. What happened?" He shrugged as if to say it wasn't much, but they could see that the words were tough to get out. Almost as if he hadn't spoken of it in a long time, which in truth, it was. Ben was a loner even before the tragedy that had taken his parents and their deaths had isolated him further and made it harder for him to form real bonds of friendship. Helen had done much to draw him out, as had Anders, and he felt safe with them, comfortable in showing them who he was.

"I was at Oxford when it happened. I was doing my PhD at the time, happy in the knowledge that I'd spend my days in a lab, researching oncogenes. The Dean calls me into his office one day and there was a police officer there. He was telling me that there'd been a fire and that my folks were gone, but I couldn't understand, couldn't comprehend what he was saying." Ben finished his drink with swallow and grimaced at length. He held out the empty beaker to Helen, who topped it up for him.

"There were no answers," he said, thanking Helen with a smile. "No one knew why. They couldn't find the cause of the fire and that hurt more. Their death's were senseless enough as it was, but the fact that there was no empirical reason that explained what happened hurt more. It took me a long time to move past that." He looked at Anders, a great sadness in his eyes. "I don't know what drives you so hard to do what you do, but I understand it. Every death deserves an answer and I play a part in that." Anders stood up and embraced Ben, a tear running down her cheek.

"You most certainly do," she said softly, as Helen joined in, embracing the pair of them.

"Group hug," she said tearfully and made to speak further, but Anders' phone rang. It was Mal.

"Fire at Temple Church. Get over here now."

Chapter 8

Jonathan made his way to London with ease. Once he'd slipped his tail, it was a short walk to the train station and within a few hours he was hidden among a throng of humanity. He saw his face on the front pages of the evening newspapers, but no one paid him any heed. No one really looked at you in London. Jonathan was non-descript, plain face, average height, average build, mousy hair. He could be anyone.

The susurrations were louder in London, the darkness imbuing the city with its sickness. Buckland guided him with his messages, but once he was set on his course he needed no further help. He ditched the phone, tossing it into a waste bin as he walked past. He wanted to be alone. At least, as alone as he could be when every shadow and demon slithered from the dark to speak to him, their efforts more insistent since he'd freed Sarah.

He found Melissa quickly and she took his breath away with her beauty. When he'd remembered her the other day, Jonathan had recalled every detail, but he'd forgotten how alive she was. Melissa radiated life, every pore of her being radiant with thrumming joy. His heart broke once more and he felt angry at not having freed her sooner. As she walked down the street, chatting with friends, a Hen Night sash round her shoulder, he followed closely. Close enough to reach out at times, but she never saw him. If she did, she would leave again. They always did. He enveloped himself in the shadows and Melissa never once looked at him. She was filled with the vibrant invincibility of the young, tempered by a vulnerability only they can't see.

She was his first. His true love. The one for him. It was through her that his infatuations grew, his sickness spread. Raised in a happy household, Jonathan had no reason to be as he was. No moment to point at and say, "that's why he is sick." He woke up one morning and saw the world in a different way. The bright lights dimmed, the joy of life leached from him. Then he saw Melissa and knew she could save him. But now he had to save her. Free her from the insidious darkness before it wreaked irreparable damage to her soul.

He watched as she danced. As she drank and laughed. He watched as she was taken home in a drunken state and he watched as she slept.

Before she woke, he left. He had work to do.

Temple Church was located near Embankment and was nestled among ancient houses, courtyards and gardens. Built by the Templars it had served the two Inns of Court for hundreds of years. It was so delightfully hidden that you had to know of it to seek it out. It was not something that you stumbled across. Made from the palest of stone and with a small cobbled yard surrounding it, the church was corralled in by houses that overlooked the beautiful building.

Jonathan saw none of this. He missed its regal beauty and majestic presence, focused as he was on his work. Since leaving Melissa, he'd been busy. Struggling through the narrow streets with his luggage he knocked on a house that overlooked the yard and waited patiently as the owner, a frail old man, answered the door. Johnathan gave him a push, stepping into the house and taking the side of his head to ram it into the wall of the hallway. His violence had been so quick and brutal that the old man hadn't made a sound as he slumped to the floor.

Kicking him aside, Johnathan walked down the hall to the kitchen where he heard the sounds of tea being poured. An old woman was humming to herself as she put the kettle back into its base and Jonathan attacked her with equal venom and force. Moments later, he quickly moved to the front of the house and pulled his luggage off the street. He felt nothing for the people he had killed. He saw himself as setting Sarah and Melissa free, but did not love the old couple. He didn't need to free them. He set about his work and then waited. Turning off the lights, he moved a chair to the bedroom window so that he could look down on the yard below. The sun rose to its zenith and then sank below the rooftops, stealing the light away with it. Still he did not move.

He watched while a group of excited people lay candles in the yard and decorated the area with white canna lilies, delicate petals strewn around the floor. Had he not seen darkness in every nook and alley, he'd have realised how beautiful it was. A crowd of people gathered, dressed in satins and silks, hats and heels. The atmosphere was jovial, a night time wedding at Temple Church a rare event, reserved only for those of the Inner Temple or children of a member.

Jonathan watched dispassionately as the groom stood outside with his entourage. He felt nothing, his heart a steady, rhythmic beat. As they were ushered inside, his pulse quickened. Melissa was brought to the yard in a horse drawn carriage, hooves clipping loudly off the brick walls. She looked stunning, her red hair flaming in the candle light, Ivory satin shimmering as she was helped from the carriage by her father. He helped to smooth her skirts and Jonathan heard the sound of the church organ being played as they awaited her arrival. After a brief pause, Melissa took a deep breath and walked into the church, elegant and composed.

Jonathan almost stopped then. Almost. But he didn't.

After all, he had a calling.

The yard was empty when he dragged the old man onto the street and carried him to the yard. The carriage was nowhere to be seen having been ushered aside to allow pictures to be taken outside the church afterwards. Jonathan's hands were sticky from the honey that he'd poured over the corpse, his limp body now stiffening as rigor mortis crept in.

Finally reaching the yard, he placed the man cross legged on the floor by the entrance, propping him up with some bricks he'd brought with him. Taking a bag from his shoulder, he emptied it over the corpse, feathers swanning out and sticking to the honey. An old skull clattered to the floor, decorated in a macabre fashion and he placed it carefully in front of the old man, facing the Temple entrance.

Checking that he was still alone, he sprinted the twenty feet to the house and scooped up a crate of bottles containing spirits with cloths jammed into the tops. Still alone, he rushed to the side entrance and jammed a wedge into the door, the noise drowned out by the enthusiastic singing from inside. Moving to the main entrance, he jammed another wedge into each wooden door and stepped back, taking a deep breath as he readied himself. Shadows and darkness whorled around his vision, becoming ever more excitable as he reached for one of the candles on the floor and lit the cloth tucked into a bottle.

Flames shot high as the spirit soaked cloth gleefully ignited. He hurled it at the door and the bottle exploded into shards of glass, spilling the alcohol and setting fire to the old wood easily. He lit the remaining bottles and threw them through the windows, screams of rage and then pain erupting from the congregation. Hammering at the jammed doors, the wedding guests pleaded to be let out and, as Jonathan backed away, he noted with satisfaction that they would not escape, flames billowing from the windows, reaching to the sky in seething anger and fanatical turmoil.

"Goodbye my love," he whispered, watching the inferno with regret. "I'm sorry I couldn't free you sooner."

Chapter 9

Anders arrived at the scene as the fires were eventually brought under control by the Firemen. They'd struggled to get their hoses to the Church as the streets to the Temple were too narrow for their trucks. The ancient temple was a shell, forlorn and sad. Embers sparked and glowed with a dull hostility at its tragic fate and the firemen who had been unable to save it. The roof had collapsed, though the brick remained largely intact. Too hot to go near, Anders could see a mass of charred bones through the wreckage. She couldn't begin to estimate how many had lost their lives to the fire, but could see far too many limbs and skulls. Her eyes were drawn to the smaller ones. Children. She shuddered at that, images of Cassie and Aaron coming unbidden to her mind. Any trace of tequila in her banished by the tragedy she witnessed.

Barry and Mal were already on scene and in deep conversation with a sergeant from the Met. She walked over just as he was pointing to the old man covered in honey and feathers.

"I saw that," he said. "And called you guys. Can't be anything other than another entry." He looked pale and she could see that he'd recently been sick, small stains spotting his uniform. She didn't blame him.

"How do you know?" asked Mal. The sergeant ran his fingers through his hair as he recalled happier times.

"I bought the Grimm tales for my boys. The proper ones. They loved it. That," he said, pointing again to the feathered man. "Is Fitcher's bird. The skull proves it. The story was about some evil sorcerer who was locked in a church during a wedding and burnt alive with the guests." He looked at the old man once more and paled further, his skin turning ashen.

"Excuse me," he said and ran off, hand clutched to his mouth. Barry turned to Anders, his face a mask of fury.

"A damn wedding," he muttered. "Happiest day of your life." He stalked off to speak to the firemen. The fire extinguished, he wanted them to stop spraying the crime scene so they could get some evidence before it was washed away. Mal watched him go, his features full of sorrow.

"I'm at a loss," he said. "Five million to kill one person you can almost see. Someone snaps and lashes out. But this? This is something else. It's an atrocity, pure and simple." Anders lay a comforting hand on his arm and looked around. Officers and SOCO's were busy tending to the scene now that the fires were out, but something nagged at her. She walked around, surveying the scene.

"This isn't about money," she said absently, glass crunching underfoot as she walked around the remains of the church. She closed her eyes, picturing the scene. She discounted the old man. The fairy tale was window dressing. Walking back to Mal, she looked at the buildings around her.

"This is personal," she said. "If it's personal, then he wants to see it." She kept looking, searching the houses for something. Or rather the absence of something.

It didn't take long.

Chapter 10

Jonathan watched as the flames rose to the heavens. His offering to Melissa. He had set her free and was thankful. From his window seat, he watched intently. The fire roared and growled as it tore into the building, rendering it asunder. Above the flames, he could hear screaming and his heart rejoiced at the friends that would be with Melissa.

He watched in the dark as the fires were tamed by the fire teams, their desperation turning to relief as they won a hollow victory. The Church that had survived the Great Fire of London was reduced to rubble and ash. The surrounding buildings had been saved and for that, they were grateful.

Jonathan watched as the police arrived. He saw two large men speak to officers and coordinate the site. The bigger of the two was a hunter and the darkness seethed at his presence, offended by him. The shorter man was brighter, the darkness more fearful of his presence. He continued to watch from his vantage point, confident that he would not be seen. He wanted to see Melissa one last time as she was taken from the wreckage, so would wait until that moment, happily biding his time. He would see her at peace and move on to his next love. He had a calling.

The shadows suddenly recoiled, angry and scared as another entered the yard. She was diminutive, but her essence stretched out around her. Leaning forward, he strained to watch this sinuous woman, tempered with steel and forged in fire. He couldn't fathom her out, unique as she was. She wore darkness like a cloak, a seething, torrential mass enveloping her, yet she shone with such a brightness that it lanced through the dark. Whereas the largest of the men was a hunter, she was a predator. The quiet whispers at the edges of his hearing grew into shouts and screams. He ignored them. He'd found his new love.

Long ago, his father had read a fable to him. It told of Donkeyskin. A daughter to a king who disguised herself in a cloak of donkey skin to escape his attentions, only taking it off when her true beauty was recognised by another. The story wormed into his mind and Jonathan was awash with giddiness at his next undertaking. He would stalk this woman, this Angel of Righteousness, and take her when she least expected it. He knew what he would do, his fervent imagination giving rein to his madness.

He pictured her bound and gagged as he took a knife to her soft, delicate skin. He would slowly peel it from her, careful so as not to ruin muscle. He'd skinned cats and dogs in his youth and had mastered the art of taking the skin whole. He would do it to her. He would keep her face intact though, so that he may preserve her beauty. Then he would take the skin from a donkey and sow it to her, the head worn as a mask. He closed his eyes as he imagined how she would look. Only he would know her true beauty underneath, the world horrified by his deeds, recoiling in terror from this woman. He didn't want to set Anders free. He wanted to keep this one.

He watched as she prowled the scene then froze as she started looking at the buildings around the court. The offices around the church were empty, their lights off. The houses weren't. They were occupied and the occupants were watching the horror below. With a start he realised that his house was the only one with no lights on and no gawping neighbours.

She scanned the houses, her gaze intense and fierce. She then turned to his, bright green eyes scanning the building until she settled on Jonathan's window. She seemed to look directly at him and he saw the flapping of wings from her back as her cloak of darkness unravelled. Panic coursed through his body and he shot up from the seat, knocking it back in terror. She saw him move and ran to the house, calling for the large men to follow her.

He hit the staircase hard, sliding down the steps rather than taking each one, only too aware of the banging on the front door. It burst open as the giant crashed through it, barely slowing as he hit the door. Jonathan grabbed the railing and used his speed to spin round and head for the kitchen, throwing a chair behind him as he ran. He was rewarded with an expletive and a smashing sound as the big man tumbled.

Risking a glance back, he saw the woman in pursuit. Fear jolted him forward and he raced through the kitchen, pushing open the back door and finding himself in a courtyard, impeccably manicured and tended. He was blocked in, tall walls surrounded by even taller houses. He scrambled over a hedge and spied a cluster of steps leading to the roof of the house opposite. Aiming for the stairs, he turned quickly to see the woman gaining on him, the two large men just coming out of the house.

Breathing hard, he pelted up the steps three at a time and found himself on the roof, a hundred feet from the cobbled streets below. The darkness crept around him, narrowing his vision as he ran to the opposite end of the building, desperately hoping to find another ladder to lead him to safety.

Skidding to a halt, he realised that he was trapped. He turned to find the woman walking towards him slowly, her breathing even and steady. She raised her hands in a gesture of faith.

"I just want to talk," she said. "I saw your work in Liverpool. The Blood Eagle. It was impressive." He saw the lie. She was wrapped in darkness, not light, slithering around her soul. As she walked towards him, he saw her true form, dark wings unfurling behind her, flapping loudly in the dark. He looked at her and saw retribution. He knew his mistake when he'd fantasised of taking her. Like Lucifer, she'd fallen from grace and that fall would continue, deeper into the depths of a Hell he shrank from.

She stopped, sensing his decision and, before she could catch him, he turned and leapt into the darkness. It enveloped him as he fell, but it was not the familiar embrace he knew so well. The darkness that wrapped itself around him was Death, full of brimstone and suffering.

In that instant, he realised that he was not free.

Chapter 11

"I meant to ask," said Mal as he poured Anders some more wine. "How did you know? Back at the fire." They sat in a private room at Dinner, a luxury restaurant nestled inside the Mandarin Oriental at Hyde Park. The hotel was the most luxurious Anders had seen, Edwardian grandeur at its finest. As the sun set low over the park, the hotel exterior was lit with hundreds of spotlights, highlighting the intricate masonry that gave the building such character.

Within the hotel, lay one of London's premier restaurants, opulent in style and serving European food from as far back as the Fourteenth Century. Mal had booked them into a private dining room with large hand blown glass pieces hanging from the lights, red embossed leather walls and glass panels that gave them a view of the park. They'd ordered a tasting menu and enjoyed the delights that were brought through, sampling all manner of delicious foods.

Anders sipped her wine, the large goblet dwarfing her hand as she enjoyed the fruity aromas emanating from the glass. She gave an elegant shrug of her shoulder.

"Blind luck," she replied. "He was sitting in the dark and part of the roof to the church collapsed some more, throwing sparks in the air. I saw him in the sudden light. Recognised him." Mal shook his head in disbelief.

"That's some lucky break," he said. Sipping from his glass, he eyed Anders over the rim before putting the wine down and appraising her openly. "You look stunning," he said. Anders blushed at the complement.

She'd spent the day with Cassie and a very bored Aaron looking for something to wear as they went into shop after shop, eventually settling on something from Karen Millen, a dark purple dress made of shimmering satin that hugged her figure perfectly. Finding a matching shawl and some shoes with a heel that she knew she'd regret later, she treated them all to some ice-cream. She then bought

Aaron some Avengers action figures by way of apology as she and Cassie had their nails done in a beauty parlour, Aaron re-enacting some of his favourite scenes from the movies.

"Thank you," she said, keen to move the topic away from work as more delectable delights were brought through for their tasting. One of the waiters stared at her bare shoulders, the scars a dull colour in the dim light, hastily averting his eyes as Mal gave him a challenging stare. Anders indicated the plush surroundings they found themselves in and smiled at Mal.

"You must have blown a year's wages to bring me here." Reaching forward to try some of the food, Mal chuckled. He'd made some effort himself and wore a suit instead of his usual jeans and check shirt. He looked awkward in the outfit, but pulled it off and looked handsome.

"I am a Deputy Chief Constable, you know," he replied. Anders sighed heavily.

"Ah yes, all of the power, none of the money."

"Not all of us are as wealthy as you are if Jesse is to be believed," he retorted, a mischievous glint in his eye. Anders tipped her glass to him.

"You shouldn't believe everything he says."

"But his stories are so fun," said Mal through a mouth filled with food.

"I will hurt you," replied Anders good naturedly. Mal gave her a sardonic look.

"Not with that dress on you won't."

The evening passed all too quickly. They laughed and joked, flirted and enjoyed each other's company. As the wine flowed, their inhibitions evaporated and they constantly found reason to touch, to linger, to revel. It never bothered Mal who she once was. Sat there in front of him was the most stunning woman in the room, one that every other man openly stared at, first at her beauty and then at her scars. She was oblivious to the effect she had on people around her and Mal delighted that she was here with him.

He talked openly and freely, not hesitating to tell her of his past. The family he'd once had, the tragedy they'd met in a car accident that had ripped them from his life. He told of his grief, Anders seeing the pain and loneliness that still haunted him. She saw that it hadn't broken him, though it had come close. He toyed with the slender neck of the wine glass as he spoke.

"My wife would always say that we live our lives under the night sky. When good things happen, a star shines brighter, the night less dark." He sipped from the glass, savouring the taste. "She likened the bad things in life to a star twinkling out. As you get older, some of us live under a dark sky, others get a bright and wonderful night. The Aurora Borealis if you like. That guy at the church? He lived under a black sky." Anders reached over and squeezed his hand.

"And you?" she asked quietly. He gazed at her for a moment, an ineffable sadness in his eyes. Eventually, he spoke, his voice soft.

"Somewhere in between, I guess."

Sensing his own melancholy, Mal changed topic and they were soon laughing and teasing each other once more, closer now that he had shared his loss with Anders.

As they finished their deserts and polished off another bottle of wine, Mal asked for the bill and then turned back to Anders. Her cheeks were slightly flushed from the alcohol but she still looked radiant. He wasn't yet ready for the night to end.

"Fancy another drink somewhere?"

"I'd be delighted," she said and they stumbled from the restaurant in search of a taxi. Even in her rather too tall heels, she only came to Mal's shoulder and she leaned into him as he put an arm around her, guiding them down the street. She was happy to be led this night, content as she was.

Hailing a cab, they slid into the back seat as Mal gave directions. Anders loved moving through cities at night. They buzzed and sparked and truly came alive and she enjoyed watching the streets as they drove to the bar Mal had suggested.

It didn't take long to get to the Phoenix. It was nestled in a corner near Oxford Circus and gave a shabby chic vibe. Anders chuckled as she stepped from the cab, earning a few wolf whistles from the queue waiting to get in. She turned to Mal as he unfolded himself from the vehicle, amusement crinkling her eyes.

"Little overdressed aren't we?"

"Nonsense," he said gruffly and led her to the front of the queue where the doorman let them straight in, Mal shaking his hand in greeting as he walked past. Inside, Anders could hear Country and Western from a live band in the floor below and grinned at Mal. He smiled back and leaned closer to speak in her ear.

"I know the owner. Helped him out a few years ago. Drink?"

"Tequila," she said and Mal rolled his eyes. Making their way through the packed bar and looking rather incongruous in their clothes, Mal took her downstairs where a table had been reserved for them. "Little presumptuous don't you think?" said Anders. "What if the date had gone terribly?"

"Then I'd come here anyway and drown my sorrows," replied Mal and went to the bar as Anders settled into her seat and watched the live band. They worked the crowd well and the dance floor was full of revellers enjoying the music. Mal returned with a bottle of tequila and a handful of shot glasses that he lined up, filling each one as he straightened them out in front of them.

"See you in the middle," he said, shouting to make himself heard over the noise. He took the glass closest to him and downed it quickly, turning it over and slamming it down before reaching for

233

the next one. Anders did the same and they guzzled three shots in quick succession, the taste making Mal grimace.

"Never did like tequila!" Anders pulled the lapels of his jacket towards her and he leaned forward for a kiss, one hand reaching round the soft material of her dress and resting around her firm waist. It was all too brief for his liking as she pulled away and slid out from the table. She looked at him as she poured some more tequila, giving him a challenging look.

"Don't be a wuss," she said and slid the shot glass over the table towards him. Downing it quickly, he took her offered hand and allowed himself to be led to the dance floor, Anders swaying rhythmically to the music as she found a spot she was happy with.

Mal didn't care that he couldn't dance or felt awkward in his suit. He was smitten and enjoyed the moment as she pulled him close and they danced for what felt like hours, all thoughts of Buckland and his madness pushed aside as they focused on the here and now, the world narrowed to just the two of them.

Eventually, the night came to a close and Mal led her from the bar as they locked up. The owner had come out to greet them and ribbed Mal mercilessly over his attire as he ushered them from the bar. Out on the street, Mal hailed a cab and hesitated as it pulled up next to them. Anders felt a slither of adrenalin snake through her as she guessed his intent.

"Would you like to come back to mine for some coffee?" She laughed openly at his clumsy attempt to keep it cool and lay a hand on his chest.

"I'd be delighted to," she said. Mal rolled his eyes as his phone rang and he reached into his pocket to see who it was. He frowned as he saw the number and stepped away to answer the call. Anders waited, the cool breeze whistling down the street making her wrap her shawl more tightly round her shoulders. Moments later, Mal stepped back to her, a look of apology on his face.

"I'm so sorry, that was McDowell. He wants me over there now." Anders felt a stab of disappointment and also annoyance at McDowell as she stepped closer.

"You want me to come?" she said. Mal shook his head.

"No. I'd rather McDowell not see us together. Not yet anyway." He hesitated then. "Tomorrow night?" he asked hopefully.

"I promised Aaron we'd build a Roman fort tomorrow. Monday night? Come round and I'll cook you dinner." Mal's eyes narrowed.

"Can you cook?" Anders slapped him playfully.

"No, but Cassie can and I'll pretend I did it." He grinned and leaned forward, taking her in his arms as they kissed once more. This one wasn't so brief. Eventually the taxi driver beeped his horn and Mal shot him a warning look. Grumbling as Anders stepped into the taxi, he closed the door behind her and waved goodbye. Anders returned the wave and sighed contentedly as she settled in her seat and told the driver where she wanted to go.

Feet sore from dancing in her new shoes, Anders slipped them off and curled her feet under herself as she stared happily through the window. She liked Mal. He was warm and kind with a gentle demeanour that hid a fierceness when provoked. He could be grumpy at times, but his gruffness was a front. He treated people well and his team loved him. She thought that maybe one day, she would love him too. They'd both suffered such loss that their greatest strength would be their empathy, their understanding of what the other had endured.

She didn't realise, as she pondered on her evening and contemplated some future with Mal, that she would never see him again. They had shared their last dance and stolen one more kiss from the night.

Week 4

There's been so much written about me these last few weeks. To some, I'm a saviour. I've lifted the veil we cower behind and shown the truth of the world. To others, I'm a monster. I'm the embodiment of Lucifer himself, inciting others to kill, murder and maim. This vitriol is written by high minded idealists. They miss the point with their words. This isn't about me. This is about us as a species. It isn't time for idealism. It's time for realism.

I walk among you. I see everything. I see society eroding away in a mere three weeks. That's all it has taken. Three weeks to sow terror, to make you afraid of your neighbour. That stranger walking towards you. Is he about to enter the Competition? Will you be the next entry?

If I can do this in three weeks, how strong was our society anyway? Was there really such a thing as civilisation, as humanity? The revolution continues. We grow strong. We are legion.

Take arms against class. Take arms against those who would bracket you, put you in a box and say "this is your worth. This is where you belong." You are powerful. You are mighty. You are a creature of this world. We took millions of years to evolve to now. We survived mass extinction events and have earned our right to be here. We lose that right as we turn from Natural Selection, believing ourselves above such petty competition, but we need to embrace Survival of the Fittest. Weed out the weak. Nature selects those best adapted to survive. Every entrant proves this. Every death, natural selection in action. The only law, the only order, is that which is governed by nature herself.

How dare we take it upon ourselves to impose our will on nature. We are the embodiment of it, not her masters.

This week, we had an unprecedented number of entries. I promised five winners and next week, we shall have ten. One entry caught my eye. The Big Bad Wolf and his three little pigs. Such art. Such understanding of our glorious work. I had to meet the creator. We were kindred spirits.

When I met him, he was not the creator. He was not capable of such beauty. He took credit for another's work. Worse, he was the man your society sent to catch me. Law and justice made flesh, upheld by you for his virtuous work.

But we are here to tear down society. To live in a world of natural law and real justice.

*I decide to tear this symbol down. To tear **him** apart. This week's theme is serial killers. I have my favourite. We all do. The Washington Whipper. He would tie his victims to a cross in his basement and lash them with his cat o'nine tails, tearing flesh from body. Why? Because he could. Because he understood the natural order of the world as it should be. It's not about strength. It's about willingness. That is the ultimate form of natural selection.*

I take this man in his own home. This Mal Weathers. I shove thousands of volts of electricity through his body and he collapses in a twitching heap. I set up my cross and drag him to it. He's wearing the trappings of society. A suit. Dressed up like a peacock. I tear this from him and he wakes, screaming and bucking against his restraints. Vile anger and vitriol spews from his mouth. He curses me and swears vengeance. I laugh, for his anger is hollow, his threats empty.

I have my whip. Like the Washington Whipper, I feather my cat o'nine tails with barbs, the better to tear flesh with. I am clumsy with my first few attempts. I barely scratch the skin, but I improve. He curses me, but does not scream. Eventually, I get the hang of this skill and, with new found respect for the Whipper, I set about my work. I tear chunks of flesh from the police man. This embodiment of society. I tear it and him to shreds.

Eventually, he screams. Oh, how he screams. His living room is soaked in his blood, pieces of torn flesh plastering the walls and still I continue. He struggles some more, but he weakens as I expose bone. The barbs catch and stick in them and I pull with effort to remove them, scratching and cracking bone.

His struggles lessen and soon stop. Sweating with the effort, I toss my whip to the floor, blood and gore soaking its length.

This world cannot touch me. Society and civilisation, by its very nature are too weak, your ideals too soft. You will not catch me. The next person you send will be held back by your morals, limited in capacity.

I am not limited. My morals are linked to our true spirit and being. Natural selection. It's not about strength. Survival of the Fittest never has been. It's about willingness. Our species revolution is all about willingness.

Chapter 1

Mal's flat was clean and sparsely furnished, though dark wooden floors and pastel walls gave it a comforting warmth. It looked like someone stayed there, but not that someone lived there. He'd moved in shortly after the accident that had killed his wife and son and never made it a home, his love for them a ghost that haunted every room.

Anders stood outside the door to the flat. Behind her, Barry and Duncan paused. No one wanted to be the first inside. They knew what they would find. Anders' hand shook as she inserted a key into the lock. She'd taken it from the janitor and it scraped noisily as the key brushed against the metal. Pushing the door open, she gathered her courage and stepped into the flat.

The smell of death hung heavy in the air, an iron tang of blood mixed with the fluids released from the body at the time of death. Anders knew Mal was dead before she saw him. Her world stilled as she entered the living room and saw the horror of Buckland's work. Her own scars tingled and crawled on her back. The Washington Whipper had done the same to her, but she had been lucky to escape.

There'd been no such luck for Mal and she fought back tears as she saw him, his body rent apart, his face a mask of blood and pain. Barry and Duncan followed after her and stopped, unable to speak. Duncan cried freely.

"Everyone out," whispered Anders. Barry made to protest, but saw the look in her eyes. He gave a curt nod and helped Duncan out. Anders followed, closing the door behind the pair as they stepped outside.

Alone, she put her back to the door and slid down, great tears wracking her body in debilitating convulsions. She sobbed, face in her palms as she grieved for Mal.

She sat for a long time on the floor, not caring if she contaminated the crime scene. She let the grief pour out and then gathered herself. She built a wall around the pain and composed her will, breathing steadily as she sought to control herself.

It took some time.

Finally ready, she took out her phone and made a call. Getting the answer she wanted, she stood up and opened the door. Helen and Ben had joined Barry and Duncan and she could see that Helen had been crying. Ben looked distraught.

"I'm so sorry love," said Helen and embraced Anders. She nearly lost control for a second time then, her grief bursting from her mental walls like a dam, but she kept herself in check.

"We can't go in there," she said. "Not yet." Helen gave her a puzzled look, but helped Anders into a coverall and made sure that she had all of the equipment. Just as she finished, Cooper arrived. She'd taken a disliking to him in her job interview but knew that he would provide legitimacy for the investigation.

"Everyone, this is Cooper from Her Majesty's Inspectorate of Constabulary. He's here to make sure we don't fudge anything and invalidate the scene." Anders handed him a coverall and, wordlessly, he put it on. As the team made ready to go back into the flat, Anders shook her head.

"Just me and Cooper," she said. "None of you should have to do this." They made to protest but acquiesced. Anders was now in charge. At least, until she was replaced. She turned to Cooper, who suddenly looked nervous. He'd read the blog on the way, but reading about something and seeing it were two very different things.

"Ready?" she asked and he nodded, unusually quiet as she passed him bags of equipment. She turned to Barry. "Make sure we're not disturbed. Start canvasing the rest of the building, get Jesse to check the camera feeds. You all know the drill. Keep busy."

She turned and stepped back into the flat, not pausing to allow herself a moment of panic and fear. She heard Cooper gag as he saw the horror and told him to take a seat on a bar stool in one corner. Shakily, he turned to find the stool and sit on it, keeping his eyes from the bloody carnage that surrounded him like a nightmare. Anders took out her headphones and put them in, plugging the end into her phone.

Finding the music App, she hesitated, her finger hovering over the keypad. Through her white coverall, the dark purple of her polished nails showed through. She'd had them done especially for Mal. She knew that the moment she played the music and walked the scene, not only would she remember every facet of this room, but she would be forced to replay the barbarism, acting out the killing of Mal over and over again.

In time, her memory of Mal alive would fade, but the memory of his death would linger forever.

Cooper watched Anders as she slowly walked around the room, her face a mask of concentration. She stared at Mal Weathers, taking in every detail. He'd have run screaming if it was him. Standing in a room with your former boss' corpse, analysing his death, one that should have been her death but for one loose buckle. He wasn't sure he should be here, but knew Anders had made the right call. He'd be the one to sign off that the evidence was clean and impartial. It wasn't a precedent he wanted to set, but in light of what was going on, he made an exception. At some point soon, he'd have to make a decision on whether to let what was now her team continue or whether to recommend to McDowell that he find a new team.

Pondering his decision, he absently watched as Anders started taking photographs, each flash highlighting the blood stained walls and sticky flesh that was starting to putrefy. He felt sick to his stomach. Deciding to ignore the scene, and trusting Anders completely, he took out his tablet and started some work, doing his best to block out the chamber of horrors he found himself in, but failing miserably.

Eventually, Anders approached him. She'd done as much as she could and was ready to leave.

"We're done," she said. "SCO can do the rest." He put his tablet away, glad to leave the room. Anders looked tired and worn but he sensed something behind those green eyes that he couldn't quite read. As he slid from the stool, he dialled a number and waited a few moments until the receiver picked up.

"She's finished. I'll bring her over to you now." Anders gave him a querulous look, getting a reply from over Cooper's shoulder as he hastily left the flat "We're seeing McDowell and the Home Secretary as soon as you've scrubbed up. We need to decide what we're going to do with you."

Chapter 2

Anders spoke little on the way to the Home Office. Her mind still reeled from Mal's death and her carefully constructed defences kept threatening to crumble. Cooper parked near the building and they walked the rest of the way in silence. McDowell was waiting for them in the foyer and rushed to greet Anders, holding out both of his hands to take hers.

"I'm so sorry," he said, grief tearing at his face. "We knew each other for many years. It's so…so…" He was at a loss for words, so Anders helped him out.

"Senseless Director. Last week, he used a word to describe the Temple Church killings and it keeps playing in my head. Atrocity. What happened to Mal was an atrocity." McDowell took a deep breath and ushered her into a conference room next to the foyer. The Home Secretary, Justine Barrett, waited for them and she offered her apologies also. Anders found it less sincere. She was saying the words, but was there for one purpose and that wasn't to grieve some guy she'd met once before.

Taking a seat, Barrett led the discussion.

"So we're here to review the case and decide on how we are going to move forward from here. We've a press conference in twenty minutes and the world is watching. Personally, you've all royally fucked up. What the Hell were you doing faking an entry?" She beat the table with the palm of her hand as she spoke, anger twisting her features. McDowell answered before Anders could.

"Mal came to me with the plan and I ok'd it. We both felt that it was worth a shot if there was chance of contact."

"He made contact all right. Bits of him are spread all over his living room and the photo is there for everyone to see."

"Justine, a little sensitivity please." Cooper had spoken so quietly and softly, that he demanded attention. It was strange for Anders to see him take the opposite approach to the last time she'd been here, but this time he wasn't playing a role. His words sliced through Justine's anger and she huffed an apology, pulling her tailored jacket together haughtily.

"You spoke to him last night," said Anders, using the silence to speak. "Tell me." McDowell's eyes narrowed briefly at her tone, but he answered her anyway.

"We'd set up a burner phone. It went off."

"So why didn't he tell any of us?" McDowell spread his hands in a helpless gesture.

"He was worried that Buckland would bolt if he saw too many people. Figured it was best to go it alone and call you guys as back up when he needed it." His words stung, but Anders recalled his look as he hung up on McDowell at the end of their date. She knew that Mal would try and play the hero.

"So where's the cell phone now?" she asked. McDowell shifted uneasily in his seat.

"Mal took it with him. Buckland sent a text saying he would be in touch." Anders bit her tongue, curbing the anger that flowed through her. Calming her voice, she still heard the grief in it as she spoke.

"So Mal kept the cell phone and Buckland used it to trace him back to his flat." She wanted to say more, to berate his and Mal's stupidity, but McDowell knew it. His face greyed and he slumped back in his seat. Cooper spoke, his voice firm yet gentle.

"We can all decide who shoulders the blame at a later date Miss Anders. You found little of use at the crime scene and we can deduce that the phone has gone if you didn't spot it there. The question we all need to discuss, is who leads the team and whether the same team carries on." Justine made her case, almost hissing in anger. The last time they had met, she had been friendly and warm, but Anders could see the pressure Justine was now under and it was breaking her.

"First off, your team lets a suspect escape so he can drive to London and set fire to an historical church filled with almost a hundred guests. Then you fake a crime scene and wind up with your Deputy Chief Constable murdered in a most public way. You know what my answer is." She sat back and glared at the group, daring them to argue with her. McDowell gazed at his thick, scarred knuckles, reminding Anders that he'd started out on the rough streets of Glasgow and risen to Director General on merit alone. He was a bruiser by nature and stared hard at Anders, weighing her up. Cooper kept his council, happy to let McDowell come to his decision.

"Assistant Chief Anders is yet to sully her name in this case. We can keep the team going, promote her and present it as a new start. I keep my team." He turned to Barrett and spoke pointedly. "My very successful team, and you get a new face." Justine leaned forward and jabbed a finger at Anders.

"You want her to lead the team? The press will have a field day. Not only is she transgender, she's American. The public will never accept her."

"She's the best option you have. No one else is more qualified," butted in Cooper. They started bickering among themselves until Anders cut them off. Her voice was filled with steel, the force of her will dominating the trio.

"I don't care what the public think. You want to find Buckland and put an end to these killings, give me the damn team. You can bitch and moan as much as you want, I don't care. Put me in front of the press, let them see me. Buckland whipped Mal to death because he knows I'm on this taskforce. Why else would he have done that, other than to destabilise us completely? You won't find many takers for the job after what happened to him anyway."

"Aren't you worried Buckland will come after you?" asked Justine, resignation in her voice. She knew she'd lost the argument. Anders gave her a cool gaze by way of reply.

"Seems not," said Cooper jovially. "Let's go meet the press."

Chapter 3

Anders had always hated this part of the job in the States, but in Britain, the press were more invasive, more aggressive and happier to sell papers using lurid headlines. Camera's buzzed and lights flashed as she took the stage with the Home Secretary and Director General of the NCA. Justine spoke first. She told of the terrible loss the police had suffered and gave several platitudes to the deceased. Anders watched dispassionately as Barrett spoke, aware of every eye on her. She'd spent a few cursory minutes in the bathroom freshening up, but knew she looked tired and worn out. She tried to keep her emotional turmoil below the surface and focused on her breathing.

They were sat behind a long table covered in a dark blue cloth, microphones pointing towards each of them, a ring of reporters from around the world, faces intent, salacious almost. Written press, TV and internet. The whole world saw them live.

McDowell spoke next and he told of his grief at losing a dear friend. He spoke of his determination to catch Buckland and see justice brought to him. He vowed it would be swift.

"To that end," he said and gestured to Anders. "Assistant Chief Constable Anders will be promoted to Deputy Chief Constable and take over the dedicated task force. She has had an exemplary career working for the FBI in America and has been their most successful agent for over a decade. We are delighted that she has returned home to her native Britain and can be here to support us in our darkest hour." The flashing of lights intensified as their focus turned to Anders. She kept her face neutral as McDowell continued to list her achievements. Eventually, he opened the floor up to questions. Several dozen hands shot up and McDowell chose those he knew.

The first to ask was a reedy man with a high pitched nasal voice who worked for The Times. He carried a notepad and pencil in his attempts to resist the tide of technology.

"Why didn't she lead the team from the beginning?" he asked.

"She has only been in the UK for a few months. We wanted her to acclimatise to the law here and get used to our policing before giving the Deputy Chief Constable her own command. Her work to date has been outstanding." The reporter gave a sly grin.

"So it's not because she used to be a man then?" The crowd erupted and McDowell called for order, his thick Scottish accent booming across the room. He scowled at the reporter and made a stout and passionate defence of Anders.

Hours later, Lucy and Anders watched the news on the TV in her room. McDowell was listing Anders' achievements again and berating the reporter for his narrow mindedness. The YouTube footage of the reporter quailing under his verbal battering had already reached a million views and Anders sighed heavily. She hadn't wanted this. She came back to the UK to get away from the constant glare of the public. Not because she was transsexual, but because of the Washington Whipper. Her career had become a public fascination, the stories growing ever longer and filled with myth. Each had a kernel of truth, but she wanted to keep Aaron and Cassie away from this. She wondered if she had done the right thing. She had enough money to never work again.

"I could walk away," she said as Lucy muted the TV. She looked healthier each day and swung her legs from the bed, leaning on Anders as she tried to walk around the room, each step an effort of will. Lucy grimaced at Anders.

"You don't seem like the walking away type." Anders gave an irritable sigh.

"It was selfish of me to take this job in the first place. I came here to give Cassie and Aaron a better life." Lucy paced further, Anders propping her up, helping her if she slipped. They moved in silence for a while, Lucy's grunts and panting the only sound. Eventually, she made her way to the bed and fell back heavily, exhausted from her efforts and reaching for her tablets. She gave Anders a frank look as she helped herself to some chocolate.

"I've always been ridiculed in the Force for my faith," she said. "Like it doesn't have a place among the worst that humanity has to offer, but I've always felt that, when you see such terrible things, our faith becomes more important than ever." She lifted some pillows behind herself with her one good arm, clearly practised at the technique now and settled back, content to be more comfortable. She turned back to Anders.

"I look at you and I know you were put here by God to do what you do. To take on the most base and most despicable of us all. Jesse said you were righteous and he has no idea how right he is." She indicated Anders' scars. "You pay a heavy price, yet you keep coming back. Why is that? Why do you fight so hard?" Anders gave it some thought, picking idly at her now chipped nail polish.

"I guess because I can't sit by and let people suffer. I'm a lapsed Catholic, so I have all the guilt, none of the absolution." Lucy smiled at her, tired eyes drifting shut.

"Footsteps in the sand Anders. There's always one set when times are toughest," she said, paraphrasing a well-known parable. Anders gave her a smile, happy to wait for her to drift off to sleep. Lucy continued to speak though, the drugs slurring her words slightly. Anders couldn't tell if she was lucid or high.

"Do you think Buckland is evil?" she asked.

"I'm not sure I believe in evil as an entity. We're all capable of both good and evil deeds. What Buckland is doing is most certainly evil. I don't think evil has a face, just people." Lucy smiled at Anders' response.

"Evil is real, I think," she replied. "It's beautiful and seductive, drawing every lost soul to it. They say the Devil is terrifying, a huge beast with horns and cloven feet, but I think they're wrong. A fire is beguiling, filled with light and warmth, but get too close and you'll burn."

"I think that most acts of evil aren't seen as such by those who commit them, so you may well be right," answered Anders.

"Did you know that Lucifer actually means Light Bearer?" Anders made to reply, but Lucy kept talking, her voice becoming quieter as sleep took her in its gentle embrace. "It's the Morning Star. Lucifer was the Morning Star that was banished from Heaven along with those Angels who had joined his rebellion. A third of all Angels. They refused to bow to man, to accept God's son as their ruler and resented Him giving us free will. The Book of Revelation tells of a war in Heaven, where the Archangel Michael defeated Lucifer and threw him to Earth."

She was quiet for a long time. Anders, thinking she was finished, made to leave, but Lucy spoke again.

"Dead Sea Scrolls," she said. "There's a War Scroll and it tells of the Sons of Light who fight the Sons of Darkness here on Earth. The war will never end. It will always need those who fight against the Sons of Darkness." She gave a deep sigh and rolled to her side. "Alfazon," she mumbled and drifted off to sleep, leaving Anders to contemplate her words in silence.

Anders stayed with Lucy a while longer to make sure that she was asleep before leaving. Outside the hospital, she took off her jacket to enjoy the sun and held it over her arm as she walked past the London Eye and made her way along the bridge towards parliament, taking a right when she crossed the Thames and heading for Scotland Yard. She ignored the stares and whispers as she passed strangers on the street. They may be unfamiliar to her, but she was front page news to them.

Arriving at the building, she saw Jesse leaning over the rails by the river, smoking a cigarette with a thoughtful look on his face. She reached him just as he saw her and gave her a sad smile.

"Hey boss. How you holding up?" Anders leaned on the rail and faced the water, not looking at Jesse.

"I'm ok," she said. "It's been a tough couple of days." Jesse grimaced and threw his cigarette into the water.

"I know. I saw the news footage." He sobered up and lay a comforting arm around her. "I'm sorry about Mal. He was a decent guy. I know you two were close." Anders leaned briefly into his embrace and they shared a moment of friendship together. She gave his hand a squeeze and moved away, suddenly business like.

"Right, let's go meet the team," she said and strode towards the building.

"You gonna make me take the stairs again?" called Jesse as he hurried to catch up.

Chapter 4

Anders stood in front of the forty or so people that now occupied the Hub. She'd managed large teams before and enjoyed the thrill of the hunt, but this time, all she felt was a great sadness at the loss of Mal. Most people stood, leaning on walls or desks and faced her with blank expressions, waiting to see what she would do. A few sat on chairs and they were the original occupants of the Hub. Abi, visibly upset, comforted Helen as she sobbed quietly, a tissue pressed to her nose as she grieved. Anders wished that she could grieve so openly.

Ben sat next to Duncan and Barry, taking comfort from their presence. His eyes were red and raw. Jesse stood behind Anders, giving her his unofficial support as she addressed the group. Most hadn't known Anders beyond her being the "quiet but fit one" or "the intense one". Most had found her intimidating and so had steered clear. They now gazed at her with open curiosity, her past now splashed over the tabloids and many were changing their previous appraisal of her.

"I'm not Mal," she said. "Nor will I try to be. Buckland is still out there and we need to find him. Whatever it takes, we will find him. And I'll only do that with your help and support. Stay focused, stay alert and stay sharp. I want every detail reported to me, no matter how insignificant you think it is. I want ideas, I want creativity and I want you to think outside of the box. Be autonomous, but you get back to me." She turned to Barry, who sat up smartly as if being addressed by a commanding officer.

"Where are we with the building checks?"

"Three more found boss. Nottingham, Surrey and City Centre. I checked the city one this morning and have sent a crew to the Nottingham and Surrey sites. No luck. Deserted and abandoned warehouses or estates."

"Which means what?" asked Anders. She knew the answer but wanted the team to find it. One man put a nervous hand up. He looked about twelve to Anders and spoke with a stammer.

"He…he knows we're ch, checking his buildings." Anders gave him her best smile.

"Good work Harry," she said and he glowed with pride that she knew his name. "Buckland knows how we're finding his locations. The explosion tipped him off."

"Or his son did," said Duncan.

"More likely that. We still tailing him?" Duncan shook his head.

"We didn't get the warrant through."

"Get a tail on him, I'll get the warrant." Anders had Jesse put on the projector and they started working through the murders linked to this week's theme. Jack the Ripper seemed to be the most popular and it took a long time sort through the entrants. Anders assigned everyone their jobs and set them to it. As the group went about their work, a bustle of noise and activity in their wake, she beckoned the original team into Mal's office.

She felt a pang of sorrow as she walked in and saw the first aid kit she'd used on him still on the desk. He'd hated his office and had rarely used it. Her eyes found the cabinet that she knew would be full of his shirts and jeans and she steeled herself against the pain that ravaged her, biting it back with venom.

Barry, Duncan, Helen, Ben and Abi followed her in, Jesse entering moments later and closing the door behind him. Anders sat on the desk, unwilling to sit in Mal's seat and looked at them all. She knew that she had no choice but to be honest with them.

"You all know Mal and I had a…thing." Barry was the first to speak.

"We all know. Don't mean you need to be taken off this case because of it. We've already spoken and decided that it stays with us." Anders gave them all a grateful smile.

"Thank you. That means a great deal to me. In terms of practicalities, Mal spent the evening with me last night. He received a phone call on his cell at one twenty two in the morning from McDowell. He'd been contacted by Buckland." There was a sharp intake of breath as she spoke, a collective shock rippling through the team.

"Mal met with McDowell and decided to keep it to himself until he had something more concrete."

"Buckland traced the phone didn't he?" asked Jesse. Anders nodded.

"What was he thinking?" asked Duncan, more in frustration that anger.

"The same thing he was thinking when he barrelled into a house rigged with explosives or asking you to make a fake crime scene," said Abi. "He wanted to stop Buckland. Mal hated him with every fibre of his being for what he represents. The very opposite of what Mal did."

They thought on that for a moment, each recalling a different memory with Mal that they would treasure. Eventually Anders spoke, her voice soft in the silence.

"Buckland's blog came out a day early because Mal forced his hand. He killed him but didn't want the body found before he'd written about it and published his photos. We all know what that means."

"Someone tipped him off," whispered Abi, a horrified look at the bustle of activity outside the office. "But I thought only us lot knew." There was an awkward silence in the room as realisation dawned on them. Anders was the first to speak.

"It's no one here," she said. "Let's be clear on that. But we need to be vigilant. Barry, I want you to find the pressure points in what we did last week. Who could have known? Follow the evidence." He nodded, a thoughtful look on his face.

"I'll need Jesse to help with that." Anders looked to Jesse and he nodded.

"I'm about done with the registry, so should have some time spare."

"Good. Ben, help them out too. You're good at analysing frameworks. Helen, will you be okay without Ben for a while? I can chip in if you need." She nodded her head and spoke quietly, grief infusing her emotions as she spoke.

"I can get by with the SCO team. I'll let you know if I need more help." Anders thanked her and then dismissed them all.

"We've work to do. Let's get to it. Every lead we cross off the list is one lead closer to Buckland." As they shuffled out, she asked Duncan to stay behind. He'd removed the sling from his arm, but it was still swathed in bandages. Anders sat him on a chair and took the one opposite, still sitting on the same side of the desk, Mal's chair an ominous presence in their periphery.

"You applied for the same post as me," she said bluntly. Duncan nodded, happy to keep his council. Anders ploughed on. "Was that your only issue with me?" She didn't need to say more. They both knew what she meant. He raised his hands in a placatory gesture.

"I don't give a shit about that other stuff. You took my job, plain and simple." He spoke truthfully, but Anders pressed on.

"What about now?" she asked. He responded quickly, having thought about it a great deal over the last three weeks.

"You should have been given Mal's job, not the one I applied for. We're all good, you and I."

"You still want my old job?" Duncan gave a grimace.

"I do, but not if it means you get horribly murdered and I end up with your job." Anders laughed and held out her hand. Duncan took it awkwardly in his left and gave her a lopsided grin.

"Assistant Chief Constable Phillips. How does that sound?" Duncan gave a nod of approval.

"I could get used to it," he said.

Chapter 5

Anders pushed herself hard. Sprinting through the trees, she startled some deer and they galloped away as she burst from the woodland. Heart beating rapidly, sweat poured from her as she ran, cranking up the speed with every kilometre covered. She ran from her grief, from her pain. Focusing on her body, she ignored her aching muscles and tested her limits as she crossed the ponds and hit the roads, coming to the Richmond Hill gates ten minutes before they opened. Impatiently, she did some stretching exercises as she waited.

The warden was late that morning and he didn't greet her with his usual smile and good cheer. She gave it scant thought as she sprinted through the gate and made her way through Richmond. Passing a newsagent, she saw the owner putting out the papers on the racks at the front and skidded to a halt. She was the focus of every tabloid and broadsheet. Most had photographs of Anders from the news briefing, but one had the entire front page dedicated to the picture of her clutching Aaron as she escaped from the Washington Whipper, covered in blood, her face a rictus of rage and anger. Her heart sunk at the sight, her first thought of Aaron at his new school. Above the picture, the headline was both inflammatory and lurid.

Transsexual cop; hero or psycho?

With a heavy heart, she finished her run and stepped quietly into the flat. Cassie was up and pacing the kitchen. She hadn't slept and her make-up from the previous day was smudged. She'd also been crying.

"I'm so sorry," started Anders as Cassie rushed to her, gripping her tightly. "I never wanted this to happen. Has Aaron seen it yet?" Cassie sobbed and nodded her head. The morning news had been filled with tales of Anders and the Washington Whipper, how Buckland had copied the killings and how Anders now ran the team to chase him down. Coupled with her past, the British press were having a field day.

Anders held Cassie for a long time. Eventually, she managed to gather herself and pulled from Anders' embrace.

"Sorry. It's just, seeing that picture again brought it all back." She picked up the remote and started flicking through the channels, snippets of conversation blurting from the TV. They were all focused on one thing. The first channel started with a well presented reporter standing outside Scotland Yard. He was rattling off a lengthy list of criminals that Anders and her team had killed during her manhunts in America. Cassie clicked the remote to another station.

…sounds like this woman, or man, or whatever you're meant to call *it,* is some kind of vigilante…

…how is she any better than the person she's hunting…

…send a killer to catch a killer that's what I say…

…so let's talk about this transsexual aspect. Is she mentally stable?...

…it's a disease, plain and simple. A sickness of the mind…

…she may be pretty but that just makes her more of an insult to all of the real women out there…

…the results of our poll are in. We asked whether you would sleep with Deputy Chief Constable Anders and you all answered with a resounding…

"Switch it off," said Anders quietly. Cassie turned to her, anger colouring her cheeks. Anders had done so much for them and she hated to see her publicly derided for a choice made twenty years ago that made her whole as she saw herself.

"Don't listen to them. They're all assholes." Anders smiled at her venom.

"There's only two people in this world whose opinion I care about and that's you and Aaron. Do you know if he's told anyone at school about me?" She nodded her head.

"First day at school. You saw his painting."

"Ok. Both of you take the day off. Go back to work and school tomorrow. If it's too much, then we'll move on." Cassie shook her head fiercely.

"We can't keep running. It'll die down eventually. Catch Buckland and they'll all forget about it soon enough. Besides, it might mean they start looking at people like you in a better light." Anders sighed heavily.

"I don't want to be some figurehead. I just want to go to work, catch bad guys and come home to be with my family. Is that too much to ask?" Cassie smiled sadly.

"I guess it is," she replied. "Go see Aaron. He'll be dressed by now."

Anders made her way to his room and found him sitting on the bed looking upset. She sat next to him and kissed his forehead.

"Hey you," she said. "How you holding up?" He gave her a look with such big, sad eyes that her heart almost broke.

"Is that nice man dead?" he asked. Anders reflected that he was far too young to know about death but reasoned that not many seven year olds had been through what he had. She'd promised never to lie to him, so spoke the truth.

"He is, honey."

"I liked him," Aaron said, his voice full of sadness. Anders forced back her tears.

"I did too. Very much so."

"Did my dad do it?" he asked, his voice full of fear. She gripped him tightly.

"No sweetheart. Your daddy is gone. You know that. He won't come near you again." She knelt on the floor, facing Aaron and tilting his head so he could see her.

"Things will be tough for a short while. People will ask you lots of questions about your dad and say lots of horrible things about me." He gave her a soulful look, his eyes older than any man three times his age.

"Walk tall, stand strong. That's what you said to me when you saved us." Anders held out her little finger.

"I gave you a pinkie hug too," she replied. He took her finger in his, a ghost of a smile flittering across his face.

"Catch the bad man Bumble. Make him pay."

Chapter 6

Buckland strode confidently down the hospital corridor. He smiled at those he passed and walked with purpose. He gathered a few strange looks, but most ignored him. Reaching his destination, Buckland turned to the group of people he walked with and told them to wait. Used to his command, they obeyed as he counted off the room numbers until he found the one he wanted.

She was asleep as he entered, so he closed the door behind him quietly. He saw her gaunt features, her ruined arm and her pale complexion. *She's a fighter*, he thought. She had died several times but had fought back. In his new world, she would have done well. Now, however, ravaged as she was, she would only drag others down with her.

Natural selection in action, he mused as he lay a felt pouch on the table beside her. Opening it, he took out a syringe and a small, glass vial. The label identified the clear solution as insulin and he jabbed his needle through the foil cover and filled the syringe.

She was supposed to be dead. Someone, anyone, from NCA was meant to die that day. The fact that she had survived galled him. It was an affront that he could not allow to stand.

She stirred as he lifted the sheets but did not wake, the morphine dulling her senses and rendering her close to unconscious as she slept. He lifted the bottom of her top, exposing the belly button. In the womb, the umbilical cord had joined mother and child, giving sustenance and removing waste. It was the first connection to life, the ultimate symbol of our nature.

Buckland pushed the needle in, slowly but with assurance. The needle mark would be difficult to find if they thought to look for it. He filled Lucy with insulin, the hormone diffusing into the subcutaneous fat below the skin and leaching into her blood, the high dose causing hypoglycaemia within minutes. She had battled so hard against her injuries that her blood glucose levels were already dangerously low.

Her signals weakened and Buckland allowed himself a moment to saviour the feeling.

Seconds later, he left the room, closing the door behind him and whistling a jaunty tune as he re-joined his team.

He left the hospital with a skip in his step. People would analyse his words and dissect his deeds, but the all missed the simple truth when they looked for meaning in his actions. He just enjoyed killing. Inciting others to the same thrilled him just as much. As chaos ruled and his website was flooded with entrants his heart soared with real emotion and meaning.

Life's good, he thought as the sun shone on his face and he was absorbed by the crowd, invisible as always.

Chapter 7

Anders drove to Scotland Yard in her rusty pick-up truck and parked next to the gleaming patrol cars in the underground car park. She had debated going on the train, but her jog along the street had made her feel uncomfortable with the stares she was receiving. She felt like she did at the beginning of her transition. She was too used to walking through the world as a woman, but she could see people looking for tell-tale signs of her previous gender. She pushed her doubts aside as she parked. She had more important things to deal with.

She didn't bother to lock her truck and walked along the concrete corridor to the Hub. She was met with the sound of bustling activity and frantic work. It had become a default state at the Yard and each week the number of killings grew. They had to manage that as well as follow every lead on where Buckland might be.

Anders enjoyed the thrum of activity, feeding off its energy and vibrancy. Since Mal had been killed, she sensed an urgency and resolve in the group that she hadn't before. Calling a meeting, she stood next to the projector and waited for everyone to assemble. She'd even invited the Met Commissioner, Dawkins, down and he slunk at the back, happy for Anders to take the lead but pleased to be kept in the loop.

"Good morning," said Anders when everyone was gathered. "Let's start with the open cases linked to the website, move to any new ones that opened last night and then get to Buckland."

It took a while. She'd set up individual teams to chase any new entries and each one now had three separate cases. She had half reporting to Duncan and the other half to Barry. Abi was running profiles on each case and Anders thought she'd have to help her out, such was her workload. Eventually, they moved on to new cases in Britain and she assigned them to new teams, Dawkins happy to use his men for the London ones.

After that, Jesse collated the data for Europol and Interpol and laid the markers on the map, the projector showing hundreds of red dots on the wall. It shocked the group into a contemplative silence. Anders assigned several more to liaising with the local departments worldwide and made a mental note to ask McDowell for some more support there.

"Last item is Buckland. Jesse, you collated all the registries yet?" He gave her a big grin.

"All done as of this morning! We've done the most up to date consensus going and deserve a reward from some government department somewhere for doing their damn job!" A ripple of laughter sounded in the room. They'd all had to help at some time or other and it was a tedious, labour intensive job. It would also free up hundreds of man hours to Anders. She led the round of applause as Jesse stood to take a mock bow.

"Three more buildings to check," he said. "One in Brixton, near here, one in a council estate in Leeds and the other in Bath." They had checked dozens of buildings and holdings where the paper didn't match the IT records and it was often a case of poor paper work or an empty shell of a building that gave no evidence.

"Where in Bath," asked Anders, intrigued. Jesse looked at the screen briefly.

"Royal Circle," he replied. Anders paused for a moment, planning her next move as the group looked on in silence.

"Ok," she said. "Duncan, you take point here. Contact Leeds and have them search the estate there then get to the one in London. Barry and I will get to Bath and check that one out."

She dismissed the team and was joined by Barry as she made her way to the parking lot. He was dressed in his usual combats and a tight fitting black t-shirt that served to emphasise the enormity of his bulk and paucity of body fat.

"You want me to sign out a vehicle," he asked as he caught up, hooking a rucksack over his shoulder.

"No, it's ok. We'll take my car." A horrified look crossed his broad face.

"You want to drive down the motorway in that heap of rust?" Anders gave him an evil grin.

"No, I want *you* to drive down the freeway in that heap of rust, while I sit in the passenger seat and do some work." He grimaced at her as they neared the truck and she tossed him the keys. The car groaned and creaked as he forced his bulk into it and spent several minutes coaxing the vehicle to life. Leaving the parking lot, the suspension complaining about the speed bumps, Barry gave Anders a pointed look.

"That's a very pretty Versace watch you have there, all buckled up on the inside of your wrist like you're still back in the army. How much did that cost you?" She gave him an unimpressed look, doing well to hide her smile.

"Enough," she replied haughtily.

"Damn right enough. Enough to buy a brand new car that's how much that watch cost, several new cars actually. This piece of scrap metal pass its MOT? You bribe someone to sign the certificate, or just show your gun?" Anders reached behind and lifted a tablet from Barry's bag, refusing to take the bait.

"I like this truck," she said. "It has character." She swiped the tablet to unlock it and started going through her emails as Barry crunched through the gears.

"You mean temperamental, stubborn and a pain in the arse? They're not good characteristics."

"Eyes on the road soldier," replied Anders and settled in her seat, shoes off and feet on the dashboard as Barry grumbled his way out of the city and headed for Bath.

It didn't take long for Anders to sort her admin out and she closed the tablet and tossed it on the back seat, leaning forward and switching on the radio. It looked new and expensive and cost more than the truck did. Which didn't say much. She tuned it to a news station in time to hear Francis Buckland conducting an interview.

"…that's why the House of Lords has agreed, in principle, to suspend Habeas Corpus for any individual attempting to enter the competition should Parliament vote in favour of this legislation tonight." He was interrupted by the interviewer.

"The competition your brother set up." Anders could hear the exasperated tone in Buckland's voice as he replied.

"I've been through this in a dozen interviews. I've worked closely with the home office and NCA to do everything in my power to bring him to justice. I've been instrumental in suspending Habeas Corpus and also in ensuring the Royal Decree rescinding my brother's Lordship. I'm as horrified by his actions as any rational individual and renounce him and his deeds strongly, without reservation and without compunction. The sooner he is brought to justice…"

Anders switched off the radio and sighed heavily. She hated politics and police work. They were often poor bedfellows.

"He's on dangerous ground suspending Habeas Corpus," said Barry. Fundamentally, it was the right of the individual to a trial.

"There's still judicial review," replied Anders absently as she watched the countryside speed past. Green pastures and fields greeted her and she felt a weight lifted as they left London in the rear view mirror. "Besides, it's been suspended many times before. Seventeen ninety three after the French Revolution, Eighteen Seventeen, even the First World War. The last time was back in seventy one to try and tackle the IRA. The anti-terror bill pretty much does that anyway. It's just an attempt by the government to put people off entering the competition."

Barry gave her a sidelong look.

"I thought you only came back here a few months ago. You go and learn the British Judicial system just like that?" He clicked his fingers to make his point. "You're a scary woman Anders." She gave him a cheeky grin.

"That's why you like me so," she said and he gave her a pitiful look.

"In your dreams little one, in your dreams."

"In that case, keep your eyes off my butt then."

"It is kinda huge. Must be all that chocolate I see you stuffing your face with."

They bantered good naturedly as they made the journey to Bath. The journey should have taken a couple of hours, but the traffic held them up by another two. The conversation naturally turned to more sober topics and, as they stopped for a refill, Barry gave Anders a sly look as he chewed on a sausage roll.

"Don't think I've not see you sneaking into most of the empty buildings we've found. My cameras have caught you poking around in the dark." Anders gave him a guilty look.

"Just doing everything I can," she said. He nodded in agreement.

"Had a Captain just like you back in the forces. Wanted to do everything, be the best at everything, lead by example. Burnt out before his time. Pushed too hard." He looked at Anders pointedly. She looked tired and worn, but he could see the fire in her. She wasn't going to give up. She gave him a sad smile and finished her sandwich, washing it down with a bar of chocolate and mineral water. Barry turned on the CD player and, to his surprise, found Disney songs playing through the speakers. He turned to Anders with a delighted grin.

"It's for Aaron!" argued Anders, failing miserably to justify her CD collection. "Besides, nothing wrong with a bit of Disney." Barry shook his head.

"I worry about you, I really do."

"So what do you listen to then?" Barry muttered something under his breath, Anders teasing and prodding until he spoke clearly.

"Opera. Maybe some West End." Before Anders could rib him further, her phone rang. She picked it up, had a short conversation and hung up. Sighing heavily, closing her eyes and tilting her head back, she spoke quietly to the night

"Lucy passed away this morning. No autopsy yet, but doctors think it's most likely a clot from the surgery or something from the explosion they missed."

"Shit," said Barry, his tone giving more meaning than a thousand words. They drove in silence for almost an hour, each contemplating losing yet another member of the team. She'd been sour and sullen with Anders, but was opening up and they were becoming friends. Barry had also spent some time with her, and though they had only known her for a few weeks, their friendship had been forged in fire. It was strong and they felt her loss deeply. Eventually, Anders spoke, her voice quiet in the cab.

"Alfazon. That's what she called me the last time I saw her. The last thing she said." Barry gave her a puzzled look.

"Alfazon was an Angel who sided with Satan and was cast out of Heaven when they lost. After he fell, he renounced Satan and now walks the Earth, atoning for his sins." Barry chuckled.

"Pegged you for a fallen Angel did she?"

"Something like that." As they drove on in silence, Anders reflected on Lucy's last words. Whether they were spoken through a drug addled haze or with lucidity, Anders felt that she should be upset with the comparison, but knew that there was a kernel of truth in what Lucy had said. Barry, sensing her mood, kept his counsel and pushed on through the traffic laden motorway in silence.

Eventually, they arrived at their destination. Some of the places Jesse had identified turned out to be normal households with families or couples that had simply slipped through the system. Others had been more promising. Abandoned farmhouses or small holdings, but none had yielded anything of use.

Barry pulled up near the Royal Circle in Bath, the battered truck looking out of place among the regal splendour. The Circle was a ring of Victorian houses facing inwards to a grassy knoll and ringed by a road that branched off at each compass point. In the centre of the knoll were some large and ancient trees, proudly defying the advances of the city. Anders loved Bath, steeped in history as it was. Everywhere she turned, there would be an old Roman construct or Tudor dwelling. She vowed to bring Aaron to the city and show him the Roman baths.

They were here for a different purpose though and walked up the hill to the Royal circle in silence as the sun meandered below the horizon and a soft dusk took a gentle grip on the city. Turning round, Anders could see the twinkling city below them, great swathes of green pebbling the city centre. She gave a satisfied sigh at the view and took Barry's hand in hers, his massive paw dwarfing hers.

As they approached the knoll, they were just another couple, out enjoying a walk along the cobbled streets and alleyways, come to view the famous Royal Circle. Barry sat and leaned against a tree while Anders cuddled up to him.

"Number twelve," said Jesse in Anders' earpiece. She scanned the buildings, noting that most of them were now flats. They'd been bought many years ago and turned into apartments for more profit. Number twelve hadn't, the usual tell-tale sign of several buzzers on the side of the door absent. They chatted away amicably for half an hour as the sky darkened and the street lamps came on. The night was hot, a stifling, muggy heat, so Anders took off her jacket and lay it beneath her, now sitting opposite Barry and taking out a pack of cards. Just an ordinary couple enjoying the night. Barry was engaging company and the pretence wasn't hard.

Eventually, they agreed that the house was empty and, under a gibbous moon, sauntered over to the building. A large oak door barred their entry into the house and Barry pulled out his lock picking equipment. Anders scanned the now quiet street as he worked and, within moments, he had secured entry. Opening the door quietly, he slunk into the house, Anders following him in. She pulled out a pencil light and they found themselves in a large kitchen. It looked like it hadn't been occupied for some time, dust collecting in a faint burr over the units.

The rest of the house was abandoned and they did a thorough search before switching on the lights.

"Empty," said Barry in frustration. He called the Hub and spoke to Duncan as Anders walked slowly through the house. It was decorated with exquisite and expensive furniture. Each hallway and room was filled with carvings, paintings and artefacts from all over the world. One room held wooden sculptures from Africa and she traced a finger along a frightening mask from the Chokwe people of the Congo. In another room, an oriental theme prevailed with a large terracotta man encased in a glass cage. She whistled in admiration. The house may be unlisted anywhere, but someone clearly cared about it.

Making one last sweep, something in the hallway caught her attention. Barry switched off his phone and caught Anders muttering under her breath. She walked back into one room, came out and went into the next.

"Other properties were occupied by families. Had a fair old shock when the Police turned up. What are you doing?" he asked as she kept pacing back and forth. She curled a finger at him and he followed her into a study, every wall lined with bookcases housing hundreds of hardback books on law. Anders pointed to the wall behind a large desk. It was the only one that wasn't occupied by shelving.

"That wall is new," she said. "There's a ten foot space between the two rooms that doesn't match." She gave him an appraising look, taking in his massive height and build. "Fancy doing some home wrecking?" He chuckled.

"We don't got a warrant for that." A twinkle in his eye suggested he didn't care so much about that.

"You show me what's behind the wall and I'll show you all the warrants you could need." Grinning, he reached over and pulled the desk backwards. It was heavy and old, but he moved it as if it were made of cotton. He flung it onto its back, scattering pens and paper everywhere and kicked out a leg, the wood splintering under his assault.

"Mind yourself," he said as he peered closely at the wall before stepping back and swinging the table leg at it. The force of his blow cut through the plasterboard and he almost lost balance as the unexpectedly thin panelling gave way easily. A few more swings and he'd cleared a large section of wall, his hands grabbing chunks from the plaster and tossing it behind him. Covered in soot and dust, he whistled as he saw what was inside the opening. It was a large safe that seemed to glower at them menacingly as they shone their torches on it.

"That's a TXTL60. You're not getting in there anytime this century." The safe was roughly six feet high with a control panel on the front and a large metal wheel. Anders studied the panel and phoned Jesse.

"Hey boss," he said. "I'm sure you're not phoning me to ask me out on a date. It's ok, I've moved on."

"TXTL60," she said, ignoring his lame joke and staring at the panel. "Can you hack in?" She waited as he tapped quickly on his keyboard, whistling as he worked.

"Nope. Not from here anyway. It's one of the best on the market and entirely self-contained. You'd need someone there and I'm not sure anyone could do it, not even me. I'll contact the company that makes them and see if they can help us out."

He hung up, Anders and Barry waiting in an easy silence. They were used to long waits. It was part of the job. Eventually, Jesse called back.

"Okay, you're gonna need to find a bed for the night. They won't send someone round until the morning." Anders rolled her eyes in frustration.

"Give me their number," she said. Barry chuckled. He wouldn't want to be the poor sap who answered this call.

Thirty minutes later, a nervous employee turned up. He wore dark blue overalls and thick glasses that he constantly squinted through. He spoke with a stammer and Anders showed more patience with him that Barry would have. He prowled behind the poor man who knelt in front of the safe and applied a cable to the control panel, his hands shaking with nerves and glancing at the damaged wall that Barry had smashed through.

"Easy there Mike," said Anders gently. "Barry's just a big softie, all wrapped up in a mean looking package." She winked at Barry as she spoke and he stopped his pacing. Mike found his stillness more intimidating and, with trembling fingers, tapped in a twenty digit code to give him access to the safe. Eventually, he was done and looked up at Anders with a nervous smile.

"All done Miss. Just turn the handle and you're in." Anders straightened up from where she had been leaning against a wall, reading a book, and thanked him.

"Remember, Mike, that you have agreed to confidentiality. You cannot say to anyone what you have done here until we ask you to present evidence in a court of law. Are we clear?" He gulped and nodded, stammering his understanding. Barry led him out as Anders stood in front of the safe. Reaching forward, she turned the wheel and was surprised at how easily the door slid open.

What was more surprising was the putrid smell as a brown pungent liquid seeped from the safe, sloshing over her shoes and oozing onto the floor. The door suddenly swung open further as a semi decayed corpse slid from the safe, its flesh half rotted, chunks sloughing from the skeleton as the movement disturbed its metal tomb. Its fingers were mashed to a pulp and someone had taken a mallet to the skull, shattering it into a hundred shards.

Barry arrived just as the skeleton gushed from the safe and recoiled at the smell, holding his hand to his mouth and nose. He saw the mess congealing around Anders' feet and she gave him a frustrated look.

"Dammit. I really liked these shoes."

Chapter 8

Anders gave her shoes a rueful look as Helen bagged them for evidence. Sealing the bag shut, Helen gave her a sympathetic look.

"Good excuse to go shopping," she said and looked pointedly at Anders' feet. She wore some running shoes that she'd found in her car and the brightly coloured trainers looked at odds with her dark trousers. Anders had phoned Duncan and told him to get Helen and Ben to Bath as quickly as possible. They'd arrived within a couple of hours and Barry had buzzed them in as soon as he saw their approach.

In the orange glow of the street lamps, they looked like ordinary tourists, newly arrived and carrying large suitcases. Anders had told them to come without making a fuss or alerting the neighbours and was pleased to see them. Though Ben was young and ungainly, his work was unmatched. Helen was equally gifted and knew how to get the best from Ben. They were an excellent team. Helen had even managed to draw Ben out from himself a little over the last month and Anders could see a real difference in him.

He was on his knees peering into the safe and sifting through the congealed sludge that the corpse had festered in while Helen looked at the body itself. Barry had taken pictures before they'd arrived and his face was a mask of distaste at the smell.

"Why's it all half rotted like that?" he asked.

"There was enough oxygen in the safe for some decomposition, but that soon ran out. The corpse was then left with anaerobes," replied Helen absently as she moved the corpse a fraction only for more skin to sluice off, taking flesh with it and revealing bone underneath.

"Time of death is going to be difficult," muttered Ben, his head still stuck in the safe, the light from his torch sucked up by the dark gloop he had one hand in. "No insects were able to get to him, so I can't use succession. I can work out how much oxygen would have been in the safe and perhaps link that to the level of decay." His voice echoed from the safe as he spoke.

"You're looking at stage one decay easily, but parts of stage two and three as well," said Helen, pointing to the internal organs that were now mush, the liver and kidneys no longer identifiable.

"So at least three weeks," said Anders. "Even if we can't pinpoint the exact time, we're looking at a minimum of three weeks."

"Easily," answered Helen. "Longer with the lack of oxygen in the safe."

"It's disgusting is what it is," said Barry succinctly. "You got his brains leaking out of his skull and his manhood all swollen up in three different parts. When I die, just cremate me, ok?" Anders patted his arm reassuringly.

"Don't worry hon, I'll burn you to a crisp. But first, you gotta help me get all those pieces of skull into that box there." He gave her a long suffering look and pulled on his extra-large coveralls that needed to be specially made for him and got down on his hands and knees to help. There were only the four of them on the scene, but Anders had contacted Cooper and used FaceTime to film the scene for him. He'd paled visibly in the bottom corner of the screen but agreed to have just the four of them assess the scene initially before using a full SCO team. Though he had no authority to allow such things, any review would go through him. Anders wanted to be certain that anything they did would hold up in court.

Anders was keen that as few people knew about this as possible. Though she trusted her core team, there were far too many people leaving and joining the task force every day that she couldn't be certain one of them would leak the news to the press. If this house was linked with Buckland and this murder to him, then she didn't want anyone to know that they had found it, though she was sure Buckland would find out sooner rather than later. The fact that this corpse had been hidden intrigued her. It hadn't been posted on the Fifty Two Weeks of Murder site, so she was sure it was something that he didn't want found. If it really was him of course. It could just be some horrifying coincidence.

The teeth of the corpse were shattered and the flesh from the fingers too putrescent to get fingerprints. She and Helen had agreed that the best way was to reconstruct the skull and then hope that the face was known to their data bases. As they worked to gather evidence, Barry grunted irritably.

"I joined the police force to catch criminals, not spend time on my hands and knees looking for bits of skull. Ah, found something." Anders looked over and shook her head.

"That's a piece of dirt." He tossed the grit back into the slop and searched again. Though he grumbled, he was diligent and helped Anders recover more fragments. When they could find no more, he stood up and started to remove his coveralls.

"Oh no you don't," said Helen. "You're going to need to help me move this body, reseal the safe and clear up this mess. Maybe Buckland, if it was him, won't notice the body was found." Anders smiled as Barry gave her an evil look and zipped his coverall back up.

"You owe me," he said and Helen gave a cheeky smile.

"I'm sure I'll think of some way to pay you back," she said, her eyes roving his broad chest and narrow waist. He blushed and set about helping her, muttering darkly under his breath. Helen helped Anders remove the main portion of the skull, cutting the spine just below the third vertebra. Her work done, Anders took off her coverall and picked up the dark case that held the fragments.

"When you guys are done, get some rest and I'll see you back at the Hub." They all gave varying forms of acknowledgement and she stepped out into the street, grateful for the cool air and dark night. As Anders made her way to the truck, she gained the odd look of recognition, but no one approached her, preferring to scurry off instead. She hoped word wouldn't get out that she was in Bath and tip off whoever owned the house, but had little choice.

She made it to her truck quickly and gunned the engine, letting it turn miserably before starting. Putting her bag on the passenger seat, a battered old Stetson in the foot well caught her eye. She'd worn it a great deal in America and had become something of a trademark, her fiancé ribbing her mercilessly that she belonged in some old Western. She'd not worn it since that night in Washington and Aaron had claimed it as his own, running round the flat with a sheriff badge and plastic pistols in a holster. He must have left it in the car when Cassie had taken the truck a couple of weeks ago. She held it for a few moments, an uncharacteristic moment of hesitation, before sliding it onto her head. It still fit pretty good.

She switched on her CD player and put in a Tom Petty CD, chuckling at the cliché she must have looked in her truck as she turned the volume up until it was loud enough to keep her awake. Pushing the truck beyond its limits, she then sped down the motorway to London, her mind focused on the task at hand. She couldn't let it wander, for it would take her, inevitably, to Mal and then to Lucy. She couldn't afford to grieve. She would though. When this was over with, she would grieve as she always did. Fully and painfully. She'd suffered so much loss in her life, she was accustomed to its icy grip, a permanent companion to her. Anders would let her emotions crash over her defences and knew that it would ebb and flow, pummel her with guilt and hurt and then let her rest, rushing in when she least expected it, wreaking more devastating pain. Eventually it would fade like the tide on a beach to leave smooth sand behind that would be rewritten with a new story, though the dull ache of loss would always remain.

Arriving back at Scotland Yard, Anders grabbed the box from the passenger seat and made her way to the Hub. The space was empty, the late hour having chased away anyone working overtime. She'd also given Jesse the task of taking everyone to the pub to toast Mal and he'd done his job well, knowing why she needed to have the area to herself.

She checked her office quickly, scanning her emails and messages for anything urgent and then made her way to the forensics lab. She set the bag to one side for a moment and took out a sterile needle and some yellow collection tubes from the equipment store. Sitting on the stool, she rolled up her sleeve and tied a band around her arm, just above the elbow. Tapping the Basilic vein until it pulsed visible, she pushed the needle in and collected a sample of blood. Her movements were swift and well-practised. Once the bottle was full, she swapped it over and collected another sample. Finally, she removed the needle, swabbed the area and held some cotton wool over the puncture wound until the bleeding stopped.

Whilst she did this, she perused Helen's shelves of equipment and gathered what she needed. She'd arranged an appointment with Charing Cross Hospital upon her arrival in the UK, but they'd been slow to respond, so she was happy to do this herself for the time being. As a transgender woman, her liver and renal function had to be tested as well as her haemoglobin, lipid and hormone levels to make sure that they were all within range. Helen had been happy for Anders to do it in her lab and had even offered to do the tests for her. Doing them now helped to calm her mind and focus on something other than Mal and Lucy. It would make her work more quickly on the skull fragments.

Anders' potassium was a little high and her liver function was at the lower end of the range, but she attributed that to stress. She'd check again in a week. Tidying up after herself, she put the waste into a biohazard box and the reagents back into the neat and orderly rows Helen liked.

Putting on a fresh set of coveralls and surgical gloves, she took the bones from her bag and laid them on the metallic surface. Helen was exceptionally fussy about how her lab was managed and the table gleamed with cleanliness. The bones, chunks of dried flesh and brown, rotting viscera looked like a macabre jigsaw puzzle as she laid them out, counting them as she did so.

"One hundred and four pieces," she said with a grimace. Whatever had crushed the skull had been heavy and whoever had done it had used that weapon repeatedly in their rage. She knew that they would have missed many fragments in their haste and guessed that several pieces wouldn't fit as well as she would have liked due to the savage nature of the killing. The brutality would have crushed some bone to microscopic shards and the teeth were too fractured to piece together accurately enough for dental records.

Her first job was to clean the fragments and she took photographs of the bone before cleaning them, keeping all the collected gore for evidence. Eventually, she laid the pieces in order of size and put in her headphones. When working on puzzles, she liked to stand and be able to move, preferably to some beat. It was the opposite technique to her meditation of a crime scene, but for her, equally as useful in focusing the mind. She picked up the largest piece of skull, essentially the lower half with the jawbone smashed off and scanned it closely as "Uptown Funk" sounded through her headphones. Looking at the pieces around her, she picked one up and found a match.

Singing to herself, she started piecing together the skull, dancing and singing softly as "Happy" followed the previous song. Lost in her own world, the skull started to take form. Hours passed and she didn't notice, trapped as she was in an underground room with no windows and nothing but the glare of neon lamps above. She had her back to the clock above the doorway and didn't notice as Barry entered and put the corpse from Bath onto a steel gurney, the body bag squelching as he dumped the bag. He grinned as Anders, her back to him, shuffled to the music and sang to herself.

"Not perfect after all," he said, taking his phone out to film Anders, her singing off key and displeasing to the ear. Thinking he'd get Jesse to play that during the next briefing, he sauntered out of the lab with a whistle and a skip to his step.

Many hours later, Helen entered the lab to find Anders asleep, perched on a metal stool and head resting on her arms as she leaned onto the desk. By her side stood the reconstructed skull. There were several gaps in the bone and many teeth were missing, but she had done an outstanding job. Helen glanced at the gently snoring Anders with a new level of respect. Reaching out so as not to disturb her, she took the skull and placed it onto a Cyberware laser scanner connected to a Silicon Graphics Indy computer. On the screen, the computer placed a wire mesh over the skull and started overlaying tissue depth based upon Helen's findings on approximate age, gender and build. It was a more accurate method than the traditional one of adding clay to give depth on landmark sites, but still not perfect. She then passed the data to HOLMES and ran it through the police data bases. As she was doing that, she finally took a look at the reconstructed face on the screen and gasped in horror. The computer had the hair colour a shade lighter and the features were slightly off kilter, but there was no mistaking who it was.

Anders woke with a start at Helen's curse and gave a deep stretch, arching her back deeply as she chased sleep from her body.

"Everything ok?" she asked as she slid from the stool to see what had startled Helen.

"Come look at this," replied Helen, shock in her voice. "I think we have a new problem."

Anders stood behind Helen and looked at the monitor. The face was instantly recognisable. It had been plastered on every paper in the world in what had become the largest manhunt since Osama Bin Laden. Barely a day had passed without his face appearing on TV from news programmes to debates to daily shows.

The skull was that of Lord Michael Buckland, the very man they'd been hunting these last few weeks.

Chapter 9

Anders sat on the floor in her office and looked at the evidence around her. She'd drawn the blinds and dimmed the lights, pushing the desk back against the wall and putting a tablet next to her on the floor. She then put her phone into a dock and selected a playlist that she had made from every crime scene linked to Buckland. Playing the music, she started the process of building her construct.

She started at the beginning. Matthew Peters. Nailed to a cross on Wimbledon Common. She re-read every report, every lead, every piece of evidence. She did the same for Boyle. Chopped to pieces over forty days and nights in a shipping container. The vicar and his wife. Killed in a grotesque parody of a fairy tale.

She hesitated then.

Mal Weathers. Killed using the same method that she'd been disfigured with. Shoving her emotions aside, she read the reports, analysed the evidence and looked at the photographs, not shying from the horrific details they showed.

She read the report from Ben and Helen on the corpse in Bath. They'd had little time to gather evidence, but they had been thorough. Once done, she picked up her tablet and scoured the web, chasing her thoughts and finding links. It was time then to build her mental construct. It had taken her hours to reach this point and her stomach gnawed with hunger, but she ignored it, focused as she was.

Closing her eyes, she went back four weeks to Wimbledon common, the music helping her to realise the world as it was then. She dragged Peter Matthews from the van, beat him and tied him to the cross, hammering the nails in after shoving a ball of Buckthorn into his mouth. She wasn't alone. Someone else was with her, helping to hammer the nails in, taking delight at the bloody mess, squeezing his mouth shut so that the thorns dug deeper into flesh.

The shape was blurred. Fuzzy and indistinct, there wasn't enough evidence for her to get a clear image.

Boyle. She sliced and diced, tore finger from socket, cut limb from torso. The different grooves of the blade, tough and decisive, the other timid at first, then strong. The third cutting, weaker yet sure, steady in its work. To keep him alive, she needed help. She couldn't do it alone. Boyle wanted to die so very much, but Anders wouldn't let him. She gave Boyle constant care, set up a rotation, kept his wounds clean, showed the others how. Anders stopped then. Buckland wouldn't know how to keep him alive. But *she* would. *She* showed them how.

The Vicar and his wife. Anders made the steel boots, heated them up, but needed help to hold the wife's legs still as she put the boots on her. The poor woman screamed and the acrid smell of burnt flesh and hair clung to Anders like a stain. It took a long time to beat the Vicar. To break every bone, but Anders swung the bat hard and fast. Stopping, she remembered every break. Someone else broke that bone. Too tall for that angle. A shape blurred next to her, swinging the bat with glee. Smaller, not as strong. Then another, raining blows with strength and fury.

Then came Mal.

Alone in her office, tears of anguish streaked down her face as she whipped the skin from his back. She tried to block out his screams, but her construct was too strong, too clear. She tore the flesh in strips of meat from his body until she exposed the bone beneath and continued her terrible work. She sobbed quietly in the now dark office but would not flinch. She paused, rewound, re-whipped, covering every angle until she knew the story of his death more intimately than she had known the story of his life. The memory would be seared on her brain as if she herself had committed the atrocity. She would carry the guilt of his death forever, and, in the dark, with music filling the room, she played a requiem for his soul.

Several hours later, exhausted from her efforts, she climbed stiffly to her feet. The music had been on repeat and she switched it off, erasing the Playlist from the phone. Taking a moment to gather herself, she headed to the door, slightly unsteady on her feet, and made her way into the Hub. The place was eerily quiet, the only sound coming from Jesse's keyboard as he tapped away, lit only by a single lamp.

"Hey," he said when he saw her. He looked tired, but his energy levels were high. "You have any luck in your weird dream world thingymaboby?" His question alerted Abi, Duncan and Barry and they came scurrying from Abi's office, clearly having been waiting for her to finish. Anders gave them all a tired smile.

"I think I know who did it." she said. "Get McDowell and the team. We're ending this today."

Chapter 10

Anders stood by the projector waiting for Helen and Ben to make their way from the forensics lab. McDowell was being Skyped and his picture showed at the bottom of the screen. He looked like he had been dragged from sleep and his suit was a crumpled mess. The rest of the team looked shattered, except for Barry, who looked bright and alert. He'd slept on Abi's sofa while waiting and passed mugs of hot coffee around. Anders accepted hers gratefully and munched on a bar of chocolate as she waited for Ben to fold himself into a seat. At the back of the group, the Met Commissioner, Dawkins sat slouched in his chair. He exuded an air of authority and calm, his silver hair and crinkled skin immaculately kept. Word had it that he was next in line for McDowell's job when he retired.

"Thanks for coming," she said as Ben gave her a shy nod that he was good to go. "I've kept this meeting small as we need to move fast and I don't want any leaks. Helen, did you get what I needed?" Helen gave her a sad nod. She'd had Lucy's body sent to her lab and found the needle mark in the belly button. It was exceptionally difficult to spot and would only be found by those looking for it. Anders turned to Jesse and he gave her the thumbs up. He'd finally found the documents for the house in Bath.

"As you all know by now, we found a body in the house in Bath. Jesse has come up with the goods once again and we can see that the house has been part of the Buckland family estate for generations. Only now, it belongs to Francis, not Michael. The body in the safe is Buckland. We can't confirm that one hundred percent yet, but we can do that easily enough, given a little time." She clicked on a remote and the projector showed some archive footage of Lord Francis Buckland. He was giving a seminar in Oxford on Law, the students enraptured by his passion and vigour.

"Michael's brother. The good egg, if you will." She clicked the remote again and showed footage of Francis on the BBC news last week. He was just as impassioned, but there was a slight shift in tone. His speech in Oxford had been about how the law was there to protect everyone, to allow society peace in which to thrive and grow. Here, he was making an argument for a return of the death penalty.

"...the last execution took place in nineteen sixty four. It was abolished for murder at that time, the only punishment by hanging given to treason until nineteen ninety eight. Since then the rate of murder has only increased..."

"...actually, the murder rate has declined sharply since two thousand and two..."

"...there will always be a blip, a time when murder rates peak and decline, but on the whole, there has been an increase. The justice system is letting people down..."

Anders turned to Abi, who was frowning.

"There's a change there," she said. "His attitude to the law has changed completely."

"I think his attitude is the same as it's always been," replied Anders. "Around the same time as Michael is divorcing his wife, Francis' dies in a car accident. I've read the reports and there's no way her brakes should have failed like that." Realisation was dawning on the group as Anders piled on the evidence.

"Matthew Peters. Buckland's first victim. He'd known Francis since they were children. The two people, Matthew and his wife, who could tell the difference between Francis and Michael were dead. The body in the safe isn't Michael. It's Francis." A stunned silence settled over the room as everyone digested the information. Michael had killed his brother, hidden the body and then assumed his place. He'd been hiding in plain sight all along. McDowell swore loudly, the sound coming clearly through the speakers.

"I've been keeping him up to date on the search for his brother," he said angrily. "He's been the one making sure we had extra funds to pursue him." Anders shrugged.

"Either he didn't think he'd be found or he enjoyed the sport." Anders gave him a look of sympathy as further realisation hit.

"That's how he knew about Mal," he said, ageing suddenly, his vibrant energy leaching from him. "He's dead because of me."

"There's more," said Anders, unwilling to dwell on that fact. "I think Lawrence, his son is helping him out, but also his wife." Abi gave a snort of derision.

"Not her. She's devastated by this whole thing."

"She fooled us both Abi," replied Anders. "Unless she's been living with her head in the sand these last few weeks, she'd have seen her ex-husband on the TV. Boyle took at least three people to keep him alive. Lady Margaret trained as a nurse. It was also Lady Margaret Buckland who visited St Thomas' yesterday to open a children's ward. She could easily have slipped into Lucy's room. Occam's Razor. The theory with the fewest assumptions is the one we go with. This has the fewest assumptions. Helen, what are your findings?"

Duncan groaned in shock as Helen spoke, her voice quiet in the group.

"I checked Lucy's body just now. There's a needle mark in her belly button. Very small. Toxicology is running now, but I don't think it will show anything. Insulin would do the trick and the hormone would denature then break down quickly so as to be untraceable. I may find slightly elevated levels, but nothing conclusive."

McDowell spoke in the silence that followed.

"I'll have a warrant drawn up for you now. You can take Buckland in his brother's home at Kensington. There's not enough for the other two beyond circumstantial evidence."

"We can still take them in for questioning and hold them for thirty six hours," said Duncan. "Might give us time to find something."

Dawkins stood up and brushed lint from his trousers. His voice was grim but filled with satisfaction.

"I'll have two armed units escort you. When can you leave?"

Chapter 11

Buckland's property was located at the Academy Gardens in Kensington. He occupied the bottom two flats of an exclusive residence and Barry had the gate keeper open the gates as Anders drove through and parked the patrol car. Behind her, two large vans screeched to a halt and out poured two units of armed officers. They wore vests with Police emblazoned across their chests and carried Heckler & Koch machine guns with clear magazines that showed clips filled with bullets. They moved with a grim silence and were followed by two men carrying a large tube with handles that would be used to break down the front door.

Anders opened the boot to the car and tossed Barry his Heckler & Koch. He plucked it from the air with practised ease and checked the chamber before holstering a pistol. There was a nervous tension in the group as Duncan stepped from the car and struggled into a vest. Everyone knew what had happened to Lucy and were wary of further traps. Anders appraised the property, which Jesse had gleefully told her was worth over five million pounds, and figured Buckland wouldn't care about such niceties. After all, that was the prize for one winning entry.

In silence, they moved to the front door, a large, oak panelled entrance that would take some blows to knock in. Anders signalled the two squads behind her and bade the entry team to step forward. One of them put small explosives on the hinges and stepped back whilst the other two moved forward. The manoeuvre was well practised and they moved with intimidating efficiency. A quick glance to Anders and they were given the go sign.

The doors buckled as the compact explosives warped the hinges and the blow from the metal tube took the door clean off, the metal shearing as if made from melted butter. Anders burst through the smoke as the entry team stepped aside.

"Police! Put your hands up and stay where you are. We are armed," Anders yelled as she found herself in a large open plan room. It was huge and housed a banqueting table and an open fire that burned heartily despite the summer heat outside. The space was bright and well lit, natural light streaming in from large windows. It was also empty and Barry followed Anders through the room and into a long corridor, both checking for any signs of traps, yet moving quickly, guns raised to their shoulders.

Racing along the corridor, they scanned each room as they passed, Anders signalling those behind her to secure the room properly. The flat was elegantly decorated, wealth obvious but not overstated. They had little time to admire the surroundings as they pushed on. At the end of the corridor was a large study area and it was here that they found Buckland.

He was leaning against a large desk that dominated the room and had his hands in the air. He was dressed in a bespoke suit, elegantly tailored to show his broad shoulders and trim waist. His dark and grey speckled hair was neatly combed and he glowed with good health. He was grinning as Anders entered and covered the space quickly to him. The world slowed for a moment as she saw Buckland, images of Mal's ravaged body flashing through her mind. Her finger tightened on the trigger. The only thing protecting Buckland was her training and her desire to see him punished through the judicial system he so brazenly mocked. He saw the anger in Anders, felt the flutter of wings in the darkness and knew how close he was to death. He brushed the fear aside, his discipline stemming from class and breeding.

"Welcome!" he said. "How may I help you today Miss Anders?"

He protested as Anders spun him round and pushed him forward onto the table, pulling his hands behind him. Barry checked the room as she read him his rights, keeping her voice neutral as anger coursed through her. Barry glanced at the laptop on the desk and looked nervously at Anders. She quickly picked up on his vibe.

"Something wrong?" asked Buckland, staring hard at Anders. He was no longer the composed, charming, handsome and athletic man Anders had met in Parliament. He'd warped and twisted, his mask removed, showing the true madness that lay beneath.

Barry turned the laptop round so that Anders could see the screen just as Jesse spoke through her headpiece.

"We have a problem," he said, his voice tight with worry. "It looks like every device that's been used to look at the website over the last four weeks has a virus that's just been activated, some kind of Trojan horse. Smart phones, tablets, even smart TV's. Doesn't matter if it's Windows, Android or Apple. They're all showing the same thing. I can't override it. Three of my screens are buggered."

Anders stared at the laptop as Barry took out his phone and checked. It no longer responded to his commands and he couldn't switch it off. It showed the same scene as the laptop. In one corner of the screen, an image from a small drone was showing Buckland's house, the police car and two vans parked outside. The feed was live. Above it, Buckland had written three sentences and they sent a chill down her spine

Burn it.

All of it.

Set the world on fire.

Chapter 12

Anders paused for a moment to work out her strategy. They had to get Buckland to Scotland Yard and secure him.

"Duncan, Barry, get Buckland to the car. We'll ride in the middle, armoured van in front and behind. Barry, you're driving. Take a wide route, not the direct one." They hurried through the house as Anders gave her orders to the armed units. Normally, they'd secure the house and have it made safe for evidence collection, but their priority was to get Buckland to the safety of Scotland Yard.

Anders hung back for a moment as they raced through the house to the cars. Taking her phone out, she quickly dialled Cassie, having not used her phone to view the site. The line was dead and she sighed heavily, knowing Cassie must have been looking at the website on her phone. She tried Aaron's. He had an old Nokia that wasn't connected to the internet. She'd told him he could have a smart phone when he was older and he'd always been fine with that. When you have nothing, getting anything is a blessing. He answered on the second ring.

"Hi Bumble," he said, happiness in his voice at her calling him.

"Hey there Aaron," replied Anders. "How are you?"

"I'm ok. I've been making cookies with Cassie. I made one with extra chocolate for you." Anders smiled and hated herself for not being able to be there with them.

"That's great honey. I look forward to eating it. Is Cassie with you?" There was a sound of conversation in the background as Cassie took the phone.

"Hey, wassup?" she said.

"Are you at home?" Anders asked, keeping the urgency from her voice.

"Yes. Why?"

"Keep Aaron away from the news. Lock the door and don't let anyone in. Do not leave that flat, you hear?" Cassie suddenly sounded worried.

"What's going on?" she asked, her voice tight with fear. Anders sprinted from the house, knowing that she had held everyone up.

"No time to explain. Just stay in the flat and keep the door locked. Don't let Aaron see your phone either." She hung up just as she burst from the flat and sped to the car as Barry folded himself into the driver's side.

Running from the house, Buckland was pushed into the back of the patrol car, his handcuffed arms bending painfully as he sat on them. It didn't affect his mood and he grinned at his escort.

"This is fun," he said. "So much more fun than I thought it would be." Duncan sat next to him in the back and told him to keep quiet as Jesse gave them a quick update.

"Fires in Brixton, Camden and Croydon. Rioting has started already. I'm looking at the feed now and they're not taking anything, just setting stuff on fire. Hang on, you've a large group heading your way. I can see it on the website. Get out of there and hang right."

Barry reversed quickly and gunned the engine as he waited for the lead van to exit the gate. Jesse had linked their radios to the same frequency and they listened in as he gave directions. Speeding from the courtyard, Anders could see an angry mob sprinting towards them. They were hurling abuse and throwing stones at the vehicles. There were men and women of all ages and types, but they all shared one common factor. Anger and rage.

"Not sure if they want to kill him or set him free," muttered Barry as a large rock cracked a window, making Duncan jump nervously. Jesse started reeling off a list of cities around the world where rioting had started. Barry negotiated his way round the traffic with skill, following the path set by the police van in front, the rear vehicle following closely behind. Anders turned to Buckland and spoke to him through the mesh that separated them.

"What have you done?" she asked, knowing the answer but wanting to hear it. He smirked at her, his patronising aloofness grating.

"It's been a busy month Miss Anders." He leaned forward, his eyes cold and full of menace. "The poor. The disaffected. The abused, spurned and the lost. People from all walks of life who feel let down by their standing in the world. All they needed was a cause. I gave them one."

Anders recalled the London riots in twenty eleven. What had started as a protest at the death of Mark Duggan had turned into simple looting by those who wanted what they felt should be theirs, regardless of whether they had earned it or not. The true cause of the protest had been lost amidst the looting, but Anders was well aware of how a simple spark could spiral out of control. Buckland had provided a spark and created enough unrest that it would catch fire all too easily.

"In every major city around the world, they've been waiting for my signal. They believe, Miss Anders. They believe most passionately." She gave him a contemptuous look.

"But you don't." He shrugged, neither denying nor defending his beliefs.

"Maybe not Miss Anders, but this sure is fun." Just then, Barry and Duncan's phones chimed. It seemed that Duncan had been checking out the site on his phone as well. His eyes widened in fear as he saw a message scroll across the screen. It showed the convoy making their way through the early evening traffic, the images being screened live via the drone overhead, guided by someone unseen. Above the feed, scrolled a simple tag.

One Hundred Million Pounds For Anyone Who Rescues Lord Buckland From The Oppressors.

Chapter 13

Darren Snow rode passenger in the lead truck. He was sweating nervously. In the dimming light of the evening, he could see an orange glow lighting the sky, black smoke coiling around the throbbing light in sinuous menace. The group of men and women at Kensington had scared him more than he thought they would, but the constant images beaming to his phone of his convoy had him panicking. Every turn they made, an overlay on the map changed, indicating possible routes back to the Yard. And possible ambush points. Next to him, Frank rode through the traffic, sirens blaring and ignoring traffic signals. They were making good time back to the safety of Scotland Yard, but every street and corner seemed to hold danger, roadblocks disrupting their progress, projectiles hurled at the windows. The glass held firm, but they all twitched nervously at every noise, loud in the confines of the van. London felt like a war zone.

He clutched his Glock tighter and jumped when his phone chimed. Frank gave him a worried look as he read out the new message.

"Jesus," he said in his thick Scouse accent. "We're going to have the whole damn city after us." Darren wiped sweat from his brow and looked again at the phone, mesmerised by the convoy he was part of. Ahead, at Chelsea, the rioting had started and the roads were blocked. Frank avoided a car that swerved straight for them, narrowly avoiding being rammed off the road. The street ahead became jammed as the car skidded past and crashed into a lorry, causing it to dovetail across their path. On the radio, Anders' voice guided Frank.

"Head for Battersea, we'll have to go across Tower Bridge and circle round. Keep changing direction, don't stop, don't indicate and don't slow down." Frank followed her commands, smashing through one road block and speeding across Battersea Bridge on the opposite side of the road, Darren holding on for dear life. His eyes kept going to the screen on his phone.

One Hundred Million Pounds.

He could do a lot with that. Maybe his girlfriend would stop moaning at him about his gambling debts. A hundred million would shut her up. Actually, screw her. With that kind of money, he would just leave. See how she liked him then. He'd get loads of women. Go to Vegas. *Always wanted to go there*, he thought. A screeching brought him back to focus as a large truck was parked across the road and Frank hit the pavement to avoid it, honking his horn and desperately trying not to hit any civilians.

Anders' voice came through the radio, calming and soothing, giving them the confidence that they would get through this. Darren couldn't understand why everyone liked her so much. Sure, she was fit, but she was a fucking transsexual. What the hell did *he* know? They were just mincers pretending to be women. He'd come across loads on the beat and most of them were rotters. Mingers, the lot of them. He looked at the screen on his phone again and saw Anders leaning out of the car and taking aim, not caring about the traffic hurtling around her. She fired a shot at the drone and the image on the screen went blank. *She was pretty badass though*, he thought as a new image came on the screen from another drone.

One. Hundred. Million. He looked over at Frank. He was an arse. Always looking down at Darren, always giving him grief.

Anders was guiding them back across the river, over Tower Bridge. The huge towers in the middle looming overhead as they crashed through the barrier and started making their way across just as the two sides were rising. Frank gunned the engine and crossed to the other side, wheels bouncing over the narrow yet widening gap.

One Hundred Million.

Darren made his mind and steeled himself. Switched the safety on his Glock to *off*.

"Sorry Frank," he said and shot him through the temple, blood spattering the windows, the noise shockingly loud in the small cab.

He grabbed the wheel and twisted, hoping to stop Anders' car and get Buckland out, but misjudging the speed of the van. It flipped at the sudden turn, spinning through the air as it rolled and landing with a sickening crunch.

Chapter 14

Barry crossed the gap a split second after the lead van. All three vehicles were riding within a metre of each other to make sure they crossed the gap over the river and stayed together. Before Barry could widen the distance between the vehicles again, the van ahead turned sharply and flipped. Too close to avoid the change in direction and sudden loss of speed, Barry drove straight into the side of the van, knocking it further and causing the tail end to spin and hit their own car, flinging it sideways. The rear van crashed into the first one and they both spun.

Anders lost sight of the vehicles as their safety bags burst open and cushioned their impact as the car bounced into the blue steel railings at the side. They held firm and the car wrapped itself around them in violence and fury, the car absorbing the impact and buckling under the stress as it was designed to do.

The world blanked for a moment as the windows shattered, covering them all in glass. The sound of shearing metal eased and was soon replaced by a buzzing in the ears as Anders pulled herself from the wrecked car, amazed that she wasn't badly hurt. Barry fell out behind her and they rushed to the back to check on Duncan. He was reeling from a cut to the forehead but his eyes were clear and his focus sharp.

Buckland had dislocated a shoulder as his cuffed hands had yanked and pulled behind him. Barry felt little remorse as he dragged him from the car, Buckland groaning in agony at the pain. Anders moved to the trunk and leaned in. The boot had been torn clean off, but the contents were still in their straps. She pulled the Heckler and Koch out, the attachments on the weapon giving the stubby rifle an air of menace, brimming with ill intent.

She ducked down as she heard the ricochet of bullets from the concrete around them. Barry had dragged Duncan round the side of the car and he peered over to see who was shooting at them.

"One of the armed unit guys," he called, looking calmly around. The bridge behind them was now raised at too steep an angle to climb so they were effectively trapped. Anders peeked over the car and saw one of the officers striding towards them, rifle raised to his shoulder and firing wildly. He would be there in seconds. She tossed her gun to Barry and he caught it deftly.

"On my mark," said Anders. "Three, two, one." She leapt out from shelter, sprinting across the road and catching Darren's eye. He turned his rifle to her, tracked her movement briefly and pulled the trigger.

Barry's gun fired first and Darren's bullet missed Anders as he spun with the impact of Barry's shot. The bullets tore through his chest, fragmented against the ribcage and shredded his heart. Darren was dead before he hit the ground.

Anders kept sprinting, moving quickly to the two vans that were strewn across the bridge, just before the barriers leading to the North side of the Thames. To their left was the Tower of London and on their right sat a squat, ugly hotel. On the other side of the barrier, people were getting out of their cars to see what was happening. Some, sensing an opportunity to make some money, started moving towards the accident. The truck that Darren had flipped lay on its roof. The van was warped and twisted and she could see a pile of bodies lying on the ground, broken limbs and torso's a sickening sight. A few of the officers started to move and she yelled at them to get clear. She could smell petrol and saw it leaking from the tank, a jagged tear along its edge. The engine had cut when it had crashed, but she didn't want any stray sparks to set it off.

The other truck was on its side, the back flush against the edge of the bridge. She saw movement in there as the men inside started hammering at the door, trying to get out. Anders turned to see Barry heading towards her. He tossed her a belt with clips, spray and baton attached and passed her a Glock. Duncan was dragging Buckland across to them.

Shouts sounded from across the barrier and she sensed that the crowd there was building up the courage to do something rash. As Buckland was pulled to her, she passed Duncan her speedcuffs and told him to cuff Buckland's ankles, effectively immobilising him. She leaned down to him and grabbed his chin as he lay resting against the railing, a pale sheen on his face at his dislocated shoulder.

"You try and run, you go off with anyone trying to collect your pretty little reward and I will kill you." Buckland looked at Anders and felt real fear, saw death in her bright green eyes. She held his gaze a moment longer before turning away.

"Duncan, get a crowbar and open the door on top of that truck." She pointed to the one on its side that was jammed against the railing and started to run towards the one with the leaking fuel tank. It had taken the brunt of the crash and several bodies both inside and out weren't moving.

The noise on the bridge was deafening as the crowd ahead of them gathered its courage, much like an old Saxon shield wall. Anders had seen it before in New Orleans. A few of the bravest would make the first move and the others would follow, emboldened by the stupidity of the mob. She knew that she had moments before something happened and needed to get everyone off the bridge fast.

The world slowed then. She saw it but couldn't stop it. Couldn't quite believe it. Arcing through the air was a bottle with pale brown liquid inside and a strip of cloth stuffed down the neck. The end of the cloth was lit and it hurtled towards the van before Anders could get there. She turned and yelled for Barry, just behind her, to get down as the bottle hit the van and exploded, droplets of flaming petrol covering the vehicle and igniting the exposed petrol tank.

The explosion knocked Anders from her feet and she was flung backwards, landing painfully on the floor. A sharp jab in her rib told her she may have cracked it and another pain in her arm lashed her with agony as a shard of metal pierced the flesh. Her head swam and her vision blurred. It didn't stop her hearing the screams though, as the men inside the van were roasted alive, black, acrid smoke broiling from the vehicle as metal and flesh popped and cackled.

She felt Barry drag her to her feet and leaned on him momentarily whilst she cleared her vision. Her arm bled freely. The metal shard had torn right through and Barry quickly ripped his shirt and tied it round her arm, tight as he could manage. She flexed her hands and tested her movement, giving him quick thanks. She checked on Duncan, seeing him crouched on the side of the van, pulling with his crowbar to open the door so the other team could get out.

Beyond that, she saw a stream of men and women climb over and under the barricade and start sprinting to the van. Their faces were contorted in anger and bile having worked themselves into a frenzy and built up enough courage to come and claim their reward. Some looked like believers, a hint of fanaticism about them. What really chilled Anders was how varied they were. Office workers mingled with Goths who ran with builders. United by one purpose. There seemed to be hundreds of them, but most were simply filming the attack on their phones or cowering from the rage. A few had blanched at the smell and violence of the burning van and turned away.

"We need to keep Duncan safe," said Anders. "Try not to kill anyone, but do it if you need to. Stick together." She turned to Barry and he gave her a steady look.

"I ain't letting any of these punks get Buckland," he said. His voice was calm and steady. Anders couldn't think of anyone else she'd rather have by her side right now.

They sprinted to close the gap, making sure they got past the van Duncan was on and give him time to get the men out from there. Barry fired some warning shots above the heads of the crowd and a few more faltered and turned. Anders saw another Molotov Cocktail being lit from the rear and fired her Glock. The bullet shattered the glass and covered the assailant in flames. His screams cut through the noise but Anders felt little pity for him.

A few more turned back, sickened by his burning torment, though there were still almost thirty men and women heading for the pair of them, covering the distance quickly. The first to reach Barry found the stock of a machine gun smashed into his face and went slack, tumbling to the ground as his momentum took him past the veteran soldier. The second was hurled backwards, causing those behind to stumble as Barry stepped forward, his massive fists beating them back further.

Anders opened her baton and swung quickly at the first to reach her, a woman in a business suit who snarled at her as she lunged forward. Anders' baton smashed her temple and she fell, eyes rolled up in their sockets. A sharp pain coursed through Anders as the swing opened her wound further, but she ignored the pain and stepped forward, constantly moving, spraying and punching those who came near.

"On your six," she yelled to Barry and he turned to meet an attack from the rear. They were being swamped by sheer numbers. Barry protected her right flank and she his left, but they were quickly being subdued. A brick flew over the group and crashed into Barry, the blow cracking his collarbone with a loud snap. He grunted, but his right arm was now useless, his flank undefended.

Another brick flew in, but he managed to avoid it, sweeping up the one that had hit him and clubbing an attacker. Anders knew they were beaten. There were too many of them. They hadn't wanted to use their guns. The sight of two police officers mowing down civilians would be screened around the world for years. She had to hope that they had fought long enough to show that there was no alternative. They'd still lose. She would be killed on the street by an angry mob, but maybe they would suffer such loss that the attackers would flee. Or she would take as many out with her as she could, a flutter of wings as the darkness within her bared its teeth.

Two large men charged her at the same time. She stepped into the closest man and thrust upwards with the handle of the baton, cracking his chin. Spinning under his arm, she took her gun from its holster and aimed over him to the second man, finger on the trigger, safety clicked off.

A deafening roar of machine gun fire splintered the air as Duncan finally freed the men from the van and they clambered out, forming a solid line that walked forwards, firing an entire clip above the crowd, who disengaged and ran. Anders lifted her finger from the trigger and saw Barry lower his own weapon. He'd also reached the point at which firing his weapon may be the only way to survive. She ran back to the safety of the line and saw Duncan dragging Buckland behind them.

"Thank you," she said, relieved at their rescue. She was breathing heavily, the pain in her ribs spearing her every breath with white agony, cuts and bruises from the attackers peppering her body with pricks of pain. She pointed to the barrier. "We'll need to cross that and find transport. I can see a bus near the back. That's where we're heading. We'll need a circle with Buckland and Duncan in the middle. I'll take point. Barry, you good?"

He grunted in distain at her question and stepped to her side as the men formed around them. She grinned at him, exhilarated at their survival.

"Let's go," she said, and led them forward. They were attacked frequently, stones flew at them and all manner of projectiles, but they held firm, moved swiftly and with purpose. No one broke the line, held in place by Anders and Barry. The group bristled with machine guns and this stopped all but the most foolhardy from attacking them. Those that did were beaten off and left on the street, bloodied and bruised. They made it to the bus and clambered aboard, Anders taking the wheel and smashing her way down the river, London burning around them. Buckland's acolytes had started the fires, but more and more had rallied as the night wore on, whether to loot or in the belief that the world order could be changed. A pall of smoke hung in the city air, besmirching the darkening sky, fire flickering up to greet the night.

As they approached Scotland Yard, Anders could see down the street to the Palace of Westminster. It was ablaze, the oldest symbol of democracy in the modern world a pyre to Buckland and his teachings. Anders hated the man even more in that moment, beyond what he had done to Mal. Hated him with passionate fury. It was all a game to him, teasing those in need, those in suffering, for his own sick fantasies.

She looked in the rear view mirror and saw him staring back at her, a smirk on his face. Even though he'd been caught, it was still going as he'd planned.

Chapter 15

Anders stood behind Jesse and watched the news reports come through. It seemed as if the whole world was on fire. They'd fought hard to get back into the Yard, surrounded as it was by thousands of supporters of Buckland and those who would see him hanged by the same death penalty he was pushing through the House of Lords. They had clashed with each other and the riot police surrounding the building had been helpless to prevent it. They stood in a ring around the building, preventing entry and trying to protect it from the rioters, fires blazing in the street, rocks hurled at the windows and officers. The noise was a deafening wave of anger and rage, a physical force that was barely absorbed by the layers of concrete and steel that separated them and those in the hub.

Three of Jesse's screens showed Buckland's website, the drone now focused on Scotland Yard as it hovered high above, the commandeered bus parked at an angle across the entrance, now providing protection to the main entrance. They were effectively locked in, the only escape through the underground car park, which was protected by steel shutters. Helen was tending to Barry's wounds and Ben fussed around Anders as he stitched up her arm. He was no surgeon and the wound would heal in a crooked scar. Abi had hugged Duncan fiercely as he entered, saying how proud she was of him. He'd held his own and had not faltered.

"The army has been called in. They'll restore order in a few hours." The voice came from McDowell who was on one of Jesse's many screens. "Buckland has wreaked havoc, but he's achieved nothing more than death and misery. This time tomorrow, everything will be just as it was." Anders shooed Ben away as he tried to put a bandage round the wound. She stuck a large plaster on it and spoke to McDowell.

"I'll speak to him anyway, see if we can't get this damn virus shut down." McDowell nodded his agreement. There was nothing left to say. Anders took an earpiece from Jesse and put it in her ear.

"Take care," he said. "He's one sick son of a bitch. Don't let him get you all twisted up." Anders gave him a tired smile. She couldn't remember when she'd last slept.

"I'll be fine." She tapped her earpiece. "Keep me posted."

Anders walked to the interview room, gathering her thoughts and focusing her mind. Her rib hurt and she could feel it grate every time she moved. She knew she would have to check it out sooner rather than later but pushed her pain away. She was covered in bruises and cuts from the attack on London Bridge, but had suffered worse. Far worse.

She tapped in the code for the interrogation room and entered to find Buckland sitting on the metal seat, cuffed to the table and staring blankly at the wall ahead. As she entered, his eyes focused on her and he gave an insidious smile.

"Miss Anders," he said. "I'm so glad I killed Mr Weathers and made you the boss. You're much more interesting." Anders ignored his taunt and sat opposite him. He continued to speak, "You found me much more quickly than Mr Weathers did. I'm impressed."

"It was Mal's work that led me to you. We simply continued with his investigation as he had it," she replied, keeping her voice neutral. Anger seethed below the surface at what he had done to Mal. She struggled to control herself and it was through sheer force of will that she didn't attack him where he sat. Buckland smiled and gave her a patronising look, the effect distorting his handsome features.

"You do yourself a disservice. Mr Blackwell should be arriving soon. I believe that I cannot be interviewed without my consent until I have spoken to my attorney." Anders leaned forward and bared her teeth.

"I spoke with Mr Blackwell earlier. Seems he has declined to represent you. Would you like me to find you another attorney?" Buckland shrugged as if without a care in the world.

"Never mind. How goes my revolution?"

"Habeas Corpus. Why abolish it? Doesn't that make it easier to throw you in jail?" Anders wanted to keep changing topic, put him off guard.

"I'm sure my trial will be too good an opportunity for the likes of McDowell to pass up." Anders leaned back in her seat.

"Shame you couldn't get that capital punishment deal back up and running. I'd love to see you hang for the suffering you've caused." Buckland gave her a steady look.

"Pull the lever yourself no doubt." Anders flicked some dirt from her nail. Pretended to consider the comment. Deciding he wasn't going to get an answer, Buckland folded his arms across his broad chest and waited for her to speak.

"It's just chaos isn't it?" said Anders eventually. "Take away more rights on one hand, offer them more incentive with the other. Nice little hornets' nest you've stirred up." Buckland looked pleased with himself as she spoke. In that moment, she saw him for what he was. He wanted to rip and tear and burn. No reason. He cared little for revolution, just pain and suffering and misery.

"Your little revolution will be over by the morning. Army has been drafted in, martial law declared. As it always would. You knew it would never happen, you just wanted some legitimacy, some aspiration to a higher purpose for people to follow you in your sick games." Anders put her hands on the desk, showing him her bloodied knuckles. "I want to know where your son and your wife are and I'd like to shut down your website before any more innocent people are killed."

Buckland looked surprised for a split second at the mention of Lady Margaret, before hiding it behind his mask of superiority.

"My ex-wife I believe." Anders inclined her head at his correction.

"What I don't understand is why you didn't dump the body?" It took a moment for him to realise that she was talking about his brother.

"Didn't think you'd find the house and then the safe. Did you have fun chasing me up and down the country? I will admit, I was annoyed at my son for being so careless, but I guess it was fun to see your officer blown into little pieces." Anders visibly controlled herself with an effort of will, fists clenching on the table. Buckland noticed the reflex and chuckled.

"What is it you say? Walk tall, stand strong, isn't it? Lucy was a fighter, I'll give her that." An icy chill of fear rippled down her spine at his words. She'd only ever said that to Aaron. Buckland saw her look and gave a triumphant smile. "The advantage, Miss Anders, of being on the committee that set up this wonderful taskforce is that I know where everyone lives." He looked at her with hooded eyes and raised his hands, the noise of the steel chains through the hoop suddenly loud in the room.

"Please remember Miss Anders, that I have a higher purpose," he said, aping his blog in a mocking tone. "When you do what I do, you become more than an individual with an ideology. You become an entity. And as an entity, I, no, we, are legion."

Anders shoved her chair back with such force that it clattered off the wall behind her, aghast as he spoke, a snarl spearing his smile. "The Devil wants his share Miss Anders. We're here to collect on his behalf." She tore from the room, Buckland's cackling following her as she left, and took out her phone. Dialling Aaron as she moved, she cursed when there was no reply. The phone rang ominously. Aaron was proud of his phone. It never left his side.

"Jesse?" she said out loud.

"On it," came his voice through her earpiece. "Barry is hooking you up with an exit strategy. Got you a bike." She gave him Aaron's number.

"Keep trying," she said, sprinting through the Hub. Abi and Helen give her anxious looks as she passed and grabbed some Aviators from her desk as she headed for the parking lot. Careening down the corridor, she saw Barry, Duncan and Jesse by the entrance. The barricade was down, thick metal doors barring the way. Barry was struggling into a vest, his broken collarbone making the task difficult. She also saw Ben trying to fit himself into a vest and helmet that was clearly too big for him. Anders shook her head.

"Don't do this Ben," she said. He gave her a lopsided grin as he buckled the straps to his helmet.

"You may be the only person I've met smarter than me, but I'll be damned if you're braver." Anders hugged him briefly, unable to speak.

"Over here," called Jesse and pointed to a police motorbike resting against a large truck. The top of the vehicle had a hose attached and a large tank filled with water below it. Jesse was settling into the seat behind the hose as Duncan switched on the engine.

Anders sprinted to the bike and gunned the engine. Barry approached and handed her a Glock. She looked at his bandaged arm.

"You don't need to do this," she said and he smiled at her.

"Would you do this for me?" he asked. They both knew the answer and she was glad that the Aviators hid her emotions. He gave the signal and the metal doors started to rise, a cacophony of noise reaching them as the chaos from the riots outside poured through. Jesse gave Anders the thumbs up as Barry picked up a riot shield with his good arm and trotted alongside Duncan's door as he drove the van out, Ben strutting alongside Barry and shielding his weaker side. He looked tiny and petrified, but held his chin high, shouting a battle cry that was soon lost to the noise.

Within moments, a stream of people started to enter the parking lot, gleefully seeing a way in to claim their reward or kill Buckland. Either reason didn't matter to Anders as they swarmed in. Jesse turned the hose on and sprayed the crowd, knocking them from their feet with the force of the jet. A few tried to duck under the spray and were bashed aside by Barry as he protected Duncan who drove forward, Ben using the huge shield he carried with purpose. Together, they cleared a path out from the building, but the streets were overflowing with a mass of seething humanity.

The van was quickly swamped and the hose could only push so many back. Anders spied a gap in the crowd as Jesse sprayed them and spurred the bike forward, the vehicle responding to her touch with a snarl. The bike roared through the crowd. A few men tried to knock her off but were thrown back by the hose. She burst from the rioters and found herself on the street. Looking in the mirror, she saw the van overrun by the hateful mob and prayed for their safety, guilt at leaving them behind tormenting her.

She pushed the bike hard, leaning in to the corners and hitting the bridge, Parliament blazing behind her as she sped to Richmond, her arm starting to bleed again with every turn of the handle. Panic gripped her and she forced it down, pushing the bike beyond its limits. She wore no helmet, relying on the shades to protect her eyes, hair whipping around her as she passed through red lights and swerved around abandoned cars. The slightest knock and she'd be instantly killed at the speed she was travelling.

In her ear, the headpiece sprang to life, barely audible in the wind.

"It's Helen," came the voice. "I'm trying to call Aaron for you, but I'm not getting through. There's no patrol cars nearby either. I'm sorry."

"Are they ok? Back at the station?" she yelled, the wind snatching her voice away.

Anders wove through some burnt out cars and an explosion from a petrol station nearly knocked her from the bike. She didn't hear the reply and a static in her ear told her she'd lost contact with Helen. She was engulfed in a tide of despair, fear clawing at her. She knew the look Buckland had given her in the room. It was the look of a hunter catching his prey, the look of the spiteful practising cruelty. She pushed the bike harder again, not caring for her own safety.

Around her she saw looting and destruction on a scale not seen since the Blitz, but she ignored the wanton damage.

A short while later, but what seemed like hours to Anders, she arrived at her block of flats and skidded to a halt, leaping from the bike and reaching for the Glock she'd tucked into her belt. It wasn't there, having fallen off during the ride. Hoping she wouldn't need it, she rammed her way through the front door and hurtled up the stairs. At the top, she slammed open the stairwell door to find them in the hallway.

Lawrence Buckland and Lady Margaret stood by the lift, waiting for it to arrive. Anders had moments to take it in. She saw the surprise on their faces, saw the bag Margaret was holding, a bloody sickle poking out from it, saw the spots of blood that freckled their clothing, saw the gun in Lawrence's hand.

Saw the door to her flat at the end of the corridor.

It was ajar, the lock broken and splintered.

In his shock at seeing Anders, Lawrence wasted precious seconds before raising his gun. Anders wasted no time. She sprinted towards Lawrence, a look of surprise on his face as he saw her coming. He managed to raise his weapon in time to fire one shot, the bullet piercing her shoulder, white hot pain tearing through her swifter than lightening. Rage drove her on and she moved to within lovers touch.

She reached out, grabbed the gun and, with the other hand, slammed his elbow up, cartilage snapping as the joint was smashed the wrong way. He dropped the gun and she caught it, firing her reply, the sound concussive in the narrow corridor.

Lawrence screamed shrilly as the bullet took out his kneecap, the bone shattering in an explosion of pain. The second bullet removed his manhood and he mewed simperingly as he tried to crawl away. A third bullet shattered his spine at the waist.

Lady Margaret, shocked at the speed of the violence, dropped her bag, grabbing the sickle at the same time. With consummate ease,

Anders took it from her as she spun around Margaret, one arm taking her neck, the other holding the sickle to her stomach.

"Please," whimpered Lady Margaret. Anders had stared into the darkness for a long time. She knew it intimately. Her light shone in the dark to protect those in need. A different light shone now. Righteousness. In his madness, Jonathan Sanders had seen it in her and now Lady Margaret saw it as Anders pulled the blade across her torso, the cold steel opening her stomach and spilling her intestines to the floor. She screamed in pain as Anders tossed her aside.

The brutal violence had taken mere seconds.

Anders dropped the blade and walked to the door at the end of the corridor, ignoring the screams that followed her. Blood poured from the wound in Anders' shoulder and her rib had certainly snapped in the explosive movement. She felt the two pieces rub against each other painfully. Stitches torn, the wound in her arm bled freely and her vision swam, the world suffused with numbing cinders of agony. Anders ignored the pain, the fatigue and her failing body. She was consumed with dread. She knew what she would find beyond that door and hesitated, unsure whether she would survive what she would see.

Steeling herself, she pushed the door open with a trembling, blood soaked hand and entered the flat.

Moments later, cries of grief filled the hall as Anders was torn apart by loss of the most desecrating kind.

Acknowledgments

Writing a book is a long, solitary process, but you can't do it alone. Without Emma, Josh and Wilson, there would be no book. Emma for driving me on to be better, Josh for making me prove that I could do this and Wilson for listening to all of my crazy ideas, even though he didn't have a choice. You are my family and I love you without reserve or measure.

I'd like to thank those who read the manuscript and didn't judge me too harshly or get worried about my state of mind. Lauren, Brooke, Fiona and, of course, Patrick, whose brutal honesty made the book immeasurably better.

A special mention to John as well. His enthusiasm forced me to try harder at making it something that I could be proud of.

For my Spanish lessons, Caroline, Kimberly, thank you. For red penning the work, a thank you to Didier. My jokes are terrible, so I relied on Sophie to help me out with her Top Ten Jokes.

Finally, a shout out to Louise. You know why. Have at 'em girl.

About the author

Owen lives in London with his wife, son and retriever. Originally from Wales, he moved to London for a short stay fourteen years ago. He works in a school in Wimbledon as Head of Science. He's often found on Wimbledon common walking the dog and plotting his next book, the retriever being a good listener to his more outlandish ideas.

Follow him on Twitter on;

@ojnichols1

Or Facebook using;

o.bd@hotmail.co.uk

Or even;

www.owennichols.co.uk

for interviews, latest news and more!

Don't miss the terrifying story behind Anders' ordeal at the hands of The Washington Whipper.

This short story is available exclusively on Kindle

17034570R00174

Printed in Great Britain
by Amazon